A PRINTZ HONOR BOOK

A BANK STREET CHILDREN'S BOOKS JOSETTE FRANK AWARD WINNER

A NEW YORK PUBLIC LIBRARY BEST BOOK FOR TEENS OF 2018

A CHICAGO PUBLIC LIBRARY BEST BOOK FOR TEENS OF 2018

A *BOOKPAGE* BEST BOOK OF 2018

AN AMELIA BLOOMER BOOK LIST 2019 SELECTION

A YALSA BEST FICTION FOR TEENS 2019 TOP TEN SELECTION

"A book everyone should read right now." —***NEW YORK TIMES BOOK REVIEW***

"A vital and heartbreaking story that brings together the #MeToo movement, the effects of gun violence, and the struggle of building oneself up again after crisis." —***ELLE***

"Equal parts heartbreaking and hopeful." —***BOOKPAGE***

"A moving, unfortunately timely, and gut-wrenching story that will stick with you." —***BUSTLE***

"This is one for the ages." —**GAYLE FORMAN,** author of the #1 bestseller *If I Stay*

"Caletti's novel dazzlingly maps the mind-blowing ferocity and endurance of an athlete who uses her physical body to stake claim to the respect of the nation." —**E. LOCKHART,** *New York Times* bestselling author of *Genuine Fraud* and *We Were Liars*

"More than bittersweet . . . It will nestle inside your brain as well as your heart." —**JODI LYNN ANDERSON,** award-winning author of *Midnight at the Electric*

★ "Remarkable." —***BOOKLIST,*** starred review

★ "A timely novel." —***KIRKUS REVIEWS,*** starred review

★ "Powerful." —***PUBLISHERS WEEKLY,*** starred review

★ "Annabelle exemplifies persisting nevertheless." —***BCCB,*** starred review

A HEART in a BODY in the WORLD

ALSO BY DEB CALETTI

Girl, Unframed
The Queen of Everything
Honey, Baby, Sweetheart
Wild Roses
The Nature of Jade
The Fortunes of Indigo Skye
The Secret Life of Prince Charming
The Six Rules of Maybe
Stay
The Story of Us
The Last Forever
Essential Maps for the Lost

AND DON'T MISS

He's Gone
The Secrets She Keeps
What's Become of Her

A HEART in a BODY in the WORLD

DEB CALETTI

SIMON PULSE
NEW YORK LONDON TORONTO SYDNEY NEW DELHI

This book is a work of fiction. Any references to historical events, real people, or real places are used fictitiously. Other names, characters, places, and events are products of the author's imagination, and any resemblance to actual events or places or persons, living or dead, is entirely coincidental.

SIMON PULSE
An imprint of Simon & Schuster Children's Publishing Division
1230 Avenue of the Americas, New York, New York 10020
First Simon Pulse paperback edition April 2020

Also available in an Simon Pulse hardcover edition.

Cover designed by Laura Eckes
Interior designed by Steve Scott
The text of this book was set in Adobe Caslon Pro.
Manufactured in the United States of America
4 6 8 10 9 7 5 3
The Library of Congress has cataloged the hardcover edition as follows:
Names: Caletti, Deb, author.
Title: A heart in a body in the world / by Deb Caletti.
Description: First Simon Pulse hardcover edition. | New York : Simon Pulse, 2018. |
Summary: Followed by Grandpa Ed in his RV and backed by her brother and friends,
Annabelle, eighteen, runs from Seattle to Washington, D.C., becoming a reluctant
activist as people connect her journey to her recent trauma.
Identifiers: LCCN 2017038192 (print) | LCCN 2017049586 (eBook) |
ISBN 9781481415200 (hardcover) | ISBN 9781481415231 (eBook)
Subjects: | CYAC: Grief—Fiction. | Running—Fiction. | Post-traumatic stress disorder—Fiction. |
Social action—Fiction. | Massacre survivors—Fiction. | School shootings—Fiction.
Classification: LCC PZ7.C127437 (eBook) | LCC PZ7.C127437 He 2018 (print) | DDC [Fic]—dc23
LC record available at https://lccn.loc.gov/2017038192
ISBN 9781481415217 (pbk)

For John, Sam, and Nick.

This heart is yours.

Overhead, the twilight sky was clear. But somewhere, far away to the south, a gale was blowing toward them. . . .

—ALFRED LANSING,

ENDURANCE: SHACKLETON'S INCREDIBLE VOYAGE

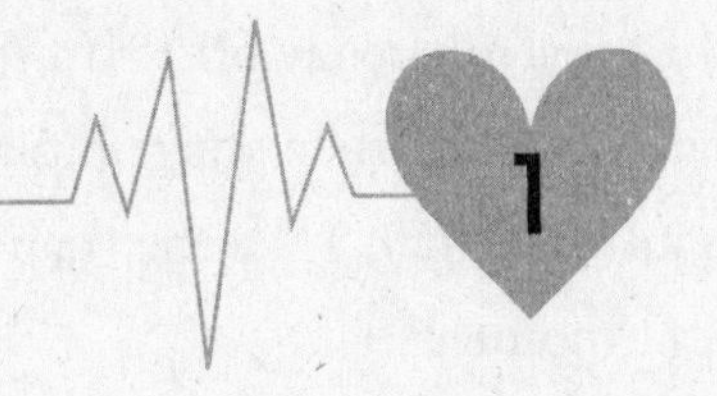

Annabelle Agnelli is trying to hold it together in the parking lot of Dick's Drive-In. After what just happened, she's stunned. Frozen. And then—imagine it—Annabelle's wrecked self suddenly takes off like a lightning bolt. She's clutching the white bag, which has the unfortunate word, *Dick's*, stamped across it in orange. Her burger is still warm. She's holding the Coke, too, which sloshes like a stormy sea as she tries to outrun the bad visions of the recent past. French fries spring loose in the bag, and it shakes around like a maraca.

Of course she's heard that saying—*A journey of a thousand miles begins with a single step.* Coach Kwan has a poster of it in his office. It shows the silhouette of a girl at sunset, running up a steep mountain path, and it's all clouds parting and God rays shining down and purple mountain majesties. There is no panic and dropped napkins and hair flying. That poster does not look like *this*.

Where is she going? No idea.

Why is she going? Well, sometimes you just snap. Snapping is easy when you're already brittle from the worst possible thing happening. It is easy when you're broken and guilty and scared. You snap just like that. Like the snap has been waiting around for the right moment.

So, now, Annabelle Agnelli is no longer trying to hold it together in the Dick's Drive-In parking lot. She's lost it. Utterly lost it. She's ditched her car entirely, and she's jogging down the sidewalk, fast, at a really good clip. Coach Kwan would be proud. She's getting sweaty and her mind is swirling, and it's all a little unhinged for the straight-A student that she is. She is a good and nice person who keeps things together, but that has been a big job, an enormous job, a job that's way, way too big for her lately.

It gets worse. Of course, this is what often happens: Things get worse and worse still. A spiral follows gravity downward. She's been running for who knows how long, and it starts to get dark. It's metaphor-darkness, but it's also just the truth. Night falls. Big clouds cross the sky, threatening rain. So many things are falling—night, rain, the last of the stuff holding Annabelle Agnelli together.

She's halfway down Seattle's busy thoroughfare of Broadway. Then she turns down Cherry, and before she knows it, Annabelle is on the path that hugs Lake Washington. It's March, which means that the sun goes down around five, five thirty. She has no idea what time it is, though. People with hunched shoulders and their jacket hoods up are walking their dogs. Little dogs and big dogs are pulled and yanked—there's no time for luxurious sniffing with the sky that black. There's a bicyclist or two or twenty, speeding home after work, their wheels *zizz*ing by her. Backpacks are slung over their shoulders. Their tight, shiny bike pants shoot past, meteor streaks of luminescent yellow. Streetlights plink on.

She keeps running. There's a little pit-pat of rain, nothing major. The burger bag is gone (in a trash can, she hopes, though she can't say for sure), but Annabelle still has the Coke, and her purse bangs against her side. She stopped by Dick's after hanging out with Zach Oh and Olivia, and so she's wearing her jeans and a sweater and she's way, way too hot. Her jacket is in the car; her regular running clothes and shoes are back at home. None of this matters.

Now, she's past Leschi and then Seward Park, and it's a little creepy out that way, with the lake a deep indigo and the big evergreens shaking their boughs overhead. This is the thing she wants to outrun: the creepiness. Not only the creepiness of Seward Park and the creepiness that just happened at Dick's, but all creepiness, all powerlessness, all moments where you feel your fate in someone else's hands.

Seriously, she should not be running in this part of the city at night. People get hurt here. Robbed. Killed. She feels a weird fearlessness. Whatever. *Come and get me*, she thinks. *Do you think I care?*

Then, she thinks something else: *I could keep going and going.*

This is where big ideas come from—a flash across the brain screen in moments when all the circuits are throwing sparks. The *where* and the *why* and the *I don't know* form the tiniest ball of cells you'd need a microscope to see.

Big ideas can lead to great things. Big ideas can lead to disaster. The cells begin to divide.

Her phone has been buzzing in her pocket. She is hours late getting home. People are worried. She brushes away the thought, but then the responsible-person guilt collides with the burn in her legs and the ache in her toes. This is a large part of Annabelle Agnelli—the weight of what she owes everyone. It makes the gears of her anxiety click and whirl. Finally, she stops. She's panting hard.

There is a park off to her left. She's lived in Seattle all her life, but she's never been out here. GENE COULON MEMORIAL BEACH PARK, the sign reads. CITY OF RENTON. She slurps down the Coke, crushes the cup. Crushing things feels awesome. She walks in a circle until her breath regulates, because she knows what will happen to her muscles if she doesn't. Her chest burns.

Help me, Kat, Annabelle thinks. *What do I do?*

Keep going, Kat answers.

See? Kat is her best friend, so she understands. Kat knows Annabelle better than anyone, except maybe a certain someone who is losing her mind right about now. A certain someone who is calling and calling. Annabelle reaches for her buzzing phone.

"I'm okay, Mom," she answers.

"Oh, God, Annabelle. Dear Jesus, where the hell are you?" Yes—*God*, *Jesus*, and *hell* in a ten-word sentence is really packing it in there, but this is Gina Agnelli. For her, being Catholic isn't just about religion—it's about superstition and safekeeping and tradition. She rarely goes to mass, but she's got the required crucifix over the kitchen doorway, the rosary in the dresser drawer, and the stack of dead relatives' funeral cards, held together with a rubber band. It's almost hard for Annabelle to believe that people are still Catholic. But the Catholic church is something that's been around for a zillion years and will keep on being around for a zillion years, in spite of the bad press and rumors of vanishing, kind of like Hostess Twinkies.

How can Annabelle believe in anything anymore, though? It'd be nice to have belief, but it's likely gone for good.

"I'm at Gene Coulon Park. In Renton?"

"What? Why? Who are you there with? Have you been *drinking*?"

Ha. Annabelle wishes. "No, I haven't been drinking! I ran here."

"You *ran* there? What do you mean, you ran there? Where's the car? Christ in heaven, do you know how worried I was? I was worried *sick*."

Worry! Annabelle's mother is always worried! She was worried even before last year, even before there was reason. Worry is another way Gina tries to keep everyone safe. Worry is a different version of prayer. Here is what happens when your mother worries: *You* become secretly worried. Anxiety plays in your background like bad grocery store music. You pace and count stuff and wake at night, your heart beating too fast. You pretend to be brave, and do stuff to prove you're not a scared person like she is. The constant worry (over your whereabouts, over certain friends, over anything and everything, but always the wrong things) bashes into your head: *You are not safe. The world is full of danger and treachery. You don't have a chance.*

Look what good all that worry did anyway.

How can you feel safe? It is a complicated question. Which is fitting, because Annabelle is complicated. Hidden behind all that nice-and-pretty, she is desperate and grief-stricken.

"I'm fine, Mom."

Of course she is not. She is most definitely not fine.

"Malcolm was trying to ping you, whatever that means! And I almost called Grandpa to go look for you, that's how frantic I was. Annabelle, you can't just *disappear* for *hours*."

Malcolm: Annabelle's younger brother. Technological genius, thirteen-year-old MacGyver. Brainiac, irritant, little buddy. Ed Agnelli: Grandpa. Nickname: *Capitano*. Former owner and boss of a frozen fish packing company, who retired and became the solo skipper of his own ship—an RV he drove around the country. Currently—their next-door neighbor. Add in Bit the dog: breed unknown. Small, brown and tan. Super-fast underwear snatcher. Also, Carl Walter: Mom's occasional boyfriend, division manager of AT&T. Rabid Seahawks fan. Still thinks Pop-Tarts and Hi-C are decent nutritional choices. Finally: Anthony. Annabelle and Malcolm's dad. Former high school athlete and runaway parent, now Father Anthony, a priest at Saint Therese's near Boston. Also known as: That Bastard Father Anthony, which is what Gina's called him ever since he left six years ago, after saying he'd *had enough*. Annabelle—she has stopped calling him altogether.

There it is: *La famiglia*. The family.

"Annabelle? Annabelle! Are you there?"

"I'm here."

"Why are you so quiet? You're making me nervous."

Oh, mothers can drive you nuts, but mothers know you.

It's now or never.

"I'm not coming home."

"What do you mean, you're not coming home? Of course you're coming home. I've got my car keys in my hand. Malcolm!" she shouts. "Look up Gene Colon Park on GPS!"

"Not Colon. Coulon. *Cu*." A wave of hysteria rises up. She almost laughs. *Cu* is an abbreviation for *culo*, Italian slang for *ass*. "But you don't need to come now. I've got a hundred and twenty bucks of birthday money in my wallet. I saw a Best Western a ways back."

"We'll be there in a half hour, if I don't get lost."

"I'm not coming home. I mean it."

"Annabelle. Stop this right now. *I* mean it. I'm the one who gets to mean it! What happened at Zach Oh's? Something happened." Gina says Zach's name really fast. *Zackos*. It sounds like the online shoe-shopping site for people who've lost their minds.

"Nothing happened at Zach's."

"Is this some Dungeons and Dragons thing?"

"Mom, no. . . ."

How to explain it? Even to herself?

She replays the scene: She is leaving Zach's. She actually feels good. She's light, lighter than she's been in months. They'd even had *fun*. Driving home, she spots the snowy ridge of the Cascade Mountains in the distance. It's so beautiful that it fills her with a Nature's Wonders surge of gratitude. Her iPod plays. It's an old song she snitched from her mother—British alternative, rising good energy, from the time of shoulder pads and big hair. *I'm alive! So alive!*

She flinches at the words, but she ignores it. Up ahead, she sees the slowly spinning Dick's sign. The delicious smell of grilling burgers marches through her heater vents. On a whim, she pulls in. She's suddenly starving. It's *so alive* hunger. It feels good.

She orders, and then slides the money through the bank-teller-ish window of Dick's. She pushes the little lever of the box for a straw, yanks a stack of napkins. She collects her bag and her drink. And then she turns around.

There are two young guys in line behind her. The one in the army jacket is obviously drunk. He half leans on his friend. "Hey, beautiful," he slurs to Annabelle. "Hey, come here."

He steps toward her. He reaches for her arm. She feels his fingers through her sleeve.

"Chad, come on, man," the other guy says.

"She's beautiful. I want beautiful."

"Chad, knock it off."

Annabelle wrenches her arm free. She tries to pass, but can't pass. The *so alive* vanishes. She stands there with her bag, paralyzed and small. The friend steers drunken Chad into another line.

"I was going to step in, in a minute," the man behind them says. He's as thin as fettuccine and wears a peacoat and a muffler. He has kind eyes. Annabelle wants to kiss him. Honestly, she'd do more than kiss him. She doesn't care if he hoards bongs or spends his days in his mother's basement, learning guitar. She doesn't care about anything except the offer of safety.

All of it—the hand, the arm, the vulnerability, the urge to kiss the saving man—it crashes like an avalanche. All of the wrongness thunders and falls and threatens to bury her alive. Annabelle wants to be strong, and strong on her own, but she has no idea how. She doesn't want to imagine that some guy can save her, because she knows that's a lie. She doesn't want to feel fear like that, or be paralyzed by it ever again. She wants to rise up, set her gorilla-mean chest right up against the chest of anyone threatening her. She wants to be the kind of woman who says *No man will ever* and *No one messes with me*, who banters about the power of her vagina and cutting the dicks off of bullies. Fierce talk. Bold, big, *back the fuck off* talk.

She'd like to even just *believe* talk like that, but she can't. It's not only because of what happened nine months ago. It's about the bigger reality here. A reality that words can't make untrue. She's five foot three. She's a hundred and ten pounds. She's a young woman. History—her own, and the world's, years and years ago and just yesterday—has told her the truth about the vulnerability of her gender. As a female, her safety, her well-being, and the light she has for the world are still often overlooked and stomped on. That is quite clear.

She is also beautiful, which means it's what people see first, and sometimes, the only thing they see, and this is power and weakness both, but mostly weakness, at least so far. And while no one has put a hand on her (this is not *that* story, though of course for many women it is)—she understands something after last year that she wishes she didn't. She understands that when push comes to shove, literally or otherwise, that she must rely on other people being good and doing the right thing. And this, as she knows—as she knows very, very well—is a terrifying thing to rely on. It's fine most of the time, but at others, it is a thin thread. The thinnest.

She feels the thinness of that thread when that man's hand is on her arm, and she realizes there is nowhere for her to go, and nothing she could do, not really, if he decided to harm her. She can't overpower him. All she has is her voice, and even that can seem as helpful as shouting into a hurricane.

She is back in that place again, that horrible place, and the fun day is gone, and the happy music is gone, and the hunger is gone, and there is only the need to claw herself from the avalanche and *get away*. And that is how she finds herself here, at Gene Coulon Park in Renton. Her mind whirled and her feet slapped and slapped the pavement and now she is standing in a parking lot, trying to tell her mother what she is suddenly determined to do.

"Annabelle!" Gina nearly screams. "Stop going silent! Tell me what is happening."

"I'm not coming home. I'm going to run and keep running. I'm going to run until I reach Washington, DC." Of course, this is crazy and impossible and doomed, even if she's a long-distance runner and has two marathon medals hanging on the doorknob of her room. It is silly, and dramatic, and naive. Also—idealistic. Of course, she has no concept of the realities here. She has no plan. No team. No training. She will fail, fail, fail. But all she can feel at this moment is how much she personally needs this. She needs this so bad.

Yes, she is *that* Annabelle Agnelli.

"This is PTSD, Annabelle," her mother says. "Don't you remember what Dr. Mann said? This is hyperarousal, recklessness. Have you been having flashbacks? You haven't been sleeping well, I know. Talk to me. No one just *does* something like this. People who do . . . they plan, Annabelle. For months. There's, I don't know! Lots of stuff involved! No one just takes off. I'm coming to get you. Stop acting crazy."

Stop acting crazy? Well, it is far, far too late for that.

2

1. The blue whale has the largest heart, weighing more than a thousand pounds, the size of an average dairy cow.
2. The heart of a shrew can fit on your thumbnail.
3. The fairy fly, a type of wasp, has the smallest heart. It is 0.2 millimeters long. You need a microscope to see it.
4. Dogs have the biggest hearts compared to their body size.
5. A human heart is the size of two hands clasped together. Imagine your own hands joined, or your hand in someone else's, because that is what hands are for, and what hearts are for: holding each other. This can be very, very hard to remember when hearts have been so broken.

After the words *so broken*, Annabelle sets her pen in the little notebook to keep its place. It isn't really necessary, because the pen is between the cover and page one. She has been carrying around this little notebook, a nice one, the champion of notebooks, for a long time, not knowing what she should write in it. Now, look. The pen is moving, and the blank page has ink on it for the first time.

She has done all the things one can do in a Best Western while she waits. In addition to writing her first words in the Moleskine, she has searched the brown laminate dresser and nightstand drawers. She has thumbed through the padded folder of nearby restaurants. She has broken the paper-band hymen from the toilet seat. She has unwrapped the little soap and used a washcloth to clean her face. She has checked the bathtub for anything disgusting. She has tried out first one bed and then the other to see which had a better view of the television.

She sits in the swivelly chair at the table by the window and stares at the rain, which is now pummeling down like God is pissed. Well, He has a lot to be furious about, if He's really up there. She hopes He is up there, but honestly, it's very hard to tell. She has serious doubts, as you might understand.

The rain rolls down the window like tears. This sounds like bad poetry, so she's probably just overly hungry and very tired and questioning her good sense. She checks in with herself. Nope. She still wants to do what she said she wanted to do. Things are a little shaky, okay, fine, but her will is strong. She can hear the steady thump of it as she gazes out, waiting for the familiar headlights of her mother's Honda Civic to turn in to the Best Western lot.

Gina probably got lost. She is probably cursing the GPS woman as Malcolm claps his hands over his ears in the passenger seat. Gina treats GPS like it's an incompetent chauffeur.

She bullies and yells as the GPS woman keeps trying and trying with her endless, robotic patience. It's like watching an abusive relationship. Recently, Malcolm decided that Gina has to pay twenty-five cents every time she swears. He has a jar on the kitchen table. He's probably got sixty bucks in there already.

Waiting is tricky, because any sort of empty time in her head fills with you-know-what and with you-know-who. She will not say his name. He shouldn't get to have a name. She calls him The Taker. She calls him this because it is the essential truth, that he is the most evil sort of thief, and she calls him this because the words are tall and slender like The Taker himself, and because the name is shorter than Motherfucking Asshole, which is what Gina calls him. The problem is—well, there are lots of problems, but this one problem is—he is not just evil incarnate, not just the most vile and vicious monster, but a human who breathed and talked and ate lunch and took notes and held her hand, even. This makes her shudder, but it is also true. Some truths you just hate. You wish they weren't true. You wish you could annihilate them with your hate, but you can't. The only thing you can do is hate them, and that doesn't seem like much.

You wish you could annihilate some memories, too, but you can't do that, either. You try. But they pop in. They pop in and pop in, like Malcolm used to do when she was studying for some really intense final in her room. He'd do it just to annoy her, and she'd want to kill him. Memories: same.

It's happening now. She turns on the TV for distraction. It is a cooking show. A woman is making béchamel for lasagna, but not the way Grandpa does it. If he saw this, he'd have some heated words for the lady on the TV. The pans and the measuring and the woman's high-energy voice aren't doing enough to help Annabelle. The Taker walks right into her head, the way she saw him the first time. He's wearing a plaid shirt and jeans. He swings his backpack off.

She doesn't know him. He's new. She's in the one and only elective class she has all year, because she's an overachiever. She doesn't know what she wants to study later, but something science-related. She loves science, all of it—biology and physiology, planet earth, the universe, creatures both animal and human. She loves the magical design of it all, the unfathomable architecture of the cosmos right down to the intricate masterpiece of the eye. Science is where you might uncover facts that explain mysteries. She loves mysteries, too, but she loves explanations for mysteries even more. To her, explanations don't ruin mysteries; they only make them more magnificent.

Something science means it's AP everything, plus orchestra (cello), cross-country (of course), friends (she's popular), books read just for fun (too many to name). There's also her job at Essential Baking Company, and volunteer hours at Sunnyside Eldercare. See? She's nice, and to old people, too. Sweet, watery-eyed ladies with tissue-paper skin. Cranky old men with hangy basset-hound ears and suspenders. They love her. She's a sweetheart, they say. She is.

She was. Like a monster, she has destroyed people. She doesn't feel like a sweetheart anymore. She doesn't know yet if that's a tragedy or a very good thing. Or both. What a loss, that her naive kindness is gone. Kindness like that is the daffodils of the world, the dewdrops, the grass stains on the knees of jeans, yet she is sick to death of being a sweetheart. Also, that kind of naive kindness is akin to standing on a busy freeway and gazing at the beauty of the sun.

The elective is Mixed Media Art. The oldest, most tiresome game is: What If. It starts here. What if she chose Drama? What if she chose Video Game Design? What if Mixed Media Art had been full? Why did she have to be so neurotic and perfectionistic that she was online the minute registration opened for students with last names beginning with *A* through *C*? An hour later, and that class would have been filled. Mrs. Diablo was everyone's favorite teacher.

The Taker walks in. He has shaggy hair and he's tall. Tall enough that everyone looks. Plus, everyone's curious, because most of them have gone to school together since Eckstein Middle School. The backpack comes off and then the new guy slides into the seat in front of Annabelle. But first, he gives her a shy smile. He slides into the seat in front of her, but first, he gives her a shy smile. He slides into the seat in front of her, but first, he gives her a shy smile. He slides into the seat in front of her, but first, he gives her a shy smile for the millionth time.

Stop!

This is actually a technique that Dr. Mann taught her. She's supposed to say it out loud, and so she does.

"Stop."

Her own voice is very small in that room of the Best Western. The crowd watching the cooking show applauds. In this strange room, which smells faintly of traveling salesmen, the clapping sounds like encouragement, even though it's only praise for the lasagna that has come out of the oven.

She is almost grateful when Gina arrives and pounds on the door.

"Annabelle! Open up. It's me."

The lock is one of those old-fashioned sorts where you slide the chain sideways, so she does this. It makes her feel like she's in a detective-thriller film, which she sort of is. Gina busts in. Her disheveled, black-turning-gray-at-the-roots hair shimmers with raindrops. She's wearing her sweatpants and a million-years-old green sweater. She tosses her purse on the closest bed. Stuff spills out. Her keys, her Maybelline mascara, a tampon.

"Thank God you're all right," she says.

Malcolm follows behind her. He looks at Annabelle and rolls his eyes. It must have been some drive over. It is late. Malcolm is in his striped pajamas and dress shoes. Annabelle sees the narrative: the hurry, hurry, hurry, the quick grab of whatever is nearest. Malcolm sits at the edge of the bed and unties his shoes. He leans back against the headboard and sighs. In his black socks, striped pajamas, and without his usual glasses, he looks like a weary businessman, fed up with the account managers in the tristate region.

"Get your things," Gina says. "I'm just sorry you wasted the money paying for this *room*." Said as if the room is somewhat beneath her, which it isn't. It's pretty nice, actually. There's Wi-Fi and a coffeemaker. Free breakfast from six a.m. until ten in the hospitality center downstairs.

"I'm not going anywhere."

"Annabelle."

"I'm not."

"You can't be serious about this! Do you know what you're even saying? Do you know how far DC is from here?"

"Two thousand seven hundred and nineteen miles by foot," Malcolm says from the bed. He's changed the channel on the television, from the cooking show to *Nova*, which she and Malcolm both love. *Nova* explains the ways impossible things work. *Nova* has answers. On the screen, a satellite orbits our earth.

"My phone's about to die," Annabelle says. "Did you bring my stuff?"

"Of course I didn't bring your stuff. If you think I'm going to allow this, you're nuts. Aside from the practicalities here, aside from the fact that it's basically, um, *impossible*, you are graduating in two and a half months. Your birthday is in five days. I had a whole surprise bowling and picn—"

"Exactly."

"What do you mean, 'exactly'?"

She didn't want to have to play hardball, but here goes. "In five days, I'll be eighteen. There's no more allowing. I'll officially be an adult."

Gina's exhale is a freight train barreling through a tunnel. Her face turns red. She throws her hands up, paces to the bathroom and back.

Malcolm is putting his dress shoes back on. Tying the thin grown-man laces. He hates conflict. She's surprised the shoes even fit. He only wore them twice that she can remember. Once to the wedding of Patrick O'Brien to Angie Morelli, her mother's oldest friend. Angie helped get Gina the paralegal job at O'Brien and Bello's Attorneys-at-Law. Malcolm also wore the shoes—

Stop!

"Excuse me," Malcolm says.

"Where do you think *you're* going?" Gina says.

"I forgot something in the car."

"It's dark out there. It's eleven thirty! We're in *Renton*."

He's got Gina's keys in his hand. Annabelle once let him drive the car in the empty high school parking lot. She hopes he doesn't try to make a run for it, too. "I'll be right back. You can watch me from here," he tells Gina.

"Be careful," she says.

Gina doesn't even keep an eye on Malcolm out the window, though. She has more than she can handle right here. The two of them, Annabelle and her mom, face off. "I know you don't understand. . . ." Annabelle tries.

"It's not that I don't understand. Of course I *understand.* It's just . . . We don't know anything about this! Do you even know what you're saying? There are mountains. Trucks. Miles and miles! Rain, summer heat coming. What're you going to do, sleep on the road? Oh my God. I can't even think about it. You, a young woman alone? You can't do that! And you're not ready for that kind of distance! You're talking, what, a half marathon *every single day*? Do you have any idea what that would do to your body? And if you ran slower, well, you can't be gone that long, in case you forgot."

"Like I could forget? And a guy in Oregon just did it in four months. Coach Kwan told us about it. We followed his blog. I know more about it than you think. And I *am* ready. Ready enough. After the marathons, halfs are easy!" This is a lie. They aren't easy. But they may be doable. "I ran eleven miles here, and I feel great. I've done the math. If I push a little, go sixteen a day—"

"What about money? What about graduation? What about *Seth Greggory*? You can't just take off. September twenty-second, Annabelle."

"I *know.* Do you think I don't know? The date is burned into my brain."

"Avoidance! PTSD symptom! This is just a momentary panic like Dr.—"

"I have more than enough credits to graduate already. I have more than enough money."

"College money!"

"How do we know if I'm even going to use it? Dr. Mann also says I put too much pressure on myself. Maybe I—"

"And this isn't pressure? This isn't changing one kind of pressure for another kind of pressure? Frying pan into the fire. Frying pan into the blazing forest fire!"

She may have a point.

"And what do you hope to even get out of this, huh? What happens when you get there? You just knock on some senator's door?"

"I haven't figured that part out yet." Annabelle pictures Dr. Mann, sitting in her office with the painting of the red and yellow mountains behind her. She has soft auburn hair cut short, a calm voice, and patient eyes that crinkle when she laughs. She wears looped scarves and the room smells like vanilla. There's a box of Kleenex and a little clock next to the couch where Annabelle sits, but Dr. Mann sits back in her chair as if she has all the time in the world. She listens. She says things like, *You don't have to have all the answers at once. You can get more information. You can figure it out day by day.*

Gina walks to the window, stares out. She folds her arms. "What is that even going to do? Huh? Really. Say you walk into the senator's office. Say you actually talk to a giant room of politicians. How does that change anything?" When Gina turns around, her eyes are teary. *God damn it. God damn it!* Annabelle can see once again what this has done to her mother, too. She's aged in the last year. She looks tired. Her sweater droops because she's lost weight.

"It's something. Something is better than nothing," Annabelle says. Or tries to say. Her voice cracks and wobbles.

Gina shakes her head. "Oh, honey."

"Mom," Annabelle pleads.

Malcolm is back. He has a fat backpack, which he sets on the bed and unzips. Inside, there are two sets of her lightest nylon track clothes, her Camel hydration pack, her handheld water bottle, and her thin rain jacket. Underwear. Socks. Her small medical kit. Her phone charger. Toothpaste, toothbrush. The knee-length Batman T-shirt she sleeps in. A Ziploc bag with a fat bunch of money in it and a credit card. He applied for that card to start building credit, as *Money* magazine had advised. Annabelle gave him that subscription when it was on his Christmas list last year.

"Here," he says. He hands her a brown bag. Inside, there are two peanut butter and jelly sandwiches packed tight in plastic wrap, an apple, slices of cheese, a few cookies, and a mostly full bottle of Gatorade. "You must be hungry."

Annabelle can't speak now. Her throat has tightened. She might cry.

"Also this," Malcolm says. Several pages of paper, stapled together. "A route. Google Maps. Cross-referenced with the one Jason Dell from Oregon did. I got it from your cross-country binder."

"Oh, butthead," Annabelle says very softly. It's an expression of love. It's her all-purpose name for him, yelled in fury, tickled in affection.

"No," Gina says. "No, no, no, no."

"Wait. These." Malcolm reaches into the backpack again. He sets her new pair of running shoes on top of the other stuff.

Annabelle can barely get the words out. "Thank you."

"We'll figure it out day by day." There'd been several family sessions with Dr. Mann, too. Malcolm sat quietly, picking at his fingernails, but he'd been listening.

Gina starts to cry. A noisy cry. Malcolm claps his hands dramatically over his ears. Annabelle claps her hands dramatically over hers.

"God damn it, you two! Stop making fun of me."

"Stop making fun of me," Malcolm makes fun in a Gina voice.

"We'll stay here with you, Annabelle, until we get past what you're feeling right now. We aren't going anywhere," Gina says as she retrieves a wad of TP from the bathroom and blows her nose.

"Mom, no," Malcolm says. "I've got to go to bed. I've got a math test tomorrow." And then to Annabelle, "Give me everything from your bag that you don't need. Tomorrow, run to the red circle on the map, and we'll reconvene." He's gone from weary businessman to CIA operative.

"Okay, bud," Annabelle says. "Thanks."

Gina is shoving the stuff back in her purse. "I hate it when you guys gang up. I *hate* it. We are doing this *tonight only*."

Malcolm's and Annabelle's eyes meet and have a conversation. In that split second, stuff is decided, a vow is made. Well, vows are often made without having enough good information.

Annabelle stands at the window and watches the arc of headlights as her mom and her brother leave the Best Western parking lot. She is less anxious than she'd have imagined, here alone in this room. Her anxiety is a quiet hum and not the heavy-metal band you'd expect, given her current plan, and given the future that awaits her. She sits at the edge of the bed, eats her sandwiches, and watches *Nova*. Planets spin and stars explode.

This is how it begins.

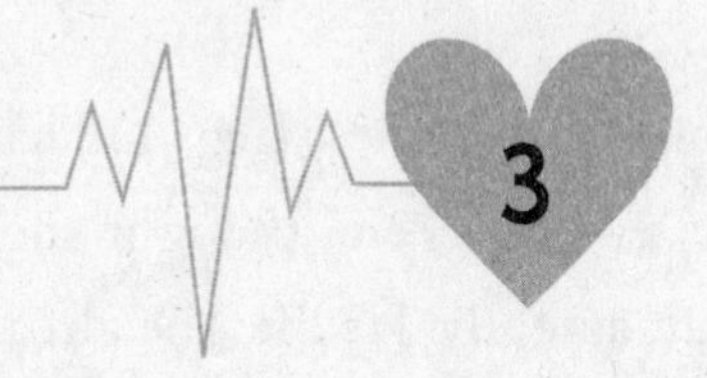

Under the big aluminum domes—a bounty. There are fluffy mounds of scrambled eggs, shiny sausage links, a bacon extravaganza. Annabelle wraps up a few bagels and muffins in napkins and puts them in her backpack. She learned this trick from Grandpa Ed, who always makes her put the extra rolls in her purse when they go out to eat. There is an array of sliced fruit laid out like a sunrise. Orange slices go in her pack, too. There are little boxes of cereal and jars of granola.

The abundance makes her feel hopeful, and so does her charged phone, and the pink-yellow light of morning. She thinks: *It's going to be a beautiful day.* Annabelle has not had that thought for almost a year now. She realizes that there have been other days when the pink-yellow light of morning made everything look hopeful, but not to her. She despised those days for their wrongness. Now, even a parking lot and out-of-state license plates and strip malls in the distance wink with hope. She feels the slightest opening inside of herself. She allows a little light in. This sounds like a religious card, but she doesn't care.

Annabelle stretches. Legs up, legs out. Bend down; reach. She's not as sore as she thought she'd be after yesterday. She feels great, actually. It's like she already left something behind. Not *it all*, of course, she knows better than that. That is something that will never happen, her whole life long. Just *something*. One tiny piece, which is a large enough event to occur, given her circumstances.

She takes a big gulp of misty March loveliness. The air is deliciously damp. Annabelle spots the arrowheads of bulbs poking up in the landscaping. A Renton squirrel scurries up the gate of the motel swimming pool, closed for the season. Spring, renewal, life! Sure, this—this expansiveness—has something to do with the recent joy of consuming bacon (she shouldn't have had that much salt), but it's also from the road ahead. The road *ahead*. Is this where the magic is? That she is, for once, not looking behind?

She is still in front of the Best Western, where it is very easy to be optimistic.

In fact, after this moment, she won't be this optimistic for a long, long time.

The slap-sound of her feet on pavement is familiar. Even way back when That Bastard Father Anthony lived with them, when she was just a kid, Annabelle would run circles in their backyard as he timed her with the stopwatch he kept in his gym bag. In elementary school, she raced around at recess, and it was all about speed, how fast she could go, the feel of her ponytail flying out behind her. Later, in junior high, after her father left and her name went from Annabelle Agnelli-Manutto to just Annabelle Agnelli, there were a lot of things to run *from*. Money problems; Malcolm in that bad spell where he peed his bed; Dad driving to the house to pick them up, and then driving away again after he and Gina argued. Dad spending less and less time with them, and how this hurt but was also somehow easier.

Annabelle started counting things then—ceiling tiles, sidewalk squares, and consonants in words. Steps. Strides. She went from speed to distance. Back in junior high, she learned that the long-distance run, tiring herself out, soothing herself with the rhythm of pace, helped the anxiety. It was like driving a screaming baby around in a car.

Back then, a three-mile cross-country event was huge. It still is—in high school, she made state. But after cross-country season ended in early November, she also just ran for herself the rest of the year. To stay in shape, but also for the nature-connectedness-science-y beauty all around outside and for the overachiever challenge of distance. Half marathons. Two marathons, just before her life went up in flames. And after it did, weeks after, when she could finally get up out of bed again, she put on her shoes. She went outside and ran. She ran until she was exhausted. She ran fast enough to blur the scenery in her mind.

When she did this, she discovered another trick. If she goes far and runs hard enough, her body hurts. She'd done this week after week even before now. Inflicting pain on herself. Punishment. That sounds a little sicko, but too bad. It is what it is. She wishes the punishment were more brutal, even though it's pretty bad already and, thanks to Seth Greggory, about to get worse. Along with the punishment, she's also doing the thing she most wants to do: flee.

Now, on this first day of her long journey, she is running along Lake Washington Boulevard again, but this time on the east side of the lake. The lake is pink-tinged with morning, and she can see the freeway beyond, and the cars lining up in their commute. School starts in just over an hour. Her seats will sit empty. People will wonder. People will worry. People will become uneasy. She shouldn't even be in school anyway. Why they let her come back is beyond her. Every day, she makes people uneasy. They look at her like she's got a bomb strapped to her chest.

To the east, straight through those hills packed with evergreens, is her destination for the day: Preston, Washington. The route ahead is filled with enticing *Westward Ho!* names: the Coal Mines Trail, the Bullitt Fireplace Trail, the Rainier Trail. Honestly, it looks a little dark out that way. It looks ominous, like the deep forests of fairy tales. Fear crawls up her spine.

You will not be weak, she tells herself. *You will not think about Seth Greggory and the future. You will not imagine jails and handcuffs*. The lecture evolves into a list of commandments: *You will not count all the miles that are left. You will not be terrified. You will not let The Taker take over every silent moment in your head. That is not him, in that car. That is not you, getting out—*

Stop!

There is a large building next to her. RENTON BIBLE CHURCH, the sign reads. CHURCH PARKING ONLY! VIOLATORS WILL BE BAPTIZED! She needs to pay attention. She is suddenly seeing problem number one: navigation. She doesn't want to drain her phone battery, but she needs that GPS woman. They are about to have a very important relationship. She almost feels like she should apologize to her, for all the abuse she's taken from her mother. This is one of Annabelle's struggles, the sense that she must apologize and atone for other people's actions.

"Let's start fresh, you and me," Annabelle says. "My mother isn't exactly the most patient person in the world, so I'm sorry. She's been horrible to you. I'll do my best to be more respectful."

"In one half mile, turn right onto Tenth Street," the GPS woman says.

"I don't even know who you are, and you're going to be with me on the biggest trip of my life."

The GPS woman is silent. She needs a name, for starters. As Annabelle heads for Tenth Street, she scrolls through some possibilities. Olive. Mrs. Cash. AJ. Big Rose.

"Loretta," she says.

"Turn right onto Tenth Street."

"Loretta it is, then."

• • •

Somewhere just after the endless Highway 900, after a lunch stop for a bagel and water, Annabelle tackles the Coal Mines Trail, which parallels a railroad track before looping through a dark and fern-filled forest. She crosses a creepy wooden bridge. It is mossy-slick, and she has to watch her footing.

As she runs through the cool, dark woods, she begins to realize how alone she is. It feels dangerous, like the trees may start talking with gnarled wood mouths and reaching for her with twisted branch arms. She gets the creeps. It is alone-in-a-parking-garage fear, alone-on-an-empty-street fear, the kind of daily fear women are so familiar with that they forget how wrong that familiarity is. The damp path has splotchy parts. Mud smacks and dots her legs. And then: She's out. She's on Mountainside Drive and suddenly, shockingly, she grasps problem number two.

Hills.

Not just hills, but serious freaking inclines. And she is not unfamiliar with hills. Of course she's run hills! But these are mountain foothills, which means they are the baby hills before she gets to the real deal of actual *mountain passes*. Already, as she makes her way up, she slows and leans forward, same as Mr. Giancarlo at Sunnyside Eldercare as he heads to the dining hall. Everything hurts. Her chest, her legs, her stomach. Probably this is also like Mr. Giancarlo at Sunnyside Eldercare, though he never complained. All Mr. Giancarlo used to say was *Get that woman out of my room*. What woman? There was no woman. Mr. Giancarlo had ghosts haunting him, too.

Annabelle shuffles. She can't go fast, or she'll never make it. She's in excellent shape, training for this even if she hadn't realized it, but sixteen miles a day could kill her if she doesn't pace herself. At home, her friends are already in fifth period. This is taking a long time, much longer than she ever imagined, which is likely going to be problem number three. Seth Greggory is not exactly going to wait.

Her phone buzzes and buzzes. Wow! Look how popular she is, now that she's not there. Now that people don't have to face her and manage their own weirdness and sorrow. Of course, it could just be Gina, checking on her every two seconds. She can't stop to look. This is her *first day*, and if she stops to look at her phone, she may just stop, period.

She can hear the freeway alongside her, I-90, humming along. Parts of the road have blind curves that scare her. She hopes she doesn't get flattened by a car before she even gets out of her own state. Man, people drive fast. Problems number five, six, seven, eight!

Finally, she sees it—a tiny town, if you can even call it a town. There's a single street with shops: a True Value and a Subway and the Preston Tire Center. She's been out here once for a cross-country meet, but nothing looks familiar. After all of this running, she's maybe a forty-five-minute drive from home.

"Help me, Loretta."

"In two miles, take a left on Alder."

"You're a real friend."

• • •

Her destination: the Secret Garden B&B, forty-two bucks a night. She booked it that morning, and she's supposed to call home the minute she gets there so that they can decide what to do next. Annabelle loved *The Secret Garden* when she was a kid. She can still remember when the robin helps Mary Lennox find the key to the gate. So, okay, her expectations were high for forty-two bucks a night, but blame Frances Hodgson Burnett. The small, sagging house in front of her has faded gingerbread trim. The porch needs painting. On it, there's a cat food bowl with dried stuff in it, and drapey cobwebs up in the corners, and a fat spider that has zero fear of being evicted. The welcome mat says only LCOME. But Annabelle is too exhausted and mud-splattered to care. She rings the buzzer. Twelve years later, an old hippie woman with waist-length gray hair answers the door.

"Yes?"

"I'm Annabelle Agnelli? I called this morning?"

"Oh! I was expecting someone . . ." Less muddy? Less covered in sweat? Less burdened, less crouched and exhausted? Someone not about to burst into tears? Someone whose life isn't essentially over? "Older. Someone older."

Clearly, the proprietor of the Secret Garden has not read or watched the news in the last nine months. Then again, Annabelle Agnelli may be utterly unrecognizable right now, even to herself.

Problems number nine, ten, eleven! She was stupid to think she could patch this thing together; stupid to think there'd be nice motels and cheap B&Bs along the way. There will be long stretches of country without *any* motels in sight.

This is why people plan for months. Her mom was right—you *don't* just take off. Jason Dell had a team that followed along in an RV. He had a logistics coordinator, a driver, and the critical emotional support he needed. He had medical supplies at the ready, the right clothing and equipment, and meals prepared for him, along with a supply of protein shakes, protein bars, water, and snacks providing the hydration and thousands of calories required to keep him going. In that RV, he could sleep the essential eleven hours a night wherever he was.

It's becoming very clear: This is a failed mission. She and Loretta can't do this by themselves.

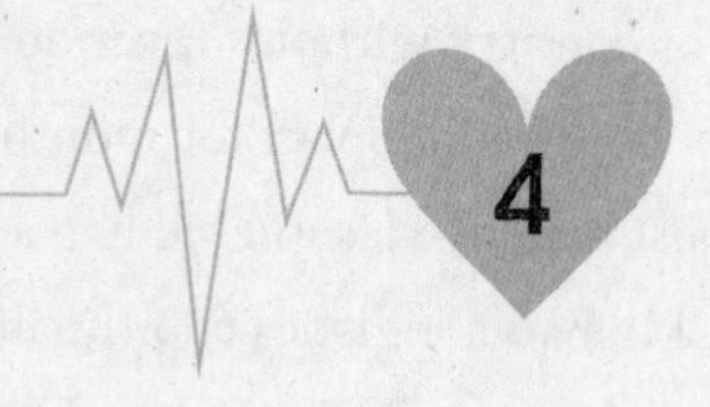

4

In her room at the Secret Garden, Annabelle rolls down her mud-caked socks. More problems: blisters at the back of her heels. New track shoes, what was she thinking? She wasn't, is the answer. The blisters are puffy little waterbeds right where her shoes hit her Achilles. Now that she sees them, they start to shout and burn.

The bed has a floral spread, and there are unnerving paintings of bunnies on the walls. A doll sits in a rocker, and a teddy bear rests against a lace pillow on the bed. The house smells like potpourri and Lysol, and something beef-stew-ish. Annabelle hears Yvonne, proprietor of the Secret Garden B&B, rattling pans downstairs. A cat meows on the other side of the door. Annabelle wants to hold the lace pillow to her chest and sob, but it's too icky to touch.

Her shirt is stuck to her back from sweat. She goes down the hall, takes the fastest shower ever, and changes into her Batman T-shirt. Yvonne agreed to launder her clothes. She imagines them spinning with Yvonne's cat-hair nightgowns.

Annabelle is supposed to call home. She checks her phone. Just as she suspected, most of those missed calls were from her mother. People at school are probably relieved she's gone. Gina is likely tapping her fingers and waiting for the apologetic call she knows is coming. I'm here, Annabelle texts. Will call ASAP.

She wants to go home.

God, what was I thinking? she says to Kat. *This was silly! I am stupid, stupid, stupid. Mom can come pick me up, and it will be like none of this happened.*

Let's not forget The Glass Menagerie, Kat says.

The Glass Menagerie?

Ninth-grade play, don't you remember?

Of course I remember.

You did this same thing when you got the lead. You brought the script home with all your lines highlighted and then you freaked the fuck out. Come on, Belle Bottom. Rally.

It's like Kat is sitting right beside her. Ever since they were the only two girls in the sixth grade who were afraid of gymnastics, they'd always been there for each other. They knew the *story* of each other from then on, which is one of the largest things you can say about another person. Kat was there when Annabelle sent the big letter to That Bastard Father Anthony a few years ago, after he shocked them all by moving to Boston to become a priest, and Kat was there to hear Annabelle's confession about her and Will on Will's dad's sailboat. Annabelle understood about Kat's mother, Patty, and her drinking, and she kept the secret of the tiny butterfly tattoo Kat got. Kat could tell when Annabelle was counting things in her head from anxiety, and Annabelle could tell when Kat felt lonely even in a big bunch of people. They knew which books the other would love and hate. From behind, they looked so similar, with their thin shoulders and long dark hair, and their same taste in clothes. But they were different, too. Kat was more funny and brave than Annabelle, but more cynical, too. Science and math were hard for Kat—she wanted to be a writer. She got antsy watching science shows; she'd throw pillows and try to grab the remote, but if you interrupted her at the end of a book, you'd pay. Differences don't matter all that much when you love someone.

There's a tap at the door. Yvonne hands Annabelle a tray. There's a bowl of beef stew, and a dish of green salad with that orange dressing on it that Annabelle can't remember the name of, and one of those chubby Hawaiian rolls that Will's family sometimes had with dinner.

"Wow, thanks," Annabelle says.

"You said you had some clothes for me?"

The clothes are wrapped in a towel. "Sorry they're so disgusting."

"Also, you wanted these?" Yvonne hands Annabelle the scissors. Yvonne's mouth is set in an unreadable line, but her words drip suspicion. "Is everything all right?"

She apparently thinks Annabelle might use the shears to slash her wrists or something, which might be an understandable assumption. Annabelle saw her own eyes in that bathroom mirror. They looked desperate, haunted. "Everything's great! Thank you!" She adds several sunny exclamation points.

This is how cheerful she used to sound when talking to Theresa, her supervisor at Sunnyside Eldercare. And to Claire and Thomas, her bosses and the new owners of Essential Baking Company, and to all her teachers, especially Coach Kwan. And Will's parents. And Nordstrom salespeople. And waiters. And every adult who maybe held some sort of imaginary report card as to what kind of human being she was. Truthfully, she used that voice with Will sometimes, too. Cheery and positive, even when she didn't feel cheery and positive. Who was that talking? Not her. Some perfect, made-up version of her. Niceness is expected of her, not honesty.

She hobbles (and this is bad, very bad, the way the backs of her heels hurt) to the bathroom down the hall.

She takes one last look at herself, but doesn't hesitate. The long brown hair—well, it has to go. She should have done this months ago. It's harder to do than you think, actually physically harder, but maybe just because her hair is still damp and Yvonne's scissors are dull. Fat lumps drop into the sink. She reaches around to the back. She doesn't give a shit, honestly, how it looks. It's a bit of a dramatic movie cliché, this sudden hacking of hair, but she doesn't give a shit about that, either. What matters is that it's gone.

In the mirror, there is her once-lovely face, looking gaunt

and wrecked. Her hair is a sad, ragged helmet, like she's the loser in the war. She looks awful. Finally, her outsides match her insides.

She sweeps what she can into the trash. Yvonne will be horrified. She'll think Annabelle is running from the law, which in a way is true.

Back in the room with the creepy bunny paintings, Annabelle touches the chopped, uneven edges of her hair. The doll stares at her from the rocking chair.

What is she doing here? What has she done?

She is lost.

She is so lost.

And she is so, so terrified.

She starts to cry. She puts her face in her hands and sobs. She tries to do this quietly. Muffled sobs are even more desperate than loud, set-free ones. She can tell you all about sobs, their various forms. Crying can be a quiet drizzle or a torrential downpour.

Her phone buzzes. Her mom is calling, Annabelle is sure. Annabelle will tell Gina to come get her. She will apologize for her stupidity and her craziness. Gina will be here in an hour. Annabelle will ask her to bring a Kid Valley burger and onion rings. The orange dressing on that salad looks like cat barf.

But it's not Gina. "Your brother has called me, like, fifteen times," Zach Oh says.

Annabelle blows her nose.

"What is that noise? Is that a jet? Are you at the airport?"

"No, I'm not at the airport! I'm in a weird horror-movie B&B, where the dolls talk."

"Malcolm told me. Forty-two dollars a night? What did you expect?"

"Disregard anything my brother said."

"What do you mean, 'disregard'?"

"Disregard! I can't do any of this. It was stupid. I wasn't thinking. I had a bad moment."

"I can't disregard! I just set up the GoFundMe. It's got, like, eighty-six bucks in there already." Zach just got accepted to University of Washington on a full scholarship to study financial engineering. He's been trading mutual funds since he was in the sixth grade, and Malcolm thinks he's a god. "Olivia is designing the Run for a Cause T-shirt. Wait. She's yelling something at me. What?" Annabelle hears Olivia in the background. "She says to tell you we're giving away the shirts with a fifty-dollar donation."

"Zach, my heels are already a mess. My legs . . ."

"You did this same thing about *The Glass Menagerie*."

Annabelle groans. Zach was the sound and lighting guy for the production. She and Zach have been friends since grade five, when they were partnered up to make puppets of Lewis and Clark. Most people come and go in your life, but Zach has stayed—through puppets and the awful middle-school play when they were talking bacteria and that one embarrassing semester they took chorus, through his dad's job loss and her parents' divorce, through the tragedy. And she's known Olivia since middle-school orchestra. Olivia was first-chair cello, and Annabelle sat behind her, a total admirer of Olivia's long hair, which is shiny as a mirror. They became even better friends when Olivia and Zach became a couple. Annabelle feels a little choked up. It's the people who know you and love you that save you.

"Malcolm wants a website, but that'll take a few days. You've got seven followers already on the Run for a Cause Facebook page, but two are dudes from Pakistan with shirts unbuttoned to their navels, and one is me and one is Malcolm and one is Olivia and two are teachers from Roosevelt."

"Oh my God, you guys!"

"Blame Malcolm."

"Why did you listen to him?"

"He's *right*. *You're* right. You need this. Jesus, it's better than—*you*, lately. Rally, Annabelle. This is . . . a reason to, you know, *go on*. Wait. Olivia wants to talk to you."

"Annabelle?" Olivia is one of those strong, efficient people who'll be the CEO of some big company after she gets her MBA. She can memorize long pieces of music, and she has one of those plain faces that turns beautiful unexpectedly, and she is so capable, she never loses her car in parking lots like Annabelle does. Annabelle has seen a different side to her, though. Like when her dad was going through chemo. Like after the tragedy. Like now. Her voice is small and full of hope. "You need to do this for you. And maybe this is the wrong thing to say, but *I* need you to do this, you know?"

Zach is back. "Hey! GoFundMe just went up to one hundred twenty-one. Coach Kwan! Thirty-five bucks!"

Someone's knocking. It is probably Yvonne again, picking up the tray of untouched food. Or else the Preston Police Department, after Yvonne dialed 911.

"I've got to go."

"Me too. Malcolm's calling again on the other line."

When Annabelle opens the door, she does not find Yvonne or the Preston Police Department, or even her mother.

"What the hell is this place? *Mi fa cagare!* I'm gonna have nightmares."

"Grandpa! What are you doing here?"

"Jesus, what is that? Looks like a cat puked on that salad. Get your things."

"Are you taking me home? I'm not sure if I want to go. I think I do. Maybe I don't."

"Who said anything about going home?"

"Where are we going, then?"

"Where are we going? We're going to DC! You run, I drive. I got the RV outside. It's been almost six months since I've been on the road, and I'm losing my mind. *Che cavolo!* Let's get out of here."

"Grandpa . . ." Annabelle can barely speak.

"Don't get all mushy on me. Get your stuff. I got a pan of eggplant parmigiana in the oven."

• • •

Yvonne seems relieved to see them go. She hands Annabelle her clothes, still damp. Grandpa has the RV parked at the end of the street. It's a big, hulking beast, with a license plate holder that reads CAPTAIN ED, and a seen-better-days bumper sticker HOME OF THE REDWOODS from the time he visited Sequoia National Park. Now, Annabelle's wet clothes hang off the back of the padded benches. Her socks lay limp over the door to the bathroom. It's like a laundry crime has been committed.

Stop!

Grandpa Ed has brought some of her things. More clothes. Her laptop. Her bigger backpack, with lots of her special stuff in it. There are a few pairs of her favorite pajamas, including the flannel monkeys in space. Oh man, tampons, too, and that's when she realizes.

"*Mom* packed this. How is it that Mom packed this?"

"Let's just say, she said some things, I said some things." Grandpa opens the oven, and great smells parade out. "I promised I'd take care of you. I promised you'd be safe. She cried. I slipped Carl Walter some money to get her a nice glass of wine and some dinner."

"It couldn't have been *that* easy."

"She thinks you'll be back in two days. Me, I know different."

He sets the pan of eggplant parmigiana on the small laminate table between them. It looks amazing. There's a sourdough loaf and butter, and a salad in a Tupperware bowl. He's gone all out. Grandpa slides a big cheesy slab from the pan and slaps it down on a Chinet plate.

"You haven't mentioned my hair," Annabelle says.

"Hair, shmair. Give me your glass." He pours her a small amount of red wine. "Don't tell your mother." Grandpa Ed believes in red wine. His father and his father's father lived to be ninety-six because of a glass of vino a day, he says.

She shouldn't drink it. Not only because she's underage. It'll be dehydrating.

"It'll help you sleep," Grandpa Ed says.

This is an excellent selling point. She used to just close her eyes and sleep hard all night long, but that hasn't happened in a while.

He lifts his glass. She lifts hers. "To—"

There's only one thing that should follow "to." Forevermore, this will be the case. Annabelle's face squinches up. She puts her head in her hands.

"*Bella.*" Grandpa Ed puts one old hand on her arm. "In San Francisco, back in the day? After Gino Maserelli—" He stops. Tries again. "After your Grandma Luna—" He's going for wisdom, but the real wisdom is knowing there sometimes isn't any.

She peeks at him and, God damn it, his old eyes are watery with tears, and then he takes out his grandpa handkerchief and honks his nose into it loudly. They just sit there in silence across from each other at the laminate table of the RV, which has traveled the country and seen better days. Viewed from above, it is a glowing capsule of aluminum, with two astronauts inside. She wishes she were one, anyway, an astronaut. She wants to propel herself into the dark and terrifying universe. Being that unanchored and that much in peril seems preferable to being here, grounded on the earth that wrecked her.

5

1. The average human heart beats seventy times a minute. But it can speed up to 220 in extreme circumstances.
2. A hummingbird's heart zooms at 1,260 beats per minute.
3. A blue whale's heart beats six times a minute. A groundhog—five times a minute when he's hibernating. A horse—thirty-eight. A rabbit—205. A mouse—670. The heart of a canary beats seventeen times in a second.
4. A study ("The Physiological Response to Fear in Unexpected Situations") found that hearts beat over six times faster when a person has been startled.
5. In real life, the Physiological Response to Fear in Unexpected Situations is a feeling that your heart has stopped altogether.

Annabelle leaves the Moleskine under the pillow of her bunk. The bunk is a narrow alcove above the RV's front seats. When she sits up without thinking, she bonks her head. She did this twice last night, not remembering where she was. Grandpa Ed was wrong about the wine and sleep—she was awake all night. This might have also been due to Grandpa Ed snoring down below on the daybed. Hour after hour, it sounded like a donkey was getting strangled.

When Annabelle climbs down from her bunk, Grandpa Ed's eyes are narrowed from morning light. He isn't used to getting up this early. There's a lot of swearing, and gross throat-clearing. He can't hear a word she says, either, because he doesn't have his hearing aids in yet. *Yeah, yeah, yeah*, he says to everything.

The plan is: He will meet her by the trailhead of the Iron Horse Trail at the end of her day. Gina wants Grandpa Ed to follow behind Annabelle in the RV as she runs. This would not only be annoying, but pretty much impossible and sometimes dangerous, since Loretta's pedestrian route is on back trails and down small, narrow highways. It will take Annabelle three days to finish the Iron Horse Trail. It'll take another two weeks to cross the state line into Idaho. When Annabelle thinks of that state line, she thinks of Kat, and the joke they had after the two of them read *On the Road*. For weeks, whenever they got in a car together, even if they were just going to get Slurpees at 7-Eleven, they'd do it.

"We have longer ways to go," Annabelle would say in a profound Kerouac voice.

"No matter," Kat would answer. *"The road is life."*

• • •

It is a different view today for Annabelle and Loretta, and the sky is blue and the air is crisp. Annabelle tries to concentrate on all this, instead of on the pain, pain, pain in the back of her heels. She and Loretta have planned a shorter run today, twelve miles. Her body needs a break. The end location will be near food and facilities.

The route takes her down the street of a town, North Bend, and on a backcountry road through a long stretch of green meadow. Now, she finds herself in a suburban neighborhood of big houses with three-car garages. The lawns are all perfect except for the one shit yard that probably makes the neighbors crazy. In the others, flowers bloom flawlessly, and there are SUVs in driveways, ready to ferry the kids to soccer practice.

It makes her think of Will, of course. And then The Taker.

"Stop," she tries, but she's weak today. Sometimes, you just need to give in. It's like the pain of punishment, when it's a craving you succumb to. The way you laugh until you cry, the way you eat until your stomach aches, the way you scratch an itch until it bleeds.

"Turn left on Eagle Lake Drive," Loretta encourages. But Annabelle can't be reached. She is in it.

The Taker. Will.

In Will's large suburban house, Annabelle and Will are in the bonus room—that vast, luxurious space where Will and Stevie played when they were little, and where they now hang out with their friends. Will lives in Bellevue, on the east side of Lake Washington, and he goes to Bellevue High. Annabelle goes to Roosevelt and lives in Seattle. The Eastside seems so foreign. Most Seattleites think so. They make fun of Eastsiders for having lots of money and for driving everywhere. The bonus room is practically bigger than the whole downstairs of Annabelle's house. Will and Annabelle sit on a leather couch that could fit eight people.

Annabelle and Will met at a football game, Bellevue versus Roosevelt, when they were both sophomores. Bellevue High is a rich school, a rich city, and the kids there win everything, every football game, every track meet, every academic scholarship. The parking lot of their school looks like a luxury car dealership, stuffed with BMWs, a few Porsches and Jaguars thrown in. After the game, Annabelle and Kat and Zander were down on the field, and so was Will. Annabelle was wearing her big puffy coat and braids and a baseball cap, and Will tugged one braid playfully and said "Pippi." A boy who looked like that, who knew about *Pippi Longstocking* . . . well, that was that.

After a year together, she still wants to put her hands on him all the time, and he wants to put his hands on her. His big arms feel so good. His butt in those jeans does. His chest is a perfect hard pillow to rest her head on. His eyes are brown and sweet, like those of a deer in a forest. God, Annabelle's attracted to Will, but they're buddies, too. They have fun. He cracks her up, and she cracks him up. They go to Shilshole Beach with friends, and they drink a beer or two at the bonfires, and they bring burritos to Magnuson Park. He sometimes runs with her in the summer when she trains for cross-country in the fall, and she goes to his spring lacrosse games. They swim at Green Lake and go to each other's houses for dinner, watching all the premium channels at Will's because Gina doesn't have them.

Will has it all. He's funny, and a good person; he's popular, athletic, and so smart. His favorite sandwich is peanut butter and honey, and he's nice to his little brother, but his mom still does his laundry and he drives his dad's old Mercedes. He's good-looking, with those brown curls and those eyes and that body, and he can get a little cocky, a little self-involved, but Annabelle and everyone else forgive him for it. She especially forgives him for it whenever she sees him write by hand; he crouches over in concentration, his arm curled and his fingers pressing hard like a child, and she loves this. She especially forgives him, too, when he comes inside and he smells like cold winter air, and also when he keeps his promises. He is serious about promises. He's going to be a lawyer, like Robert and Tracie, his parents.

Now, on this couch, they are kissing. Annabelle's cheeks are hot. She wishes they were somewhere alone instead of at Will's house, where she can hear Robert and Tracie downstairs talking and having a glass of wine. See, he has perfect parents, too. They like each other. It's like witnessing a vanishing species. They take family trips to Tahiti and Bali. They're a family you envy.

Annabelle rubs her hand on the V of Will's jeans. She loves him and wants him, but he also seems a little distant right then, as he has been lately. She's trying to reach him, to bridge the distance. She can sense the unspoken rules, all right. Making him feel wanted and desired is part of what's required of her. But she also just plain *likes* rubbing her hand on the V of his jeans. She's forever in a spinning round–ness of who she's supposed to be and who she really is, what's expected and what she really wants. When you spin like that, things get blurry.

Will grabs her wrist. "Annabelle."

"What? What's wrong?"

"I think we . . ."

Of course, he doesn't need to say much. She reads his eyes, and suddenly she knows she was right about what she feared was coming.

"I think maybe we should . . ."

"Oh, God."

"I love you, Belle. You know I do. But my mom and dad think we're too serious, you know, for our age. They think—"

"*They* think?"

"Well, they're probably right. I mean . . . we should have other experiences, with other people. You've only been with me and Chase. I've only been with you and Sarah and Catherine."

Annabelle's chest caves in. Tears gather, and one rolls down her face and drops off her nose like an unlucky mountain climber.

"Is that what you want?"

He doesn't say anything more, so she knows the answer. "Pip," he says. This is her love name. "Please don't cry. Shit."

"I'm going."

"Don't go yet. Don't go like this."

"I can't . . . I'll call you later."

She can't deal with leavings. Not after That Bastard Father Anthony. A vanishing like that could make you feel the deepest sort of unseen and unwanted, and suddenly she is feeling those same things again. It's a horrible trick, the sense that her value is being sucked down the drain, like when the plug is pulled from the tub and the dirty water goes down. It's a lie, but maybe it isn't, so she flees down the stairs and then realizes she forgot her purse. Ugh! Embarrassing. She runs back, snatches it from the couch, and then rushes past Robert and Tracie, those traitors, in the kitchen.

She drives home in a haze of tears. Her heart is being squeezed in a big, mean fist. Cruel words like *No one wants* and *There will never be* poke at her bruises.

She wipes her eyes. She is not the sort of person who will lose her mind with abandonment and jealousy. There will be no crazed calls and tormented letters and drive-bys. No, Annabelle handles things. She studies for tests early, and keeps a training log of her running, and her nail polish bottles are arranged in an orderly rainbow in her bathroom drawer. What's done is done! Right there as she drives, her efficient, internal employees get to work. They erect barriers and fences, hammer up giant gates. Back there, behind them, is her heart.

There are guards, too. She can feel them inside, getting in place.

She ignores Will's calls that night. She ignores his messages, even if he's crying in one of them.

Take that.

As a power move, it is so lame—rejecting his rejection.

The next morning, she aches with sadness. But she picks something really cute to wear to school. It's a new shirt that she and her mom bought when they went school-clothes shopping, one she hadn't worn yet. Money is tight, and so she rations the new clothes. But this is an emergency, and emergencies are when you use your rations. She chooses cute heels, too, clips her long hair back. None of this is about replacing Will by attracting someone else. It's just about feeling good and powerful again. In terms of power, though, beauty is like glass, isn't it? Shining, but transparent and easily marred. A shard of glass can draw blood, but a fist can shatter it, too.

"Look at you, Belle Bottom," Kat said at school that morning. "You survived. You are the Phoenix!" They'd been on the phone for hours the night before, Gina interrupting with feed-your-heartbreak homemade macaroni and cheese and bowls of ice cream. Kat listened to Annabelle cry and go on, same as Annabelle had done after Kat and Noah broke things off.

Here is where the memory starts to really hurt. Will, Kat, her own rejected self—each fateful piece sears her. Now, as she runs, Annabelle's heels scream in pain. The suburban houses fly past. With every step, those blisters flame, and she lets them, because there he is.

There's The Taker, in Mixed Media. The class stands along the long back counter, hunched over tubs of gray pulp-filled water. They are making paper. The next step is to dip the wire frames in the muck. The Taker is next to her. He's so tall. She's aware of his presence in some energy-way.

"Yum, ashy bone soup," he says as he dunks the frame in.

This is not some big foreshadowing moment. He's just being funny. And it *is* funny, because that's what it looks like. "Delicious," Annabelle says. "Fine dining."

"Oh no. Your cute shirt," he says.

She looks down. He's right. There's a gray splotch. But she hears the compliment, too. She forces a grimace. "Can't take me anywhere."

"Note to self: Only take Annabelle to the drive-through."

"Ha," she says. She smiles. It's sweet. There's been so much shy grinning at her, it's even kind of bold. He doesn't seem to talk that much to anyone.

And after what happened with Will, it's kind of nice, the little flare of energy, the flirtation. The way he sees her, and notices her. She can't tell if he's weird or cute.

She says this to Kat at lunch. "I can't tell if he's weird or cute."

"If you're asking that question, you know the answer."

"Cute?"

"Weird."

"We shouldn't do that. It's mean. We don't even know him. Who is 'weird,' anyway? Only every person who will do great stuff in the future."

"Georgie Zacharro," Kat says.

Annabelle groans. In the sixth grade, she was nice to Georgie Zacharro. You were supposed to be nice. He followed her around for the whole school year. It gave her the creeps. *He* did. She told Mr. Riley about it. This was hard to do. She wasn't sure if this was a legitimate problem, even though it *was* a problem. *He just likes you*, Mr. Riley had said. Georgie Zacharro's right to like her, to step into her space, was greater than her own right for him to stop, apparently, so she didn't say anything more about it. She felt bad and ungenerous for bringing it up at all. She also felt weirded out and mad every time Georgie Zacharro lurked around.

"Sometimes weird is your gut talking to you. The point is not him being weird or not being weird. The point is that you feel uncomfortable, and you're trying to talk yourself out of it because you think you're supposed to be *nice*," Kat says, unwrapping a granola bar. "Anyway, if Will hadn't just called things off, you would never have asked that. Don't be desperate."

"I'm not being desperate! I'm just . . . regaining my mojo! Like you said last night."

"Mojo isn't just about boys."

"Mojo is sometimes about boys."

"Ugh!" Kat concedes. "Hey, I brought you that Meg Gillian book." They are on to more important things. "You're going to love it, but I don't know if you'll like the end. I won't say anything more, but it sorta just drops off."

"I still have to give you back *Deer Hollow*. God, I can't wait for the movie."

"We can be like those Star Wars fans who camp in their sleeping bags to be first in line, even though there'll be us and, like, four other people. Hey, Zach and I are going to your meet today."

"You are? You guys! Are you sure? It's all the way in West Seattle. It's raining." Also, cross-country meets are not the most exciting thing ever. Lots of waiting around at the finish line.

"It's always raining. Zach has that big golf umbrella his mom got at Costco." They both crack up because they immediately know what's funny about this—the idea of Zach's mom playing golf.

She smells it all—Kat's orange blossom lotion, chocolate bits from the granola bar, the waft of cafeteria pizza. She sees it all—the red scratch on the underside of Kat's wrist as Kat hands her the Meg Gillian book, the brown and blue shine of the cover. Now, it's all in front of her: the slight tang of weed coming from The Taker, the muck of wet newspaper, the orange stitching on The Taker's denim jacket, and the flash of red of Mrs. Diablo's nails as she claps her hands. *Ten minutes! Let's wrap it up, folks!*

She sees herself, smiling back. Flirting, almost.

She is felled. Literally. Her toe catches on the tipped edge of the sidewalk, and down she goes. The thoughts make her feet lose coordination. The brain circuits skip, and she is on all fours, her palms stinging, her knees burning. Those internal employees who used to keep her safe are long gone. Laid off, fired. Who wants to stay in some thankless, impossible job? The factory is now a ghost town, with abandoned buildings and FOR LEASE signs. Her internal landscape is bleak. A dry wind whistles through.

She *smiled back*. She *flirted*.

Annabelle is down on her knees. A woman runs across her front lawn. "Are you okay? That sidewalk! I've called the city three times."

The woman reminds her of Tracie. She has a similar haircut with the same blond highlights, but she has warmer eyes. It's expensive hair, unlike Gina's. Gina goes to Supercuts and colors her grays in the kitchen sink. She wears the plastic gloves that come in the box and there are black splatters in surprising places for weeks after.

"Oh my God! Sweetheart." The woman's voice goes from compassionate to alarmed as she takes in the fallen girl with the chopped hair. "Oh, God. Your ankles . . ."

Annabelle looks. There are bloodstains rising up from her burning Achilles. The ignored blisters have burst. They have scraped, scraped against her shoes for miles. It's bad.

"Do you need to call someone? Are you all right? You shouldn't even be walking, let alone running."

Annabelle can hardly look at that woman. She can't bear to see that face that reminds her of Tracie and everyone else who hates her. She doesn't deserve this woman's compassion.

Annabelle gets up. Brushes the small bits of gravel from her palms. "It's okay."

"Honey! That does not look okay."

"It's a . . . condition. I have medicine for it."

It's a terrible lie. The woman looks doubtful. "Do you need a ride? I don't have to pick up my son from school for another half hour."

"Thank you. But no worries! I live around the corner."

"If you say so." The woman looks relieved. She's actually backing up. Annabelle can only imagine what the woman sees. A bleeding, haunted girl with a crazy-person hairdo. She is right to be freaked out.

"See you around. Thanks again!" Annabelle says.

She limps, and Jesus, dear God, a scorching burn rises up her legs. Her palms sting from the fall.

To keep going—it seems a little sick. A lot sick. Of course she knows this. She doesn't need Dr. Mann to tell her so.

It's hard even for Annabelle to understand. But she feels this in her heart and soul and with every searing and burning step: A crime must have a punishment, and this is part of hers.

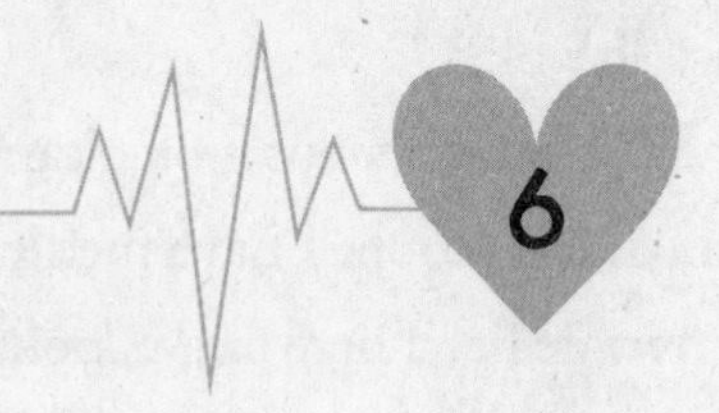

"Holy moly," Grandpa Ed says. "You look like Vinnie Lucchese after Gino sicced his dog on him. We're going to a doctor."

"Food. Water." Annabelle collapses onto the padded RV bench. Her head spins from exhaustion.

"Yeah, here, that, too." He hands her a full bottle. "But we're finding a doc-in-a-box. Jesus, you're bleeding all over. Let me get a towel."

The towel is from Grandpa Ed's trip to Niagara. There's an embossed photo of the falls, meant to hang over the stove railing decoratively. She holds the wet cloth across her ankles as Grandpa Ed backs out of his spot and hits the accelerator. Well, *hitting the accelerator* is actually the RV lurching and climbing slowly to thirty-five. Everything rattles—pots, pans, Annabelle's eyeballs. Something in the oven slides and bangs and slides again.

"Ah! *Broccolo!* I forgot to turn off the ziti. Can you reach the oven from where you are?"

"Ouch, ouch, ouch." After the half marathon she's just run, the thought of food makes her nauseous. In a few hours, she'll be starving, but right now, even the smell of the food could make her vomit.

"From where you are! Did I say move? I said, don't move! You're lucky I don't take you to the hospital and sign you in."

They're in the small logging town of Edgewick. People are going about their regular lives. She remembers the world. She's been in her head, deep in memories, lost in a pain universe, and the world seemed like a faraway thing. But, look—business as usual.

The doc-in-a-box is next to a gas station and a feed store. When Dr. Ohari cleans her wounds, it hurts like a motherfucker. There is no other way to put it.

"Any pus or fever, I'll want to see you back here. Needless to say, you should stop until these have healed. Use the antibiotic ointment under a loose bandage. Replace the bandage if it gets wet or dirty."

"Pus or fever," Grandpa Ed repeats. Annabelle shuts her eyes against the pain. She concentrates on her hatred for the word *pus*.

"Do you understand the long-term issues of a cross-country run like you're planning? Muscle damage, oxidative stress, enlargement of the heart, knee damage, hip and pelvis misalignment, should I go on?"

"You tell her, because we sure as hell—"

"I don't know who's in charge here, but—" The doctor is

eyeing her hair. "Emotional well-being is critical to physical health."

"Hey, now," Grandpa Ed says. His chest puffs up.

"You must remember that the heart is a muscle, too, and it can get as stressed as the others."

"Tell me something I don't know," Grandpa Ed says.

"Thank you, Doctor." Annabelle lifts herself from the table. "I've gotten advice from my physicians at home." Lies are flying out her mouth right and left.

"She's gotten advice from her physicians at home," Grandpa Ed says. He looks like he's about to punch out Dr. Ohari.

"Well, then. Take this to the front desk." Dr. Ohari hands them a receipt and a pamphlet entitled *Instructions for Wound Care*. "Good luck to you," he says, as if bestowing a dire prognosis.

"Fa Nabla!" Grandpa Ed says the minute they're outside. He sticks his forearm flat against his chest in disgust. Ooh, it's a low blow: *Go to Naples, I can't stand you*.

Annabelle leans on his arm as she hobbles back to the RV. "You're such a liar."

"What? Me? You are! 'My physicians at home.' Bella, Bella, you got the Agnelli Curse."

"The Agnelli Curse?"

"Silver-tongued liars. Gets us into a world of trouble, gets us out of a world of trouble."

"I thought you were going to take out Dr. Ohari back there."

"Nah. He doesn't bother me."

But he does a little, Annabelle can tell. And it's not just that Dr. Ohari poked at Grandpa Ed's substantial pride. Dr. Ohari worries Grandpa Ed. This whole thing does. The Taker and Seth Greggory do. Annabelle can see it on his face right now. But Grandpa Ed is not just a reckless guardian with a madwoman on his hands. He has made calculations, Annabelle knows. He is choosing what he thinks will give her the best chance of survival. This is no easy task when each of her hands holds a grenade.

"I could eat that ziti straight out of the pan right now."

"Thatta girl."

Grandpa Ed returns to the very spot they left. She may be a silver-tongued liar, but she will not be a cheat. They are parked beside the freeway. That night, when trucks speed past, their headlights flash, and the RV trembles and shivers against their power. They are comets and meteors burning past her little capsule; they scorch up her very skin as she tries to sleep. They sear and singe images on her retinas: furious screams, wails of sorrow, the slow, mournful crawl of cars. The destroyed shoulders of Robert and Tracie. The crushing guilt. The wrong fact of her existence.

Her heart still pumps blood. Every day, her heart pushes and thrusts and pumps its gallons and gallons of life-stuff. The next day: again. The next day: again, and again. She *is* a criminal. Her socks have been rinsed, but they are tinged pink as they hang to dry over the bathroom door. She sees them—two still, white ghosts, hovering near the ceiling.

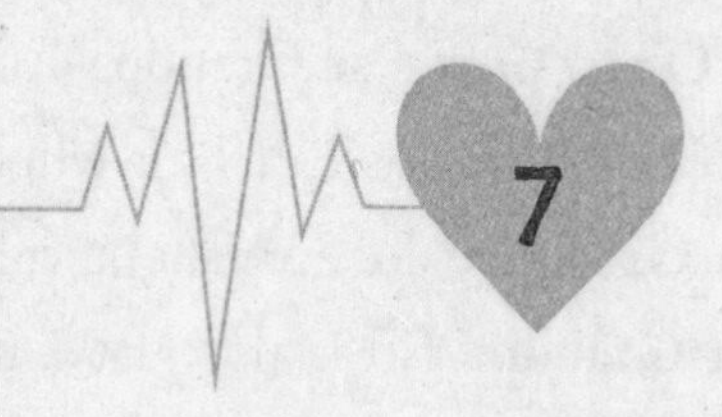

1. Though the heart weighs less than a can of soup, a healthy heart pumps two thousand gallons of blood each day.
2. A kitchen faucet would have to be turned on full force for forty-five years in order to equal the amount of blood pumped by a heart in a lifetime.
3. Looked at another way: During an average life, the heart will pump nearly 1.5 million barrels of blood. This is enough to fill two hundred train cars.
4. In spite of all that power and force, there are only one and a half gallons of blood in the body at a time. And you only have to lose two liters of it—one bottle of Diet Coke—and it's over.

Annabelle promised both her mother and Grandpa Ed that she would take a few days off, that she would wait until her blisters healed before she runs again.

But she has the Agnelli Curse. She is a silver-tongued liar.

She is also driven by something that is beyond all sense. She is compelled by a force that has no reason. Call it guilt, shame, a need for redemption. Call it terror or courage. Call it the human spirit, trying to rise.

Call it stupidity, given the condition of her feet. Still—call it the deepest of desires smack up against a lost cause.

It is very, very difficult to sneak out of an RV when a grandfather is sleeping right on a pullout bench below. It requires some advance planning. Seth Greggory would call this *premeditation*. In this case, the planning involves a note she wrote to Grandpa Ed the night before. Also, sleeping in her clothes. She packed her pack when Grandpa Ed was brushing his teeth and gargling with Listerine before bed. She's got energy bars and fruit and a dinner roll stuffed with cheese slices, so she'll have breakfast and lunch.

It also requires a little luck, which she gets: On the table, she spots the juice glass ringed in burgundy. Grandpa Ed's second glass of wine before bed. See? She is stressing him out. However, he is snoring hard. His mouth gapes like a cave.

Sneaking out also requires some disgusting stuff—not brushing her teeth, peeing outside. And, gross—changing her bandage out there and leaving the old one on the steps to the RV door. *Forgive me*, she says in advance. This is such a familiar phrase that she should have it tattooed on her wrist, or maybe over her heart. She wraps her feet in so many bandages, it's like she's wearing snow boots. She'll hobble like Mr. Giancarlo the whole run if she must.

In the next three days, Annabelle will become very acquainted with the Iron Horse Trail. She'll be on it for forty-two of its nearly three hundred miles. If Grandpa Ed doesn't disown her after her jailbreak, he'll meet her at a state park on the Snoqualmie River on day one, at a bend in the Yakima River on day two, and just off of Cabin Creek Road outside the small town of Easton on day three, her eighteenth birthday.

In its former life, this trail was a working railroad. Now, it's home to some of the most desolate land in the state. She isn't likely to see many humans out here, only coyotes and gopher snakes and worse.

This morning, past the Cedar Falls train stop, Annabelle runs on a friendly path of crushed rock bordered with trees, all bright green and yellow with baby leaves unfurling. The antibiotic cream slathered on her feet comes with a nice pain-numbing element, and so the scorching fire of the day before is just a burning hum. The abundance of bandages makes her clump along, though. She has loosened her laces and stretched her old running shoes to accommodate them, but she still feels like a C-grade zombie. She worries about a new ache in her hip. She hopes it isn't the start of Dead Butt Syndrome—tendonitis in the *cu*, basically—something Coach Kwan warned them about. She'll have to make sure to add some crunches and leg lifts to strengthen her abdominals and her glutes.

Zombie feet, dead butt, haunted spirit—pieces of her are dying off already. This is only the third day of her run.

Fourth, if you count the hours after fleeing Dick's. It feels like so long ago.

As she shuffles forward, she taps her thumbs to each of her fingers. She's aware of other pains and pulls in her body, all potentially catastrophic. Her chest fills with anxiety, same as a sinking ship fills with water—it rushes in and then rises slowly. That morning, she'd read about this route, and she knows what's coming: a pitch-black train tunnel. Two and a half miles of complete darkness. After that, twelve miles, all uphill. Punishment enough? No way. Not by a long shot.

Don't believe everything you think, Kat says. Or maybe that's Dr. Mann, meeting her eyes and smiling before fetching her glasses to make their next appointment.

It is a bad, bad moment to get the text. Annabelle almost doesn't look at her phone, because she's sure it's Grandpa Ed, fuming mad, or Gina, or even Malcolm, with news that the GoFundMe is up from yesterday's four hundred sixty bucks. But she's alone out there, except for Loretta. The bling of the text sounds like reassuring company.

It's Geoff Graham. Geoff is her friend. They used to be on the cross-country team together. He has a T-shirt that says *Like Jeff, but Geoff*, but nothing seems funny anymore.

Heard what you're doing. That's awesome.

Nice, huh? So nice. But the text socks Annabelle in the gut. It almost bends her right in half.

Annabelle stops. She thinks she spots the tall, gaping

cement arch of the tunnel up ahead. She has no flashlight or headlamp. The timing sucks.

God damn you, tunnel. God damn you, Geoff, sounds like Jeff. God damn you, Taker.

It is what it is, Annabelle tells herself.

It's a phrase she often finds comforting. It reminds her to accept the truth rather than struggle against it. But now, it sort of pisses her off. Sometimes, *what is* is something that *shouldn't be*. It should *never* have been. It only *is* because of messed-up reasons going back messed-up generations, old reasons, reasons that don't jibe with this world today. Sometimes, an *is* should have been gone long, long ago, and needs to be—immediately and forcefully and with not a minute to lose—*changed*.

She is more than pissed off. Actually, it fills her with fury, the way people can protest and shout and write letters and yet, the *is* stays an *is*, and bad, bad stuff can still happen and happen and happen. There are no words for this. It's unbelievable. It is a travesty. It is a communal mark of shame.

She's standing in front of that stupid tunnel now and, wow, it's dark.

"I am coming for you, tunnel. You are not coming for me," she says out loud. She gives the worst of the worst gestures she's learned from Grandpa Ed—index fingers stuck aggressively out. Literal translation: *I'll kick you so hard, your buttocks will end up this far apart.*

She runs. She's inside. The tunnel has a high ceiling and curved walls, and it is roomy enough for a freight train, but the walls close in. It is too dark to even see the end. And it's cold in there. She's suddenly freezing. A chill draft whips down its length.

Annabelle shivers. It's so frigid and so utterly and completely dark that she forgets about the pain in her feet and in her butt and even, for a moment, her heart. If she hears or feels a bat, she will have a heart attack. Something wet plops on one shoulder and then her cheek. There's more dripping. She speeds up.

Annabelle's feet echo. Goose bumps ride up her arms. She thinks she hears something, and then she's sure she does, because all at once it's upon her. It's a bright light, coming close, growing large. For a second she sees the stone walls around her before his headlamp blinds her. It's just a man on a bike. He says a cheery and surprised "Oh, hello," and then he is gone. It's black again.

Two and a half miles is a long way in complete darkness. Of course, she's gone a lot farther in places much darker than this.

Geoff Graham.

She sees him that night. He opens his front door. He grins. He says, "Hey, chips! Thanks." He squeezes the bag in appreciation. "No one else brought anything. Losers." There is music—

But no, before that.

Way before that.

Geoff Graham is over by his car in the Roosevelt parking

lot. He's there with Trevor Jackson and Zander Khan. Zander pushes Geoff good-naturedly, and Geoff shoves him back. They're laughing. Talking loud. Annabelle leans against Gina's old Toyota, waiting for Kat. Last week, Roosevelt lost to Ballard High in the District Championship, so the cross-country season is over. Now, Annabelle's back to her regular work and volunteer schedule, and she's going to give Kat a ride home. Kat's always late, it's annoying, and right then this is the biggest problem Annabelle's got. Kat better hurry up. Annabelle needs to go home and change for work.

It's late fall. The trees along the sidewalk near the school—so recently a burning orange and red and yellow—are losing their last leaves. A few drift down as she waits. The air has the smoky smell of the end of October. Fall always smells like a campfire.

She can't miss him, coming her way. The Taker. He's just so tall. Annabelle feels embarrassed for him, but she doesn't know why. He hasn't talked to her in Mixed Media for two days, and then he was absent, but here he is now. She wonders what's going on. He grins like he's up to something. This makes her nervous. But curious, too.

"Hey," he calls.

Geoff looks over. She notices this quite clearly, the way Geoff stops the joking and laughing and pushing. The way he watches, now that The Taker has caught his eye.

The Taker is holding a pink envelope. A card. A card that's on its way to her. Her embarrassment grows.

She feels . . . She doesn't know. The tiniest bloom of regret. She has started something that she'll now have to undo. *You can smile at a boy, and he'll think you're in love with him*, Gina cautioned back in the sixth grade, after Georgie Zacharro. This meant: *It's your job to keep guys in check*. Her first thought when she sees that card coming toward her is that she has somehow misused the nice-and-beautiful power-not-power she has. She wielded it recklessly, unleashed it on the vulnerable without entirely meaning to. It sucks, the way that her power is at times not enough and too much at others.

"For you," The Taker says. And then he does something that makes her uncomfortable. Well, the whole thing does, but this is worse. He bows. It's one of those odd actions that Geoff Graham and Trevor Jackson and Zander Khan would never do because they'd know it was odd. In fact, Trevor and Zander are also looking her way now, along with Geoff. And they are nice guys, so this is not threatening or mocking, just—it's unusual enough to make them wonder.

"Wow," she says. "Thank you."

She's not sure what to do, but he seems to be waiting, so she opens it. On the front of the card there's a vase of flowers dropping petals onto a tabletop and floor. Inside, in elaborate script: *An honest mess is more beautiful than a perfect picture.*

He waits.

She's a little stunned, because he seems to have understood something about her, the actual her. He isn't just seeing the pretend girl she feels like so much of the time, the girl who tries to be so perfect, perfect, perfect. At least, he notices something real about her that even Will never did. Yet the message and this card are too much. It's too much for this high school parking lot with beeping horns and laughter and buses idling by the curb.

"The other day, your shirt . . ."

She'd totally forgotten. This gives her some context, some way to respond. What a relief. She laughs a little. "Aww," she says. "Hey, thanks."

"No worries."

He blushes like mad. "That's really sweet," Annabelle says. She wishes Kat would hurry up.

"Hey, I gotta go. My bus."

"Thanks again," Annabelle says. "That's really sweet," she repeats.

"See you."

"See you."

He lopes toward the second bus, takes the stairs in one leap. The buses pull away. Trevor gets into Geoff's car, and Geoff reverses out of his spot. Zander jogs in the direction of home. Annabelle tucks the card in her notebook.

When Kat finally appears, Annabelle doesn't tell her what happened. That night, though, Annabelle looks up The Taker online. What is she expecting to find? No idea. There are only pictures of him and friends from his old school in Vermont. In one, guys wearing backward baseball caps lie goofily on classroom desks; in another, a group of kids wearing American

Revolution–style three-corner hats stand on a lawn. There's an awkward homecoming photo, and a cat playing in snow, and his dad and him holding rifles at a shooting range. There's a close-up of a big breakfast. There's him and his mom dressed up and standing in front of a fancy hotel. She's a good foot shorter than he is, but has his same shaggy hair.

Annabelle is wrong to judge him without knowing him. So what, he's awkward—he's new at their school. He seems sweet. The only card Will ever gave her was for Valentine's Day. It showed a beagle holding a box of chocolates and said *You're my favorite treat dispenser.*

She should repay The Taker for this kindness. She should at least ask him about himself. She should at least be friendly and nice.

Still, she throws the card away in the garbage can in her room. She shoves it way down. It doesn't seem far enough. The card makes her feel bad. She takes the can out and dumps it in the trash.

"Do the kitchen one, too," Gina calls.

In that dark tunnel, Annabelle can barely breathe. Besides the bats and the dripping water, she imagines things on the ground, ready to spring at her ankles. She imagines a man, his back flat against the wall, ready to seize her when she passes. He is there, and then there, and then there, with his reaching arms. She swerves away from his hands. She picks up her pace, because she pictures another man behind her, trying to catch her. He's back there somewhere, getting closer. He's gaining on her. She needs to hurry.

There is danger above, below, around, behind. Darkness wiggles its horrible fingers and tries to grab.

When she sees the tiny pinprick of light that means she's near the end, she feels relieved but not relieved enough. She can almost hear the man's steps behind her.

The circle of light grows. It brightens as a new day does. In spite of the long ordeal she just endured, it feels like a sudden embrace. She runs another mile or so away from that awful place, and when it is no longer visible behind her, she slows, and then stops.

She sets her palms on her knees. Pants. She takes a long drink of water. She wants to feel victorious, like she faced that freaking tunnel and won. She is, after all, out in the sun, with the tunnel behind her. But way down in there, inside of her, the something-someone still chases. It does not have the immediacy that it did in the tunnel. She cannot hear the man's steps or feel his breath on the back of her neck, but he still lies in wait.

Turned up or turned down, the feeling is permanent. She survived something big, and when you survive something big, you are always, always aware that next time you might not.

8

"What am I going to do with you, huh?" Grandpa Ed's accent flares whenever he gets emotional. He came to this country when he was twelve, from the town of Gallarate, province of Varese, in northern Italy. Patron Saint of Gallarate: Saint Christopher, who watches over travelers, children, and bachelors, and protects against storms, holy death, and toothaches. Grandpa Ed's Saint Christopher medal is tucked into the plastic sleeve of the RV's visor.

"Che palle!" Translation: *What balls.*

"I'm sorry," Annabelle says.

"You're not sorry," he says. "Don't give me sorry."

"I'm a little sorry."

Mostly, she's relieved. She was so happy to see the RV right there at their chosen meeting place by the Yakima River. She worried he might get mad enough to leave her stranded. Annabelle has seen the way he and Gina fight. Someone is always saying something too honest, and voices rise, and then one of them stomps off. They'll pretend the other doesn't exist for a week, even if they see each other getting the mail. But maybe things are different with children and grandchildren, because Grandpa Ed's upset at her fades quickly. It seems like she gets a million chances with him.

"How'd it go?"

"Fine. Good." She won't add to his worries with the truth. "Butt hurts."

"Yeah? You give me a pain in my *culo*, too. Let me see the feet."

She's already unwrapping the bandages. Grandpa Ed winces. "Jesus."

"I thought you were in the fish-packing business. You saw guts."

"I was the businessman. I was the numbers guy."

This is hard to believe when she has to tell him a million times how 2,700 miles divided by sixteen equals five months, give or take. "It's actually feeling a lot better, even though it still looks gross."

"It's healing, Bella Luna." She likes when he calls her this. Luna is her middle name. Her grandmother's name. Annabelle never met her—she died when Gina was seventeen. But Annabelle has heard stories. How her grandmother had the love of fifteen mothers. How she could put Grandpa Ed in his place with one look. How she could ward off the *malocchio*, the evil eye, with a prayer and the dip of her pinkie into a bowl of water sprinkled with a few drops of olive oil. Sometimes,

Annabelle thinks her mom and Grandpa fight because they both loved the same person so much.

"I almost can't believe it's healing, but I guess it is."

"Okay. Buckle up. We've got to move. There's a state park nearby. I already scoped the place out. Can you believe it? A cop drove by and told me we can't stay here overnight! What's the problem, I'm gonna rob something?"

"A beaver," she says.

"Yeah! That's about all a guy could steal out here."

"No, I mean, look. I see a beaver."

She points. He's right there, scurrying out of the river. He disappears into some brush, and then he's back again, carrying a big branch that looks way too big for him.

"That's a heavy load," Annabelle says. The beaver tugs and pulls. What he's trying to accomplish—it looks impossible. He doesn't look all that smart, to be honest, choosing something so huge. "Why'd he pick that one?"

"We don't know what he's doing, but he knows what he's doing," Grandpa Ed says.

It's a shame that they have to move. The river is winding and scenic, like a picture of a river. It's calendar-page perfect. The snow is melting, and white rapids splash against picturesque rocks, and spring gives the late afternoon a sweet yellow light. It's all science and beauty and nature, minus the messed-up stuff of the human world. It's one of those moments where you imagine quitting everything and staying right there. Annabelle has a lot of those moments lately. Of course, they are all just a fantasy because of Seth Greggory.

The RV rumbles and lurches away. The state campground isn't as inviting as the river. It's woodsy and shaded, and the dampness of winter still lingers. Grandpa Ed finds their spot, yanks the parking brake.

"Look! People are camping. It's March and freezing cold. I can't imagine it."

Annabelle forgets who she's talking to for a second. Before he bought the house next door to theirs in Fremont, Grandpa Ed drove around the country and stayed in places like this for years. Now, he's as cheerful and flashy as the winning slot machine.

"Party central," he says, snapping his fingers. "Viva Las Vegas."

"Wow, you sure perked up." Annabelle peeks out the window. "All I see are some zipped tents and a camper with a 'Keep Portland Weird' license plate holder. They're probably granola-eaters on the run from the law."

He raises his eyebrows at her.

"Forget I said that."

"Strangers are friends you haven't met yet," Grandpa Ed says. He sounds like sweet Mrs. Parsons from Sunnyside Eldercare, not Grandpa Ed, with his big nose and his hair combed back, wearing his Seahawks sweat suit. "They invited me over for a cocktail."

"They? Who?"

"The lady with the camper. I saw her when I checked out the place this afternoon."

"Wow. Go get 'em, tiger."

"Dinner's in the oven. Help yourself. I'm going to get changed."

"You better." His sweatshirt says *Property of Seattle Seahawks* and looks like he used it as a shirt/apron combo.

"You should clean up and come with me."

"I can barely move."

"There's a kid your age. A grandson. From Portland."

"No, Grandpa."

"C'mon . . ."

"Stop it. No boys."

"Bella. What'd I say, you're getting married tonight? No. I said, come say hello, be friendly. Be a good neighbor."

"*No boys*. No way."

"You gonna close off that part of your life forever? Huh, Sister Mary?"

"I don't want to talk about this anymore."

"Suit yourself."

After a good half hour, he comes out of the bathroom. What the hell! He's wearing black slacks and a dress shirt, and he smells like he's been attacked by a cologne squirter. His hair is floofed up to hide his hearing aids.

He snaps his fingers, and the little door of the RV slams shut.

• • •

Annabelle hurts all over. She stretches, concentrating on her glutes to help the pain in her hip. Then she takes Grandpa Ed's pan out of the oven, lifts the foil, and eats the roast chicken with rosemary potatoes as she stands against the counter. She's still wearing her disgusting clothes, but she's starving. Lately, she's a machine, energy in, energy out. She likes feeling like a machine. It would be great to be made out of metal parts that have no feelings, only a job to do.

Annabelle eats while checking her phone messages and texts. They've piled up. There are even a few e-mails. This is what happens when you drop your life. Next, she returns calls.

"Carl Walter drove me over to Dick's and we picked up your car," Gina says. "We're lucky it didn't get impounded. I called the manager, and he said 'no problem,' but Carl Walter was still in Boise until today. I finally got in touch with Mrs. Garvey. You'd think she was the governor and not the principal of Roosevelt High, after how many messages I left and secretaries I had to talk to. They're excusing the unexcused absences. Don't be mad, but I forgot to call last week, because, you know, I had a lot on my *mind*. Then she tells me she hopes you'll be at the graduation ceremony, that missing it would be unfortunate, given the situation, and I totally get it, but what a bitch! *Unfortunate*. She had the balls to say *the community needs*—"

Annabelle has stopped listening. At the word *community*, she's out of there. Her mother loves her and she loves her mother—honestly, she'd have never gotten through what she has without her—but sometimes you wish even the people you love would go away. Not for long, not forever, just long enough to have a little quiet. Annabelle gazes out the little window of the RV. Night has fallen. She wonders what that beaver is doing now. It's spooky out there. But she sees the camper from Portland across the way, lit up and glowing like the moon.

"And blah blah, more something, more nothing, babble, babble, babble, but he said it was fine, as long as you're back by September twenty-second—"

"What?"

"Seth Greggory. Weren't you listening? This *is* important."

"A big truck passed and I couldn't hear."

"He said it's fine if you leave the state. I was worried, you know."

"Okay."

"So, that's good."

"Okay."

"You don't have to snap, Annabelle. Um, I'm dealing with your whole *life* over here? A box for you from Amazon came—"

"Oh, yeah. Remember? Those watercolor pens I needed for school. I'll pay you back. Better yet, I'll give you my bank passwords."

"There's no need for that! You'll be home after Idaho, in, what, twelve days?"

"What do you mean, I'll be home after Idaho in twelve days?"

"What do you mean, what do I mean? Your grandpa said you guys agreed to only cross the state line into Idaho, and then he'll drive you back."

"Agnelli Curse. He lied."

"What do you mean, he lied? He can't have lied!" She's shrieking. Annabelle actually has to hold the phone away from her ear. "The only reason I'm agreeing to this madness is because you'll be back in less than two we—"

There's a rustling sound. Now her mother's voice is muffled, protesting from a distance with words she can't make out.

"Don't worry, I'll handle her," Malcolm says.

"God, Malc, what'd you do, wrestle her?"

"Six hundred," he says.

"Six hundred what?"

"Six hundred dollars! The GoFundMe."

"You're kidding. That's a fortune."

"Well, two hundred came from your old bosses at Essential Baking, Claire and Thomas. And didn't you work with an old guy, Giancarlo?"

"Mr. Giancarlo. At Sunnyside."

"Must be his daughter. Jennie Giancarlo, seventy-five bucks. Seven hundred will probably only get you halfway through Idaho, if we don't count what you already spent, but we've barely started getting the word out."

"Malcolm, I've got my college money."

"Don't you get it? People *want* to help."

She can't stand to hear this. The kindness from her old bosses, from Mr. Giancarlo's daughter, from *strangers*—it brings a wave of shame that threatens to drown her.

"Annabelle, are you there?"

"I'm here."

"Don't freak out, but when you get to Wenatchee in three days, you've got an interview with Ashley Naches from Wenatchee High. I'm going to text you her number. Call her when you're an hour away, and she'll meet you in the library of the school."

"What? Why?"

"Per the PR campaign from your publicist."

"My *publicist*?"

"Olivia. Zach's handling financial matters. I'm covering logistics."

"You guys don't need to do this."

"We've discussed overall strategy and made a plan with Mrs. Hodges." Mrs. Hodges—the business teacher and DECA adviser at Roosevelt. "She underscored the need for publicity, and Olivia's all over it. Ashley Naches from Wenatchee High is only the first person Olivia contacted, and she jumped at the chance to talk to you."

Annabelle groans. "Malc! What is there even to say?"

"What is there to *say*? You're kidding, right?"

Annabelle's stomach feels sick. "I don't want to do PR. You know how I feel about all that." It's whooshing back. The news. Reporters, press. The days when she couldn't leave the house, even if she wanted to. The days when the phone rang and rang until they shut them all off.

Stop!

"Annabelle. It's the *Purple Panther Bugle*. This isn't CNN."

"Malc, I *can't*."

"You can. You have to. This is too big to just be about you."

"God damn it! Fine."

"You'll have to sign in at the offi—"

"I said fine! I'll figure it out."

Malcolm is not only a genius; he has the industrious, plodding patience of a tortoise crossing a desert plane. He's also her friend. "Me and Mom are going to be surprising you for your birthday tomorrow, and I know how you hate surprises, so act surprised."

He loves her. She shouldn't have snapped at him. "Thanks, butthead."

"Stop being a moron."

Annabelle listens to his serious breathing on the other end of the phone. "I love you, too," she says.

In spite of being alone all day, she wants to be alone more. She's glad the calls are done. She has no desire, even, to look at social media, to peek at what her friends are doing. The world is gone. At least, that world has temporarily vanished, and she is in another one, one that feels real and old, one that has gone on and on, no matter what is happening in that other noisy place. Terrible stuff can happen there, petty stuff can, while here, beavers still drag around sticks. Here, there is a plan that makes sense, one that's been working as it has for eons.

She takes off her disgusting clothes, rinses them, and hangs them up. She gets in the shower. Well, it's sort of a shower—a nozzle you hold over yourself. The warm water comes down.

And, then—oh, shit, shit, shit!—the warm water is coming down, all right.

"Eyyow!"

She shrieks. It is actually more of a scream, the sound a rabbit makes when it's been caught by an eagle. She holds the nozzle away from her body like it's a hose of acid rain. The sting is at her back, where her bra clasps, and it's at her neck where there was a tag, and it's under her breasts, and down her sides where the seams of her shirt hit.

She didn't see the marks. She looks down at her body. The raw places aren't even really visible, but they will be tomorrow. She should have known better than to wear that loose shirt—a cotton one, no less. Now, her skin has abrasions where any fabric rubbed and rubbed against her skin.

She leans far, far over to wash her chopped hair, but when even a drop of water hits the back of her neck where that tag was, it burns.

"Ouch, ouch, ouch!"

She gets out carefully. She pat-pats herself dry. Her ankles burn, too, but not as badly as they did the day before. Her body is on fire. She is a mess of wounds. Fresh wounds, old ones, wounds in various stages of pain and healing.

She wonders if all of her will ever feel healed at the same time.

It is something every human being wonders, probably, at some point or another.

She climbs into her bunk. She lets the sheet—*ow, ow, ow*—fall carefully over her. She sets her alarm, but then turns the face of the phone away. She doesn't dare look at that clock. She can't bear to see the numbers moving forward, five to six, six to seven, seven to eight. Eleven to twelve.

If she looks, she will see it, the time going forward to the day she gets to turn eighteen. The awful day that she gets to be another year older.

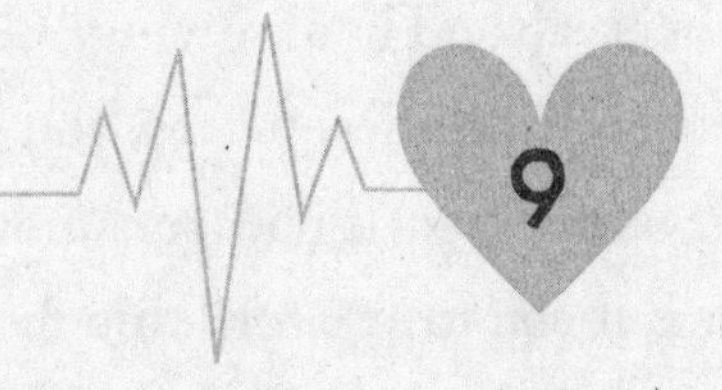

1. The heart symbol can be traced to before the Ice Age, when Cro-Magnon hunters used it in pictograms on cave walls.
2. The first time the shape was used as a representation of love was in a painting from 1250. In it, a man kneels and hands over his heart to a lady. It looks more like a pinecone than the shape we know today.
3. In the Middle Ages, heart shapes were also used to portray lily pads, fig leaves, and weapons, namely arrows.
4. On his coat of arms, fifteenth-century Italian military leader Bartolomeo Colleoni used upside-down hearts to depict his testicles.
5. Heart shapes . . . symbols for love, sex, and violence.

"Wake up, Bella Luna!" Grandpa Ed says. He whistles the happy birthday song.

She is already awake. She's been awake for a while. She closes the Moleskine, folds her pillow over her head. She's been dreading this day, as she dreads all the big days—all birthdays, not just hers; also, Thanksgiving, Christmas, and upcoming events like anniversaries, proms, and graduations.

There are lots of good reasons to be in the middle of nowhere. But she can't avoid this, her eighteenth birthday. It will bring on everyone's forced cheer. They will be trying for her, which means she'll have to try for them, too, and this will be harder and more arduous than her run today.

She steels herself, takes the pillow from her head. "I smell bacon," she says. "Do I actually smell bacon?" It's her first gift to Grandpa Ed's first gift. She makes her voice full of pleased surprise.

"My Bella Luna loves her bacon."

Her phone rings. It's Mom, Malcolm, and Carl Walter singing, *"Happy birthday to you!"* Second gift to their gift—she makes her voice delighted and grateful.

When she hangs up, she sees that there's a message and an e-mail card from That Bastard Father Anthony. A singing chipmunk holds an acorn with a candle in it. *Miss you. With love, Dad.* Olivia called late last night: *I know this is a hard day. Hang in there.* There are eight notification messages from people posting on the Facebook page she doesn't even use anymore. She counts. Sixteen more hours until this day can be considered over.

She climbs the ladder from her bunk, and Grandpa Ed hands her a big cinnamon roll with a candle in it. "Wow! Where did we get these?"

"Special treat from a friend."

A friend? She realizes that she didn't hear Grandpa Ed come in last night. She has no idea how late it was. "So, who were those people you had cocktails with?"

"Dawn Celeste and her grandson. They're from Portland, Oregon. She's a widow. They're taking a trip of the western states together."

"You said he was my age? So, why isn't he in school?"

"You should have come with me and asked him yourself, if you wanted to know so bad. Look at these babies. Plump and lush."

"The cinnamon rolls or the widow? *Dawn Celeste*—sounds like an old hippie name."

"It *is* an old hippie name. She changed it from Delores Carpenter to Dawn Celestial when she was seventeen. Look, I made you some fluffy scrambled eggs, too. *Mangia, mangia*, before the good stuff gets cold."

Annabelle wears her seamless, moisture-wicking shirt with all the tags ripped out. She squeezes out the last bit of Aquaphor from an old tube, slathers what's left onto all her chafed spots, and then covers them with Band-Aids. She needs some Body Glide, but way out here, it'll probably be impossible to find. She'll have to make due with Vaseline until she gets to a larger city.

Out on the Iron Horse Trail that morning, the sky is blue. It reminds her of the sky she sat under while watching Will's lacrosse practice. It's the shade of blue he wears in the baby picture that's framed and sitting on the shelves of Robert and Tracie's bonus room. It's the shade of blue of Kat's mother, Patty's, bedroom.

When even the sky is a reminder, you've got problems, Annabelle knows. Grief is everywhere. It's its own being. It walks beside you silently, jumps out at you meanly, pokes you awake at night. It makes tears roll down your cheeks at a blue sky.

Happy birthday, Belle Bottom, Kat says.

Remember last year? I don't know how I'm going to get through this.

An hour at a time.

Sometimes an hour is forever and sometimes it's a second.

Sometimes it's Mrs. Ysidro's class, Kat says. They both laugh. See? They have that language that comes from shared history. An hour in Mrs. Ysidro's AP Calculus was an eon.

Kat's laugh—it's the best. She laughs like a baby does. It's an all-the-way, let-it-loose laugh. It's a laugh that just destroys you with its hundred-percent-ness.

The last section of the Iron Horse Trail is flat, flat, flat. This is the real birthday gift of her dreams.

"Thank you, Loretta," Annabelle says.

She doesn't have to pretend to be delighted this time. She feels the excited relief of a snow day.

It's flat, but as she goes, she realizes that the trail isn't in the best condition. It winds through a rocky meadow, where she can still see some of the railroad track hidden in high grass. The ground is uneven. If she thinks about her feet, she'll definitely trip. This used to happen when she carried her lunch tray in the cafeteria. If she was conscious of balancing things, she'd spill her drink, or a wave of Ivar's chowder would splotch over the bowl.

Now, she sees herself carrying her lunch tray on this same day last year. All of her friends are at their table. They're all looking at her as she approaches, and she knows this means they have a surprise for her, and so she spills her water, and it splashes onto her salad.

"Happy birthday!" Kat shouts. "I know you don't like big surprises, so it's just a little one for now."

"Who doesn't like surprises?" Carly Trevor says.

"People who haven't gotten good ones." It's the millionth reason to love Kat. She has the wisdom of people who've gone through shit.

"Chocolate, chocolate, chocolate, please." Zander puts his hands together and looks at the cafeteria ceiling where the god of birthday cakes must be.

"Yeah, like, don't tell her it's a cake or anything," Zach Oh says.

Kat lifts the double-layer beauty from its hiding place under the table. *Happy 17th, Belle Bottom*. "Ta-da."

"Guys! This is so sweet!" Annabelle wasn't expecting anything until the weekend, when they're all going out to celebrate.

“That is so much frosting,” Sierra Kincaid says. “Oh my God. I’m going to have to be good the rest of the week.”

“Just enjoy the yum,” Kat says.

“Yes! Chocolate!” Zander yells, like he just found a bag of money with his name on it. “I call corner piece.”

“Eww, go ahead,” Sierra says.

They sing. They substitute insults for her name, like any good friends.

After the plates have been shoved in the trash and everyone goes off to class, Kat unzips her backpack. “I want to give you this now, on your real birthday.”

The gift is beautifully wrapped in thick green paper, looped with rainbow shades of ribbon. Annabelle hates to wreck it by opening it. “It’s so pretty.”

“Just tear it right off,” Kat says.

When Annabelle sees what’s underneath, she holds it to her chest. “Oh, wow. Thank you, thank you! I love it. I love this so much.”

She does. She brings it to her nose, sniffs the rich, dark leather. She’d always wanted a Moleskine like Kat’s. Kat writes lines in it that she wants to use in her short stories. Annabelle doesn’t know what she’ll put in hers.

“Now we’re twins,” Kat says.

When the trail exits the meadow, it turns cruel. It climbs slowly until Annabelle finds herself high, high up. The ground drops off below in a rocky lurch. It is not an easy day after all.

Annabelle shuffles and pants, feeling the pull in her thighs and calves and the press in her lungs. Ahead of her, the trail of scrubby shrubs is heading toward a monster.

Oh wow. Oh wow, wow, wow. It's a railway trestle. It's creaky-looking and made of ancient timbers, and it rises precariously from the ground that is so very far below. She will have to cross it. The railroad tracks that once ran across the trestle are gone, and now there are only thin wooden slats.

The row of A-shape structures holding up this bridge—they don't look good. They're blackened and old. They look rotted and unsteady. At the start of the Iron Horse Trail, she saw the sign labeled TRAIL IMPROVEMENT PLAN, but she thought she'd be off the route before she got to the wrecked parts.

Now, she sees the orange flags tied to various posts. Boards have been lifted off the trestle floor itself, and the handrail has been replaced in spots. She can see the new, light pine set against the dark worn wood. Worse—sections of handrail are completely missing.

Her stomach drops when she looks down.

Jesus. This doesn't look safe. Not at all. Not remotely. Gina would have a heart attack if she saw this. Annabelle may be having one right this minute. Her chest is squeezing at the sight of those gaping bits in the trestle ahead.

"Oh, Loretta," she says.

Loretta has fallen silent. Yeah, Annabelle would, too, if she'd just screwed up that big.

Annabelle taps her thumb to the tips of her fingers, one after the other. Her anxiety ratchets and hums.

Should she run fast over this dangerous bridge, or go carefully slow? Probably, she should just turn around altogether. Slow means less chance of stepping on some rotting board and tumbling to her death; fast means maybe making it to the other side before the whole thing crashes down. Going back means failure.

"It'd be closed, if it were that dangerous," she says out loud.

But look at it, she says silently to herself.

It's been one of her biggest problems, hasn't it? Assessing danger? Isn't that part of what got her into this mess, to this place where she is weirdly and surreally standing alone on a high, rotting railway trestle on her eighteenth birthday?

Danger was confusing. On the one hand, there was her mother, telling her that every street she had to cross, every car ride, every new person was a deathly risk. As a girl, too, she was told that she needed to be on guard against 50 percent of the human race, and she carried that awareness everywhere, ready to make use of it every time a car slowed next to her as she was walking, or she was driven home by the dad after babysitting. Every time she waited at a bus stop or was at a party with boys and alcohol or was just plain alone, she felt the high alert of vigilance. You could forget that some people don't live this way. Part of the population rarely even thinks like this. They just walk around without fear and wait at bus stops and go to parties.

But what are you supposed to do when you're also required to be kind and helpful as well as vigilant? To give directions to the driver in the car slowing beside you, to be polite to the father of the kids you babysat, to be friendly and fun at the party? And some of it wasn't logical. Most of the time you're fine. It was hard to hear very well through the buzz of constant watchfulness. She couldn't tell when she truly was or wasn't in danger. That voice inside that said, *Now, yes, this is it, get out!* was muffled by mixed messages. And then, too . . . you could be afraid of all the wrong things.

Because, of course, there were the other critical moments of her birthday last year. That day, the worst, wrong pieces clicked into place, and she didn't even know it. That day, the clock started ticking.

Annabelle runs. She speeds across that trestle. Well, she speeds as well as she can as she watches where she steps, nervous sweat pouring down her sides, her heart beating in terror. She tries not to look down, because down is everywhere. It's a harrowing adrenaline blend, being fearless and afraid at the same time.

10

"I heard this place is great," Grandpa Ed says. The restaurant is called Big Chuck's, and there's a wagon wheel on the roof. The freeway whizzes out front. Grandpa Ed pretends that it's just the two of them going out for a big birthday dinner, and Annabelle pretends not to see Gina's car in the lot. Actually, she can't wait to get in there. She's starving. Honestly, she could eat three or four steaks.

It makes her think of Sierra Kincaid and some girls at school, who'd eat two bites of yogurt and a carrot stick and say they were full. Sometimes, Annabelle did it, too, because you were supposed to be thin and delicate and feminine, even if your body was never those things, even if you were hungry. From the time she was in kindergarten, she heard the encouraging rah-rah about how girls can do anything, yet still there were the yogurt bites and the carrot sticks and girls looking at each other's bodies, and boys looking, too, judging. It's hard to be all that you can be on carrot sticks and criticism.

It's weird because, since her run began, Annabelle feels something different about her body and food. She was already "in shape," but she is starting to understand that if she wants to be strong, she needs to *feed* the strength. Energy and power in, energy and power out.

"Surprise!" Gina and Malcolm and Carl Walter shout when she and Grandpa walk in. Actually, Carl Walter just smiles uncomfortably. He's not the sort for loud displays in restaurants. He's the kind of guy who's quiet unless he's watching sports on TV.

"Surprise!" Angie Morelli O'Brien, Gina's oldest friend, and her husband, Patrick, also shout.

"Oh my gosh! You guys! Aunt Angie, Uncle Pat! What are you doing here?"

"Anne Lazzarini's daughter is getting married in Wenatchee, so we thought we'd drop in for dinner on the way. We're not staying." She smooches Annabelle's cheek. "Happy birthday, sweetheart."

"We *are* staying," Malcolm warns.

"Come here, my love. Give me a hug," Gina says. "Happy eighteenth, baby."

"Mom! I'm so happy to see you guys. What a long drive, just for this! What do you mean, *staying*?"

"Do you think we'd miss your birthday? We're staying the night! We got a couple of rooms at the Sleepy Inn. We thought you'd like a real bed for once. A splurge."

"I don't want no real bed. I've got a real bed," Grandpa Ed says. "Money doesn't grow on trees."

"You told me already," Gina says. "I didn't get you a room, okay? I heard you loud and clear. You're cheap, Pop."

"I'm not cheap, I'm thrifty." He's a little cheap. He hoards fast-food ketchup packets and steals the small containers of jam from restaurant tables.

"Look at all this great food!" Angie Morelli O'Brien shoves a couple of menus in front of Gina and Grandpa Ed to shut them up.

"How about some beers?" Patrick O'Brien says.

"Beers? What family did you marry into, O'Brien? Vino, vino!" Grandpa Ed is all dressed up again. He smells like the Acqua di Parma factory exploded.

"Mom and Carl are paying for their own room, but the GoFundMe is doing ours," Malcolm tells Annabelle.

"Wow, that's awesome, Malc."

There is steak, and there are baked potatoes tucked into foil sleeping bags. There is corn glistening with butter, and salads made from iceberg lettuce and tomatoes. There are presents: new shoes and a stack of moisture-wicking shirts from Aunt Angie and Uncle Pat, a new hydration belt from Mom, sunglasses and SPF 45 from Carl Walter, a pile of socks from Grandpa Ed, and a box of PowerBars, Clif Shot Bloks, and Cytomax Energy Drops from Malcolm. Three sticks of Body Glide from Zach and Olivia.

"Wait," Mom says.

There's one more gift. Annabelle opens the lid of the small box. It's her own medal of Saint Christopher—protector of travelers, guardian against storms, holy death, and toothaches. Saint Christopher is in his flowing robes and carries a child on his back. *St. Christopher Protect Us*, it says, and it's beautiful, really. "Oh, Mom. Thank you. Thank you, everyone."

It's everything she could need for now. Her family is here, and today she kicked the butt of the Iron Horse Trail. And, in spite of the dread for this day, she feels lucky. So lucky. Annabelle knows you should never forget that part.

After she blows out the candle in the large sundae, Grandpa Ed starts waving his arms.

"Over here!"

Maybe Grandpa Ed has arranged another birthday surprise. Annabelle tries to see who he's waving to, but it's hard from where she's sitting. The servers are taking dessert orders, and Uncle Pat is walking around, insisting that everyone get what they want, since he's picking up the tab.

An older woman with a long gray braid and a flowing gypsy dress is coming their way, and behind her is a guy about Annabelle's age. He's every Portland-Seattle hippie cliché: his brown hair is a mess of curls, and he wears a Value Village–ish striped jacket, a looped scarf, and a cross-body bag.

It's a birthday surprise, all right.

She's going to kill Grandpa Ed. She doesn't care how good he's been to her since the day she was born. Sure, she brought him to kindergarten for show-and-tell. Sure, he wore a paper hat with a painful elastic strap under his chin for every kiddie birthday party they ever had, and sent them cards with five bucks inside on every Valentine's Day no matter where he was in the country. But she's going to beat him with his own bag of Caputo flour.

Grandpa Ed is suddenly the life of the party. His cheeks are flushed, though maybe it's the wine. "Dawn Celeste, everyone!" he says, like she's a Vegas lounge singer entering the stage. They should maybe all applaud. She hands Annabelle a pan of cinnamon rolls covered with plastic wrap. Another pan of cinnamon rolls! God, how many does a person need, even if they're delicious? Really, really delicious! As delicious as the ones at Essential Baking Company, where she used to work. Annabelle feels sorry for the guy, the grandson, following behind Dawn Celeste in her Age of Aquarius dress. He must feel so awkward and humiliated.

But he doesn't seem awkward and humiliated. He's as mellow as a country road, and, shit, what is he doing? He's handing her something and smiling. A *present*?

"Hey."

"Hey," she says.

"I'm Luke Messenger."

"Annabelle."

"I know. I heard about what you're doing. It's awesome. This is for you."

It's a cassette tape, the kind you don't even see anymore, tied with a shoelace to a small cassette player. The player can hook to your waistband. There are earbuds. The wire is crinkly, like they've been used for years.

Luke grins. Shit, shit, shit! It's one of those grins that causes your heart to bump around, a grin that says you both share a secret.

Malcolm wiggles his eyebrows up and down. She's going to kill him, too. He's going to get it tonight, smothered with his own pillow from the Sleepy Inn.

Grandpa relays the story of how they met at the campground. Dawn Celeste tells everyone that she's a retired social worker and perpetual wanderer, and Luke is a college student on hiatus. They took off from Portland a few weeks ago, and are going to go wherever their mood takes them. Grandpa says stuff that makes Dawn Celeste laugh. She seems to be laughing a lot. Her toenails in those sandals are painted the color of a tangerine. It's too cold for sandals. Gina smiles the tight smile of an Italian countess in a Renaissance painting. Luke Messenger just sits back in one of the red padded chairs of Big Chuck's with his hands folded across his chest, calm as the setting sun.

After a while, Aunt Angie and Uncle Pat have to go, and the party breaks up. There are thank-yous and hugs and *Happy birthday, sweetie*s and *Be careful out there*s and good-byes.

"Hey, thanks again," Annabelle says to Luke Messenger. She can at least be polite.

"No problem. Hope you like it."

"Where are you and your grandma going next?"

"Idaho."

"Oh, great! Have a great time."

Great, great. Just great! Idaho! *Their* Idaho. She is going to kill, kill, kill Grandpa Ed.

It turns out, she doesn't have to. After everyone leaves, Gina yanks Grandpa Ed's sleeve. "Pop, I need a word with you."

They are over by the defunct cigarette machine. Gina gestures like a street-corner mattress sale guy, and Grandpa Ed looks pissed. There are words like *family celebration* and *stranger* and *Annabelle* and *You know how she feels* and *Ease up, Gina, Christ.* Also *Idaho* and *liar* and *You can't stop her, Gina, Jesus.*

Malcolm slurps the last of his Coke, now mostly melted ice. Carl Walter sits at the table with them. He's dropping liquid onto the curled straw wrappers to make the snakes squirm.

"Long day," he says.

"Thanks for coming all the way out here," Annabelle says.

"Hey, my pleasure." He seems to mean it.

In their room at the Sleepy Inn, Malcolm is bugging the hell out of Annabelle, who is sprawled on the bed in her monkey pajamas. She loves these pj's best, because the monkeys float in blue flannel space. They are monkey astronauts, adrift in the endless universe, and the best thing about them is their faces. They look nervous. Their mouths are set in straight, worried lines, which is how you feel when you are out too far, away from your planet, doing something that feels way too big. It has been an exhausting day, and she needs to get her rest for tomorrow, but Malcolm keeps asking her questions from the other bed and filming her on his phone. Now he's got it right in her face.

"What is the hardest part of running sixteen miles a day?"

"Back off, Tarantino."

"I'd rather be Wes Anderson. Answer the question."

"The hardest part of running sixteen miles a day is dealing with your annoying brother after running sixteen miles a day."

"Be serious, Annabelle."

She makes a face.

"What do you hope to accomplish with your mission?"

"I hope to discover a new planet with evidence of life. Go to bed."

"Annabelle. Come *on*."

"What? I'm exhausted. Go brush your teeth."

"After everything that's, um, *happened*, why are you running from Seattle to Washington, DC, Annabelle Agnelli?"

"I have to do *something*."

He clicks off the video recorder. "I'm going to bed."

She hears him in there, the bathroom of the Sleepy Inn, *shoosh-shoosh*ing his teeth with his brush. He is a serious and devoted tooth-brusher. He takes on all the parental tasks for himself that Gina's a little sloppy about. He even flosses. On school nights, he's in bed by nine thirty exactly, and allows himself a half hour to read, lights out by ten. He eats his broccoli without complaint. He writes *Multivitamin* on the shopping list that's attached with a magnet to their fridge.

When they turn out the lights on this night, though, Annabelle can feel her brother lying awake, and he must feel her lying awake, too, because now there's his voice in the dark room. Dark, anyway, save for the red smoke-detector button and the occasional swoop of headlights from the road outside.

"Happy birthday, Annabelle," he says.

"Thanks, butthead."

"Sorry Mom and Grandpa fought."

"No worries."

"Sorry Grandpa brought that guy."

"It's okay. He didn't mean anything by it."

"Sorry about . . ." It's quiet. Outside their room and down the hall, there is the rumble of the ice machine. "Everything."

"Me too." She doesn't bother to tell him that he should not be sorry, that he is not responsible for any of those things. She doesn't bother because they are both chronic apologizers, and chronic apologizers know that *sorry* is also just sorrow for the general state of the world. Annabelle and Malcolm lie there for a long while. She is so exhausted, but far from sleep. "Hey, butthead?"

"Yeah?"

"How have things been at school? Has that kid Derek been giving you any more trouble?"

"Not Derek, but this other guy, Sean."

"I'm so sorry, Malc."

"He's just stupid."

"He doesn't try to hurt you or anything, though, like Derek?"

"Nah. He's just a moron. Some people are always going to be stupid and mean."

This is true, so true, but this is still her last thought of her eighteenth birthday: She has wrecked so much for so many people.

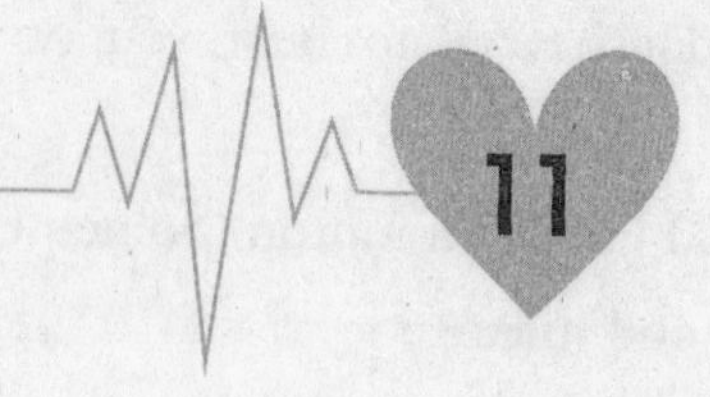

1. The small, withered heart of Marie Antoinette's ten-year-old son is kept in a crystal urn in a French church.
2. The Polish composer Chopin's heart was smuggled in a booze jar out of Paris and to a Warsaw church, where it was then stolen by Nazis before being returned.
3. Twenty-two embalmed hearts of popes are on display at a church near the Trevi Fountain in Rome.
4. The mummified heart of Saint O'Toole was kept in a cage on display in Christ Church Cathedral, until someone stole it.
5. There is a strange fascination with disembodied hearts.

For a day and a half, Annabelle runs on a brutally hot road, WA 970, through Cle Elum. She is smothered in slick, sticky Body Glide. Every truck that whips past gives her a near-death experience. This is how opossums must feel, the ones that make it across the road. Sweaty relief, plus the cold fear that makes the hair stand up along your arms.

Next, there is endless flat farmland, stretching like a yellow sea. And then, for two days, she is on a forest service road. Loretta keeps her entertained with names: Cougar Gulch (eek), Roaring Ranch (nice), Beehive Road (adorable), Swauk Creek (where gold was discovered in 1873, she read that morning).

Finally, today, farmhouses begin to appear, and then come the gas stations and feed stores that mean a city is about to materialize. Her day's run is almost done, and all she wants is food, water, rest, and a break from the day's monotony. She spots the always welcome sight of the RV, parked in the driveway of the Squilchuck Mobile Home Park.

"They're letting us stay for free," Grandpa Ed says.

Where to park overnight is one of their largest concerns, they quickly discovered. You can't just plop an RV down anywhere and stay. Even if they overlooked private property and sheriffs writing citations, most of the highways feature narrow shoulders, in a landscape that gets so pitch-black at night, any car rushing past would likely kill them all. So now, Malcolm, logistics coordinator, and Zach, financial manager, organize their sleeping location every day, texting her each evening with the details. From the open doorway of the RV, Grandpa Ed hands Annabelle a bottle of water.

The cap is already off. They've got this routine down. She takes big, grateful gulps. Grandpa Ed sits on the step. He picks up a little piece of wood and a knife.

"Are you *whittling*?"

"What, where's the problem? Gotta have a hobby while I wait."

"I thought only hillbilly grandpas did that, not Italian ones. What is it going to be? It looks like a large raccoon dropping." Annabelle should know. She's already seen bunches of those.

He ignores her. "Did you text the girl from the school paper?"

"I'm not feeling well."

"You're feeling fine."

"My stomach aches. I'm going to call Olivia and cancel."

"Che cavolo!" Translation: *What cabbage!*

Annabelle calls Olivia, but she doesn't answer. A moment later, Annabelle's phone buzzes, and it's a text from her. You're not canceling. I just called and told Ashley Naches that you're an hour away.

I'm sick, she types.

A text from Zach bleeps onto her screen. You're fine. Remember debate, sophomore year? The silver, baby.

Ugh! Okay, all right! In the tenth grade, before their debate competition, Annabelle told Mrs. Lehwalder she had a stomachache and had to go home. Mrs. Lehwalder gave her a pep talk and a Pepto-Bismol, and Annabelle ended up winning a medal.

"Hurry it up," Grandpa Ed says. "You're supposed to meet somebody, you meet somebody."

• • •

The stomachache is real when she walks through the hallways of Wenatchee High. The problem is, every high school looks pretty much like every other high school. At least, she's hit with the fluorescent-light-ness of the place, the locker-lined hallways, the smell of sweat and lunch-bag apples and cafeteria cooking. She can sense all the other stuff you find at any high school, too—the bravado and insecurity and self-consciousness and pretending. Big posters are taped to the walls. They have images of basketballs and say GO PANTHERS! She made signs like this at her own school. Her and Sierra and Josie Green and other girls. Mostly girls, which makes her think that boys should make the posters for the next few hundred years until the poster score is even.

She sees The Taker by the—

Stop!

On the stairwell, there is The Taker—

Stop!

In spite of the physical pain of the last few weeks, Annabelle realizes what a relief it's been to be in forests and farmland and even on highways. She understands why Dr. Mann kept suggesting yoga and meditation. These are all ways to be *away*, to set aside the images that scream and pummel. Everything here is a reminder. She has no idea how she ever managed to be in school. Well, truth is, she *wasn't* managing, was she? She wouldn't be here if she had been.

Stop! Now, it's the open doorway to that classroom, where she can see The Taker in front of her in Mixed Media.

Stop! Another open doorway to another class with The Taker, winter quarter of AP English Comp.

Stop! The trophy case, because next she's smacked with the memory of walking with Will through his school. He shows her his name on the plaque from their state championship lacrosse win. *Immortal*, he says. *Until you graduate and junior varsity becomes varsity, and* they *win, and you're outta here.*

Stop! The library, where she is meeting Ashley Naches.

And this library looks basically like the one at her school, too. There's a long desk up front, and shelves of books. There are tables with computers, and READ posters on the walls. There is one kid, hiding from life. There is a table with four chairs. She can see herself sitting beside The Taker with Destiny and Lauren K (who was always Lauren K to distinguish her from Lauren Shastes, who was always just Lauren). They're at the library during English Comp, and he takes her fingers under the table, and she lets him.

She lets him, do you see? This was after the card in the parking lot, after the birthday gift, but her mind jumps and shoves images in front of her.

She still feels his fingers. They are warm as they grip hers. She doesn't mind. She lets him, and she likes it.

Annabelle is nervous. She taps her thumb to her fingers under the library table where Ashley Naches can't see. Annabelle feels around for the weight of the Saint Christopher medal in her hoodie pocket.

Ashley sets her phone between them to record their conversation, and she has a spiral notebook to take notes in, too. Ashley Naches has the thoroughness of a CNN reporter interviewing a head of state.

"So how do you feel about your decision to do this now that you're halfway across Washington? Your publicist, Olivia Ogden, said you've gone almost—" She checks her notes. "A hundred and fifty miles." Her publicist! Annabelle wants to laugh. Then again, she thinks of Olivia in middle-school orchestra, always first chair. Olivia has colored tabs dividing every class notebook in some personal system of priorities, and she plays Minecraft like a demon.

"One forty-two. I feel . . . I don't know. Crazy. Insane. No, wait. Don't write that."

"Okay."

"Please don't write that."

"I won't."

The librarian stands near the computer table, watching them. She made the kid who was hiding in the back corner leave, like Annabelle had an explosive device strapped to her chest. Annabelle's hands start to sweat. She can only guess what it's like to have her here.

She tries again. "It feels like the hardest thing I've ever done." But of course this is wrong too. Running 2,700 miles is nothing compared to what she's been through and what's ahead. "Um, wait. Don't write that."

"Okay."

"Just say, I don't know. Tired. Determined. I'm not really all the way determined, but that's what people will want to hear."

"Probably," Ashley Naches says.

There are more questions. How long it will take. What she did to train. What she hopes to accomplish once she gets to DC.

Ashley Naches does not ask about The Taker. She doesn't ask the thing everyone really wants to know: *How did it feel?*

"Can I take your picture?" Ashley asks.

Oh, God. Annabelle hadn't anticipated this part. She's not wearing makeup. She's gotten thin already from the run. Her cheekbones sink in like old couch cushions. Her hair still looks like she cut it with her eyes shut. "Okay. I guess, okay."

Ashley stands. She's wearing jeans and a T-shirt with a glitter butterfly on it. She is overweight but confident, wearing her T-shirt tight enough to hug her curves. *Go, Ashley! Way to love your body!* Annabelle thinks. Ashley backs up until she's under the "Great Books for Spring" poster. She hunches, snaps a few photos of Annabelle, who isn't sure whether she should smile or not. Smiling seems disrespectful.

Ashley Naches gathers her backpack and her notebook. The interview is over. The librarian locks the door behind them the second they leave.

"I have to stop at my locker, so . . ."

"Sure. Well, good-bye," Annabelle says. "Thank you."

Now, Ashley Naches looks at her hard. Ashley Naches

has warm, dark eyes, and they stare kindly into Annabelle's. "Are you, um, okay?"

How to answer this? There's an awkward moment of silence, when Annabelle searches for a response. "Not really."

"Are you going to be okay?"

Annabelle shrugs. "I don't know."

Ashley Naches does a surprising thing, then. She hugs Annabelle. She grips Annabelle to her big chest. When they separate, Annabelle sees that Ashley's eyes are wet with tears.

"Bye," Ashley Naches says.

"Bye."

Annabelle watches Ashley go. There are rhinestones in a V on the back pockets of her jeans, too. Annabelle wonders what it's like to be Ashley Naches, a girl hopeful enough for sparkles. Ashley will head home now, to her mother and father, or just a mother, or just a father, or a grandma, or two mothers, or some configuration of family. There will be problems under that roof, because there are problems under every roof. But she will not carry the guilt Annabelle carries. Seth Greggory is not in her future, and for that reason, Annabelle is hit with a longing, a bad, bad longing, to *be* Ashley Naches in her sparkling jeans, heading home to whatever her problems are. Ashley Naches, who walks home feeling sorry for the girl she just interviewed back there.

Annabelle needs to get the hell out of Wenatchee High. She pushes through the doors, and outside it is spring again, and there is Grandpa and the RV, waiting in the lot. She is so relieved to see that her new life—where she's both running and on the run—is still there. She still has many, many miles to go before Seth Greggory, thank God. She does the math. She has more than 2,500 miles between her and what's coming.

And then she sees them. A group of guys on a patch of lawn with an iron panther statue at its center. One of the boys has his hand on the panther's back, like they're pals who've discovered the real meaning of friendship. Three other guys stand nearby, laughing and talking. One of them has a denim jacket like The Taker's. His shoulders turn inward with shyness and he watches the others carefully, as if he's gauging what his own response should be.

Just like that, he's here.

He's here. The Taker, wearing that coat, walking home with those same hunched shoulders. Annabelle is driving. She's got her music on, and she's filled with the boldness from a good song. It's a few days after that card, and she's trying to be friendly. They've talked in class. He told her how he's trying to teach himself to play guitar, and about his dog named Marty, who can get into every locked cupboard. She's told him about the Almond Croissant Crisis at Essential Baking Company last weekend, and how Mrs. Chen fled from Sunnyside Eldercare and they had to call the police. He's surprisingly funny. And he knows all these cool cultural references that make her feel kind of stupid. *Like the iconic dance scene in* Pulp

Fiction, he'll say, and she won't have any idea what he means.

After her initial avoidance of Will, he and Annabelle completed the breakup dance: There were a handful of upset phone calls, the long-minutes-of-silence calls, the maybe-we-shouldn't, yes-we-should ones. Recently, the days of no contact have been stringing together into permanence. Her life is sort of like it was, just without Will in it—school, work, family, friends, running. So now, Annabelle is trying to be larger and fuller. She's training for her second marathon in November, doing extra-long runs on the weekends, and she's attempting to be open to all new experiences. *Being open* and *new experiences* are awesome, because they make her feel like she's moving on, while also serving as a *Fuck you, Will* and a *Look at all the stuff you don't know about me now, Will.*

She turns down her music, pulls up beside The Taker, and lowers her window. "Hey. Where you headed?"

"Home. Missed my bus."

"Shoot. Want a ride?"

"That'd be great."

His head almost hits the roof of her car. His legs fold in like a grasshopper's. The small space between them is suddenly filled with heat; his cheeks are flushed and there's the wet-wool smell of boy sweat and that tang of something again, maybe weed.

Also rapidly filling the car: awkwardness. Now that he's in there, Annabelle has no clue what to say to him, and she can practically hear the gears of conversational effort turning in his own head. He shifts around a lot, looks for something in his jacket pockets as if he's occupied with important business. She's filled with instant regret at having stopped. *See what happens when you're impulsive?* she lectures herself. She often lectures herself. It's like living with a cruel boarding school teacher inside your own mind.

"So, where to?"

"Ravenna Park?"

"Got it."

Whenever anyone gets in the car with her, Annabelle starts driving like an idiot. She's fine when she drives alone, but now she almost runs a stop sign, and speeds past a lady waiting at a crosswalk. He's not the only one who's nervous.

She turns her music back up to cover the uncomfortable silence. "Can I look at your library?" He gestures to her phone.

"Oh, God. Go ahead. But disregard any Raffi."

"Hey, childhood nostalgia, I get it." He scrolls, comments. One thing she's learned—he knows a lot about music. "I like, I like, I don't know, I never heard of . . ." he says. "Hey, the Clash! 'The only band that matters.'"

He's making a cultural reference that she's ignorant of again, she's sure. "Stole it from my mom."

"Hey, old people have some good music! It's not all 'Lady in Red.'"

"Hmm. I've never heard that one."

"You're kidding! What's wrong, you're not into sappy shit from the eighties? Can I play the Clash?"

"Sure."

It's "Police and Thieves." "Junior Murvin's lyrics—so awesome," he says. He sings along, stuff about fighting nations, and guns, and ammunition. She thinks he might have a thing for guns, which in her world is as rare as saying he has a thing for medieval weapons of war. Once, he dropped his backpack and a firearm catalogue spilled out, and there was also that photo at the shooting range. Who has guns in Seattle? No one she knows. Guns seem foreign and weirdly aggressive. Here, people say they're sorry when they bump into someone on the street.

The Taker rocks his head to the beat, and she plays drums against the steering wheel. When they get to the chorus, they *Oh, yeah* together. She's having fun.

"That one," he says. "The gray one with the Volvo."

"Wow, nice house." It's a big, old Craftsman, right by the park. There are three stories at least, and it's got one of those curved cupolas that would be perfect to do your homework in. One of his parents must be a serious gardener. There's the kind of mishmash of flowers that look unplanned but are oh-so-carefully planned.

She turns the music down.

"Hey, thanks. I appreciate the ride," he says.

"No problem."

He's looking right into her eyes, and she's looking into his, and he's not being shy and maybe he doesn't even like her anymore. Of course, this makes him more interesting, and he's . . . how to explain it? Different. Odd. He's maybe like a door to somewhere she's never been. Maybe weird would be interesting. Weird is definitely not Will. Maybe weird means troubled or some kind of history that isn't parents like Robert and Tracie, even though there's a Volvo.

She could kiss him. She could see what it was like and then never do it again. She thinks he might kiss her. But he doesn't. He just unfolds himself from the car and gives a little wave.

And what happened after that, well, this is what she really thinks about when she sees that boy by the panther statue. Because after that day, he started hanging out with Annabelle and her friends. It was her approval of him that let him into their circle, which is horrible right there—the "let" and "allow" by superior people. She was one of them, the superior people. She floated around in the privilege of her popularity without giving it a thought. It was wrong.

After the day she drove him home, he sat with them at lunch. Geoff Graham invited him to play guitar when his band, Shred, appeared at Café Hombre on Wednesday nights when no one was there. Kat helped The Taker with a paper on *The Scarlet Letter*. Everyone could tell he liked Annabelle. She liked being liked. It wasn't a big deal, the liking, until it was.

Even after he joined their group, though, The Taker

hung back in a way that's hard to explain. Annabelle would catch him watching her and her friends, same as that boy on the grass is doing now, making sure he doesn't do anything to shame himself from the circle.

Annabelle flings the door of the RV open, slams it shut behind her. "Get me outta here," she says.

Grandpa Ed sits in the driver's seat, window down, listening to NPR and whittling.

"Looks like you survived the paparazzi."

"The librarian made everyone leave." Okay, this is an exaggeration. *Everyone* was one lonely kid reading *Dune*. "She locked the doors. She couldn't wait until I was out of there."

"Bella Luna. Did you ever think that maybe she was trying to help you? She booted everyone out for your own privacy. To make you comfortable, *capisce*?"

She scowls. He's saying the same things as Dr. Mann. That her perceptions skew reality. That her guilt does.

"Floor it," she says to Grandpa Ed.

He does. His little wooden raccoon turd slides from the console and rolls under his seat. It clatters every time he makes a turn or the slightest swerve. Roll, clang. Roll, clang.

The noise in her head is worse. There are a thousand wooden raccoon turds rolling and clanging. All she wants is to get back where she now belongs: the trail. Where the only sounds she hears are her own steps, and Loretta's calm voice, and streams gushing and birds tweeting, and trees creaking and crashing, and the occasional creepy animal sound.

She hears her own heart on the trail, too—its guilty beating. Out there, though, she can trick herself. It is not evidence of her going forward. It is not the sound of her own clock, moving her to the horror of what's coming. It's the base thrum of a trucker's radio. It is the purposeful thump of hooves. It is an ancient drumbeat, old as time.

12

Annabelle has just turned left onto East Morris Road, very near the Washington State border, when everything turns to shit. Pardon the expression, but there is only one good way to put this. The much-anticipated marker ahead does not bring her the joy she thought it would. No. Instead, after three and a half weeks of this, her first month, she's suddenly despondent. Beyond exhausted. Disgusted and fed up and aching with the madness of it all.

For God's sake, look around. What does she see? That's right! Nothing. Nada. Zero. Zip. Nothing but a flat road and dry grass. What about over there and there and there? Same, same, same! It is an entire continent of dry yellow grass. Hey, wait—there *is* a RAILROAD CROSSING sign, falling halfway over like it can't stand to be upright any longer, either. There are also the exciting thin metal posts with the flashers on top, so drivers don't veer off into ditches because of pitch-blackness or sheer boredom. Oh, wait. Look! Wow, awesome! There is a thrilling orange bush. Also, the smallest scrub of trees, whoopee, way, way off in the distance, though you have to squinch your eyes to see them.

Add some heat. Add suffocating heat that drenches your back in sweat and makes you stink like a caveman. Put a mean burn in your calves that's been there since last week. Set a curl of doom in your stomach. Add the fact that this—this exact picture, the yellow, the dry—has been what you've been looking at for days and days and days. Twenty-seven days, to be exact, where every day feels pretty much like the last. One month, which is only the first of four and a half more like it. The good news: This pretty much is the hell you deserve.

But, now, here are more reasons why it all falls to shit in this spot. There's a crossroads. Puh-leaze—she can't even count all the times in the last few weeks when nature or weather or some animal provided some annoying double meaning. She is irritated and peeved and just plain *over it*, over every metaphor from storm clouds to raging rivers, and she used to love metaphors. Nonetheless, there it is. The road curves. It is a decision. *WA 27* is painted on the street like a quiet but firm invitation. It is only five miles (and she has no idea when five miles became an *only*) to the state line. It would be so easy to finish and then come back here, where WA 27 loops right back to home. All she has to do is make a call to Grandpa Ed to tell him she's done.

And, oh, she is so done. She is done for many, many reasons. She is tired. She and Grandpa Ed have reached a point of togetherness where everything the other person does drives you utterly mad. Of course, she is grateful, so grateful, for everything he has done, but can she discuss for a moment the way he picks his teeth with a toothpick? How about the annoyance of toothpicks in general? Who uses toothpicks anymore? No sane, non-gross person, that's who. Only old guys. Is there a toothpick factory just in existence for old guys?

And let's not start about the evening Listerine gargling or the morning throat clearing, which sounds like her neighbor, that dick J.T. Jones, trying to start up his decrepit Mustang. Or, the snoring, which no amount of pillows folded over your head can drown out. Or burps that smell like salami and wine and fill the whole RV with the smell of salami and wine. Or the dry Stella D'oro cookies with their cement frosting, which he raves and raves about and manages to find even in the most remote locations. Or the sheer routine of him. How every night when he pours the juice glass of wine, he says, *Vino, good for the heart.* We *didn't need no Internet to tell us that.*

Wait. She must also address the anchovies. Long, flat anchovies in oval tins, and curled-up anchovies pressed against their glass jars. Anchovies on crackers, anchovies on pasta. Anchovies in salad dressing. Small salty fish with tiny fishy bones every freaking place she looks. He has an entire cupboard of them, she swears. Must stock up for emergencies! In the event of a nuclear war, do not fear: There will be anchovies on Ritz crackers for El Capitano and his loved ones.

And, she is driving him insane, too, she knows. She sees

how the muscle in his cheek works when she unwraps the tape from her ankle and it makes the loud *scriiitch.* She has heard the sigh when he sees her stinky running clothes soaking in the sink. She suspects he takes his hearing aids out on purpose, to get a little needed distance from the sound of her just being and breathing. There is a pillow over *his* head when she leaves early in the morning. Whenever she talks to Gina on the phone, he slams out the RV door and goes for a walk, even if it's a dark and moonless night. Once, she heard him pissing outside rather than coming back in before they'd hung up. He blows a disgusted sigh through his nose when she seems to be feeling sorry for herself, though, honestly, what does he expect?

She is done, too, because Gina made a good case for it the night before. When Gina makes calm sense, Annabelle often listens to her. Annabelle loves *calm* plus *sense*, because in her life, that is like a rare desert flower that blossoms only once a year. Gina is hoping and praying that this will be Annabelle's last day. *Look*, Gina said. *You ran across the entire state. Can't you call that the accomplishment? Isn't that good enough right there?*

Annabelle is done because of pain. She is done because of monotony. For the last few days, she's been in eastern Washington, and sure, there's the beauty of the Palouse of eastern Washington, until the endless, unchanging, ceaseless, tedious, flat beauty of the Palouse of eastern Washington makes you want to kill yourself.

She is done because Montana is coming, and that will be worse.

She is done because she misses home. At least, she misses her own bed and her clothes and she really misses Bit, their dog; the way he'd be so happy when she'd come back. His tail would wag like a flag in a storm. He didn't care about anything she did that was wrong or unsightly. She could wear plaid with plaid or tell him the truth or have bad breath, and he would still be just present with his accepting swiveling backside. God, she loves him.

She misses eating what she wants, when she wants. Plain old cereal or drive-through burgers or Skittles arranged by favorite color while studying. She talks to Zach Oh and Olivia practically every day, Malcolm, too, but she still misses playing video games and watching stupid TV instead of hearing how the GoFundMe is doing and who said what on the Facebook page she's too chicken to look at. She even misses Zach Oh's mom, who wakes him up every morning though he sets his alarm, who always nags him about getting his homework done though his homework is always done. She is sort of mean and angry-faced, and Annabelle often feels sorry for Zach Oh, but right then, she misses his mother so much that her heart is heavy and hurting with it.

She is done because what she is doing, this whole idea, is pointless. That's the biggest thing. Why is she doing this? She has lost track of the why. Seth Greggory is still out there, and her future is still her future, and nothing she is doing will make anything change, if it hasn't already. Look at the horrors that have already happened and happened and happened, and *nothing.* Same, same, same. More, more, more. If such horrors can happen to classrooms of *kindergartners*, little first graders with little pink rubber boots and sweet butterfly backpacks, there is no hope. *Nothing had been done.* Kindergartners. *Nothing.* Beautiful, beautiful children.

Annabelle sits down. Right on that ground, at the cross between East Morris Road and WA 27. A hot wind blows. She leans her head on her arms. She is too tired and defeated to cry.

She knows what Kat would say. *Just one more day. Go one more day.*

She can't go one more day.

So she fishes out her phone. She could call Dr. Mann. She could call Zach or Malcolm, who will talk her out of this, who will remind her that her Facebook page now has four hundred followers, and that her GoFundMe is up to two thousand bucks.

But everything has gone to shit, so she calls Grandpa Ed. At least, she tries to call Grandpa Ed, but her phone has no service.

Insert a great deal of expletives here. Also, some foot kicking, which basically just stirs up a lot of dirt that sticks to her sweat. It is tantrum-y but feels great. Awful and horrible, but kind of good. She throws a rock. She usually has terrible aim (she hated the baseball unit in PE), but the rock pings against the RAILROAD CROSSING sign in a way that is unusually satisfying. She throws another and misses.

She is pissed off at her phone. She is angry in general. She is not nearly angry enough, she realizes. Because, my God. She should be furious. She should rage like mad every day. Her rage should start at The Taker and extend to every single way her body is legally controlled or left unprotected. Her anger has been buried under goodness and guilt and fear, but it's a shame, because people with real power get angry. People with real power tell other people what they think, right to their big scary-ass faces.

All right. Shit, all right! She has no choice but to go on to the meeting place of the day, West Chatcolet Road, Worley, Idaho. Grandpa is probably in Worley now, checking out all four of its streets so he can give her the lowdown of the place in excruciating detail. The excruciating details of Worley will sound pretty much like the excruciating details of every small town they've been in so far. How much can you say about a post office, a church, and an Ace Hardware?

So, that's it. She's done. Even Loretta has fled. Saint Christopher is probably breathing a sigh of relief. It's pretty clear which direction Annabelle Agnelli needs to go, though, because it is definitely not WA 27. She turns left onto South Marsh Road, where, incidentally, there is no marsh. There is no water whatsoever, nothing remotely blue except the sky, which is also the same in every direction, not a cloud in sight.

Next, East Calumet Road, Rockford, Washington. From there, she'll turn on Chatcolet, and then she'll be at the border, and then it'll be over.

• • •

She sees the turnoff for Chatcolet Road up ahead. It's right next to a farmhouse, which is all white and picturesque, with barns and outbuildings. There's a majestic row of grain silos, too. It's weird, because she also thinks she sees some people out by the juncture. A little huddle of them, like they're waiting at a bus stop. She hopes it's a bus stop. If it is, maybe she'll get on the next one. Maybe she'll just ride that bus to wherever it's going. The idea is so appealing that she briefly indulges in one of those fantasies that momentarily feels real. She smiles at the bus driver so he doesn't suspect anything. She chooses a seat by the emergency exit. She'll just keep getting on buses and trains and planes until she's in sunny Mexico, even if Seth Greggory will have none of that.

The people in the little huddle are looking at her. Well, sure, you would. It's probably not something they're used to seeing, a girl in running clothes coming down this empty road in the middle of nowhere. Of course, it's not nowhere to them, but still.

The people are really staring. She counts—one, two, three, four, five, six. Plus a kid. Plus a dog. It's probably the whole town. The staring is a little awkward. She feels like the alien landing her UFO in the crops. She wants to tell them she's come from a peaceful planet, but, obviously, that's a lie.

Wait a second. Wait just a second, here. They are shouting now. Jesus! This is scaring her. But they look happy. They start jumping up and down.

They are calling her *name.*

Go, Annabelle!

Oh my God, oh my God, she thinks. She is horrified, and embarrassed. But, wait—maybe Zach Oh or Olivia or someone has relatives out in Worley, Idaho. That's it. Stupid Zach called up some aunt of his, and the aunt called her friends.

A woman reaches out her arm. She's holding a baggie, and it's full of orange slices.

"Wow," Annabelle says. "These are for me?"

"Don't stop. Keep going!" the woman says. She's wearing mom jean–shorts and a plaid sleeveless top.

"It's okay. I can stop. Thank you. You're here for *me*?"

The little kid—he has shiny little-kid hair, and little jeans with a little cowboy belt—is holding a balloon. It's made of red foil and has a fire truck on it. It sags a little. "Go ahead, Jonathan," another woman says. Her hair matches the color of the dry grass, and she is stout as a bale of hay. "He thought you'd like this balloon from his birthday party. To celebrate your crossing."

"I can't believe it. Thank you," Annabelle says to the boy as he hands her the balloon. He hides behind his mother's legs. "I don't know what to say. Do you all know Zach?"

"Zach?"

"Zach Oh?"

"We know you. From the *Spokesman*."

A man hands her a newspaper folded in half. Hey, newspapers! Who even knew those existed anymore!

Annabelle looks down at the page and sees a photo of herself.

It's the one Ashley Naches took of her in the high school library. The paper is the *Spokesman-Review*, but the byline reads *The Wentachee World*, and, yep, there's Ashley's name. Her article in the high school paper has hit it big in eastern Washington.

"You go, sweetheart," another woman says. "You're right near the border. It's up there where that truck is parked. We thought you'd like to know when you made it. Otherwise, you can't really tell."

"I'm—" Annabelle swallows. She can't speak. Even if she could, she doesn't know what to say. She might cry. She's overcome.

"Go, honey," the blond woman says. "You can do this."

"We heard about what you're doing. We heard about what happened," the man says. "You are lifting us. We are lifting you."

It is one of those vaguely religious things people say that sometimes creep you out, but now it's kind of nice. Actually, it's really nice. It's so nice, she can't even believe it. She feels choked up. She is holding the balloon and the bag of oranges. It is hard, so hard, but she sees Dr. Mann in her brown leather chair, urging, and so she takes this kindness, too.

"Thank you," she whispers.

"Go!"

She does. She runs. The fire truck balloon hovers and bobs behind her. She is fighting back tears, but she has forgotten all about quitting. Up ahead, there's a man in the white pickup truck. He leans out his window and waves his arm.

"Right here!" he shouts. "Right here is where it changes."

"Thank you!" she yells back. "Thank you."

She doesn't know exactly when her foot crossed the border, bringing her from one state to another. But the man is right.

This is where it changes.

13

"I can't believe it," Annabelle says to Grandpa Ed, across the table of the Coeur d'Alene Casino Resort Hotel restaurant. A big pink slab of prime rib sits in front of her.

"That there's the horseradish." Grandpa Ed points to a little silver cup of fluffy white stuff. "It looks like sour cream, but if you put it on your potato, you're gonna be sorry." He bites the end off of a fried shrimp.

"Thanks for the heads-up. This is wild, isn't this wild? It feels wrong."

"If fried shrimp is wrong, I don't wanna be right," Grandpa Ed says. "Cheers to you, crossing the border into Idaho."

"Cheers." They clink soda cups.

"Ashley Naches is a really good writer," Annabelle says.

"Front page, Bella Luna."

The picture is pretty bad, though. Annabelle's hair has grown out some, but her eyes look absent and hollowed out. She looks haunted and vulnerable. The article is between a piece about a rash of carjackings in parking garages, and an ad for *Jerome Machet, DDS. Your Gentle Dental Friend.* But she is surprised at Ashley Naches's words and how tender they are. *It is something that could have happened to anyone, but it didn't happen to just anyone. . . .* It almost makes Annabelle sound like someone worth rooting for and believing in.

And, now, a few nearby people apparently do. Six residents of Rockford, Washington, and seven members of the Coeur d'Alene city council, plus the mayor, also met her by Grandpa Ed's RV in Worley. They gave her a bottle of Martinelli's sparkling cider and a gift certificate for dinner and two rooms at the Coeur d'Alene Casino Resort Hotel. Another teen reporter, Jax Jones from Coeur d'Alene High, took her picture shaking hands with Mayor Ellis. The fire truck balloon hovered next to her, trying to get in the photo like Sierra Kincaid always does.

"It's weird, though. I keep feeling like someone should just haul me off to jail right now."

"Stop it, kiddo."

"Look where we are."

Outside the restaurant window, there's a giant teepee and a beautiful lit pool. Through the wide doorway of the restaurant, she can see the blinking rainbow lights of slot machines, and there's the ringing and clanging of a win. Okay, honestly, there's only a handful of people out there, and one guy in the restaurant, and the waitress seems tired, but still.

"*Che figata!* I can't wait to sleep in a real bed."

"That's not what you said back at the Sleepy Inn. 'I've got a real bed.'"

"That was different."

"How was it different?"

"Mind your own business. Hand me one of those rolls, would ya?"

"Because Mom was paying then?"

"That's got nothing to do with you."

"Why do you two always fight? I mean, what about *la famiglia*?"

"You love, you fight. You fight, you love." This makes no sense, but whatever. He saws his roll open. Slaps on the butter.

"But *why* do you fight? Is it a big family secret?"

"No secret. I told you."

"You never told me."

"I told you a hundred times."

"Something about Nana."

"She was sick. With cancer. Your mother thinks I should have made her see a doctor sooner. Nana kept saying she had a backache. Her stomach was bloated out like a balloon. . . ."

Annabelle is silent. What was she thinking? They were so happy a minute ago. God, she really has a way of messing things up. She could spoil a parade.

"You don't think I tried? I tried. You can't make someone do what they don't wanna do. And you can't always stop 'em from what they're gonna do."

"Yeah."

"Right, Bella Luna?"

"Right."

"Capisce?"

"Yeah." It's a hard thing to hear. Or, at least, to truly believe.

"Look, they got that molten lava cake," Grandpa Ed says.

Oh, wow, the room is fancy. If she were a movie star, this would be the room she'd get. Wait, maybe if she'd just gotten married, because, look. There are rose petals all over the bed, and a silver ice bucket on a stand.

She checks the place out. It's so roomy that she flings out her arms and walks around like that. You could fit five people in the shower. Or maybe just two active honeymooners, haha. She opens the cap of one of the little bottles on the bathroom counter and sniffs. Yum. There's shampoo and conditioner, but also lotion and rectangle soap and round soap and bumpy, massaging soap and a shower scrub soap. It is a party of soap! In the closet—awesome, a robe! First order of business: She takes a shower and puts that baby on.

She lies on her back on the bed in her white robe. The bed is still made, and she just lies there with her arms out and her feet together, like the Jesus on the cross that hangs over their kitchen doorway. The flower petals are all around her.

Annabelle smells like lavender. It's astonishing, really, how she's a different person from the one who was just standing at the crossroads, kicking dirt and flinging a rock at the railroad sign.

She is a different person from the defeated Annabelle, the giving-up Annabelle. She is sort of a victorious Annabelle, lying among rose petals on the honeymoon bed of the Coeur d'Alene Casino Resort Hotel. You never know what a day will bring, which is both the good news and bad news of life.

She has decided to keep going, as anyone could tell by her closed eyes and calm expression. She realizes that all big decisions are ones that must be decided and decided again. She imagines that when you fall in love, you must decide to be in love a million times or more, and when you go to college, you must decide again and again to stay in college, and the same thing is true when you decide to run across the United States of America after a horrible tragedy.

When you are a person who cares for any other person, you must decide and decide again to care, she also understands. Her friends and family have. Grandpa Ed has. Her mother has. In spite of the fighting and blame, he comes to dinner and they celebrate the holidays together. In spite of the fighting and hurt, Gina invites him to dinner and to celebrate the holidays together. They hang in there with their love.

Annabelle holds a rose petal to her nose and smells. Oh, it's so beautiful and rose-y. It smells like what it is, deep red and velvety. When you are a human being, you must decide and decide again to go forward. You must, or you won't move from the worst that life offers to here, the bed of the Coeur d'Alene Casino Resort Hotel.

Crawl, walk, or run: *forward*.

She falls asleep. She is so exhausted, she conks off right there. It is astonishing how untroubled she looks, in her white robe with her eyes sweetly shut, the rose petal still balanced on her nose. The man back in the truck at the border had been right: That was where things changed.

The problem is, they will change and change again. Good to bad to good to bad, the universe spins, which means morning then darkness then morning. She hasn't forgotten her future, but, still, she is in the *good*. She has been lifted by strangers, and lifted, too, into sleep. The dream is something about silos and a truck and a yellow field, no longer desolate but full of color.

14

1. There are song titles featuring hearts in various locations: "The Heart of Dixie," "Heart of Asia," "I Left My Heart in San Francisco."
2. There are songs about "Hearts on Fire," and "Foolish Hearts," and "Cheating Hearts," and "Wild Hearts," and "Whole Hearts." There's a song about a "Precious Heart" and a "Rebel Heart" and a "Second Hand Heart" and a "Heart of Gold."
3. Hearts do a lot of stuff in songs: "Heart Skips a Beat," "The Heart Wants What It Wants." "Two Hearts Beat As One" while "Two Hearts [are] Breaking."
4. There are the songs that speak of the darker truth: "Hearts of Stone," "Wooden Heart," "Ugly Heart," "Cold, Cold Heart," "Jet Black Heart." There are at least fifty-eight versions of songs titled "Heartless." This does not seem like nearly enough.

• • •

Loretta is taking Annabelle through the narrow piece of north Idaho, which sticks up like an index finger. "The panhandle"—yes, she gets it now. It's an awesome place, even if the trail climbs in elevation and she feels the wrenching through her whole body. After each of her Idaho runs, she is sore in unexpected places from the strain of the upward climb—through her chest muscles and abdomen, the back of her neck. She's had totally wrong perceptions about Idaho, which just goes to show, you should never judge unless you've been there.

What did she imagine? The easy images she'd been handed—potatoes, corn, boring stuff. But Idaho itself is awesome, at least from what she's seen. There's lots of cool, beautiful water (Lake Coeur d'Alene, Anderson Lake, Swan Lake, the Coeur d'Alene River, which she runs alongside through most of Idaho). There are brewpubs with lots of meat on the menu (she skips the elk steak). There are perfect temperatures (she's not there in the winter).

"This panhandle feels like a shortcut through an entire state," she says to Grandpa Ed.

"It's the nice little almond in a big biscotti," he says.

Maybe it's because her trek through Idaho is only seventy-four miles, about five days of her trip, but she's feeling great. She's in a routine. She gets up early, writes in the Moleskine, and then takes off. She enjoys the beauty that is the water-filled, sparkly spring-ness of Idaho. There are cheery kayakers and bicyclists and crews of friends carrying rafts. On a day of straight-up forest trail, she definitely sees a white-tailed deer. She thinks she sees a wild turkey. She keeps a count of bald eagles, and then loses track because there are so many.

She knows that there are also cougars in those woods. Grizzlies, too. Every trailhead has a sign explaining what to do if you see one. If an animal wants to get you, it will get you, though, won't it? Isn't her life proof of that? This is something she struggles with as she runs. This is the question she must answer. How do you feel safe when there are grizzlies in your midst? Perhaps, your only real hope is not crossing paths with one in the first place. She carries a soda can filled with pebbles so the sound will ward off any dangerous creatures. She willfully ignores the fact that a soda can is nothing against a grizzly.

She spots flashes of The Taker in the dim grottos and murky hollows where the bears and the cougars might be. There are his bitten-down cuticles, and the way she once accidentally embarrassed him.

You nervous? she asked, laughing, holding up one of his hands.

The expression that crossed his face—it was shame, but deeper than shame. Fury, maybe.

So what? You get freaked out at a four-way stop. She knew he liked her, but it seemed like he hated her a little right then, too. And then there was the time he stormed out of class after he pronounced "awry" *awe-ree* when he read aloud, and everyone laughed. The walls shuddered when he slammed the door.

The next day, Mrs. Lyons and Annabelle and the whole class, really, pretended it hadn't happened, though you could feel the energy of pretending in the air.

Kat is also in the damp shadows of the forest. Annabelle sees her, jumping up and down and screaming alongside Annabelle's family at the finish line of Annabelle's second marathon that November.

Go, Belle Bottom! You're almost there! You can do it!

She sees Kat sitting at that back table of Essential Baking Company, reading and eating an almond croissant, drinking green tea as Annabelle makes complicated coffee drinks for the other customers. She hears Kat at lunch one day, saying, *I like his smile, though.* His—The Taker's. The *though* tells more than the *like*. Kat is trying to be generous. Then she changes the subject to something safer. *I got the new Alice Wu at the library, but the cover sucks.*

These small details spring out from the thickest brush and shadows, but the larger pieces stay crouched in hiding, and the largest piece of all lurks in the deepest, darkest cave, pacing and putrid. While she's here in Idaho, at least, the worst memories are in the distance, and Seth Greggory is in the distance, because there may be grizzlies, but the can shakes, and it sounds like *stop, stop, stop!*

After every sixteen-mile stint in Idaho, Grandpa Ed is there just as he's promised, in the location her "team" has scoped out.

"Look who's back. My little Jesse Owens."

"Who?"

"*Mi fa cagare!* Read your history!" *Mi fa cagare*: statement of disgust. Translation: *It makes me poop.*

After her run, Annabelle takes a long nap, and then they find a brewpub, or she eats an enormous pasta dish that he's fixed. She checks in with Malcolm and Zach and Olivia about the plans for the next day. She calls her mother. Gina, seeing that she hasn't died yet, has cut down her daily calls from ten or twelve a day to two or three. This may also be due to the anxiety medication she's now on, according to Malcolm. For a few weeks after Annabelle left, he said, Gina kept waking him up to see if he was breathing. Their house was filled with those protective saint candles you get at the grocery store for a few bucks. Gina made the two of them say lengthy safety-prayers before dinner. Malcolm finally told her that if she didn't get help, he would go and live with That Bastard Father Anthony at the rectory of Saint Therese's. *Have a good run tomorrow, and enjoy the scenery*, Gina says. If Annabelle didn't also hear Gina trying very hard to breathe deeply, she'd have thought her real mother had been abducted.

Grandpa Ed has been in a fabulous mood, too, since they've crossed the border. After the raccoon turd, there's been no more whittling; instead, he's been spending lots of time on a laptop he bought at Best Buy on a trip into Coeur d'Alene. Man, he loves that thing. He's on it all the time. He loves it so much, he always seems in good spirits lately. It's the magic of technology, Annabelle thinks.

"All right. Look what we got to look forward to. Roundup, Montana," he reads to her after dinner. "Site of the Great Centennial Cattle Drive of 1989."

"1989? Wow. Historic."

"Celebrating Montana turning a hundred, okay? Don't be a smarty-pants. Almost three thousand cattle ran through the town. Two hundred covered wagons. *Che figata!* Thirty-three hundred horses over six days."

"Sounds like Panama City Beach during spring break."

"Twenty-four hundred cowboys and cowgirls."

"Yee-haw. Imagine them in bikinis after a few Jell-O shots."

The only serious downer through Idaho: her team. The Facebook page has hit a plateau of 540 followers, and the GoFundMe donations have stalled. There's an emergency Skype meeting that night, after Grandpa Ed leaves to "get a little fresh air." He does this every evening now, and he comes back rosy-cheeked and pleased with himself, whistling some old-guy tune. At first, Annabelle thought he was hitting the tavern, but tonight, they're in Black Bear, Idaho, on Yellow Dog Road and there's not a brewpub in sight. In fact, there is nothing in sight except for the forested darkness of Shoshone County.

"Nice hair," she says to Zach Oh, when she sees him on her phone. "Desert dune during a windstorm."

"Hey, I didn't say anything about yours."

"I gave him some gel," Olivia says. "It gives him some lift."

"Next, she's going say you chew too loud and tell you not to go out with certain friends," Malcolm says.

"He doesn't have any friends," Annabelle says, and she and Olivia crack up.

"I'm glad *some people* are in a good mood," Zach says. "Because *I* am not in a good mood, okay? The last commenter on the Facebook page was selling weight-loss powder, and the one before that was a middle-aged predator dude with chest hair."

"We need new content," Malcolm says.

"It's true. We need new content," Olivia says.

"Minus expenses, the GoFundMe's at eleven hundred bucks, give or take. Eleven hundred bucks will barely get you to North Dakota, with gas, food, and the new shoes you're going to need at the rate you're going through them. This is a crisis, gang." Zach looks like the young CEO of the startup. His new, hip hair says *I got this*, but his fretful face gives away the fact that the whole deal is crashing and burning.

"You've got to start posting stuff, Annabelle," Malcolm says. He's holding his phone so they can see up his nose.

"Malcolm, gross."

"Your followers *want* to be part of your trip," Olivia says.

"Everyone else on *USA Crossers* has a blog. They show where they are on their route. They take photos," Malcolm's nose holes say.

USA Crossers is the site dedicated to everyone who has run across the USA. Only about three hundred people have done it so far, ever since the first lunatic tried it in 1909. This was Edward Payson Weston, who walked from New York to San Francisco in a hundred days. More and more people are making the trip, though. Ten to twenty are doing it right now with her, including another teen, Elena Callas, who's raising money for ALS, an illness her father has. Also crossing right now: a Desert Storm vet running for immigrant rights and a college student raising funds for National Parks preservation.

"I don't get why you won't just let us send out a press release," Olivia says. "Did you even read the one I wrote?"

"I've been busy."

Olivia exhales in frustration. Olivia always paces when she's on the phone, so in Olivia's Skype corner, Annabelle gets a whizzing tour of Olivia's room. A paper lamp shoots by, and then a poster of Amelia Earhart standing by her plane. "The media would pick this up in two seconds!"

"No."

"Why? Come *on*, Annabelle," Zach says.

"No! That's like me asking for something. That's me drawing attention to myself."

"Exactly!" Olivia says.

"If you don't get it, you don't get it."

"She's okay if it happens accidentally, but not if she goes out and looks for it directly," Malcolm's nose holes say.

"Elena Callas has twelve thousand followers, and she got a parade in Denver," Zach Oh says. "Because people *know*."

"I'm not in a competition with Elena Callas. I just want to make it all the way."

"You're not going to make it to South Dakota if we don't get the word out and get more money," Zach says.

"College fund, I keep telling you."

"College fund is for college." Malcolm has disappeared. His voice is firm, but it sounds far away, and all she can see is an image of his bed.

"I don't even know if I'm going."

"You're going," Zach says. "End of story. And you need to *speak*. You can't waste this opportunity. You're going to fucking say things that need to be said." Zach never says *fucking*. His mom would have a stroke if she heard him. Annabelle almost laughs, but he's clearly upset. He's upset because the tragedy has also affected him, of course. Olivia, too.

"At least contribute to the Facebook page," Olivia says. "Elena puts up photos of all the people she meets along the route. Buddy shots, arms around each other. Feel-good stuff. Like when a store plays lively music or a restaurant shoots out smells of garlic."

"You're going to be great when you get your MBA," she tells Olivia.

"We need to release the video," Malcolm says, as if he and Zach and Olivia are kidnappers with a hostage. "It's our secret weapon."

"What video?" Now Annabelle's worried. "This isn't some terrible montage of baby movies and news footage, is it? Come on, guys. I'm not exactly Elena with a sick father."

"Annabelle. This is no time to be silent. I mean, we *need* this. The world is a fucking disaster right now, and this is one thing we can do something about. I know you understand this! I get why it's hard, but come *on*." Two *fucking*s in one day. Zach is losing it. Zach Oh has a 4.0 grade point average, and you can see how he got it. He's a surprisingly passionate guy. Then again, after the tragedy, he had nightmares so bad, his mom slept in a chair in his room.

"My mission is personal."

"Annabelle?" Olivia says gently. "This *is* about you. But also . . . me. All of us. And . . . my little sisters. Every woman. Every person, but especially—every female person."

"It can be personal *and* global," Bit the dog now says. At least, it's Bit's big face and crazy teeth that she sees on-screen now. Malcolm is holding him up and trying to make his mouth move like he's talking.

"Bit!" she cries. "I miss you, baby!"

"Stealing Kleenex and eating underwear is not as much fun without you," Malcolm says in a Bit voice. Bit is squirming like a caught trout.

"I'll put it up tomorrow," Zach says, but no one is paying attention anymore.

"And the eating of your own poop, Bit, how is that going?" Annabelle is acting like her old self for a minute. This is how she used to be. Having made-up conversations with her brother and her dog.

"It is going deliciously. And I am scooting my butt along the rug like a champ."

"Way to go, bud," Annabelle says.

This is also how she used to be. Taking the sun and fun wherever she could get it. Ignoring warnings. Letting stuff pass. Completely overlooking the critical words.

Like *video.* Like *secret weapon*.

15

Two weeks later, Annabelle and Grandpa Ed are at a truck stop in White Sulphur Springs, Montana, when the waitress pauses before setting down the menus.

"You look familiar to me," she says, narrowing her eyes and looking at Annabelle hard. The café is in a little white building with a sign in front that says EAT. It reminds Annabelle of the food Gina bought after That Bastard Father Anthony left—the no-frills, say-it-like-it-is cans and boxes you get on the bottom shelf of the store: *Cola. Beans. Rice Cereal.* But now it's *Two Eggs* and *Pancake Stack* and *Biscuits and Gravy.* The waitress is wearing a burgundy Grizzlies football jersey, which has a bear paw clawing down the front of it. After the harrowing time Annabelle has so far spent in the huge and endless state of Montana, this feels like just another bad omen.

Annabelle kicks Grandpa Ed under the table, and he scowls. *No way*, the scowl says. And maybe he's right, because how can this woman even recognize her from the news reports of almost a year ago? She doesn't look like that same girl in the school photo of her that they always showed. The girl with the long hair and bright eyes and the shining future.

"Where you guys from?"

"Seattle." Annabelle waits. She wonders if this will help the server's memory click into place.

"Long way from home."

"You can say that again," Grandpa Ed says.

Menus are set down. Water gets trickled into glasses. Coffee poured. It has been forty-three days since Annabelle took off like a frightened squirrel back at Dick's in Seattle. She has run 698 miles. For the last fourteen of those days, 222 of those miles, almost a third of her trip, she has been running on THE LONESOME HIGHWAY.

The Lonesome Highway is perfectly named. There, you can run for miles along yellow prairie and never see a car, and at night, it's pitch-black as a coal mine. Deep space has more light. Deep space has more action. Occasionally a star explodes, but on the Lonesome Highway, the only thing that exploded was one of Grandpa Ed's tires, and now they are riding on the thin, small spare.

There is no Wi-Fi on the Lonesome Highway. No regular phone service. Talk about lonely. She'd give anything to hear Gina telling her for the millionth time to wear her reflectors. And who knows what's going on at home. Grandpa Ed checks in at whatever motel he can find with phone service, but it's a quick *We're fine, you're fine, good-bye* as the motel lady eyes him with impatience.

Things have changed again. The bliss of Idaho is gone. The bad stuff is winning. The Taker is. Seth Greggory is. Fear is. If nature abhors a vacuum, an imagination adores one. Out there, road stretching to road, the occasional jagged ridge of snowy mountains in the distance, it's a playground for her thoughts. They run wild, tumble, and fight, like elementary school kids with a substitute recess teacher. The whistle blows, and she yells, *Stop!* No one listens.

There is The Taker, and The Taker, and The Taker. He stares at her. He sticks out his tongue and waggles his fingers in his ears. *Did you think you could forget me?* he taunts. Isn't that part of the reason for what happened? So he would never, ever be forgotten, and never, ever be overlooked?

I win, he says. He does. He has gotten the final word, hasn't he?

Against that blank landscape, she and The Taker are in Mixed Media, and they are cutting images from design magazines. She can see his magazine, open to a two-page spread of a beautifully landscaped yard, with lit trees and a lit fountain set into a rock wall.

"That looks like Will's house," she tells him. It is the first time she's mentioned Will to him. After the breakup, it feels good to pretend that Will is just a passing thought, even though he's still actually in her head every two minutes.

"Will?"

"My old boyfriend. His parents were attorneys."

"Wow. Fancy. And what happened to Will the Boyfriend?"

Will the Boyfriend—it's said with the sort of sarcasm that's actually jealousy. A person's jealousy is a bit of a thrill until it becomes a monster.

"He thought we should see other people. We were getting 'too serious.'" She makes the quote marks with her fingers.

"So Will is rich but stupid."

"Aww," she says, lightly, teasingly.

"Take this, Will and Will's fancy house." He slices the page with his scissors. It is silly and dramatic, not ominous. They laugh.

"His parents were nice," she says. "Until they encouraged him to break up with me."

They both look down at the page now cut in half.

"I have a hard time talking to you, you're so pretty," he finally says.

And she loved it, didn't she? She just soaked it right in. How awesome, buffed up by a few compliments. Her worth was restored. The thing is, the shameful thing—he never made her feel like she was the dirty water going down the bathtub drain. He wanted her. He desired her. She used him, she thinks now, and look what happened. She was a pretty and nice girl-object to him, and he was an ego boost to her.

It's okay to flirt, Annabelle, Dr. Mann says. *And to feel pretty.*

And to be nice. None of those things mean you're inviting someone to harm you.

The Lonesome Highway is like one big movie-theater screen.

And it is always a horror movie.

Annabelle blames this part of the trip on Loretta. It's unfair, though, because Loretta is only looking out for Annabelle's safety. If Annabelle ran on US Route 12 and not the desolate 200, she'd be facing blind curves, and navigating tight spaces next to guardrails and steep, forested cliffs. A truck zooming along could pick her off in one second. This almost sounds better than what is happening: The Taker, killing her slowly.

The Lonesome Highway may be a safer route, but it is clearly not free from danger. Livening up the action of the Lonesome Highway: two roadside memorials, with plastic flowers and photos of a dead woman and a dead man, killed in automobile crashes.

One dead woman, one dead man. When she sees the second set of plastic flowers and the poster, weather-beaten and faded, *Always in our Hearts*, Annabelle stops right there. She bends in half. It's as if someone socked her. She crouches down by the photo. The woman is so young. She is blond and pretty. Her smile is kind. Annabelle cries.

She tries to call Dr. Mann later that day, but Annabelle's phone still has no service. Everything is dead. Flat, desperate, empty. Lifeless.

It is clear that this endeavor is much more about the head

than the body. Well, it's about the body, too—she's had to ice her knee every day in the last week, plus take a few anti-inflammatories. But you can't bring down the swelling of despair with a bag of frozen peas and a Tylenol.

The French toast that the waitress brings is big as a dictionary. Grandpa Ed's corned beef and hash looks like the many blobs of roadkill Annabelle has seen. He digs in, and she has to avert her eyes.

"I *know* I've seen you somewhere recently. Maybe you just look a little like my niece. That's probably it," the waitress says. "Where are you guys headed?"

It's the usual truck-stop talk, Annabelle guesses. *Where are you from?* and *Where are you going?* are probably the most essential things to know about a person.

"DC," Grandpa Ed says.

"Wow. Long trip. You guys drive safe and get yourselves out of Montana fast. We've got a bad thunderstorm coming tomorrow. You don't want to be out on the road in *that*, unless you want your bells rung."

"Electroshock therapy," Grandpa Ed says, and stares right at Annabelle, who stares right back at him.

"Zzzz," the waitress says. She slashes her arm across the air. *Gone like that*, her arm says.

Maybe there *is* just bad electricity in the air, because, that afternoon, Annabelle's mood gets worse. And Grandpa Ed's mood gets worse. He wants to find a place to fix that tire, but he's having trouble finding a garage that's open. It's Sunday. *Che cazzo!* he says. (Don't ask.) On any other day, Annabelle would have been on the road for hours. But she'd shut off her alarm. She went back to sleep. They went to the truck stop for breakfast. She is taking a "personal day," like Gina occasionally does at O'Brien and Bello's Attorneys-at-Law. This is Annabelle's second one since she crossed the Montana state line.

Her will is leaving her. Each day's run takes longer and longer. She doesn't know if she can go on.

Annabelle has fallen into a depression on the Lonesome Highway, and who wouldn't. *Fallen into a depression*. It sounds like a misstep causing a tumble into a dark and dangerous crevasse, which is exactly what has happened. Grandpa Ed has fallen in, too. He hasn't taken a cheerful evening walk in a week and a half, ever since phone service disappeared. *You're a hard worker, Bella Luna*, he said. It's his highest compliment. *You aren't a quitter. We know that. But you can stop whenever you want*. She doesn't know if this is him saying, *Please stop*. Saint Christopher just swings silently from the lamp by her bunk where she hung the medal. He's keeping his mouth shut.

More numbers: There are more than five hundred miles of Montana yet to go. It's almost the same amount of miles that she's come. The state lines are the big prizes along the way, but this one seems so, so far away. She's lost track of why she is doing this. It's easy to lose things on the Lonesome Highway. A tire, a life, hope. Your sanity.

Her depression is laced with anxiety.

Each step forward means she gets closer to Seth Greggory. Her mind bings and shrieks like a pinball machine.

They spend the rest of Sunday at Hal's. Hal's is really Hal's backyard. Hal sprays the tire with soapy water to locate the bubbly leak, splotches on some rubber cement, sticks in a plug, and charges them fifty bucks.

"Fifty bucks! You think I don't know a criminal when I see one? *Mortacci tua!*" Grandpa Ed says as they drive off. He gestures with his flat hand.

Mortacci tua: Your feeble ancestors. Take that, Hal.

That night, Annabelle lies in bed and listens to the rumble of distant thunder as Saint Christopher swings over her head ominously, like a vial of incense during mass. If this is the supposedly big storm, even it is a disappointment.

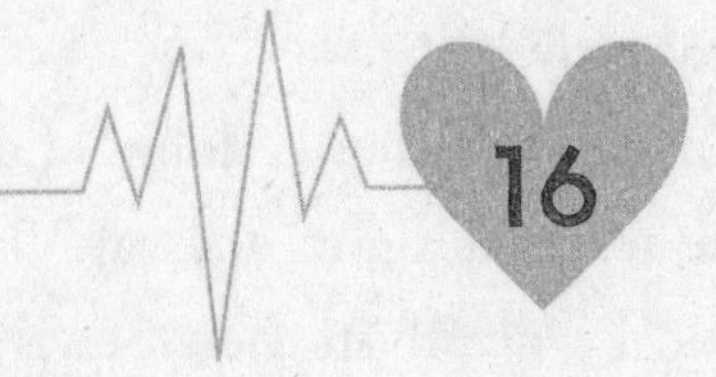

1. Louise de Quengo, who died in 1656, and her husband, a knight named Toussaint de Perrien, were buried with each other's hearts as an act of love and devotion.
2. In a story traced back to 1150 AD, a husband forces a wife to eat her dead lover's heart out of fury and revenge.
3. Love and devotion, fury and revenge—enough said.

Grandpa Ed opens the door of the RV, steps down the two metal stairs, and surveys the sky.

"Well?" she shouts.

"Get down here and see for yourself."

She is wearing her old Batman T-shirt that goes down to her knees. It's on its seventh day, which means they better find laundry facilities soon. The sink-rinsing and air-drying just isn't the same as a good tumble in a machine.

She climbs the stairs and stands next to him. They're

parked on Cemetery Road (cruel, but true) where the dry grass blows pleasantly.

"Sunny as the day is long," he reports. "We'd better check the forecast again anyway." It's flat out here. Lightning could be deadly to her. She'll be the tallest thing on the ground.

"I already did. The waitress was wrong, or else, that was the big storm last night."

"I didn't hear no storm."

"There was, like, two seconds of thunder. The forecast only shows a few clouds, is all. Who do we trust, locals or forecasters? I mean, locals named this place Cemetery Road. Where's the cemetery, anyway? I don't see one." Annabelle taps her fingers with her thumbs. "It doesn't look like a storm to you?"

"Nah. Look. Not a cloud in sight. But this is your call, Bella Luna."

She groans. How can you believe in thunderstorms when all you see is a mostly clear sky?

"Hey, I got a surprise for you when you get done today."

"A plane ticket home?"

"Nah. You get one of those after you get to DC."

"Why did I start this? Why am I even doing this?"

This morning, he does not blow air out of the side of his mouth at her whining. He's patient. He's riding his own roller coaster of endurance. He puts his hand on her shoulder. "Why does anyone do anything impossible? To be bigger than the big bastard."

"I'm not bigger."

"Yeah? Who is standing here? You, or the bastard?"

She has not forgotten about the tape and the tape player and the old earbuds that Luke Messenger gave her on her birthday at Big Chuck's, way back in Washington. Big Chuck's seems like a lifetime ago. The cassette is tucked down into her pack, where she keeps her private stuff. There's the acceptance letter to the University of Washington, folded up small. There's the new Alice Wu novel, pages crisp and cover tight and unopened. There's the *Thinking of You* card with a long handwritten message that Father Anthony sent after the tragedy. There's the small crucifix on a chain, given to her by Pastor Jane at the funerals. It doesn't represent God to her so much as a piece of herself that still holds out hope. You might say that this is true for all of the things in that corner of her pack. Hope not for someone or something specifically, but a general kind of hope. A hope that she might one day have hope.

Annabelle has been afraid of music, and books, too. Music and books stir up emotions. They make feelings rise and clatter and wreck, and sometimes that's dangerous. But music can make *you* rise up and clatter and destroy when you need to, too. And, today, as she finally leaves the Lonesome Highway to face the next five hundred miles of Montana, Annabelle needs to rise.

This is about perseverance, not about Luke Messenger, who she will likely never see again. In her mind, he's got a big X over him, as do all boys. As does flirtation and infatuation and love and sweetness and generosity and openness and belief and trust and safety, basically all the good stuff. Maybe it's a smaller X than she thinks, because she is a tiny bit curious. How can anyone sit at a birthday party for her, Annabelle Agnelli, just sit there with his hands folded across his lap, looking relaxed? Maybe the music will give her clues into someone who she'll never see again. This is the tiniest bit of boy fun at a safe distance, same as wondering about a cute movie star in a *People* magazine.

There is much arranging and scooting. The tape player rides on her hip, and the cord of the buds has a short in it, so the speaker annoyingly shuts off in one ear unless she settles it just so.

"See you later, Lonesome Highway. It wasn't nice knowing you," she says.

Outside of White Sulphur Springs, the land is all hilly green, and she passes farms and tractors trundling up dirt roads. It's going to be a hot day; it's already warm out. In the pastures, there are giant bales of hay—some upright, some tumbled on their sides. It looks like a chessboard of a sore loser. There's the great smell of cow shit in the air. The smell of cow shit lifts her spirits.

"Hey," she says to a bunch of cow ladies who watch her along a fence. One moos at her. "I am glad to share the world with you," she says.

She presses the button and the music plays. Whoever is

singing is runnin' down the road, trying to loosen his load, with a world of trouble on his mind, and the music reminds her of the flag-waving Americana Heartland stuff Father Anthony used to listen to while mowing the lawn, just before cracking a cold one. This was before the days of the Blood of Christ, in the time of the Brew of Budweiser. She maybe sees why Luke Messenger is so mellow if he listens to this.

Next up, a song called "Road to Nowhere," which is quite fitting, given what surrounds her—miles and miles of ranch fencing, and then brown and green and yellow hills marked with green scrub. Occasionally, she feels the rumble of ground and she'll look over her shoulder as a semi passes her. The *whoosh* makes her hair fly into her mouth and cools off the sweat on her skin.

After the dark but somehow upbeat "The Passenger," and then "The Distance" *(He's going the distance, he's going for speed)*, and then the not-mellow-at-all "Highway to Hell," she sees the theme. She realizes it's not just a mixtape he had lying around, but one he made just for her.

It's silly, but her cheeks grow warm. Her cheeks are already warm from the heat of exertion and the April sun, but this is an actual blush.

She presses stop. She flings the buds from her ears.

She feels like she's suddenly left the party. Everything goes silent. The beat and thrum had been awesome, actually. But now it's a party gone bad.

Stop! Stop, stop, STOP!

She checks her distance: eight miles already. A mile faster than usual, thanks to those songs. Still, kindness like that from a boy is unwanted. And it's not the sort of *unwanted* of romantic comedies, where it means they'll end up together in the end. This is unwanted-unwanted. This is a she-can't-even-look-at-it unwanted. This is an absolutely-no-way unwanted.

Now, with the music off, there's just wind, and rustling brush.

Wait, though.

What is that? She thinks she hears something.

She stands very still. Was that a rumble? No. Please, no.

She listens. She can't hear it anymore. The sky is sweetly blue. This is her anxiety talking, and the post-tragedy sense of doom. She's nerve-racked, because of the waitress and the mixtape and her own certainty that things are always about to go terribly wrong.

Just in case, she'd better hurry the heck up to Bair Reservoir, where she's meeting the RV. A storm would be very dangerous out here where lightning travels fast.

She eyes the landscape as she picks up her pace. Nope. It's calm. She was imagining things.

Still, going that fast felt good. It was because of that music. She let it back in, and it was awesome, not awful. But, wow. That must have taken a long time, to make a tape like that. She pictures Luke Messenger's shoulders hunched—

There's a rumble and a crack. Shit. Shit! There's no doubt about it now. God damn it, the waitress was right after all. She squinches her eyes and sees them, the clouds, creeping over some low-lying hills.

Jesus. She's got to *hurry up*.

When thunder roars, go indoors, Gina always told them. And now this plays in a loop inside Annabelle's head. *When thunder roars, go indoors. When thunder roars, go indoors.* Those clouds—they are definitely moving in her direction.

She runs hard. Her feet slap the road. Where to? Just forward, until Grandpa Ed shows up in the RV. He's bound to come back for her the second he hears that thunder.

She flies. It's the pace of a sprinter, not the pace of a person running sixteen miles a day. It's a good way to get injured. *Plink.* A drop lands on her arm. *Plink-plink.* More, on her shoulder. It reminds her of that first night, when she fled from Dick's. But that was home rain, city rain. Shelter was everywhere if you needed it. Here, the clouds gather and darken, and it's just her and them.

This is the problem with danger, isn't it? You can even be warned and ignore the warning. Danger can seem far away until the sky grows dark, and a bolt of fury heads straight toward you.

In an instant, everything changes. The rain is coming down, and the clouds are an unfurling carpet of gloom. The asphalt highway is a shiny, wet black. The heat rises from it like steam in a sauna. In all that open space, she is the sole upright creature, an easy mark.

God, what were they thinking? Why had they taken this

chance? How could they have been so *careless*? Where is Grandpa Ed? The noise, the rain, the sky—he knows by now that she's in danger. She doesn't want to waste a moment, but she fishes her phone from her pack. Her fingers don't work. She's shaking. She is out here all alone, and the lightning will find her.

She's surprised there's even service. Still, Grandpa Ed's phone only rings and rings and rings.

She tries again. *Ring. Ring. Ring.*

Something's wrong. Something besides this storm.

It's eerie when a sky moves toward you. She is getting drenched now.

There's a deep rumble, and then a shattering crack. Holy hell. Her only chance is to outrun what's coming. She knows she needs to seek shelter. Every long-distance runner knows that the goal in a storm is to get to a safe place as soon as you can: a car, cover, any refuge.

It's a deluge. Her hair is soaked. She's wearing compression socks to help with the recent swelling in her knee, and they are soaked, too, and so is her shirt and shorts and pack and even her shoes. She can feel wetness down to her skin. But she has no time to wade in her own misery. She flies against the rain, eyes fixed on the horizon, hoping to see the hulking form of the RV coming to save her.

The rumble that follows is the largest and loudest yet. And then there is a huge and thunderous *boom*, one that makes her rib cage rattle and shreds her nerves. There is a *pop* and a *crackle*. It is like a firework; it is like—

Stop!

She can't think about this now, but of course she does think about this now. A *pop* and a *crackle*, and she is there, and she sees—

PTSD, Annabelle, Dr. Mann says.

She sees—

She wants to cry. *Rumble, crash!* She is a sitting duck.

Stop!

She does cry, now. She makes awful, animal sobs. She is scared. She is worried about Grandpa Ed. There is no house or gas station or shelter. How do you hide, what will cover you, what will save you? Nothing, sometimes.

Her chest heaves, and tears are running down her face along with the rain, which drips off her hair.

BOOM! Crack, pop! There's a jagged bolt of brightness, and then another. More than one across this flat, flat land.

"Please," she cries.

She wants to crouch down right there. It seems the only thing to do, to crouch and huddle, to not be big and tall. To be small. She knows how to do this, how to be small and quiet and nice, hiding under the radar. But crouching is not the answer here. Crouching does no good. The ground charge will move through her body regardless, entering at the lowest point, shooting through her heart, exiting at the highest.

Another rolling rumble, and a thunderous *crack*. She is a moving target.

"Please, please," she begs. A tiny realization edges in: In

spite of all the times she thought she wanted to, she doesn't want to die.

"Please come, Grandpa."

Annabelle is crying, and rain is falling on her face, so it is hard to tell if it is her own imagination again, or if she truly sees something in the road ahead. She squints. Yes. It's a little square of white. A little square of white, getting larger.

Coming *closer*. Someone is coming! Grandpa Ed! A rise of relief presses her forward. And, then: *crack!* The lightning crashes right next to her. She is in a shooting gallery—

Stop!

As the vehicle in the distance gets nearer, though, she is starting to understand. The shape is wrong. Even though her face is so wet that it's hard to see anything, she sees that. The shape is wrong, and maybe even the color. What's coming is not the bright white of Captain Ed's RV. It is a murky yellow-white, with rounded corners.

Does it matter? It doesn't matter. She waves her arms. She probably looks like the victim of an accident, someone struggling into the street with their injuries—

Stop! Stop! Stop!

She waves. She waves and jumps. It is not Grandpa, but some stranger is safer than being a mark for the monsters of lightning all around.

The wipers of the approaching camper are flicking madly as the rain beats down. It won't miss her, will it? They will see her, right?

She shouts and jumps.

None of it is necessary, though. The camper slows to a stop. And now the driver's side window rolls, rolls, rolls down, and a head pops out.

"There you are! God, get in!" Dawn Celeste says.

Dawn Celeste says?

The camper door flings open. There is the calm, curly-haired Luke Messenger, in a warm, dry flannel shirt and jeans.

He spots the earbuds, still jammed into her waistband. He smiles.

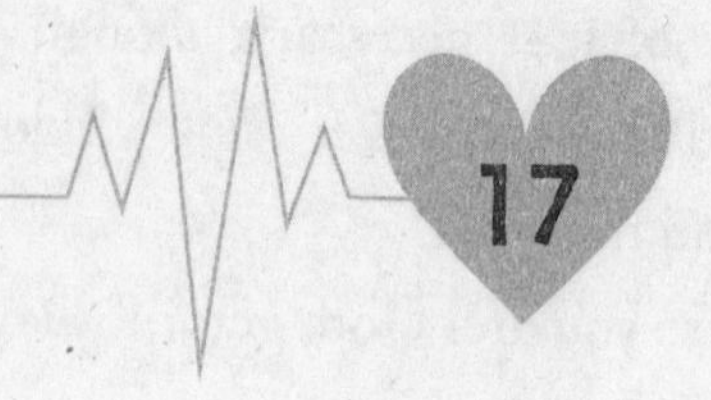

"'We're on a ride to nowhere, come on inside,'" Luke Messenger sings.

"Highway to hell, more like it," Annabelle says. "I don't understand. What are you guys doing here?"

Dawn Celeste turns the big camper in an arc and heads out. She drives that baby with the easy confidence of a trucker. "I got a call from Ed. He knew we were doing some hiking in the Lewis and Clark National Forest. His tire blew out on the way to get you. He said he just got it fixed, too."

"Wow. Well, thank you," Annabelle says. She says *Wow. Well, thank you*, while taking in the facts: Grandpa is okay, but Grandpa and Dawn Celeste have been in touch all along. They were in Idaho when she was in Idaho, and now they're in Montana, and now, here she is, with them in their camper. Her anxiety zings. Every part of her is dripping, too. So much water runs down her face and off her clothes that she is standing in a little creek of her own making.

"Luke, get the girl a towel. Sweetie, go in the bathroom and get that wet stuff off. We've got a change of clothes here for you, I'm sure. Luke?"

"I'll get some. Hang tight." Luke tosses her a towel. It's a little damp and smells of soap. She has a brief moment where she thinks maybe she got hit by lightning after all. She got hit, and now she's in some dream state where Luke Messenger spoke the lyrics she was just listening to, and has now handed her a towel that has the scent of pine trees.

"Oh, that's okay." Annabelle will absolutely not change her clothes. Her current plan is to stand still and say little until this ride is over. "I can change as soon as we get to Grandpa's. I really appreciate you giving me a ride over."

"Honey, it's going to be a while. You don't want to catch cold in those clothes."

"A while?"

"He has to go all the way back to Helena. Either that, or go to Billings. He said he's not going back to the asshole who fixed it before. And he can't go much farther on that spare."

The relief at seeing the camper, the shock of seeing Dawn Celeste and Luke Messenger, is now turning to something else, some squeezing in her chest. There is squeezing in her whole body—the compression socks, her shoes, her lungs, her heart. Maybe this is cardiac arrest. Maybe the fear and the run and the nearness of Luke Messenger are killing her right now, even if that lightning missed her.

Luke Messenger is not saying much. His back is to

Annabelle. Really, he's just as calm as a cypress. Annabelle stands there, feet planted on the ground like she's riding the subway. Something smells like wet dog in that camper.

Oh, God. Maybe it's her. She sniffs. It *is* her. She smells like wet dog! She eyes the latch of the camper. She'll take her chances with the storm, which is something you sometimes say when you're finally out of one. She will fling herself to the road and roll neatly away like a spy in an action movie.

She's maybe having a panic attack. She is pressing her fingers to her thumb, one by one, one by one, fast-fast-fast, on both hands.

Luke Messenger turns. He holds a steaming mug with a tea bag string draped over the side. He takes her by the shoulders and sets her down on the couch. It's plaid, but covered with a purple-and-red quilt. He hands her the cup.

"You're in shock," he says, which pretty much sums up the last year of her life.

She is wearing a pair of groovy lounge pants of Dawn Celeste's, and a Bob Marley sweatshirt of Luke Messenger's. Okay—she changed clothes! It's fine. It does not mean anything. She will give them back and she'll be out of here as soon as Grandpa shows up. From now until then, she will pretend that there is a big wall between her and them. Words and stuff can pass through it, but the wall renders every word meaningless.

It's strange, but after they arrive at Bair Reservoir, a small lake set into desolate, camel-hump hills, after she texts her mom to let her know she's safe but can't talk, after Dawn Celeste and Luke empty a bunch of gear—pillows and fishing poles and backpacks and jugs of water—from a spare bunk, she lies down at Dawn Celeste's insistence. And then, she sleeps like a baby.

Fear is exhausting, and so is a run like the one she just did. But something else loosens and relaxes her, too. It's the way the sheets are at first cold and then warm, and it's the way they smell a little smoky, like camping, a scent that represents both freedom *and* safety. It's the way that she has been tucked into her enclosed little bunk-cave. Just outside of it, there are two people who are completely at ease and satisfied with where they are. So she drifts off and sleeps hard. It's only in some part of a dream, a dream of Grandpa Ed and Dawn Celeste and a campfire, that Annabelle wonders now about those late-night walks he's been taking. And the joy and obsession he's had with his computer.

Even in her dream she wonders if Grandpa Ed is in love.

When she wakes in that strange place, all the comfort flees, and she's hit with overpowering anxiety. Annabelle Agnelli has always been—even before the tragedy—burdened by what she owes people. She worries if she's inconveniencing them. She's supposed to give and not take. Every Christmas, Dad/Father Anthony used to make her and Malcolm buy a present for a poor child, and Gina always said stuff like, *I don't need anything from anyone*. And when old Italian relatives like Great-Aunt Maria or Great-Uncle Frank shoved money secretly into her and Malcolm's hands, they knew what they were supposed to do. *No, no, no*, they would say. *Take it*, the old relative would respond. They'd go another round or two of protesting and insisting, until the relative would finally say, *Come on. Buy yourself something. Don't tell your mother*, and then they'd get to finally, gratefully answer, *Thank you so much.*

So Dawn Celeste and Luke's generosity now—her imposition, sleeping in their bed, taking up their time, wearing their clothes (she hasn't been in a boy's sweatshirt since Will)—it all dumps a profound distress upon her. Her emotions pace. She realizes she didn't finish her run. She had a mile and a half to go. She is cheating, being here at Bair Reservoir. Anxiety flees to rules and order for comfort, and she's broken a rule today, being here without running here. She badly, badly wants to tap her fingers, but she doesn't want anyone to see. She links her hands together and squeezes.

Dawn Celeste does not ask Annabelle if she is hungry; she just sets a plate with a fat tuna sandwich on it on the table. Inside the camper, it looks a lot like Grandpa Ed's RV, but not. There are woven curtains, and a colorful striped rug on the floor. There's a painting of an old man in a purple robe over by the door. The empty space under the bench seats, where Grandpa stores his water and wine, dry pasta and tins of anchovies, is open, and it's been made into bookshelves, with a wooden band across the front so none slide out. It's tidy, except for all the gear emptied from her bunk, which is now stacked around the bench seats.

"Thank you. Thank you so much."

"Look outside. You'd never even know there'd been a storm."

Dawn Celeste is right. Annabelle can see the blue of Bair Reservoir sparkling away with tiny diamonds of cheer. It does not match her mood. After she finishes that sandwich, she'll call Grandpa Ed to get her out of here, and fast.

"Luke thought he'd try to fish. A guy out there said the twelve- to fourteen-inchers are biting. Trout. Do you like trout?" Dawn Celeste munches chips out of a bag, brushes the crumbs off her cushy chest.

"Oh, I do. Yes." No. Lots of little bones. Those eyes staring at you.

"Maybe we'll have it tonight, then, if he's lucky. We eat late, hope you don't mind. Late as Europeans, around here."

"I should probably check in with Grandpa. I'm guessing he'll be back before then to pick me up."

"He called while you were sleeping. The tire is shot to hell, and no one in Helena seems to have another that'll fit his rig. Can you believe it? Of course, most of the snowbirds don't come out this way until July."

"What did he say, exactly?"

"It'll probably be a day or so. You okay to stay here with us, sweetie? Ed thought that might be best, so you can stay on track."

"Oh, that's all right. I mean, maybe I can just—" She waves her arm around. There's no *just* out here, unless they drive her all the way back to Helena.

"We can drive you to Helena if you want," Dawn Celeste says, reading her mind. "But Ed thought you could go forward from here, and he'll meet us whenever he's done."

"I couldn't possibly. I mean, I'm sure you have places you want to be."

"Honey, *Montana*," Dawn Celeste says, as if this is some sort of answer. "Does it look like we have a train to catch? We don't have an agenda. We go where we're interested in going next. I hope you'll relax. Consider this your own home. Books, food, you help yourself."

Annabelle is rarely relaxed anymore, not even in her own house. So here, her panic is rising. It's a tsunami of dread and obligation and the knowledge of bathroom use in small places. Sometimes she snores. She has woken herself up with a surprising snort. Already, she has smelled like wet dog and dripped on the floor, and changed out of disgusting clothes, and is wearing no makeup and has chopped hair.

"I have to—" she says.

Dawn Celeste waits.

"Go back."

"Go back?"

"To the um . . ."

"The um?"

"The spot."

"The spot? The spot where we picked you up?" Dawn Celeste's voice quickens and her eyes are bright. She is using the same excited cadence they use when trying to decipher what Bit wants when he sits and stares at them.

"It's a mile and a half or so back," Annabelle says. "I'm, it's, cheating. To be here. To go on from here."

"You want to go back now? We could start there tomorrow. You've had quite a day."

"I'm just going to . . ."

Dawn Celeste waits.

"Do it right now, you know? Just . . ."

"Whatever you want. In the country of my camper, everyone decides for themselves. We'll be here when you're done. Let me find you some shorts and a T-shirt."

Her plan is to jog casually until she's out of sight and then flee. It gets a little hazy after that.

A mile and a half takes no time at all. She runs a little past the spot where she thinks they picked her up, just to be sure. She has enough to be guilty of; she has cheated enough people of the things that matter most to them, without cheating about this, too.

The silk basketball shorts she now wears are enormous, and the T-shirt is silk-screened with a rising sun. The T-shirt must be Dawn Celeste's, because it smells like cinnamon and vanilla, and the shorts must be Luke's, because even with the drawstring pulled tight, they are large enough that she must clutch them around her middle as she goes. They are so long that they graze her shins like a skirt.

The road is empty, and her run is officially done, so she steps from the highway and into the yellow grass, still damp from rain. She sits in a patch of pebbles. She is a strange sight—a small rising sun in a field. She puts her head in her hands. How has her life come to this? The air smells like wet tar and shower-soaked earth. She thinks of that same smell one night in December, just before Christmas, the night of the winter dance.

They go as a group. Kat says it's always more fun that way, compared to when everyone pairs up. First they go to Benihana for dinner. They sit around the grill in a half-circle while the chef chops madly and simmers the beef and vegetables on the grill and makes the jokes he's likely made a hundred times. Zander Khan tries to order a drink and looks like an idiot. Zach wears a pink tie to match Olivia's dress. They're all a little too loud, and the other diners are giving looks, and Annabelle tries to shush them like a Goody Two-shoes. The Taker sits by Josie Green, who's also new this year. She moved in next door to Geoff. They'd be a good couple, really, The Taker and Josie, with her shy smile and plaid skirt and suspenders, her hair dyed jet-black.

They have green tea ice cream for dessert, which everyone pretends to like, and then they pile back into their cars. Splitting the check so many ways took a long time, and now they're late. They have to park way out by the chain-link gate and walk a long distance to the gym. That's when Annabelle smells it—that wet asphalt, damp-earth smell. It had rained while they were in the restaurant. She's wearing high heels, new ones, and a green satiny dress that clutches her hips and dips down to show the top of her breasts. The green matches her eyes. She feels beautiful in that dress. She saved her money for half of it, and Gina paid the other half. She's only had one other dress this fancy, the one she wore to Aunt Angie and Uncle Pat's wedding, but that was a little-girl dress and this is a young woman's dress, and she walks carefully on that wet pavement so she won't slip and ruin it.

This is Annabelle as she used to be: anxious, careful, responsible, but with moments of confidence, twinkles of flirtation. Love of life, a bright smile, a snort of laughter, a sense of belonging with her friends. She's aware of The Taker walking closely by her. He bumps her elbow and knocks into her shoulder, as if it's due to accidental nearness. He's wearing a dark suit, with a crimson tie. His hair is slightly slicked at the sides.

The doors are open, and the sound of the band spills out. Mr. MacKenzie, the shop teacher, takes tickets. They stand around awkwardly in a group until Drew Gilliam joins them, jokes around, and then asks Sierra to dance.

"Destiny," Geoff says. He crooks his finger, and then he and Destiny go to dance, too. The band is playing an old Coldplay song, "Yellow." They're butchering it. Yet, those words. *Look at the stars. Look how they shine for you.*

The Taker grabs her fingers. "Come on," he says.

It's one of those awkward songs—part slow dance, part

fast. What are you supposed to do, sway or bob? But The Taker puts his arms around her waist, and she clasps her hands around his neck. They are mismatched in height, and so he hunches.

She's aware of Kat, next to her. She is dancing with Zander, but they've most definitely decided to bob. Zander is doing a goofy shoulder-shimmy that makes Kat punch him. Kat catches her eye, lifts her brows in a question. Annabelle makes a face. *No way*, she answers.

But now, she's aware of something else. The Taker, very close to her, body to body. He's humming the song.

"They're butchering it," she says.

"What?"

"They're butchering it."

He still must not hear her. "'For you I bleed myself dry,'" he whispers into the soft place behind her ear.

And here is the part she has never told anyone, and that she hopes to God she will never, ever have to tell anyone, but she felt his hard-on then, pressed against her. She should have stepped back, maybe, but she didn't know what to do. It seemed up to her to be polite, as if his erection was a social blunder she should overlook out of generosity.

And why not overlook it? Why even assume it was personal? He danced with Josie Green, too. Maybe he had one then. Hard-ons are generally friendly, she knew. They aren't even particularly particular. But now, whenever she thinks of it, she is filled with guilt.

Now, whenever she thinks of it, she is confused about what she did and didn't cause. She is confused about desire, and her own desirability. She is confused about her own sexuality. It should be hers to wield as she wishes, she knows this, but why—even if she isn't wielding it, exactly, even if she's just being herself—is there the sense of a shameful invitation, or even an invitation at all? She knows she should be able to invite if she wants to invite, to say no if she wants to say no, yes if she wants to say yes, to allure or not allure, to just simply feel good about what her body is and does and how it looks. She is supposed to be sure and confident about those things, but how can she possibly be sure and confident about those things? There are so many colliding messages—confidence and shame, power and powerlessness, what she owes others and what is hers—that she can't hear what's true. And after the hard-on, she is left with a terrible remorse about that green dress and her body inside of it.

There is so much remorse that she is queasy. Remembering the hard-on, she might throw up. The tuna in the sandwich is trying to make the final swim of its life. She stands, and tries to shake it off, though maybe throwing up would feel good. Maybe she'd be ridding herself of something gross, even temporarily.

She breathes through her nose. Out in that yellow field by the side of the freeway, she thinks of Kat.

I miss you.

I miss you, Kat says.

Annabelle starts to cry. *I am sorry for every time I was a bad friend. Remember in the sixth grade when I didn't give you a valentine?*

I didn't give you one. We were fighting.

And what about that time I didn't come over when you needed me to?

I didn't tell you how bad it was until later.

Kat's mom, Patty, had been drinking and raged at her. Kat wanted Annabelle to come over and spend the night. But Will's parents were going to be gone, and they had the rare chance to be alone.

I am so sorry. I'll never forgive myself.

I think you need to get out of this field in the middle of nowhere in Montana.

Kat sounds so wise. Like she's gained all the important knowledge that there is. But, then again, she'd always been wise.

The storm has passed, but you'd never know it, the way regret rains down.

18

As much as she might want to, Annabelle cannot stay in that pasture like a lady cow. So, she gets up and heads back to Bair Reservoir and to whatever might happen next. Her back is arched with fatigue and sorrow, and she clutches Luke Messenger's shorts around her middle. Now, she definitely looks like Mr. Giancarlo of Sunnyside Eldercare during that unfortunate attack of colitis.

There is a little dot on the horizon. A moving dot. She squinches her eyes. She probably needs glasses. The dot is growing a bit larger. *Now what?* she thinks. It's probably a raging bull coming to gore her, or a Harley Davidson racing to slice her in two.

No. It's slow, whatever it is.

From that distance, the figure is serpent-y, with wavy anemones on its top half. It's a creature, walking out of the sea. It's a man. A solitary man. Now, she sees that the anemones are messy curls and the creature is Luke Messenger.

"Hey!" he calls.

Shit! A warm wind whips through the valley. The yellow grass sways. He's huffing and puffing right in front of her. A drop of sweat hightails it down Luke's forehead and drops right off his nose, like those goats that fling themselves from cliffs.

"Hey."

"How do you do this? I tried to jog a mile out here and I'm dying. My chest is burning. Jesus, I'm out of shape."

He doesn't look it. Forget she thought that.

"Well, your sweatshirt must weigh two pounds. And . . . cargo shorts? All those pockets. Pound and a half. Boots! *Hiking* boots. Might as well wear two toddlers on your feet."

"So, sleek as a seal, like . . ." He nods toward her own clothes.

"These are not my fault."

"Mine either. I'm not exactly the silky-basketball-shorts type. They were a Christmas present from my father, who played forward for his college team."

"If he also gave you a jersey with his old number on it, I can see why you're out here with your grandma."

"That was for my birthday," he laughs. He doesn't say more, and she respects that. She's glad of it, too. She doesn't want to hear the whole history of him. Wanting to hear the whole history of a person, wanting to know their story, lured by the mystery of what you don't yet know—it's gotten her into plenty of trouble.

Stop!

Why'd you guys move from Burlington? It sounds so nice, she asked The Taker.

My dad got a research job here, at the university. I was glad we moved. I hated my old school.

Why?

Private school. Lots of rich kids who lived on the lake. Acted like they were hot shit. My mom wanted us to get out of there. She thought I was friends with a bad crowd 'cause this kid I know robbed an old guy.

"Are you okay?" Luke Messenger asks.

"Sure."

"Mim suggested I come and check on you. I don't know. She was worried you'd run off or something. Hey, I wouldn't have wanted to be out in that storm today."

"It was crazy. Um, I don't want to be rude, but I've got to run back. You know, the whole way."

"No problem."

"You can walk, maybe?"

"Hell no. I got my second wind."

He jogs backward.

She can't help herself. She laughs. He looks so funny, with his wild hair bouncing. "What are you *doing*?"

"I'm going the whole way like this."

"You're going backward the whole way. Why?"

"I'm standing by."

• • •

Annabelle paces outside, along the edge of the reservoir. At least, she thinks the reservoir is out there. In the dark, the lake is black plus black. She hears the ripple of water, a gentle shush against the shore.

"Relax," Grandpa Ed says. "It's not like I stuck you with the Manson family."

"They're in there." She eyes the camper.

"Of course they're in there. Relax. You're cutting out." Annabelle swears he makes the fake crackling of bad phone service. Then he's gone.

"Cutting out, my *cu*. Agnelli Curse," she says to the dead air of the phone.

When her phone buzzes right in her hand, she thinks she misjudged him and he's calling her back. But, no, it's Malcolm. She's so happy. The connection has been so bad since Idaho that she's only been able to have two-second conversations, if that, with Malc, Mom, and her "team." But, hey, she'll take two seconds. Malc on the phone now—it's like seeing her fellow astronaut when she was sure she was lost in space.

"Butthead!"

"We heard about the tire. Bummer," he says. At least, that's what she pieces together. It sounds like: *eard tire ummer.*

"Malc, it *sucks*. Get me outta here."

"He'll be back tomorrow. You'll be running down Highway Twelve, and Grandpa will be parked at Martinsdale Colony."

"Martinsdale Colony? I'm picturing sci-fi pods of extraterrestrials."

"It's a sect of Hutterites. Super awesome. Similar to the Amish, but they embrace technology," Malcolm says. Or something like that. His voice cuts out at every third word. "They were happy for you to park there. No problem. And they run the state's biggest wind farm, which is über-cool."

Gina is shouting something in the background.

"What'd she just say, Malc? I swore I heard '*YouTube sensation*.'"

"Um, she said *you two are sensational*! You and Grandpa Ed."

"Tell her I love her, too. I really miss—"

"Gotta go. You're cutting out."

Maybe she's losing her mind, but she swears he makes a fake crackle, same as Grandpa Ed. All of these long, lonely runs are making her paranoid.

It'd be bad enough to be stuck with strangers in a large house, let alone in this ten-by-thirty-foot box. They will ask her questions. The tragedy will sit all around. It will lie heavy in the air. They will wonder how it felt, and what's it's like to have Seth Greggory in her future.

"Could you get ahold of him?" Dawn Celeste asks.

Inside, the windows are hazy with steam, and there is the warm, tomatoey smell of chili. Luke Messenger pulls a pan of corn bread from the oven.

"Yep. He's still in Helena."

"Smell," Luke says. He waves the pan under her nose.

"Yum. Did you make that?"

"Me and Jiffy and a half cup of water."

After dinner, they play cards. Dawn Celeste claims to be the gin rummy champ of the century. There's the quiet snap of cards as Luke deals. There are loud groans of losing, the cheer of a win. Luke pounds the table after two victories in a row. No one asks her anything. She doesn't ask much, either. They're just . . . having fun.

"The only one who ever beat me three for three was Sammy Jackson," Dawn Celeste says. "There was gloating."

"He sounds like a sore winner," Annabelle says.

"She. Luke's friend," Dawn Celeste clarifies. Annabelle is sure she hears the emphasis that means *girlfriend*. She relaxes even more, even though Luke's eyes are really blue, and he wears one of those woven leather bracelets she always likes.

"Two out of two, that means you serve dessert," Dawn Celeste tells Luke.

"She makes up the rules as she goes," Luke tells Annabelle.

"We'll have to see where Annabelle stands." Dawn Celeste sits back and folds her arms over her chest. She's changed into a caftan but wears a pair of fuzzy socks on her feet.

"It will be the true test of character." Luke fishes in the cupboard. He plops the packages down on the Formica table. "Red Vines or Twizzlers?"

Annabelle grimaces. "Oh no. I sense this is a dangerous question."

"Yeah, just whose side you're on, is all."

"Red Vines are insubstantial." Dawn Celeste bites the head off of a Twizzler.

"Twizzlers are the Taco Bell of candy." Luke smells a Red Vine like it's a fine cigar.

"I'm Switzerland," Annabelle says.

She is aware of their sleep sounds: a rustle of sheets, the sleeping bag Luke prefers, unzipping to let the cool air in. Annabelle is wide-awake. She needs her sleep for the run to Martinsdale Colony tomorrow, and this day has felt like a month of days. But she just lies there with her eyes open, listening to the almost-silence. Strangely, though, her body is still, and her mind is quiet. She can hear the calm lap of the reservoir waves against the shore.

Anxiety is like being in freeway traffic all the time. There's the constant sense of dodging and darting, seeking your chance to cut in, the irritation of others pulling ahead of you. You hit the accelerator; slam the brakes. You scout and scan for danger. Here, though, there is no traffic and no freeway. There is gentle company and books on shelves. There is quiet. There's fun. Dawn Celeste has a laugh that sounds like a pot bubbling over. Everyone gets to do as they wish.

How weird, she thinks, that there are people who maybe don't feel this thing, this endless buzz of nerves and fear and responsibility and control. It is so relaxing without it. It is restful. Maybe she could make any choice and it would be okay. Maybe she could quit her big job of being responsible for everyone else's feelings. Dr. Mann has suggested this before, but it sounded like a crazy, unreachable goal.

She closes her eyes now. Just for a second, she imagines it—letting go. Handing the heavy stuff back to the people it belongs to. When she does, she gets the most peaceful feeling, as if there's a cool and reassuring hand on her forehead. She is safe and okay and the storm is out there somewhere, but not here.

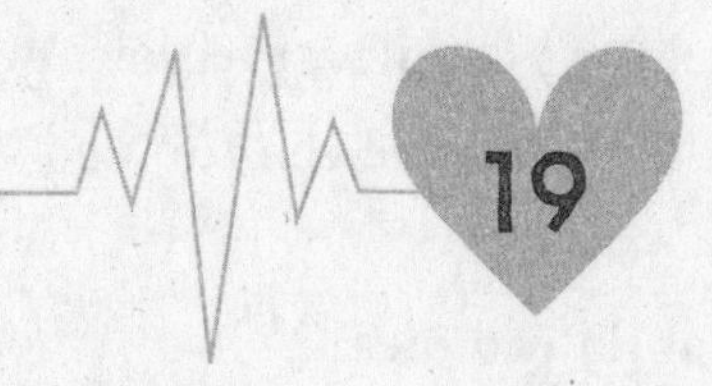

19

1. The human heart shuttles blood through sixty thousand miles of blood vessels.
2. In one day, the blood travels a total of twelve thousand miles.
3. Every day, the heart creates enough energy to drive twenty miles. In a lifetime, that is enough energy to fly to the moon and back.
4. Running 2,700 miles cannot repair hearts that have been destroyed.

"What are you trying to remember?" Luke Messenger asks.

He's up early with her. Dawn Celeste's method for washing and quick-drying clothes—pressing them between two towels, and stomping on them like wine grapes—worked amazingly, and so now Annabelle's back in her crops and her mesh tank, and Luke is giving the silky basketball shorts a try. He's trying to run alongside her on the dry, desolate Highway 12. He'll definitely slow down her progress, and there is no way he'll make the entire sixteen miles. But in Dawn Celeste's country, everyone gets do what they want to do, and that means he can run and Annabelle can ditch him when she needs to.

"What do you mean?"

"You're holding your hand like this." He demonstrates. He forms his fingers into the number four. "Sometimes I do that if I have to remember what to get at the store."

Caught. "You do that, too?" She laughs. "I was trying to remember some things I read that I didn't have time to save or write down."

"What things?"

"It's going to sound stupid."

"No it won't."

"Just some facts about the heart."

"Like the heart-and-soul heart, or the organ in your body?"

"Kind of both? It's just . . . in there, and we never think about it. But when you do, you realize how important it is. It's terrifying, you know, how much we count on this fist-size muscle."

She doesn't know why she's blurting out this stuff. Probably, it's because her runs are usually so lonely. On regular days, the only voices are hers and Loretta's.

"Yeah," he says. "That's cool." He means it, she can tell. He looks like he might want to say more but can't. The road is flat, but he's laboring as if he's going uphill. He looks funny in those basketball shorts, honestly—the most unlikely point guard ever.

"I don't know. I'm thinking it might be something I should study, if I get the chance."

"Urph," he says.

"Are you okay?"

His face is kind of purple. He clutches his own heart now. He stops. He's breathing hard. "I'm dying," he squeaks. "I don't know how you do this. My chest is burning. I've got cramps in every cramp-able place in my body."

"Your voice sounds like a mini horse if a mini horse could talk."

"Oh, *burn*."

"Come on, race you!"

"Cruel. You're cruel." He's getting farther and farther behind.

"Hey, you went a half mile," she says over her shoulder.

He's bent over. He waves his hand, indicating that she should go on without him. His John Muir National Parks T-shirt looks well-meaning but defeated.

Annabelle feels bad, leaving him back there. But she's still in Dawn Celeste's country, where everyone gets to do his or her own thing.

What would happen if she set it *all* down, not just the little guilts and responsibilities, but the biggest one? She thinks of Dr. Mann asking that question. Dr. Mann's hands are folded in her lap, and she quietly waits for a response, the tranquil painting of the mountains behind her seemingly waiting, too. *If you set down the guilt, what else might you feel?*

As Annabelle runs Highway 12, alongside miles of ranch fencing, and the occasional cattle barn and farmhouse, she tries to envision it.

She sets down the fact that this has all been her fault. She tells herself this instead: It is The Taker's fault and only The Taker's.

It's like trying to imagine any falsehood: that the sun revolves around the earth; that humans can fly; that the world is nonviolent. Still—go with it. Let it go, and what is there instead?

Sorrow. Enormous, crushing sorrow.

And something else. What is it? *Go closer, and look at it*, she tells herself.

Oh my God: fury. Uncontrollable, explosive *rage.*

Jesus.

She doesn't know if she's strong enough for all of that. Her guilt and shame are almost a familiar comfort, compared to the depth of that sorrow and the breadth of that anger. The shame is a horrible acid ball in her heart. But that sorrow and that rage might incinerate her, same as that storm yesterday, with its lightning bolts speeding through this flat land, looking for the one thing still standing.

She can tell she's getting close, because she sees a row of windmills in the distance, their white arms spinning with quiet industry. Wow, there are a lot of them. She tries to count. Eighteen, twenty? Now, she spots the sign: WHEATLAND COUNTY.

She doesn't know if she'll even meet the Hutterites while parked in the far corner of their land. She'd be curious and a little nervous to do so. As she turns down the road to the colony, though, they aren't who she sees first, and neither is Grandpa Ed. Today, it's Dawn Celeste with the bottle of water. Her sundress is a fireworks show of color.

"Ed will be here in a couple hours. He decided to get some filters changed while he was there. Luke's inside, and so is lunch. We've already had a tour of the place. I'm sure Luke would love to show you around. It's amazing, the communal sharing. But the sexist religious stuff . . . Not a fan, Annabelle, not a fan. Male managed. The women walk behind the men. 'Working for each other is the highest command of love.' Working for *each other*, or for *him*, Mr. King Big Man walking ahead? *Equality and respect* are the highest command of love. But it *is* a work of art out there."

Dawn Celeste is right, Annabelle realizes. Now that she really looks, now that the land is not simply her day's chore to cross, the fields roll and stretch below the large sky. It's the most unimaginably beautiful painting. Far off, she can see the Hutterites' long barns, and rows of apartments that look like portables.

"I get a little heated," Dawn Celeste says. "I was a proud bra burner and equal rights marcher back in the day, and I still am. I can't believe we're even talking about stuff like this in this day and age. But, you! You must be exhausted! You don't even look it. You look like you jogged down a driveway."

Annabelle chugs from the water bottle gratefully. "I feel good. Some days are better than others. I think my bladder may be leaking, though. The one for my water supply? Everything's damp in my pack, and I ran out before I was halfway."

"Hey, I know all about a leaking bladder," Dawn Celeste says. "Especially when I laugh hard."

Annabelle laughs now, too.

"No worries. We've got some duct tape that'll fix it right up."

Inside the camper, Luke is stretched out on his bunk, reading. He holds up his book. "You killed me. I can't move. Mim made you some lunch. It's in the fridge."

"What're you reading?"

"*Endurance*, by Alfred Lansing. It's about Ernest Shackleton, the explorer. He's kind of doing what you're doing, but in Antarctica. And with a team of lost crew members and sled dogs. Don't ask about the sled dogs." He pretend-shudders.

"Oh no. Sled dog burgers?"

"Exactly. I'm almost done. Last pages."

"I shouldn't interrupt, then."

"Hey! You know rule number one. You must be a reader."

"I thought rule number one is 'Don't tell the ending.'"

"Wait. Rule number one: Hate the movie version."

"Probably, all our rules are rule number one. We can get a little hard-core."

"Always judge a person by their shelves. To fold or not to fold the pages."

She laughs. "Definitely."

"I have this friend, Skylar, and he's always all, 'Who *reads,* dude?' And I'm like, 'I feel sad for you, man.'"

"Oh, I know."

"Hey, you've got to see this place. Martinsdale Colony is its own universe. I met Ken, one of the preachers. He said to come over when you were ready and he'd give another tour."

"Great."

He waves his book. "I've got to see if they survive."

"I have never seen so many turkeys in my life," Annabelle says.

"Well, there are three thousand of them. We sell them to the whole valley. Ray's our turkey man, and his son, Charles, is our turkey boy. Chicken eggs, they go to three Walmarts in Billings and Laurel."

The colonists speak German with each other, and Preacher Ken has a German accent—*well* and *we* sound like *vell* and *ve*; *the* and *they* are *ze* and *zey*. The turkeys—well, *they* sound like three thousand Grandpa Eds gargling Listerine. God, they're ugly, with their plump white bodies and red heads and drooping wattles, which resemble inflamed scrotums, if she's being honest. Not that she's ever seen an inflamed scrotum, but still.

Preacher Ken shows them the chicken house, egg sorters,

milking machines, grain silos, and communal kitchen. It's basically a huge working farm. The women wear boxy blue dresses and polka-dot kerchiefs covering their hair, and the men wear jeans and plaid shirts and cowboy hats. She spots the blue of the women's dresses and kerchiefs in the crop rows of the eleven-acre vegetable garden.

What appeals to Annabelle most is the calm order of the place, the sense that the crazy world is out there, but it isn't coming in. The colony is hidden. It's *away*. "If it wasn't for the 'church every day and twice on Sundays' thing . . . ," Annabelle says to Luke as they walk back down the gravel road where Dawn Celeste's camper is.

"Yeah. It's cool out here, but that'd be a bummer."

"Also, that the guys get to wear regular clothes and the women have to cover their heads and wear the heavy dresses."

"Hide those dangerous bodies," Luke says.

"Yeah, no kidding. But being away from the world like this . . ."

"Permanently, though? I mean, I'm on hiatus on this trip with Mim, but I wouldn't want to do it forever."

"I wouldn't mind."

"Well, the world kicked your ass."

It's one of the most truthful things that anyone has ever said to her about what's happened. And it means something to her. It means something because they haven't had to have some big talk about it. It's a simple statement of fact.

He has said something truthful, so she does, too. "I don't know what to do about it."

"Kick the world's ass right back."

"How?"

He laughs. "How? That is so funny."

She makes a face. "Why funny?"

"You're kicking the world's ass right now."

20

"I told you I'd bring you a surprise, didn't I, Bella Luna?" Grandpa Ed waves the uncut half of the dry salami.

"Salami, Ritz crackers, and Swiss cheese, family tradition," Annabelle explains to Dawn Celeste and Luke as Grandpa Ed passes the plate. Dinner is at Grandpa Ed's, a thank-you for the lightning storm rescue. From their parking spot at the end of the dirt road, just inside the gates, she can see Martinsdale Colony. Now, Annabelle knows what's over there. She imagines the thousands of turkeys and chickens, the cows, and the hundred and fifty rosy-cheeked adults and children, settling in for the night. The sun drops, and the earth glows with a warm, orange light. It's strange the way thirty square miles can look like heaven or hell, depending on what the weather blows in.

"Can I help?" Dawn Celeste says. Annabelle notices that she's wearing lipstick. Also, a skirt, and a colorful scarf tied over her shirt. No fuzzy socks tonight.

"You sit down. I got it handled."

Dawn Celeste munches a Ritz hors d'oeuvre. "Delicious, Ed. Where do you get good salami, huh? This is the real deal."

Grandpa's cheeks flush with pride, or maybe it's just the wine. She's speaking his language. He lifts the lid of the pan on the stove, and steam escapes, along with the rich, juicy smell of chicken saltimbocca—little jelly rolls of chicken breast stuffed with spinach and prosciutto.

"Light the special candle, will you, Bella?"

She meets Luke's eyes and rolls hers. The candle is just a straw-wrapped Chianti bottle with years of wax drippings down its neck. She hunts for the matches, *schwick*-strikes one, and lights it.

"I can't believe you've got dimmers," Dawn Celeste says as Grandpa turns the lights low.

"Hey, I'm a romantic guy."

Luke and Annabelle meet eyes again. This time she makes hers large and horrified and he grins.

This is their last night together, and everyone is relaxed and laughing. Dawn Celeste and Luke are doing impressions of Luke's parents, and their rigid disapproval of anything that doesn't follow their plan. Luke's mom and dad are both attorneys, same as Will's parents, Robert and Tracie. It's weird, but then again, Will and Luke aren't the same person. She can't imagine Luke ever playing lacrosse, and Will didn't really read books for fun.

"They were running this boy into the ground! He was taking SAT vocabulary classes since he was five."

"Well, true. I did have the SAT Math Concepts shower curtain in my bathroom."

"Oh my God!" Annabelle laughed.

"It paid off! I graduated high school at sixteen. But, then, one year shy of an MBA . . ."

"He decides he doesn't want an MBA, which I could have told everyone since he was three years old."

"My Bad Attitude is my MBA," Luke says.

"Nonsense," Dawn Celeste says. "You just finally said what you needed."

"When I told them I was taking a year off, they lost their minds."

"When we told them he was taking a year off to travel the country with *me*, they *really* lost their minds," Dawn Celeste says. "My daughter, she was always more like her dad. Jim was a businessman, died too young. Driven as the day was long. But now her son has my blood, it seems."

"Kids. What're you gonna do," Grandpa says.

"Are you going back to school?" Annabelle asks Luke.

"Oh, yeah. I'm seeing about transferring my credits from University of Oregon to Oregon State College of Forestry."

"Land management. The other side of the courtroom from his parents." Dawn Celeste chuckles.

"I'm not into it for the rebellion," Luke says. "That doesn't do much for me. Just . . . Have you ever heard that Willa Cather quote? 'I like trees because they seem more resigned to the way they have to live than other things do.'"

Annabelle hasn't heard that, but she loves it. "Nice."

"You ever go to Sequoia National Park?" Grandpa Ed says. "Now there's—"

It's almost hard to hear the rap at the door. But Dawn Celeste sets her hand on Grandpa Ed's arm to quiet him, and they all listen, and sure enough, someone's knocking. The dinner dishes are stacked in the sink, and the candle wax is dripping onto the Formica table, and the wineglasses only have the last puddles of red. It's late.

When Grandpa Ed opens the door, Annabelle can see the truck with the round headlights lighting the road. Two young women stand outside. They're in their heavy blue dresses, with their heads covered in blue kerchiefs.

"I'm Ruth, and this is Elisha," the heavyset young woman says. "We were hoping to meet Annabelle Agnelli?"

"Here," Annabelle says. She sounds like a student at roll call.

"We were hoping to talk with you."

"Oh, sure."

She shuts the door behind her. She's a little nervous about why they want to speak with her. Outside, there's the smell of night and dry grass. She almost thinks she can smell the moon, golden and otherworldly in the sky.

"We have this. For you," Elisha says. Their blond hair almost glows in the darkness. Elisha hands Annabelle a loaf of bread, wrapped in a cloth. It's still warm.

"We were excited that you're here," Ruth says.

"*She* was excited," Elisha says.

"You were excited, too!"

They are giggly and nervous. It reminds Annabelle of when she and Kat met Alice Wu at University Bookstore that time.

"Ruth has watched your video a hundred times."

"My video?"

"On YouTube."

"My video on YouTube? I didn't know I had a video on YouTube."

"You didn't *know*?" Ruth says. "I can't believe it. It's pretty new, but it's really popular. *Really* popular."

"I've been out of touch with—" It sounds so ridiculous. "My team."

"I'll show you." Ruth has a cell phone in her pocket.

"You have cell phones here?"

"Well, at first we only had six for the whole community, but then people started sneaking them in and now everyone has one except my mother and Elisha's mother."

"Ruth sent six hundred texts last month," Elisha tattles.

"Six hundred!"

"We get really good Wi-Fi, too."

Annabelle can barely concentrate on the conversation. She can only think: *video. YouTube. Really popular.* She can only think: *That waitress. The one at the truck stop. That's why I looked familiar. She saw it, too.*

"My brother lives on the outside and pays my bill," Ruth says. "But, look. Here you are."

Uploaded by Malcolm. Ruth pushes play, and there is Annabelle. She's on the phone of a young woman from a Montana religious sect, on a moonlit night, on the spinning and ever-changing earth. She is on the bed of the Sleepy Inn, wearing her monkey-in-space pajamas.

She's going to kill Malcolm.

What do you hope to accomplish with your mission?

I hope to discover a new planet with evidence of life. Go to bed.

Annabelle. Come on.

What? I'm exhausted. Go brush your teeth.

After everything that's, um, happened, *why are you running from Seattle to Washington, DC, Annabelle Agnelli?*

I have to do something.

She sees it the way other people might: her thin, serious face, her big eyes. Her chopped hair. She looks destroyed. She sees the lonely motel room that speaks to a mission. And the way she goes from teasing and joking to sudden seriousness. She sees the way those words have solemn weight . . . *I have to do* something. It sounds like a vow. It sounds like a vow every single human should make.

"It just . . ." Ruth clutches her heart. "It got me."

And then she sees something else. The number of views. An astonishing number. *Sixty-eight thousand.* She can't breathe. There's a long scroll of comments, too. She catches the words *brave* and *end this madness* and *everyone must do something.*

"We wanted to say, God bless you."

"Your strength inspires me," Ruth says. She takes Annabelle's hands and squeezes.

A shiver runs up the back of Annabelle's neck. It's the kind of shiver that tells her things are changing once again. She is stunned. She wants to cry, because her heart aches. She can't tell if it's a good ache or a bad one, and so she just holds Ruth's hands and squeezes back.

Annabelle is in some weird shock.

"How is it possible that two girls way out here saw a video that my stupid brother made in a motel room weeks ago?"

"So much for being cut off from the world, huh?" Luke says. "They saw that before you knew it even existed. So did seventy thousand other people."

Annabelle and Luke stand outside the parked RVs as Dawn Celeste and Grandpa Ed say good-bye.

"It's so bizarre."

She and Luke and Grandpa and Dawn Celeste watched the video again and again in disbelief. In this most distant, *away* place, she'd been found. *She.* Annabelle doesn't even know who *she* is. Which Annabelle is the real her? The pre-tragedy girl? The girl who stands under this Montana sky? The girl in that video?

Maybe she's being told something. Maybe she's not meant to hide. God, what a terrifying thought.

"Look at that moon," Luke says.

"It's seen some things."

"Still there, through the eons."

They're quiet. They stare up. Luke feels familiar. In just a few days, she's gotten used to seeing his face beside hers. She feels close to him. But it's okay. It's possible she'll never see him again.

"Do you think our grandparents are doing it?"

She socks him.

"Ouch! Hey, I'm going to get up early tomorrow and see you off, so this isn't good-bye."

"Great," she says.

"It's funny. I'm going to miss Martinsdale Colony."

"Me too."

Probably, it's not Martinsdale Colony she'll miss, but she shoves that thought away. It's been great, amazing, to have someone her own age around, someone who doesn't just see the burnt wick of tragedy when he looks at her.

"I'm impressed, you know? My friend Owen thought he was a YouTube sensation when forty-six people watched him play the ukulele."

"I hate my brother," she says.

"Good night, Annabelle. Thanks for a memorable day."

The next morning, Annabelle gets up an hour earlier than usual, and then heads out. She does not want to see Luke Messenger to say good-bye. The idea spins up a cyclone of sadness that she can't bear. After That Bastard Father Anthony, after The Taker and all that's happened, she's not up for good-byes.

When her run is finished and she returns to the RV, now parked at—oh, God—*Deadman's Basin Reservoir,* Montana, there is something on her bunk.

A book.

Alfred Lansing's *Endurance.*

21

By the time she's here—running beside the green-brown waters of Albert Lea Lake in Minnesota, watching the eerie mist rise from it, listening to the chirp of indigo buntings and eastern bluebirds—she has read *Endurance* four times.

She does not read it the way she and Kat used to read books—devouring them with the speed of two people famished for words, ideas, and beautiful sentences that make you feel *everything*. No, she reads *Endurance* the way a person might read the Bible—in small passages, repeated again and again, to help her stay grounded. To help her persevere, and understand her place in the world.

She has missed books, but she's been afraid of them, same as music. Books make you feel things hard. They hit the tender spots. Books remind her of her and Kat, but also of her old self, too, the mostly carefree self. The girl who was just so happy to come home from the library with a big stack of new stuff to read. Books were dangerous.

But this is the story of explorer Ernest Shackleton, and his twenty-seven men who survive years in Antarctica after their ship is crushed by ice, and she can't help but get swept up into it. It is 1914, in the most inhospitable place on earth, and there is starvation and exhaustion and desperation, danger and isolation, a horrible sea and unforgiving ice, and a slide down a fog-shrouded mountainside for a last chance at survival. And she is a contemporary young woman wearing a moisture-wicking sports bra, trekking in the balmy months of May and now mid-June, across North Dakota, then South Dakota, then through the southwest corner of friendly Minnesota. She is well-fed on mostaccioli and scaloppine and bananas and oatmeal. She has a full cabinet of energy bars (thanks to Zach and all the GoFundMe contributors), which are heavy with carbs for the run itself, full of antioxidants for post-run immunity boosts, jammed with protein for recovery. She does not have to fight for the smallest chunks of seal meat and penguins and worse. But the words that the *Endurance* crew wrote in their diaries speak to her.

The struggle against the sea is an act of physical combat, and there is no escape. It is a battle against a tireless enemy in which man never actually wins; the most that he can hope for is not to be defeated, she reads, before closing her eyes.

In some ways they had come to know themselves better. In this lonely world of ice and emptiness, they had achieved at least a limited kind of contentment. They had been tested and found not wanting, she reads, with ice packs on a strained muscle in her groin.

The numbers tell the story: She has been gone 107 days. It has been sixty-two days since she left Martinsdale Colony without saying good-bye to Luke Messenger. She has run 952 miles since then. She has worn through three additional pairs of running shoes. She has had four days off. Two days were due to a bout of food poisoning from a taco truck next to Dave's Marine in Webster, South Dakota. She and Grandpa Ed were both hit; oh, gross—the two of them heaving and trembling in the suddenly smaller RV. And two of those days were for a depressive episode after a fall in Bowdle, South Dakota, essentially the halfway point.

There, among more grain silos and a just-passed threat of a tornado, she twisted her ankle and tumbled onto the road, bloodying her palms and knees. She cried, like a little girl who fell off her bike, and then she collapsed with despair. It was the despair that any *halfway* brings, with the knowledge that everything you've gone through awaits again. She had such a longing for home. The person who lived there seemed long gone. Now, she was an astronaut clipped from her vessel, floating endlessly in endlessness, with no possibility of ever returning. She didn't want to be an astronaut anymore. She wanted to be a girl, but The Taker had ruined that for her.

She has listened to the tape Luke gave her sixty-nine times, once a day, and twice a day during one rough week. Near misses by semis: two. Bouts of severe cramping due to dehydration: three. More numbers: two visits from Gina and Malcolm, who flew into Miles City, Montana, and Bismarck,

North Dakota, necessitating extra driving for Grandpa Ed but gaining them five nights total in actual motel beds. Number of fights between Gina and Grandpa Ed: five. Number of eye rolls and under-table-kicks between Malcolm and Annabelle: fifty-five, at least.

Number of additional ankle twists on the rocky grounds of North Dakota's hills and buttes: four, maybe more. One infected toe. Toenails lost: bunches. Sunburns: multiple. Miles running against the wind: countless. Layers of dust, dirt, sweat on her skin: endless. Truckers, troopers, snakes, and dogs: infinite. Number of bicyclists heading toward the Badlands of North Dakota: thirty to fifty. New friends: Mary and her wife, Sharon, from Seattle—*Seattle!*—who they ate dinner with at the Prairie Knights Casino; a herd of antelope; two bison; a flock of pheasants; and two students, Josh and Rashelle, from the gifted-and-talented program at Standing Rock Community School who interviewed her and took her picture by their flagpole. Also, Dan Williams, nature photographer, writing a book about the Standing Rock reservation, who ran three miles of it with her while also taking her photo. They met when he spotted her stretching just outside of the Dakota Countryside Inn, where she and Grandpa Ed decided to stay for a real bed and Wi-Fi and a free breakfast.

And more: twelve girls and six of their parents from Aberdeen High School, South Dakota, who cheered her with signs as she crossed the border from North to South Dakota. Shia and Jo from girl's varsity cross-country at Montevideo

High, who invited her to come meet their team. The six thousand new people on the Run for a Cause Facebook page, who leave messages of encouragement that Annabelle can't bear to look at; the 1,203 people who have now given money to her GoFundMe; the three-hundred-thousand-plus people who have now watched her YouTube video, although she can't be sure they are friendly. She could have three hundred thousand enemies, aside from Ruth and Elisha back at Martinsdale—who knows. There are lots and lots of comments, but she is not brave enough to read them.

Something has happened to her and about her, and yet it is hard to grasp this fact. Her run is larger than her, and yet her daily life is mostly just her solitary steps, the rhythm of them, her daily aches, her loneliness, and the flashes of the nightmares that she experiences daily. It seems that she's become a person with a message, but she's unclear what the message is. Maybe because the message is still fighting its way through the grief and guilt to get to her.

Annabelle focuses on the daily steps, and she keeps the uproar away, as if it's happening to someone else. It *is* happening to someone else. At least, she's not yet the girl they've made her out to be.

Not this week, especially.

He's there with her every night, just as he intended. She sees him when she closes her eyes in her bunk of the RV, the Saint Christopher medal hanging over her in the darkness. She tries to concentrate on Ernest Shackleton and the men clawing their way to civilization, and she tries to give in to the fatigue that pulls her toward sleep. But he's there. The Taker. He peeks at her behind every thought. He stares. He reminds. He taunts.

He is standing by her car the week after the winter dance. She's seen him at lunch every day, and now that it's second semester, they have AP English Comp together. There's a seating chart, though, so they don't sit near each other, and there's not as much walking and moving around as there was in Mixed Media, so they don't really talk.

And, the truth is, she hurries out of class. She's *A* in the seating chart, front row, and he's *W*, so she jets. After the hard-on, after the physical evidence of some—she doesn't even know—*need*, maybe, she feels a weird urgency, some uneasy sense that she should distance herself from him. So she flies out of class, and sits at the other end of the lunch table. She rushes or lingers at the salad bar, so that she can sit by Kat or even Sierra, who she doesn't even like all that much.

But on that day, he's standing right by her car, and she can't avoid him. He's holding his clasped hands in pretend prayer, begging, and it's raining, and the bus is pulling away.

"Throwing myself at your mercy?" he says.

"Sure, no problem."

"*Merci* for the mercy," he says.

He's wearing a flannel jacket, now soaked, and a pair of combat boots that drip water on her floor mats. Combat boots are not some cliché. She wears them. Zander wears them. Kat does, and so does Geoff Graham. The Taker isn't even really wearing the odd clothes anymore. He dresses like they do. There is not some marker or sign like you think. Not until later, when you try hard to find them. His green backpack sits at his feet, and it's sopping wet, too.

"How long have you been out here?" she asks.

"Sixth period got out early." He hasn't been in her car since that day when they played the Clash.

"Wait. So you didn't exactly miss your bus?"

He tilts his head and looks up at her with mock shame. "I missed talking to you. It's like you're always hurrying somewhere."

Kat stays after on Wednesdays and Fridays for Yearbook, and it's a Friday, so Annabelle will be driving home alone. She wonders if he knows that, if he's keeping track. If he'd be standing here if it were Monday or Tuesday or Thursday.

She pulls out of the parking spot, waits in the line of cars leaving the lot. It's raining so hard that her wipers are going a million miles an hour. It's difficult to see. He's so tall, too, that she has to crane her neck to make a safe turn because her visibility is impaired.

"Can I put some music on?" He's holding her phone. What is it about someone touching your phone? It's like they're touching *you*, or reading your mind, or hunting through your most private places.

"Sure, go ahead."

"Hey, remember this?"

"Police and Thieves." She understands immediately, the way he's trying to replay the moment they had, where they were having fun, where he felt powerful, because she wanted him and he was all casual about it. And there's nothing wrong with him desiring that again, is there? There's nothing wrong with him pursuing her like this. Not really. Except that she's trying to send a message about needing space from him, and he isn't hearing it, and now it's bugging her. It's making her uncomfortable. She wanted him around and now she wants him to go away, and even though she's annoyed that he's in her car, she also worries that this wanting-not-wanting makes her kind of horrible.

"Oh, yeah," she says. She hates herself when she's not nice. And anyway, it's what she's been taught since she was a baby. Gina and That Bastard Father Anthony both drove home the message: Treat others the way you'd want to be treated. Be kind to those who are less fortunate. If you don't, BAD STUFF WILL HAPPEN.

The Taker smiles. He turns up the music. It's hard to concentrate like she needs to when driving in this weather.

"Shit," he says. "I don't know how you stand it."

"What's that?"

"This weather. It's been raining nonstop for three weeks. I'm growing moss."

"I forget you just moved from Vermont," she says. "It seems like you've always been here." She knows this is a gift, a message of fitting in. She gives it because of all the mean thoughts she just had about him. She gives it because she'd really like him out of her car.

"God, it's *depressing*, though."

"I don't know. I like it. Well, maybe not right this second when it's doing this, but otherwise . . . I mean, we're used to it. It's cozy."

"Maybe when you don't feel like slitting your wrists."

"Hey, am I going to have to report you to Mr. Curley?" Mr. Curley is the counselor they all dislike. He's known for eating rice pudding and picking at his cuticles while he talks to you about attending Whitworth, his alma mater. She's joking, but when she looks over at him, The Taker's face is rigid, and he's staring out the window.

"Nah, my mother already wants me to talk to some guy."

"Oh, I'm sorry. I thought you were kidding."

"It's stupid. Why would they pay money for some dude to sit there and listen to me? I'm fine, you know, playing the guitar and writing dark poetry, haha." The song stops. The next one begins. "Hey, Bob Marley."

"Waiting in Vain." Heartbroken man is fed up with a woman who doesn't care anymore. "Compliments of Kat and the 'Good-bye, Sucker' playlist she made me after Will and I broke it off."

"Nice."

"I saw him the other day."

"Oh, yeah? On purpose or by accident?"

"Accident. It was weird, because he lives on the Eastside.

He was at our Whole Foods getting a sandwich when I was at our Whole Foods getting a sandwich."

"Douche. Does he have a new girlfriend?"

"He misses me."

She has not told this to Kat or anyone else, even Gina, who had been waiting in the car. Annabelle wasn't really getting a sandwich. She was buying milk and coffee. They were on the way home from picking up Malcolm from a sleepover at Terrence's house, and Gina didn't want to go in because she didn't have her bra on. It was good to see Will. Really good. They hugged, and he smelled amazing—like himself. He told her about a cancer scare his dad had, and about a robotics project he was working on. His eyes got all excited and filled with light like they do. It wrecked all the good progress she'd made, making him a villain. He was just Will again, the boy she loved, which sucked. They hugged once more when they said good-bye, and he whispered that he missed her. It messed her up for a few days, and she had to give herself the hard-line lectures all over again.

Why she's mentioning this to The Taker now, though—some part of her is being evil even when she's trying to be nice, she thinks. What Dr. Mann will suggest much later—that maybe she was trying to say what she needed to say without saying what she needed to say—doesn't occur to her. The mention of Will, the joint-sandwich-buying—she's pushing The Taker away without pushing him away.

"Misses you? Too late, asshole."

In spite of The Taker's efforts, the car ride lacks the energy and fun and good feeling that it had the first time. And when she pulls up to his house, his mom is outside, fetching bags from the Volvo. Annabelle recognizes her from the photo she saw online. The Taker's mom, Nadine, comes over to the car to meet her. Nadine is nice, but The Taker is irritated, and Annabelle feels like Nadine is checking her out. It's awkward. Still, none of this seems to matter to The Taker. This doesn't stop him at all. On Friday, he is there again, with his begging hands. His begging, depressed hands.

He is there every Wednesday and Friday, never on the days Kat is there, so he clearly wants to be alone with Annabelle. It's making her furious. He won't read her signs. She is cold, aloof, talks about other boys besides Will, exits the parking lot while pushing the accelerator a little too hard. He's refusing to hear what she's not saying. She's trying to discourage him nicely, but what sucks is that he's practically forcing her to hurt him. In the evenings before dinner, she goes on extra-hard runs to try to shake off the bad feeling.

"Just say no, Annabelle," Kat says. "Tell him you can't drive him anymore. Tell him it makes you uncomfortable. Tell him it makes you late for work. Tell him you *don't want to*. God, it makes me crazy when you do this."

It's a Thursday, one of the days she drives Kat home. Sometimes, Annabelle just wants to be alone in her own car, but *sometimes* is only on Wednesdays and Fridays, when The Taker is there waiting. Annabelle is glad Kat's in her passenger seat instead of him. She loves Kat. Kat is her person. Even though Kat is pissed at her right now, Kat loves her, too.

"Do *what*?"

"This passive-aggressive shit. Just *tell* him."

"I can't!"

Annabelle swears Kat's face is getting red. "Why? Why can't you?"

"I don't want to hurt him."

Kat exhales loudly. Shakes her head. She's so mad. "So you just allow something to go on that's not right for you? He can be hurt, Annabelle. He'll be fine."

"He's depressed."

"So? Who isn't *something*? Is all of his depression dependent on what you do? I don't ask you to do certain stuff to keep *me* mentally sound."

Kat's struggled with periods of depression since her mom started drinking hard. And she's right, because, it's not all puppies and rainbows at Roosevelt High. Of course it isn't. Zander is sometimes depressed, too, and Annabelle herself is anxious, and Sierra is edging toward an eating disorder, and those are only the things she knows for sure. People have stuff; people handle stuff.

"You're just afraid of not being liked, Annabelle. You should try it out sometime. Say some bad shit. Say what you *think*. Say what you *mean*. Say *no*. Say '*I don't want that.*' See what happens."

"Oh, God," she groans. "I know what happens when

people say what they think." Annabelle is sure her mother drove her father away with her constant barrage of opinions, mostly about him.

"You know what happens when people are a bad match. There's a difference. That Bastard Father Anthony didn't leave because your mother was clear and assertive. He left because she was always picking fights with him. And she was always picking fights with him because he was aloof and distant. They brought out the worst in each other."

Not many people can get away with talking about your family like that, but Kat can. She was there when Annabelle's dad lived with them, and she was there when he left. After so much time at their house, Kat even has her own place at their table.

"Tell him you don't want to drive him anymore, or I will."

That afternoon, Annabelle works the register at Essential Baking Company. A man complains that his "expresso" doesn't have milk, and a woman in an REI jacket wants to speak to Claire about the lack of gluten-free options. After her shift, she takes the day's unsold baked goods to Sunnyside Eldercare. She reads aloud to Mrs. Alducci, and then brings her favorite resident, Mr. Giancarlo, a sugar cookie in the shape of a snowman. Throughout, her conversation with Kat about The Taker plays in her head like a radio turned down low. It bothers her. It *disturbs* her.

Things momentarily improve when she gets home. She laces up her shoes. Runs six fast, hard miles to Fremont and back. She takes a long, hot shower. Gina brings home KFC for dinner, and the red-and-white tub is in the middle of the table, and the little containers are spread around with their lids off. The spoon-fork combo inexplicably cheers Annabelle up, especially when it has mashed potatoes on it.

"Mark the calendar. We can have this again in one year. God, I can't imagine the fat calories," Gina says.

"Gross but delicious," Malcolm says, licking gravy off of the spork.

"Pass the napkins," Annabelle says. Bunches of them are already crushed and strewn around like weapons after the war.

"Annabelle, what's wrong?" Gina asks.

"What? Nothing."

"Don't tell me 'nothing.' I see when something is wrong. I know you. You were a part of me. I gave birth to you."

"Gross," Malcolm says again.

"I'm fine."

"You're trying to be fine but you're not fine. You're in a mood."

"I'll be in a mood if you keep telling me I'm in a mood."

"Is it that boy you've been driving home?"

How does she do this? How does she zero right in on the thing? Maybe Gina *does* know her. Maybe there is some creepy ESP that passes through the umbilical cord, and she'll never be free of it.

"I just . . . I don't want to drive him home anymore. I think he likes me."

"You've been acting weird since you started doing it. So tell him you don't want to! Did you tell him?"

"Not yet."

"For God's sake! Tell him!"

"I don't want to hurt him."

"You sound just like your father. You can't tippy-toe around! He'll think you like him back, and you'll never get rid of him. Remember Georgie Zacharro? You've got to be careful, Annabelle, I've told you a hundred times. Some boys, you smile at them and they think you want to have sex with them."

"Ew," Malcolm says.

"My entire school thinks that, then, Mom, because I'm a smiley person."

"You know what I mean. If you don't like him, don't encourage him."

"I don't *dis*like him. He's just *pressing*." She doesn't know how to explain it. It's a feeling, one that she doesn't know if she can trust or not. The feeling comes and goes. And it's not like anything abnormal is going on here. Boys have had crushes on her before; she's had crushes on boys. No big deal. It happens.

But this . . . There are small things. Texts from The Taker way, way late at night, ones she jokes about the next day, but that feel cryptic and intimate: Why does it seem like a forest keeps secrets? Or: Strange to think of a world with both rage and moonlight. She's caught him, too, taking a photo of something because she's in the background. He tries to linger in her car, asking her a complicated question right as they approach his house, or pretending to lose something under the seat. He smells of maybe weed and alcohol both. But, hey. A third of her freshman PE class smelled like that.

"You have to follow your instinct. Listen to the voice inside."

"Why do people always say that? Voices say different things at different times."

"Yeah, but you know when it's lying, if you're being honest with yourself. Here's where it speaks." Gina puts her hand on her chest. "Something is bothering you, you listen. Good stuff doesn't nag at you. You feel nervous in a parking lot, you get out of there. You feel uneasy at a party? You fucking leave."

"Twenty-five cents, Mom," Malcolm says.

The problem with Gina, and maybe all mothers—she could overreact, but she could also be right. It was like trying to eat the ice cream around the nuts.

That next day, though, Annabelle grabs The Taker's sleeve and pulls him aside at lunch.

"Hey, I'm sorry, but I can't give you a ride anymore. They changed my schedule at work, and I have to come in a half hour earlier. I won't have time to change and stuff if I don't just hurry home."

"Oh. Okay. No problem," he says.

She did not speak bravely or honestly as Kat told her to do.

She lied. But it's out, she's said it, and it's done. No more driving him. She's relieved.

It's over, she thinks.

She's wrong.

It's a bad week anyway. A bad, bad week, but the shores of Albert Lea Lake are boggy. Swampy, too. It's a small, shallow lake, with psychedelic swirls of green algae on top. She always looks forward to the bodies of water. Usually, they're cool and inviting, and they break up the monotony of farmland. But this lake is a little spooky. On the true-crime shows, these are the places people disappear.

She'll be meeting Grandpa Ed a few miles past the last bend of the lake on South Shore Drive. South Shore Drive will eventually turn into Highway 65, which will take her into Iowa. After he picks her up, Grandpa Ed will drive them into the nearest town of Hayward, Minnesota, population 250, where they'll stay at the Myre–Big Island campground.

She's almost at the end of her run. It is the second week in June, and the heat makes the shallow lake smell like murky stuff and old fish. She hoped the water would lift her spirits, but it's doing the opposite. She's been dragged down all day, as if her pack is full of boulders.

She sees the car coming down South Shore Drive. It is a small blue pickup. She likes to make eye contact with drivers, so she's certain they see her. No one expects that a girl will be running alongside a mostly empty highway.

He's too far away for their eyes to meet yet, though. She watches him approach. Soon, he's almost there, and she can see the man who is driving. He's wearing a baseball hat, and a T-shirt. His window is rolled down. She looks at him. He looks at her. She raises her hand in a wave.

He raises his, too. And in that split-second moment when his eyes are off the road, it happens. A deer shoots out and bounds across the highway. The truck is not even going that fast, but it is going fast enough. The driver slams on his brakes, and the back of the truck fishtails, but it is too late. There's a sickening thud. It is the horrible sound of fast-moving metal hitting the once-solid side of the animal.

The deer flies into the sky. Annabelle can hardly believe what she is witnessing, because the animal is actually in the air, like he's been lifted by a tornado. And then he lands, and it's horrible, awful, because the hit and the landing instantly turn the animal—beautifully alive and running across the road just a moment ago—into a gruesome, bent corpse. She can see the deer's eyes, and his eyes are flat, just *flat*, and blood is flowing from him.

Oh God. Oh God, oh God. Annabelle lets out a cry. She can't move. No, it's worse than that. She is sobbing, and she stands there paralyzed. She doesn't even realize she is sobbing because she is as struck as that deer. She is stunned by what she's just witnessed, how the animal was alive and then not.

The driver flings his door open. The front left side of his

truck looks like a crushed beer can. He runs out. He gets half-way to the animal and realizes there is nothing to be done.

"Shit!" he says.

Annabelle throws up. She is trembling. Now, the man really has more than he bargained for.

"Can I call someone for you, honey? Can I help you, honey? Can I help you, honey?" he says again and again.

22

1. A cockroach heart has twelve to thirteen chambers, arranged in a row. If one fails, he barely notices.
2. Squid and cuttlefish all have multiple hearts. An octopus has three.
3. The earthworm doesn't have a heart at all. Instead, it has five pseudohearts wrapped around its esophagus.
4. Only the zebra fish, though, can do the truly necessary thing: If his heart is broken or damaged or destroyed, he can grow a new one. Deer cannot. Humans cannot.

"Talk to your mother, huh?" Grandpa Ed begs. "She's called ten times. Come on, Bella Luna."

Annabelle folds the pillow over her head. She sees the deer, who flies and lands and splats, his eyes flat and blank.

"Bella Luna, look. Your brother is on the phone. He wants to talk to you. Please."

She scoots farther down into her bed.

"It's your friend Zach on the phone," Grandpa Ed says. "It's your friend Olivia."

She pretends not to hear him.

"It's Dr. Mann on the phone," Grandpa Ed says.

She doesn't move. But he climbs the ladder to her bunk. He peeks into her face. He looks like hell. His hair is boofed up and uncombed and his ears hang low and old, and he has little fluid-filled crescents under his eyes. He looks exhausted. Three days ago, he drove them from their last location to a KOA campground in town, so he could be closer to Nick's Grocery and get better Wi-Fi. She's only been out of her bunk to pee. She hasn't eaten anything but toast and polenta and bananas since the deer. Grandpa Ed is eating and drinking for both of them. He's stress-eaten most of a pork roast and he's been hitting the supply of wine and salami like it's the war and the bombs are dropping, so what the hell.

He's in over his head.

He shoves the phone to her ear. She tries to roll away, but he moves with her, and there is Dr. Mann's voice.

"Annabelle?" Dr. Mann says through the miles. Annabelle can see her, with her lovely auburn hair and her smile, sitting in her warm office with the leather couch and soft pillows and Kleenex box. Annabelle once saw her getting out of her car, a cute little red MINI Cooper, which made Annabelle love her even more.

Annabelle says nothing.

"I heard what happened."

"I—" Annabelle starts to cry.

"Oh," Dr. Mann says. "Oh, this is hard. So hard."

Annabelle sobs. Grandpa Ed is crying, too. Tears roll off his big bulb of a nose. He wipes his eyes on the back of his sleeve.

"That deer," Dr. Mann says. "He had to go run into the road this week of all weeks. The anniversary."

The anniversary. The second week of June. June tenth, to be exact. She had felt it there, black and hovering like a death sentence, and now it's here. She avoided looking at it, as if it were the *malocchio*, the evil eye, out to curse her worse than she already is.

"I don't want to look, but tell me," Annabelle says to Grandpa Ed.

"You think I wanna look? I don't wanna look."

"Just peek. Peek and tell me."

The news. What people might be saying. What people might be *feeling*. All the emotions. The news and emotions and the grief and despair on top of her own emotions and grief and despair.

"I'll do it if you answer your phone."

"No."

"You gotta. Your mother. Your brother. Your family, at least."

"Ugh. I can't talk to anyone."

"Family! They're the ones who're always gonna be there for you. You don't ignore the family. They show their love. You take their love. You feel better. *Capisce?*" He is stern.

"Okay, okay. I'll talk to the family. That's all, though. Peek."

He makes the sign of the cross, and opens his laptop. Wow, he's gotten good at it, too, the typing and technological maneuvering. It's almost funny to watch, how he still hunches over a little in concentration, like he's a new hire from the agency. He even has an e-mail account now. He's on there all the time. She asked him if he's still writing to Dawn Celeste, but he only says, "Do I ask you your business? You mind your own, I mind my own."

She waits.

"It's what you'd expect."

"Tell me."

"Articles. People talking. Remembering—"

"That's enough."

"Wait, wait, wait. This could be—"

"What?" She's terrified.

"Big. This could be big."

"Oh, God."

Her fingers tap, thumb to each finger pad—index, middle, ring, pinkie. It is not enough. She paces the small space. They are still in Hayward, population 250. By now, Grandpa Ed knows the names of the people who work at Nick's Grocery. There's Annie, and Ken, and Nick himself. She could leave the

RV and pace the few streets in town. Hayward, Minnesota's claim to fame is being the site of the world's longest horseshoe game in 1930. It lasted over five months.

"It's good. It's all good stuff."

"Okay, okay. Tell me. Only in tiny bits."

"*USA Today*."

"Holy shit! Holy shit! No more. Oh my God. Tell me you just didn't say *USA Today*." She claps her hands over her ears.

"Bella Luna. It's fine. Okay? Relax. I told you, it's good." She can still hear him, like he's above water and she's under.

"Nothing that big is good."

"I'm reading. . . . It's long. Give me a minute. It's awesome." He never uses the word *awesome*. She wants to throw up. It is horrible; there is no way to describe how horrible, having this grief and this shame and this responsibility and having it be so public.

"Does it say that I—"

"It's about what you're doing. The run."

"Oh no. I don't want this. They'll think I'm trying to get attention. They'll think I'm drawing the focus away from—" Her fingers tap, tap, tap.

"*Basta!* And stop pacing, Jesus, you're making me dizzy. Just look. The headline. See?"

He turns the laptop toward her. She summons her nerve, glances at the headline.

"'Reluctant Activist Makes 2,700-Mile Run.'"

"Heh. They got that right," he says.

• • •

"I wish I were there," Gina says.

Annabelle wishes she were there, too. Sometimes, you need your mom, even if she drives you crazy.

"I love you," Malcolm says.

"I love you, too."

They sit in silence on the phone. Most of the time, even in the worst times, *I love you* is enough.

I'm sorry, she says to Kat. *I'm sorry*, she says to Will.

Her father, That Bastard Father Anthony, calls, too. It is an awkward conversation. It's weird to have him paying attention after years of not paying attention. He asks about her run, and how she is feeling, and how she is doing, and since she doesn't know what to ask about his life, she asks about the weather in Boston.

"I just wanted you to know that I am thinking about you today," he says.

She dares to look at the comments after the *USA Today* article.

Brave.

Inspiring.

After what she's been through . . .

That YouTube video made me cry.

No one is blaming her. They don't know her, though.

She does the harder thing. She looks at the online posts of some of her friends on this day, the anniversary. God, she feels so sick. Her heart is crushed, crushed, crushed. There's Geoff Graham. He posted a picture from last year, of their group with their arms around each other. Zander posted the one from the sophomore picnic, all of them sitting around the table, happy. She's touched, because Sierra has changed her profile picture to an image of her and Annabelle at Green Lake, sitting on their beach towels. Coach Kwan has the old cross-country team photo up. There are a lot of heart emojis, lots of expressions of love and support. She doesn't see the hate and the blame, but this isn't where she'd likely find it most.

Still, it emboldens her to do another thing she hasn't been able to do—to see what she's been missing. She peeks. She scrolls back in time on their accounts. A week, two weeks. She looks at prom photos. There's Zander and Hannah Kelly, holding hands. Annabelle didn't even know he liked her. There's Destiny and Lauren K, who must have gotten back together, because there they are with their arms around each other in Lauren K's backyard. There's Zach Oh and Olivia. They never mentioned a word about going. Annabelle didn't even ask. She's mad at herself for being so self-involved.

Everyone looks beautiful and young and hopeful. There are strappy shoes and artful curls; thin, stylish ties; big smiles. Lauren K's backyard has a tableful of food. As Annabelle pokes through other stuff, she sees a lot of talk about college and next week's graduation at KeyArena and a summer camping trip. Everyone looks like they've moved on. Like they have a future.

Two days after the anniversary, Annabelle still cannot budge. She refuses to leave the RV. Grandpa Ed is getting short-tempered and stir-crazy. He complains for the millionth time that there is no prosciutto anywhere in a fifty-mile radius, when of course there is no prosciutto in a fifty-mile radius. He huffs around and doesn't wear his hearing aids on purpose. He has even visited the quilt shop in town so often that he's been invited to the proprietor's house for dinner. Annabelle is learning that he likes the company of the ladies. But maybe one lady in particular, because he turns down dinner at Mrs. Quaker's house, and shortly after that, Annabelle gets a glimpse of his e-mail, and sees Dawn Celeste's name and name and name.

Annabelle wants to help him out, to get this thing done, so they can all get back to normal life, whatever that is. But she can't move. She just can't. Her heart is a steel drum, turned sideways on the ground. Cement flows through her veins. Her legs are toppled iron pillars. She just wants to sleep.

"Bella Luna, we either gotta go forward or go back. We can't stay stuck here in the middle."

"Your voice is so loud," she says. "It hurts my ears."

"That's because you been sitting here listening to crickets chirp. You haven't even walked around the campground. Come on, at least come to Abigail's with me for breakfast."

"Uh-uh."

"I'm turning this thing around if you don't get up and run tomorrow, *capisce*?"

"You said that yesterday."

"This time I mean it."

"You said that yesterday, too."

That night, she hears him outside the RV, talking to Gina on the phone. *I can't just make her! What, I'm gonna haul her home by force?* And then: *I don't know what you expect of me*, he says. *You always think I can make things happen that I can't make happen.*

She sticks her fingers in her ears. She tries to hum all the states and the capitals.

The next day, Zach Oh calls. She finally answers, because it's preferable to listening to the fifteen messages he's left.

"In two weeks, after you get to Rockford, there's a place nearby, Cherry Valley? They have a water park, Magic Waters. They're giving you four free tickets. You get a day off and a two-night stay at the Cherry Valley Hotel."

There is no way she can fly down some waterslide with Seth Greggory getting closer and closer every minute. This is nuts. "Who am I going to go with, Grandpa Ed and our two imaginary friends?"

"That's not the point. They thought you deserved some kind of a treat."

"I can't just take a day off."

"I can't believe you're saying that right now."

"Well, if I ever decide to run again, I'll be way behind."

"The *Rockford Register Star* will be there! And you can't let the people of Magic Waters down! They're giving half price to all high school kids who show up in a Run for a Cause shirt."

"A *what*?"

She hears Olivia in the background. "Okay, okay!" Zach yells. "Olivia says, don't freak out, but when you get to Pittsburgh, the Young Feminist Alliance club of a certain university is bringing you in to talk to some students. Wait, what? Tell her yourself!"

"Hey, Annabelle," Olivia says.

"Wait. What students? What university?"

"There's been an increasing swell of support from young women," Olivia says.

"A swell of support from young women?"

"The market research from Zach and Mrs. Hodges indicates that fifty-nine percent of the contributors to GoFundMe are now young women ages twenty-four and under."

"I don't get it."

"I get it! I get it perfectly. Do you have any idea how many young women have experienced . . . well, if not exactly what you have, something like it? Someone using violence to control or silence them? Powerlessness through intimidation? Who *doesn't* feel they need a voice?"

"I'm not anyone's voice. I haven't even said anything. What university? I can't talk to university students."

"Of course you can. Every day that you go on, you say something. You say you *can* go on."

"If you saw me right now, you'd know I can't do what you're asking. Only two hundred and sixty-five people have run across the country. Who am I kidding? I can't. I have no will. I can't say anything to anyone. I don't know what I *would* say. I just want to sleep."

"Annabelle, come on!"

"The reason I was doing this anyway . . . It wasn't to say some big thing. It was just for me. To . . . *get through*."

"That's exactly the point! That's exactly what people *get*. You are not pounding another freaking message among a million messages. You're not talking, talking, talking. God, I'm tired of hearing people talk! You're doing. And you're just being your honest self, moving forward. You're not staying in old places anymore, do you see? That *is* the message. That *is* triumph."

"You should give the speech. You almost made me stand up and applaud."

"Aaargh!" Olivia screams.

Zach is back on the phone now. "You will be at Magic Waters in two weeks, wearing one Run for a Cause T-shirt. You will be in Pittsburgh in seven weeks, speaking to a few students. It's not like we didn't give you plenty of warning. You've got seven hundred miles to figure out what to say."

"What university?"

"Carnegie Mellon."

She hangs up on him.

23

The problem is, she's done things too often because she didn't want to disappoint people. Maybe if she would have said no and stuck to it, she'd be getting ready to graduate with her class right now. She'd be getting her cap and gown, and Mom would be taking pictures, and Malcolm would be trying it on while she yelled at him not to wrinkle it after all that ironing.

Instead, she is in the bunk of the RV, unshowered and smelling bad, her stomach growling but the idea of food revolting, the vision of that deer and the flesh and the blood—

Stop! Stop! Stop!

She rolls over and puts the covers high up over her shoulders. It's all too much. Grandpa Ed is on his laptop. She hears the rapid mice steps of the keys. *He* has a lot to say, anyway.

She summons Dr. Mann. She tries to remember what Dr. Mann has said again and again. *Your only job—and it's a big one—is to try to speak and live your own honest truth. That truth might shift. You might need more time to even understand what that truth is. That's it. That's the job. Trying to manage or control everyone else? Not the job. Impossible, besides.*

It is hard to believe this, it really is. Because—if she'd only been more consistent and sure . . . If she'd only maintained the distance she'd created after she stopped driving The Taker home . . . If, if, if . . .

When she closes her eyes, she sees this: herself, feeling more comfortable, more in control after the distance. She relaxes. She is friendly to The Taker again. After AP English Comp, he walks with her to her locker, even though his is in the other direction. They are complaining about the brutal compare-and-contrast paper they have to write, on the speeches of Sojourner Truth versus Chief Joseph. They are joking about the way Emily Yew always raises her hand to ask kiss-ass questions.

At lunch, The Taker saves a place next to him, and she sits there. He unwraps his sandwich.

"Ewww, onions!" She crinkles her nose from the smell.

His face flushes. "You know, I wouldn't be like that if I were you," he says. He sounds actually mad. The muscle in his cheek pulses.

"I'm sorry," she says. "I was just teasing." But he is silent. She feels awful. He is too sensitive to be teased, she realizes. Well, everyone has their thing. Zach Oh acts like a baby when he loses a video game.

She proofreads The Taker's personal expression essay. It's based on the concepts of Emerson's "Self-Reliance," and it's about how The Taker cured his loneliness at his old school through nonconformity and inconsistency. Separating himself out led to confidence and a sense of superiority that itself felt like an achievement, he writes. It bothers her, the ego in it, the way he builds himself up in his mind to look down on others. But the essay is bold and funny, and she only praises him for that. She feels wary of honestly criticizing him.

And then The Taker gets a car. And when the brakes in the Toyota have to be replaced, and Annabelle is without transportation for a week, *he* drives *her* home. He even waits around in their kitchen while she changes her clothes before they head over to Essential Baking Company.

"He still likes you," Malcolm says that night. Malcolm and Terrence were there working on a science project for school.

"We're just friends," she says.

"*You're* just friends. *He's* not just friends."

"Don't be a jerk."

"His eyes follow you like one of those haunted-house paintings. And when you went upstairs to change, he tried to look at your phone when you got a text."

"Mind your own business." Telling people to mind their own business is maybe another Agnelli Curse.

So what if he likes her? It doesn't matter. She gives in to the fact of it, being quietly adored. Who wouldn't like being adored, even if it makes her uncomfortable sometimes? She still wishes Will felt that way, even though she hasn't heard from him since the day at Whole Foods.

"Fuck!" The Taker cries, and slams on the brakes one afternoon as they leave her neighborhood.

Annabelle squeals. He turns the wheel hard and one tire ends up on the curb. She sees it, Hamilton Shiley's abandoned Big Wheel in the street up ahead.

"Did you think there was a kid on it?" she laughs, as his car bumps back down the curb.

"I couldn't see! The sun was in my eyes, okay?"

He flips down the visor in a fury. The silence is weird and uncomfortable the rest of the drive. He barely says good-bye to her after they get to her work. It's strange—sometimes she gets the feeling that he hates her. And not a little bit of hate, but *hate*. This seems crazy and wrong, after how much he seems to like her. Sometimes, her anxiety makes her too sensitive and she misreads people. Still, one thing is for sure: The Taker can't laugh at himself.

It is yet another new morning at the KOA campground in Hayward, Minnesota.

"Annabelle," Grandpa Ed says. She is not Bella Luna anymore. "We are going home if you don't run today, *capisce*? I mean it."

She is stuck in the middle, and middles are always a swamp of inertia, sucking downward. She can't go forward, because forward is more miles of self-imposed punishment—flat back-country roads plus the heat of summer, red T-shirts, and the inconceivable and undeserving support of strangers. Forward means a question-mark future. Forward is Seth Greggory.

And she can't go backward, because back doesn't fit anymore. She can't even imagine sleeping in her old bed in her old room. Who was the girl that slept there? Sometimes, she was anxious, but she was confident, too. She could be cocky; she could feel cute. She could flirt and have fun and dream about what was to come. She was popular. People liked her. She loved her bosses at Essential Baking Company, and the smell of warm pastries, and the way the old people's faces at Sunnyside Eldercare would light up when she came in. She felt life's goodness and a rosy hope all around her.

She was naive. She was a child.

Now, she is a specter in running clothes.

And she can't go backward because there is The Taker on Valentine's Day, standing next to her locker with two roses. A yellow one and a red one. He holds them out. He smirks, offering a choice.

"You know," she says.

"Which?" he asks.

"Yellow."

He gives the red to Josie Green. They would be a great couple. She keeps telling him that. She's not 100 percent sure she's glad about the red rose. There's a dark little kernel that wants him to want her even if she doesn't know entirely how she feels about him. He still intrigues her. He smiles and jokes, but there's this depressed, big ego, this overly sensitive thing that is nothing like Will. Still, the rose thing—it reassures her. She's managing it all. The dials are turned just right. See: There are dials, and she must turn them this way and that to keep things where they should be. See: She thinks it's a situation she can control, which is almost a guarantee that she's wrong.

Grandpa slams out the door of the RV. Annabelle is alone. The Taker film plays. It is March of last year. Her birthday. There are only three months left of her old life, though she has no idea. The clock is ticking.

She is carrying her tray in the cafeteria. She finds all her friends at their table. She spills her water into her salad.

"Chocolate, chocolate, chocolate, please," Zander says. He looks at the cafeteria ceiling. How many times has this film played? Hundreds.

"Yeah, like, don't tell her it's a cake or anything," Zach Oh says.

Kat lifts the cake from under the table. *Happy 17th, Belle Bottom,* the frosting reads. "Ta-da," Kat says.

And then Sierra complains about the frosting, and then they all sing, substituting insults for her name. And then Kat gives her the Moleskine. She says, "Now we're twins."

And then, other things happen.

After not hearing from Will for months, she gets a text: Thinking of you today. Miss you, Pip. She is so happy. He uses her love name, and her heart is filled with joy.

And then, something else.

The Taker is standing by her locker after school. A gift bag hangs from the crook of his finger.

"Be-elle," he sings. It's his new name for her. She doesn't mind. Half the kids in her elementary school called her that.

"What's this?"

"Open it."

She moves the tissue paper around. The bag is pretty. So pretty that it makes her nervous. It's pink and black with pink tissue paper shooting from the top. It's the kind of wrapping that's been carefully chosen, not the wrinkled tissue in a Christmas bag that Zach Oh might give.

Inside, there's an envelope. She opens it. Two tickets to see the punk band Uncut at Neumos.

"Since, you know, the Clash isn't around anymore."

"Wow," she says. "Thank you."

Two tickets. It's awkward. She assumes he expects to go together. Is this a *date*?

He reads her mind. "They're for us, but it's a group thing? My friends Lucy and Adrian and Jules are going, too." The Taker recently got a job at the QFC on Mercer, and Lucy and Adrian work in the deli section with him, and Jules is Adrian's girlfriend. Annabelle has never met them, but she's heard the stories about Adrian's band and how he and Lucy find gross stuff in the chickens sometimes. She never wants to eat a deli chicken again.

"Oh, that's awesome," she says. "That'll be fun. This is too much, but thank you."

She hugs him. He is trying to grow a beard, and the soft hairs brush her cheek as he hugs back.

"Happy birthday, Belle," he says.

"Stop, stop, stop," Annabelle says. It's useless. She is in the middle of the film about The Taker, she is in the middle of her run, and there is nowhere to go but forward. Saint Christopher seems to look at her sternly from where he hangs. Annabelle gets up to pee. Grandpa is still gone. She pours a cup of coffee and doesn't drink it. She stares out at the same trees and the same jigsaw piece of sky of the KOA campground in Hayward, Minnesota.

Her phone buzzes and spins in a circle on the table. It's a text from Gina.

Call me.

She is too tired to talk to anyone. When she opens her mouth, lava flows out. Her bones are steel girders, anchored in cement. Her arms are bird wings pinned down with rocks by mean boys.

Now her phone rings. Mom again.

Why didn't she strand them someplace with no Wi-Fi? Somewhere back in Montana or the Badlands? Here, they're in the middle of nowhere with a signal that blazes five fiery bars on her phone.

Ring, ring.

Ignore.

Annabelle shuts off her phone, but it buzzes with emergency.

She does not have the courage or faith not to answer. She has bad-image flashes that come from years of Gina spouting stuff that might go wrong, and flashes that come from real stuff that did. Things can change in an instant.

"Mom?"

"Are you all right?"

"I'm all right, are you all right?"

"Seth Greggory called."

Annabelle's stomach drops like a failed elevator, and then crashes.

"Annabelle?"

"I'm here."

"I thought I lost you."

She has no real answer to that. "What did he want?"

"He wants to make sure you're on track for coming in on September twenty-second. He wanted to remind us that the calendar is fixed."

It is horrible, the thought of him and September. Annabelle feels sick.

"Annabelle?"

"I'm here."

"Grandpa called me a few minutes ago. He's sitting in some diner eating pancakes. But he's at his wit's end. He says he's planning on turning around and driving home. And I was thinking . . . You've been seriously depressed there, honey. The anniversary, that fucking deer . . ."

"Twenty-five cents," Annabelle says for Malcolm.

"I really think you should come home. It's the right thing. You don't need to be out there doing this. You can take it easy for three months. Just . . . *rest.*"

"Rest isn't restful."

"I did something. Don't be mad."

"What?"

"I ordered a cap and gown. Just in case. Come on, honey. Come home. You've done enough."

Silence.

"Wouldn't it be nice to go to that ceremony with your friends? To sit with everyone and reflect on what you've all been through?"

"I'm not coming home," Annabelle says.

"So many people want to see you. I put new sheets on your bed. Your room is waiting for you."

"I'm finishing." Much to her surprise, she suddenly means it.

"If you insist." Gina sighs. It occurs to Annabelle that the sigh is just a little overdramatic. And Gina's words hit her worst buttons. Annabelle wonders if she's a victim of reverse psychology. Agnelli Curse, Gina-style. What has gotten into her mother? Is she now, by some saintly, heavenly miracle, *in favor* of this run?

"Did you even really order a cap and gown?" Annabelle asks.

"Oh, sweetie, I gotta go—Aunt Angie's on the other line. Burst pipe at the office. Drink lots of water, you hear me? And Grandpa said he's going to start meeting you halfway, now that it's summer, right? You need to refill the bladder, when it's this hot. And wear your bright clothes. It's hard to see in the glare."

Annabelle dresses. She pulls back her hair, which is growing long again. She eats two bananas and a bowl of muesli. She reviews the route. She leaves a one-word note for Grandpa Ed:

Fine.

She leaves the RV. Wow, she realizes how warm it was in there, now that she gets a fresh hit of June air. She looks around at where she's been the last few days. It is shady, with lots of trees. There will be other dark places, but she'll never see that particular one again.

To leave this town, Loretta takes her down Main Street. Hey, there's the quilt shop. There's Nick's. And there's Abigail's. All of the places she's heard about from Grandpa. And, wow, look. There's Grandpa Ed himself, sitting at the counter, cutting a stack of pancakes with the edge of his fork.

She runs past. She waves. A split second later, she hears him calling.

"Go, Bella Luna! Go, go, go!" She looks over her shoulder. He's practically jumping up and down in his old-man pants and polo shirt. A woman in an apron, Abigail, maybe, raises her arm and shakes it in encouragement.

It is clear right away that she's been lying in bed for days, because her muscles are tight and her joints creak like the wheels of an old shopping cart. Her lungs throb, but maybe that's just her heart, urging her to flee.

September twenty-second. Seth Greggory.

Some silly water park with kids in red T-shirts? So what. Talking to a few students at one of the top universities in the nation? Big deal. Facing junior reporters and articles in major newspapers? Practically a birthday party. At least in comparison to the real terror that awaits. She can't truly outrun her future, but you can't tell her body that. Inside, those workings are ancient. The brain shoots fear and the heart speeds and the blood pumps. Our ancient, animal nature says: Bolt when you see danger coming. It says: Race across the forest floor when you see the man with the gun. It says: Bound across the highway when the truck is coming at you.

Sometimes, 2,700 miles aren't nearly enough.

24

When the good people of the Silver Springs Golf Club in Ossian, Iowa, hear that Annabelle Agnelli, the girl who's crossing the USA after that awful tragedy in Seattle, is running right through their town, they have a big dinner for her at Bambino's restaurant. Bambino's is where many of the town's big events, both somber and celebratory, are marked. Tonight, parking the RV won't be a problem. They can park anywhere in town they please. The golf club, the post office, Bambino's lot, the Ossian City Park, wherever.

As soon as Grandpa Ed hears the word *Bambino's*, he starts rubbing his hands together, expecting cannelloni and handmade pasta, ravioli; cannoli for dessert. He has his dress shirt on, the black one with blue stripes, and his fancy trousers. Little curvy lines of Acqua di Parma are coming off of him like heat waves in a desert.

Annabelle is nervous, but she is trying to do what Dr. Mann suggested after their now-weekly phone session—to listen to what people are saying and not what she fears they are saying. To be aware of other feelings inside besides guilt. And look, there is a sign out front, which someone made with poster board and fat markers: WELCOME, ANNABELLE! OSSIAN LOVES YOU! There is a group of blue balloons, huddled together like nervous middle schoolers. What the people of Ossian are saying is that they care, they care about *her*, not what she is guilty of, and she exhales. She exhales, and what she feels is . . . a little *pleased*.

Bambino's is in a brick building right next to the fire department. The parking spaces in front of the place are all taken, but there's a spot saved with orange construction cones and blue crepe paper. Lit Budweiser signs are in the window, and inside, there's a pool table with a huge stained-glass Budweiser lamp hanging above. The far wall is decorated with enormous cutouts of football players. Grandpa Ed grunts his disappointment—there are no red-and-white checkered tablecloths, no smells of garlic and butter, no juice glasses of Chianti. But the owner, a warm blond woman with a big smile, comes to greet them, and the room is full of people—firefighters from next door, a thin boy from the *Ossian Bee*, the president of Luana Savings Bank, and the staff of Casey's General Store, Becker Hardware, and Creative Corner Salon. Everyone is *so nice*. They pat Annabelle on the back, and ask her questions that she doesn't mind answering, and they tell her that God is good. Grandpa Ed repeats his favorite joke, that he'll be the one running across the country next year.

The food arrives, and it is not pasta and veal pounded thin, but creamed chicken over biscuits, and hamburger steak and gravy with peas and rolls and mashed potatoes. This isn't Seattle food, and she realizes again how food and so many other things are different all around the country. One of the men from the Silver Springs Golf Club makes a toast, and there's the sound of clinking beer bottles. Annabelle drinks a Pepsi in a plastic cup. Her cheeks are warm from food and good feeling.

After the meal, there's the hush of a surprise, and then someone turns out the lights, and the owner of Bambino's, Sue, appears in the doorway with a cake. On it, there are lit candles, like it's Annabelle's birthday. The good people of Ossian start to sing. *Happy graduation to you!*

"We heard you're missing yours at home today," Sue says. The cake has a mortarboard on it in blue icing. Now she understands why there's blue everywhere. Annabelle chokes up. On the phone this morning, she told her mom and Malcolm that she didn't want to think about her graduation, that she wanted this to be like any other day, but now she's overcome.

"This is so nice. I don't know what to say."

Sue saves her. "Blow out the candles, sweetie, make a wish, before we eat wax cake."

Annabelle does. Her wish—well, it's private, but it involves peace and love for everyone in those graduation seats at home, and for everyone not in those seats.

She can't believe all these people and what they've done

for her. Annabelle's heart actually aches. And then one of the women from the Silver Springs Golf Club approaches. She has closely cropped brown hair, with little tendril curls framing her face. She's wearing jeans and a serious brown cardigan with a white shirt underneath, the tips of the collar fanned out like crisp paper airplanes heading opposite directions.

She grips Annabelle's hands, and stares hard into Annabelle's eyes. "I just wanted to say . . . I've thought about you every day since I heard about you. My daughter dated a boy like that in college, and if she didn't end up changing schools, who knows what might have happened. Pardon my French, but . . . *that fucker.*"

It happens again when she arrives in the village of Warren, Illinois. This is two and a half days after they watched the Casino Joe's fireworks show on the bank of the Mississipi River in Dubuque, Iowa. Warren, Illinois, was a stagecoach stop in 1851, according to Grandpa Ed's tireless Google research. The library—where Annabelle eats sandwiches from Hixter's Bar and Grill with six members of the Warren Township High School track and field team and the Warren Township librarians—sits across from the railroad track. It's right near the water tower, which is emblazoned with the word WARREN.

The students ask her questions about her mileage per day, and if she's gotten any injuries, and if she misses her parents and friends, being gone that long. A young girl gives her a gift, her own lucky coin, which the girl has carried in her shoe every time she's won a race. But afterward, one of the Warren Township librarians, Angie Canfield (descendant of Angela Rose Canfield, first female mayor of Illinois, she told Annabelle), approaches. She's a small, serious woman with carefully bobbed hair and pressed slacks and a pendant necklace you see on church ladies, but she grips Annabelle's hands and looks her dead straight in the eyes.

"I know what's coming," she says. "The trial. That boy. I don't normally use words like this, but . . . that fucker. Don't you let him get to you."

What are the people saying? They care about her. And—they're *angry.* What is Annabelle feeling, besides guilt? Something new. Because their anger lifts a rock inside of her. Underneath, it is dark and gross and slimy. But she sees it. She feels it—that worm of fury. It's large and it's creepy, and it almost looks capable of devouring her, so no wonder she didn't want to lock eyes with it before. But there it is, wriggling for its freedom.

Only *they* should be allowed to be angry, she'd previously thought. *They*, the ones who weren't to blame and who suffered the most. They got to be angry at The Taker *and* at her. But now she can't help it. The golf lady and the librarian and the commenters in the *USA Today* article—the rock lifts, and the worm wriggles out, and the fury stirs.

People plus people plus anger is how things can change.

25

1. 2,500–1,000 BCE: The Egyptians decide that the heart, or the ieb, is the center of life and morality. After death, they believe, your heart would be brought to the Hall of Maat, where it would be weighed. If it was lighter than the Feather of Maat, you got the afterlife. If it was heavier, the demon Ammut would eat your heart and your soul would vanish from existence.
2. 400–200 BCE: Ancient Greeks think the heart is the center of the soul and the source of heat within the body.
3. 100–900 AD: Early Americans, like the Teotihuacan of ancient Mexico, believe that different spiritual forces could leave the body at different times, like when you were dreaming. The teyolia, though, the spiritual force of the heart, must remain within the body at all times, or the person will die.
4. Today: It is clear that some people are without either a heart or a soul.

• • •

The fury stirs, which means stuff combines with other stuff. A neutron bonks into uranium or plutonium. There's a transformation. A revolution. It can be an explosion that ruins everything, or a beautiful power that can brighten cities. Now, Annabelle runs across the Jefferson Street Bridge over the Rock River in Rockford, Illinois. The sun is out and she's hot and thirsty already, but she's happy that Loretta is taking her through a town, because towns make the time go so much faster than the long stretches of lonely farmland or forest. Towns mean a real bed in a motel, too, unless there's a campground nearby to park the RV. Larger towns mean new supplies. Fresh varieties of PowerBars and snacks, like the fun day when your parent goes to the grocery store and you snoop in the bag with excitement.

She's crossing a bridge from West Jefferson to East Jefferson, and she's in a great mood. The little towns themselves do this, too. She imagines life in each of them. She looks in store windows. She chooses a house that could be hers.

Over the bridge, there are four lanes of cars, and it's busy, and she watches her step on the sidewalk so she doesn't trip on a wrapper tossed out a window, or a clunk of cement. Hey, there's a park down there at the side of the narrow, green-brown river. Pretty. Hmm, some restaurants, too—she sees umbrellas over outdoor tables. There's a whole bunch of bridges, not just the one she's on, but others in both directions.

Now, she's on the other side. There are lots of redbrick

buildings, and a funny red tower, with red flapping oars at the top. She has no idea what that is. Next, she's beside a long, flat building. It's a music venue of some kind, a place where bands come, and—

This is all it takes.

Great day—gone. Happy town run—finished.

Because she sees him. The Taker. This is also what he's done: given her a life sentence, these memories, these intrusive thoughts, these nightmares. In a snap, he destroys everything again and again. His car pulls up to her street. She spots it through the venetian blinds of their living room.

"I'm leaving!" she calls.

"He can't come in? He can't ring the doorbell and say hello?" Gina yells from the kitchen.

"It's not a date! I've got to go," Annabelle says, and then she's outside in the April evening.

The Taker leans across the seat and opens the door. "I would've come in. I'm not a douche."

"Not necessary. You look nice." He's wearing a dress shirt and jeans and a narrow tie. He's made too much of an effort for her not to give him a compliment, but it's true, too—he does look nice.

"You look beautiful. But you look beautiful every day."

He's in a great mood. The music is on, and he's thumping the steering wheel. "You hungry? Want to stop first?"

"Nah, I'm fine."

"We can go after."

"See what your friends want to do."

He doesn't answer. He turns up the music. "I love this part." He hits an imaginary cymbal in time to the one in the song.

They arrive and find a parking spot, and then they race across the street to Neumos, which is thrumming with pre-concert energy. There's the smell of cigarettes and weed and close bodies. Security stamps their hands. "Upstairs. Loft. Under twenty-one," he says.

It's packed inside. The Taker tosses his arm around her shoulders. "No one really cares where you go once you're in here. Up or down?" he says.

"Up is fine."

"Aww! We'll go down later if we want to dance."

The opening band, Karma, is already playing. There's purple light everywhere, and crushed bodies, and, wow, it's hot.

"How are they going to find us?" she shouts.

"Huh?" He can't hear. He pulls her close and she tries again in his ear. Someone bumps them and her lips touch his skin.

"Your friends. How are they going to find us?"

"Don't worry about it," he says.

But she *is* worrying about it. She's the sort of person who only relaxes all the way when everyone has arrived or has found their seat or has turned in their part of the group project.

"It's almost time for Uncut," she shouts. "I hope they get here."

"It's okay."

His body is next to hers in the smash of people, and he's grinning and dancing in place while she's keeping her purse close and eyeing the crowd for anyone who might look like they're looking for someone. She's never met Lucy, Adrian, or Jules, so she has no idea who she's watching for.

There's a muffled announcement. The color of lights goes from purple to blue. The crowd applauds and cheers. It's not a good venue for short people. She can't see a thing.

"Oh no. They're going to miss it."

"Something probably came up. Let's just watch the show," he says.

She shouldn't worry about his friends if he's not. Uncut plays a few songs she knows, and she relaxes and gets into it. God, it's hot, though, and Annabelle takes off her denim jacket and ties it around her waist. In minutes, her T-shirt is soaked and so is the back of his, but The Taker doesn't seem to mind. The crowd grows, and pushes them toward the center. She is in front of him now, and he loops his arms around her.

"I'm so sweaty," she says.

"I like it."

"Probably cooler down there."

In intermittent beats she can see the stage, and the singer with his narrow hips and long hair. The crowd looks like a blue-tinged swarm of bees.

The Taker is moving behind her, and she moves, too; she can't help but dance. The whole place is dancing. It is so hot and stuffy, and the air smells bad, really bad, like hot dogs plus body odor plus beer. The floor is sticky up here, too. No alcohol allowed? There's probably more alcohol on the floor up here than in glasses down there.

Annabelle might commit a crime for a drink of cold water. But as hot and sticky and stinky and crowded and loud as it is, she's having fun. The music and the atmosphere make her feel a freedom she normally doesn't feel. She's stopped worrying about his friends. She feels The Taker's body behind hers and it doesn't bother her. She likes it. He's the familiar one in this hive of bodies. His arms are around her. She leans back, sweat and all. They part only to applaud and shriek and then his arms are around her again.

It must be nearly over, but she is feeling light-headed. It is so, so hot that it is almost impossible to catch a breath of anything but the exhaling of other people.

"Wow, I've got to—" Annabelle plucks her shirt. Her hair is flat from sweat and so is his.

"Air?"

"Yeah."

"Let's go."

Go. It sounds suddenly great and vital but looks impossible. He takes her hand.

"Don't lose me," she says.

"Never."

They edge and he pushes. He says, "Excuse us," and then, "Hey, man," when one guy won't move. It's odd how in command he is in this environment. There's no following along or awkward maneuvers in this place. Maybe music relaxes him, too. Maybe he has also been carried into a freedom he normally doesn't feel. When they finally reach the front door, it's like he's successfully gotten them across a war-torn city.

They gulp air. "We made it!" she says. There's the joy of survival.

"Stay here. Don't move." He kisses her cheek. He jets across the street and into a market. She tilts her head up, lets the cool night air lift the sweat from her forehead.

He's back, carrying two bottles of cold water. It seems chivalrous. He cracks the top for her and hands it over. She drinks gratefully.

"This is the best water I've had in my whole life," she says.

"This is the best night I've had in mine. Seriously."

He tries to talk her into walking over to Molly Moon's for ice cream, or taking a drive to Cupcake Royale, but this has definitely turned into a date, and she realizes she'd better get home. He stops the car a block away from her house, though. He pulls up by the curb. The dog in the nearby house starts to bark.

"What are you doing?"

"Well, in case your mom is watching."

He leans over and kisses her. It's decisive, and she likes that. And who doesn't want to kiss after a concert? After the loud music and the heat and the surge of being alive?

But she hasn't kissed anyone since Will, and a new kiss is

always strange, and his tongue seems large and it moves in an unfamiliar way, and she's a little stunned, suddenly, at how the night has turned.

The kiss ends, and there he is, The Taker, in the seat next to her. It's unnerving, how he was someone else back at Neumos and now he's himself again.

"Wow," she says. "That shouldn't have happened."

"It shouldn't?"

"Thank you for a great time."

"Thank *you* for a great time."

"I'm sorry your friends couldn't make it. I hope they're okay."

"I'm sure they're fine. Why shouldn't that have happened?"

"Um, we're *friends*?" she says.

"Not tonight we aren't."

And he's right, isn't he? Because none of the night has been *friends*. He starts the car again, drives her down the block to her house. When she opens the car door, the dome light makes everything too bright.

"I'm saving this forever," he jokes. He has her water bottle by its neck. He waves it around.

"You're a sad boy," she says.

It's out before she realizes that he may take it wrong. He's so sensitive. But he's still grinning. He tips the last drink into his own mouth.

"Ahh," he says.

She cringes. "Gross."

"Belle," he says.

"What?"

"Just Belle."

Everyone is asleep when Annabelle goes inside. She's glad. She doesn't want to talk about how it went, because she's not sure how it went. There's the physical exhaustion of fun, but something else, too. Something uneasy. Maybe just the way she let her guard down. Maybe because the kiss felt wrong. You could have a great time, and the kiss could still feel wrong.

Annabelle lies awake in her own bed. She hears Bit snoring in the hall. It's his fault that she can't fall asleep, she tells herself.

But it isn't. In the darkness, she realizes something. The Taker never texted or phoned his friends to see where they were or what had happened. It was like he knew they weren't coming.

The thought gnaws at her. The gnaw turns to a ripple of . . . what? Confusion? Anger? She is so infrequently angry that it is hard to recognize it. And with The Taker, she's so frequently confused that it's hard to see beyond it. What *is* the confusion? She likes him, she does. But there's something shouting *Stop!* inside of her. Sometimes it's loud, but sometimes it's so quiet that it's only a weird vibration.

She's unsettled.

Uneasy. But why?

He lied to her, she understands. The friends. It's a lie.

She does something unwise, because a middle-of-the-night text, no matter what its content, sends a message. It says, *I am thinking of you at this hour.*

Were your friends ever coming? she types.

She gets an answer right away.

???

You lied to me.

Sorry, he says. He adds a weeping emoji.

And then, a moment later: Worth it. Smiling emoji.

The ripple turns to a boil. God damn him! He manipulated her, and she's pissed. But then she has another thought. Something that nags. Something that troubles her and sets her on edge.

Do Lucy, Adrian, and Jules even exist?

Annabelle runs so hard through the east part of Rockford now, she almost feels sick. She is passing Rockford High when a Hostess truck flies by so fast that it spins her pack and almost topples her.

"Slow down, you fucker! This is a school zone!" Annabelle yells.

Annabelle *yells*. She yells something she'd never yell: *You fucker!* Her face is red and her eyes are narrow slits of rage. She stops, standing on a small hill, a zit on the landscape, where the Rockford High sign sits. School is in session. She can feel the hum in the building, and the lot is full, and there are only a few kids milling around during their free period. A studious-looking boy with a wheeling backpack freezes when he sees her, like an alarmed traveler stumbling upon a piece of unattended luggage at the airport.

What does she feel besides guilt?

Fury. *Rightful* fury.

Her heart is thundering. It's a tribe of horses crossing a freeway, making it to the other side thanks to their sheer number. When it slows, she feels a little foolish. She watches the Hostess truck disappear around a corner.

She starts running again. Her step is oddly energized; her heart feels lifted. The rage rumbles around nicely. Yes, okay, there was that offensive word shouted. And pardon her mouth, she thinks, pardon the mouths of the golf-course lady and the librarian and lots of other people who are angry about violence. Cover your ears if you have to, but wow—look. The power of fury. It's happening. Stuff is combining and bashing with other stuff. The road is working its magic. The miles are. Distance is. People are. She's healing.

She's *mobilizing*.

26

Now that she's running in more populated areas, Annabelle meets with her team via Skype daily. Right this minute, her logistics coordinator is drinking lemonade in their backyard and feeding ice to Bit, which the dog chases on the lawn. Her publicist and her financial adviser are sitting on towels on the beach at Golden Gardens. Annabelle is in her room at the Cherry Valley Hotel, wrapping her knee in an ACE bandage and looking out over the parking lot. Grandpa Ed is in the room next door, taking a nap before dinner. She swears she can hear him snoring through the wall.

"God, guys. Summer must be nice."

"Hey, tomorrow you're going to get your summer in," Olivia says. "It'll be a blast! So, when you get there, you've got to go to the information center first. You'll be meeting the Magic Waters manager, Bill McGuire, assistant manager Lindsey Russell, and staff. Are you writing this down?"

"Okay, okay." Annabelle finds a sheet of Cherry Valley Hotel stationery and takes notes.

"Susan Markette, from the *Belvidere Daily Republican*, will be there, too. Photos will be taken, so smile. Also, you will see the debut of the red T-shirts, and they look awesome, if I do say so myself. Show her, Malc."

Malcolm pans across their backyard, where Gina sits in a lawn chair, cooling her feet in a blow-up baby pool. Over her bathing suit is a red Run for a Cause T-shirt. Gina sets her arms into a strongman pose and shouts, "Bring it!"

"Wow, Liv, they look great, even if the model is a little overly enthusiastic."

Zach's face and skinny shirtless chest fill the screen. "We've already sold two hundred. Also, the GoFundMe is over fifty thousand."

"Put your shirt on. I can't concentrate. I thought you said fifty thousand."

"I did."

"Fifty *thousand*? As in *dollars*?"

"You're going to have to start thinking beyond this race. You know, foundation-wise. You've got way more money than you need."

"Foundation-wise?"

There's a very loud slurp as Malcolm reaches the end of his cup. Then: "I hate when the ice hits you in the face," he says.

"Wait a minute," Olivia says. "She's not losing it."

"You're not losing it," Zach says.

"Go ahead and lose it," Malcolm says. "We're prepared."

"I told you she wouldn't lose it!" Gina yells offscreen.

Annabelle looks out the window, gazes across the parking lot into the town of Cherry Valley beyond. She thinks about what Dr. Mann said during their last phone session. She doesn't have to respond to the press of anything or anyone. She can take her time to decide things.

"I'll think about it," she says.

"I thought Mom made you get rid of all your Hawaiian shirts," Annabelle says to Grandpa Ed as they hunt for a parking space in the lot of Magic Waters water park.

"Your mom doesn't make me do anything. I told her I did, but I didn't."

"Agnelli Curse."

"Look at this beauty. You think I'd get rid of this beauty? Your grandma got this for me on our honeymoon in Maui."

"Socks with your bathing suit, though, Grandpa."

"Do I tell you how to dress? *Che palle!* Don't go sounding like your mother."

"Are you two ever going to just stop whatever is between you and get along?"

"I hope not."

"You hope not?"

"I worry. If she stops being mad at me, maybe she don't love me anymore."

Oh, love, it's so imperfect, Annabelle sees. She is thinking about her seventh-grade field trip to Wild Waves. She and Kat were fighting at the time. She can't even remember why. But she ignored Kat on purpose and hung out with Quinn Kapoor. They rode the raft together, and shared their popcorn, and Kat got stuck with Willy Zonka on the bus.

I'm sorry, she thinks.

Hey, Willy Zonka gave me a whole box of Hot Tamales, Kat says. *Next time, a trip down his chocolate river.*

"Hurry up, would ya?" Grandpa Ed says. "Don't forget our towels. Don't forget our bag."

"I haven't seen you this excited since the Sons of Italy newsletter said that Festa d'Italia would be happening when we're in Chicago."

"Best day of my life, right here."

"I thought you couldn't swim."

"I can swim. Who told you I couldn't swim?"

"You did, way back when we were by Flathead Lake."

"I said *deep water*. I said I don't like deep water. Look at this beautiful day, huh?"

He's right. It *is* beautiful, and Annabelle can maybe even see his point about it being the best day of their lives. She and Grandpa Ed are already bickering like an old married couple, but look. In the distance she can see the orange and blue and green loops and swirls of the rides. The sky is blue, blue, blue, and Grandpa Ed—in his Hawaiian shirt and shorts and socks and sandals—is whistling, and jingling his keys in his pocket. The whistling doesn't even annoy her.

What is she feeling, besides guilt?

Gratitude.

Gratitude that she's alive.

The line is long. School is out, and Magic Waters is a popular place. As she heads to the information center, she sees a huddle of people in red T-shirts. And then she suddenly stops. She grabs Grandpa Ed's arm.

"How crazy. I could have sworn I just saw Luke."

Grandpa Ed is still whistling. She socks him. "Did you put your hearing aids in? I said, I swear I saw Luke."

"I put my hearing aids in."

"He's gone now. I just saw—well, I guess other people might have that hair and those clothes. Just, it's not as usual out here."

Whistle, whistle, tweet, tweet.

"That must be the manager, Bill McGuire. The one with the clipboard."

It is. He waves them over. He introduces Annabelle to various visitors in Run for a Cause shirts. There are students, parents, and a few people from community outreach organizations. Annabelle thanks them. She shakes hands. She gets her photo taken. "Hey, wait," Bill McGuire says. "Lindsey, the swag." There are Magic Waters beach bags for her and Grandpa, Magic Waters water bottles, and two Magic Waters T-shirts, featuring a photo of the Typhoon Terror and its screaming riders with their arms in the air. Before Annabelle can avert her eyes, Grandpa Ed is unbuttoning his shirt and revealing his white old-guy boobs and slipping the bright yellow T-shirt over his head.

"Your grandma always said yellow was my color. Whatta you think?"

Annabelle thinks he should have gotten an extra-large. He looks like an expectant mother. She hopes his labor doesn't start on the Typhoon Terror.

"You look awesome."

"We have some for your friends, too," Lindsey says.

"Our friends?"

"They were just right he—"

"Hey, Annabelle," Luke Messenger says.

Annabelle is in shock. She taps her thumb to her fingers. Here is Luke Messenger in Cherry Valley, Illinois. Her stomach is flopping around weirdly and she hasn't even been on the Typhoon Terror yet. How does she feel? Glad. Glad to see him.

"I can't believe you guys are here," she says.

"When Mim called to tell me your grandpa invited us to come out, I said, 'I'm in.' I was already getting stir-crazy at home. Dad gave me a curfew when I got back. I had to get out of there before Mom started holding my hand when I crossed the street."

"Grandpa didn't tell me! I'm really glad to see you. I've

listened to your tape a thousand times. I've read *Endurance* at least ten."

"Dog steaks . . . Sorry."

"I love that book."

"I feel terrible confessing this, but I've given up my running," Luke says.

She laughs.

"We're here for a week. We're going to follow you down to Chicago and then stay and play around the city. I've never been to Chicago. You?"

"No. Never." She calculates. Seventy-nine miles. Luke and Dawn Celeste will be with them for five days.

"I hope you don't mind us crashing your party."

"I don't mind."

"Your grandpa said he asked."

Agnelli Curse. "I'm sure he wanted to surprise me. It's a great surprise."

"Awesome. Come on. Race you to the Screaming Lizard."

They ride the Screaming Lizard and the Double Dare Drop and then they hang out at the wave pool. Annabelle's having so much fun. She's drenched, and she's trekking around in her bathing suit like a little kid at the neighborhood pool. It's so hot that no one has a T-shirt on anymore. She's just herself, and the Run for a Cause supporters are, too, and all she can see in every direction is a great array of bodies splashing and swimming and sunning and having the best time ever.

"Look," Luke says. He gestures toward the winding curves of the Splash Magic River, where the riders sit in tubes and float along a moving channel. She spots them—Grandpa Ed in his palm tree trunks and Dawn Celeste in an aqua one-piece, their fingers linked, their tubes bumping as they glide along the water.

"Oh my God," Annabelle says.

"She's in love."

"She is?"

"Isn't he?"

"Oh, wow. I thought the brooding and the staring and the bursts of energy were from being cooped up with me in the stupid RV."

"She does that thing you do when you're in love, where she keeps finding reasons to drop his name into the conversation. You can be talking about going to a burger place and she'll say, 'Ed likes burgers.'"

"Really?"

"You seem shocked."

"I guess it's weird to think of him as the object of someone's romantic interest."

"I don't know. . . ."

"I mean, look."

Grandpa Ed spots them and waves. The pale flesh under his arm flaps like a flag. "Woo-hoo!" he shouts, like he's going down a rapid.

"Okay. I see your point."

Dawn Celeste waves, too. So does her underarm flab. She blows a kiss. Her bathing suit is a blue and green splash of batik. "They're happy," Annabelle says. Happiness seems like a miracle. Happiness seems like something that maybe always should be celebrated.

"I hope they don't do anything that makes us related," Luke says.

He gives her a look she can't decipher. But then he takes her fingers, same as Grandpa Ed and Dawn Celeste. "Typhoon Terror awaits," he says, and yanks her forward.

"He's giving her something."

"Tell me it's not a ring box."

"No. It's not a box. Something round? I can't tell."

"My eyes are bad. I think I need glasses," Annabelle says.

The four of them have just finished dinner in the hotel restaurant, and now Luke and Annabelle are on the second floor of the Cherry Valley Hotel, spying down at Grandpa Ed and Dawn Celeste in the lobby. They *needed a moment.* They *just wanted to say good night.* Luke and Annabelle crouch on the ground. It's hard to see around that big palm tree.

"It's, like, a little wood thing."

"A wood thing? Why would he give her a little wood thing?"

"He's putting it in her hand."

"Oh, God, we're awful."

"They're hugging. She's wiping away tears. Oh, God, don't look. Old people kissing."

"I might throw up my guacamole."

"She's holding it up to admire it. It's a wood thing, all right."

"Wait, wait, wait! Oh jeez! I know what it is! I know! He whittled that! He almost lost his thumb doing it. I thought it looked like a raccoon turd!"

"Raccoon turd of love," Luke says.

They bust up. They hit each other to be quiet. Annabelle muffles a snort, but this cracks him up, and that cracks her up, and they are both bent over and laughing silently, holding their stomachs.

"Wait—" He gasps. "Wait, wait." He's looking at her with big, round eyes of shock. This cracks her up anew.

"What?" she asks.

"You should see yourself."

"You should see *your*self."

They are round the bend, because they totally crack up again, and it isn't even funny.

"I know what the raccoon turd is!" he says.

"What?"

"A bird."

"A bird? What kind of bird?"

"Don't hate the messenger, here, okay?"

"What kind of bird," she says sternly.

"Mim has a . . . a bird. A dove. Tattoo. On her, um, lower back."

"How low?"

"Really low."

"Oh my God."

"You see everything when you're two people in a camper."

"You're telling me. But, a dove on her ass that he whittled . . ."

"It has great meaning to her. The dove, not the ass. She, like, saw one when she first fell in love with my grandpa."

"I get it. I get the tearful meaning of the dove raccoon turd."

"It's sweet! Don't you think it's sweet? Dove-ass-tattoo-raccoon turd?"

They bust up again. They laugh so hard that no sound comes out.

He is gasping. She is gasping. "Stop, stop, stop," she says. "I can't breathe."

"Good thing she didn't have, like, a mermaid back there. He would have needed a bigger piece of wood and more skills."

"We're awful. We're so awful," she says.

"You're awful. I'm a hundred percent in favor of whittled ass-tattoos of love."

"I've got to go to bed. This day has been . . ."

She feels it. The whoosh of guilt, coming in like water

through her broken ship. It wants to wreck her and toss her on the shore. *What do you feel besides guilt?* Dr. Mann asked.

Happy. She feels really happy. "This day has been . . . awesome. It has been so fun. But I've got sixteen miles to run tomorrow."

"Okay," he sighs. "Good night, then. Thanks for bringing the magic to Magic Waters."

27

It is hard to sleep. There's the air conditioner for starters—first too cold and then not cold enough and then noisy and blasting. There's the ice machine, clattering outside in the hall. There's a group of kids still swimming in the pool when it's supposed to be closed by ten p.m. There is Luke Messenger, taking her fingers at Magic Waters water park.

There is The Taker—

Stop!

Stop it, really. Will he ruin every moment of her life forevermore? Maybe not forevermore, but for a long time to come, yes, he will still be there shoving forward, reminding her not to forget him or anyone else.

Now, The Taker grabs her fingers under the library table after their night at Neumos. She doesn't exactly mind. She sort of likes the secret of it, the slow quiet of what is hidden. But he doesn't want slow, and he doesn't want hidden.

He wants to walk around the halls holding hands. He

wants to kiss her in the stairwell. He grabs her hand, he pulls her to him; she pulls away. He *presses.*

"God. It's like, you're the banana and he's the peel," Kat says.

He begins to text and call all the time.

"Who's calling you so late?" Gina says. "I don't like it."

Annabelle doesn't like it, either. It's too much too fast. She feels forced. He comes by Essential Baking Company when she's working and orders coffee. It flusters her. Once, afterward, she warmed up a raspberry muffin for two minutes and turned it hard as a baseball. Her boss, Claire, always kind and perceptive, asked if she needed to talk.

And that lie, the one about his friends the night of Neumos, it nags at her.

"What's Adrian's band called again?" she asks The Taker one night when he phones.

"Um, Loose Change."

"Do they play around here? We should go see them."

"They don't play much. And Jules is thinking about breaking things off. She says it's like she and Adrian are married. They never do anything."

"We could do something with them."

"Yeah, maybe."

"I can't believe you lied about them coming to Neumos."

He laughs. "I have my trickster ways."

"It's not funny! I don't like trickster ways. I like the truth."

He's silent.

"What?"

"I should tell you the truth, then."

"Okay." She is sitting on the floor in her room, her back against the bed. Her stomach hurts suddenly. She picks at the threads of her carpet. She feels like something bad is coming. Something bad *is* coming. Something worse than she could ever imagine.

"Remember when I told you that we moved in part because my mom thought I got in with a bad crowd? That this kid I know robbed an old guy?"

Oh God. Oh no. "Yeah."

"I was the kid."

She is silent. She doesn't tap her thumb to her fingers. Instead, with her free hand, she makes a fist and squeezes hard until she can feel her nails jab her skin.

"It's not as bad as it sounds. I mean, I didn't, like, rob-rob him. Not like, *stick-'em-up* rob him. My parents had this friend, Jim Hastings? He was a rich guy, lived alone. He used to teach at the university, too, but then his family sold some patent or something, for some kind of waterproof material, and he got rich and quit. He had this house on the water. And he kept inviting me over. Like, for jobs. To clean his pool, and paint his bathroom, and my parents thought it was great, but the dude gave me the willies. Like, he was always trying to be alone with me, and standing too close, and doing weird shit, like keeping me late to show me his rare-coin collection, and . . . ugh."

"That's awful."

"Yeah, so I finally was like, 'Fuck this. I'm not going over there. I don't care if he pays me thirty bucks an hour.' On the last day, I was finishing up this job. Spreading this big shitload of bark in his yard, and I put the tools away in the garage, and then I went in to use the bathroom and wash the splinters out of my skin, and after I dried my hands, I don't know, I just went in his bedroom and opened up his dresser drawer where the coins were, and I took all these plastic bags. They were rare coins and he just had them in Ziplocs, and I shoved a bunch of them in my pockets, and I got out of there and never went back."

"Oh, wow." She doesn't know what to say. "He had to know it was you."

"Of course he knew it was me, and my parents kept asking me, 'Why did you do this? Why?' And I didn't have an answer. I was just, I don't know. I felt like the dude violated me, and I wanted to do it back. I was drying my hands on that towel in his bathroom, and it was a white towel, and then it was smeared with dirt, and I thought, 'Good.' I was furious all of a sudden. I hated him."

"I can understand that." In a way she can.

"Yeah? You don't want me out of your life? At home, people avoided me after they heard. Not that most of those asshats were my best friends or anything before that, but still. My *real* friends ditched me. It *sucked*. Bad. It's not like I was a felon. No one pressed charges. He got the coins back. The whole thing was dropped. My parents thought it was because I was hanging out with these two guys, Kevin and Raine, and Kevin smoked pot and Raine was always depressed, but it was because I hated that dude Jim Hastings. Hated him and his creepy lips and fat fingers. He deserved it. He deserved worse, if you ask me."

Annabelle is disturbed. The man, Jim Hastings, and his fancy house, and the jobs, and The Taker and the coins and the hate disturb her. She doesn't know how to understand this story. In a way, she feels sorry for The Taker. But the story is distressing. And it is far from her own life. There is so much about the story and about The Taker that is just not *her* and *hers*. Will cheated on a test in the seventh grade and still felt bad about it. Kat's older sister, Becka, who didn't live with them anymore, got pregnant and had an abortion. That Bastard Father Anthony left them and became a priest, and Gina is so worried about stuff going wrong that she drives everyone crazy, but somehow this stuff is all above the surface, not below. She can see it and know what it is. She understands that Gina also has anxiety and that Father Anthony is emotionally removed.

She doesn't know what The Taker's story *is*. And she realizes that she really doesn't know him. The deep-down-inside him. The pieces that make him who he is. The pieces she sees—they are like foreign objects. His intensity and loneliness are, and so are the gun magazines that she sometimes sees him thumbing through during boring lectures, and the way he doesn't even seem to feel guilty for what he did. It reminds her of how she went to Kiley Tasmin's house for a sleepover in middle school, and saw a bong under her bed. Kat had to tell Annabelle what it was. She knew it was wrong, she knew it shouldn't be there, she knew it felt bad, but she didn't have a name for it.

"I'm glad you're not going to leave me," he says before they hang up.

She couldn't have known what was going to happen, Annabelle tells herself, when she thinks about his hand holding hers under the library table. There are all kinds of hands—careful ones, cruel ones, ones you can trust and ones you can't. You don't always know the difference until too late, but it's true, too, that ones as disturbed as The Taker's are rare. They are rare, she reminds herself.

Most hands are good.

Will's were.

This is a sucker punch. Her stomach reels. Her heart clutches.

Which are worse? The bad memories or the good ones?

Because now she feels Will's hands in mittens holding her hands in mittens. His fingers on her body. His fingers lift her hand to kiss it; his hands are on a steering wheel, and they cut a sandwich in half, and they hug his mom, and carry his lacrosse bag.

There is his finger, ringing her doorbell. It is shortly after The Taker tells her about stealing the coins. It is early May, and it is starting to stay light later, and she is home after work, an extra-busy shift since Claire had to stay home with her sick kid, Harrison. She and Mom and Malc had pancakes for dinner, so when she answers the door, the smell drifts out, and he says, *Mmm. Pancakes.*

She is surprised to see him. She lets him in. She can't believe he's there. She is so, so happy he's suddenly appeared like this, but nervous, too. She looks awful. Here, she thought it was a neighbor collecting signatures for some cause, but it's Will.

"Oh, God, I look—"

"Beautiful. My eyes are really happy right now."

He is in her house. He's so familiar, so terrifically familiar, it's almost like they should just go plop down in front of the TV and watch a show.

"Hi, Will," Malcolm says. He's running his finger in a syrup trail on the table, licks it.

"Gross, Malcolm."

"How've you been, Will?" Gina says. She beams at him. Annabelle can feel the wink of support she would love to give. The mood in the room lifts. They all feel happy. Or maybe Annabelle is just buoyant enough for everyone.

"We're going to—"

"Go talk. We'll be here if you need us!" Gina says cheerfully.

"Yep, we'll be here if you need us," Malcolm says. Now, he's the one who does it. He winks.

She and Will go upstairs. He pinches her butt playfully on the way up and she swats him, just like the old days. Wow, she has missed those brown eyes that look sweet as a deer's. She's missed his soft hair, and the smell of his shampoo. She's missed that easy familiarity.

In her room, he kisses her. Now *that's* the kiss she loves. Here's the boy she loves. They look at each other and smile and talk. And talk, and talk.

They make a decision that changes everything.

They make a decision that changes everything forever.

Luke's fingers, The Taker's, Will's. It is too much. Annabelle gets out of bed. She is holding her pillow. She clutches it hard. She walks in a circle around the beds and back. She walks in a circle. She walks in a circle. She walks in a circle.

28

1. Since his skin is translucent, you can actually see the heart of the glass frog at work.
2. The bar-headed goose has an unusually strong heart. So strong, the goose can fly over the Himalayas, 20,000 feet above sea level.
3. A giraffe depends on its powerful, twenty-pound heart to fight the force of gravity to get the blood all the way up its neck. Without that power, blood pressure would blow the giraffe's brains out whenever it leaned down to get a drink of water. Instead, he drinks with ease.
4. The ocellated icefish lives so far down deep in the frigid waters near Antarctica, his heart has to be five times larger than the average fish. Oxygen dissolves directly into their plasma, and so their blood is clear as the ice that surrounds them.
5. Hearts can perform miracles, too.

• • •

Annabelle hasn't slept at all, but she gets up early, before she sees Grandpa Ed or Dawn Celeste or Luke. She shoves down a breakfast of oatmeal and bananas, gets what she needs from the RV, and heads out. Loretta guides Annabelle out of town on Newburg Road, which has beautiful grassy banks with white houses tucked down long driveways. Next: the tiny town of Logan on Logan Street, and then Highway 20, with its flat yellow fields of alfalfa and corn and barley and wheat. A trucker passes; he honks and waves. Two women at a U-Pick farm stand offer her a bottle of water and a huge organic peach. They read in the *Cherry Valley News* that she'd be coming through. They ask if they can take her picture for their Belvidere Farmer's Market Facebook page.

Now, Garden Prairie, Illinois. Small houses, grand farmhouses, and the Paradise Park Campground, which would have been a perfect stop for the night, if it weren't a few miles shy of her destination: Marengo, Illinois.

She's almost there. The bottle of water is gone, and so is a lot of the water in the bladder of her pack. It's the end of June, and Grandpa Ed will soon be meeting her midway during the warmer weather, just to refuel her hydration. Tonight, they are parking overnight in the lot of the Methodist church, where the people of Marengo have the flea market on the weekends.

When she arrives, there's the RV and Dawn Celeste's rental

car, and there's Dawn Celeste and Luke and Grandpa Ed and a parking lot full of people. She is greeted by Cub Scout Troop 163, holding a big American flag. Behind them, there's an enormous red pickup truck and a huge smoker, along with some plastic tables and chairs. She smells it—barbecue. People are parking, walking over, and crossing the street with big Tupperware bowls and fat brown grocery bags. Two old ladies, who remind Annabelle of Mrs. Parsons and her best friend, Ms. Sadie, from Sunnyside Eldercare, sit in lawn chairs. Marengo is having a Methodist church parking lot picnic, starring her.

After short ribs and beans and potato salad and corn and lemonade, after the Cub Scouts present her with their most important badge, the patch for courage (featuring a boy in blue wielding a yellow shield), after she almost cries, and people clap, and the town disperses, and there is only the RV left in the parking lot, which is now cleaned up like none of it ever happened thanks to the Cub Scout troop, Luke sits on the hood of Dawn Celeste's rental car, and Annabelle sits next to him.

"You guys know how to live," Luke says. "That food was amazing. Did you have one of those brownies?"

"Yeah! More than one. Too bad you're going to miss the Union Lions pancake breakfast in the morning."

Luke and Dawn Celeste are taking off, staying overnight at the Days Inn at Annabelle's next stop, Dundee Township. "I told you, I've got to see the white cedars."

"'One of only three places where the ancient trees grow naturally.'"

"You got it. Brought to you by the Ice Age glaciers, and then nearly destroyed by man. Still surviving, in spite of all the bad shit people do."

Annabelle smiles. He says a lot to her without really saying it.

"I can't believe you guys are doing this. Taking a week out of your lives. I mean, this isn't exactly Hawaii."

"I'm just here for the white cedars. Mim's here for the sex."

"Oh, Jesus." Annabelle claps her hands over her ears.

"Don't look at the RV. Because if it's rocking . . ."

"Luke!"

"I'm actually here because it's the coolest thing I've ever been even remotely part of."

First the courage badge from Troop 163 and now this. Her eyes start to water.

"Come here."

She leans against his shoulder and he puts his arm around her. God, it feels good. She's not all nervous about it. He has a girlfriend. He doesn't talk about her much, but they don't do a lot of that kind of talking. They're always just in the here and now. Martinsdale Colony, the card games, the waterslides, the Cub Scout barbecue—enjoying what *is*. She'd almost forgotten about the here and now. But she's getting reacquainted with it. She's relaxed. She likes him so much. How does she feel? Good, good, good. So good, the guilt can't squeeze into the loop of his arm.

Dawn Celeste opens the door of the RV. Her cheeks are pink, and her long braid is over one shoulder. "Let's get on the road, Boo-Boo Boy."

"Boo-Boo Boy?" Annabelle teases. He is the least likely Boo-Boo Boy ever.

He grimaces. "Don't ask."

"Boo-Boo Boy Forester and Screaming Lizard Champ."

"Run hard tomorrow," he says.

"We know you don't like surprises," Zach Oh says that night. He's the only one at the Skype meeting tonight. Olivia is celebrating her sister's birthday, and Malcolm is having a sleepover. Zach is in his rec room. She sees a screen of Minecraft paused on his TV behind him. He's wearing his retro Atari T-shirt and is drinking a Red Bull. His mother would kill him if she saw that.

"Oh no. What?"

"It's good! It's a good surprise. Your mom—"

"Oh, God. I'm afraid."

"Don't be afraid. She's been awesome. She felt so bad about you missing graduation."

"*I* didn't feel bad about missing graduation." Which is true, but not true. She didn't feel bad about missing all the horrible stuff—the tributes, the look back at the shattered graduating class. But she did feel bad after seeing the photos of her friends with their arms around each other. The smiles, the tears, the hugging. And maybe worse—the shots of the parents, the siblings. She looked at the large image of her graduating class in their seats, wearing their hats and shiny gowns. She found the spot where she'd be sitting. Between Oliver Abbey and Riley

Allan. She moved her finger along the rows. That's where The Taker would be. That's where—

Stop!

What did she feel besides guilt?

Shame, remorse, regret, responsibility—all of the siblings of guilt.

Sadness. Grief.

"You don't sound excited."

"I couldn't hear you. You went fuzzy."

"I said we're coming to Chicago. Your mom and Malc, me and Olivia. It's kind of like a graduation celebration."

"You guys, too? How can you afford this?" Can a heart lift and sink at the same time?

"Olivia's mom had air miles. You'll be staying at a Best Western downtown, but your dad—"

"My who?"

"Your father, Our Father, haha—wait, no joke. He worked with the Catholics for Nonviolence of the Chicago Archdiocese, and they got me and Olivia an off-campus apartment of Saint Xavier's to use for the weekend."

"You're kidding."

"Last week, he had a bunch of Boston College students talking about Run for a Cause on Catholic TV."

"Why don't I know about this?"

"We just found out. Your mom told us. He's been calling her for regular updates, and he's been, what, *quietly supportive* over there. I guess the dude is showing his love in his own way."

"Wow. They've been talking? Like adults? I can't believe it."

"Have you heard from him at all?"

"An e-mail every now and then. An awkward phone call. But nothing like *regular updates*." She's kind of pissed at this magic trick, how she's gone from unseen to seen in her father's eyes, but it's also kind of nice, too. "Huh. I guess it's *progress*, right? I think I like it."

"Still, the whole no-sex thing . . ."

"Zach!"

"The point is, get ready to party in the Windy City, graduate."

"Since you don't like surprises . . . ," Malcolm says when he calls the next morning. It's nice to talk to just him instead of the whole team. His voice sounds ragged after the sleepover, like he's been screaming at a rock concert.

"You guys are flying into Chicago tonight! I already know."

"Me and Mom. Carl Walter has a division meeting in Bend. But Zach and Olivia are coming, too. And Dad-Father Anthony . . ."

"I heard. It's weird."

"He sent me a collection of *Nova* videos."

"*That's* lucky."

"He's been calling me and Mom to check in on your run. He says he has a map on his wall, and he puts pins in it every hundred miles."

Something about this—the map and the pins—makes her

remember things about her dad besides the fact that he left. How he used to hide behind the couch when they played fort with their Nerf guns. How he used to throw a bunch of dog biscuits in the air for their old dog, Rally, shouting, *Treats for no reason!* How she and Malc used to really like to do stuff with him, even if it was cleaning out the garage.

"Wow. And Mom's okay with all this? Has she turned into a new woman?"

"She's been seeing Dr. Baker every week for counseling, plus anti-anxiety medicine. She let me ride my bike to 7-Eleven and I didn't even have to call when I got there."

"That's amazing."

"The science museum in Chicago has a rocket simulator."

"Too bad not a real rocket."

"I'd go with you if you blasted into space."

"Thanks, butthead."

"And another miracle. Sean was at Nathan's party last night and he said he was sorry for being a dick."

"That's awesome, Malc."

"I think it's the corno mom got me."

"Are you *wearing* it?" A corno looks like a tiny chili pepper, but it's a small, twisted red horn, meant to ward off the evil eye and any curses to your manliness. Italian guys wear them on gold chains.

"It looks cool. Zach wants one."

"Zach *needs* one. Hey, Malc? I've got a worry."

"Just one?"

"Another one. We'll have, um, *friends* with us when you see us tomorrow."

"Is that bad?"

"Mom isn't going to like it."

"What, are they Harley guys?"

"Not quite. Remember those two people who came to my party? The ones who got me during the lightning storm? Let's just say Grandpa has a new girlfriend."

There's a moment of silence. And then, Malcolm starts laughing so hard and for so long, she has to close her eyes and wait it out.

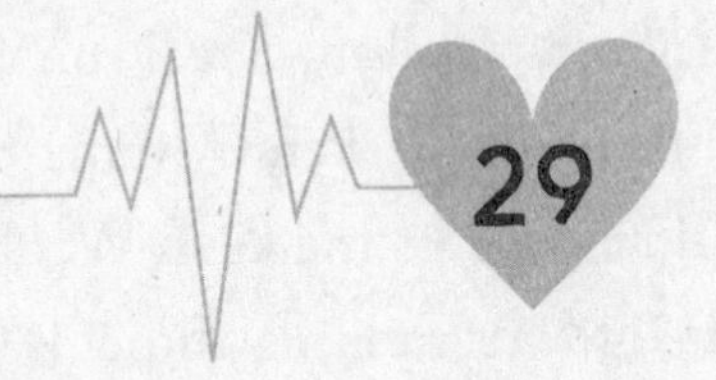

West Dundee to Parkridge to Chicago. Loretta takes Annabelle straight down Milwaukee Avenue, and across Lake Street. They take a right toward the Buckingham Fountain, her stop for the day.

She is in Chicago. She can't believe it—she's here in a city she's never been before, all by the power of her own self. Today, she feels great. It's muggy, and the air is locker-room sweaty, and her clothes are sticking to her everywhere they can stick. But she feels strong and good, and being in an actual big city is a shot of adrenaline.

Look—skyscrapers! People! The smell of grilling onions and car exhaust and heat on asphalt! A giant sea that is actually a lake, filled with boats. It is beautiful here. And now, at Grant Park, there's a wide green lawn, with a cool fountain of sea creatures shooting water from their mouths. After one day to play, after she says good-bye to Luke and Dawn Celeste and her friends and family, she and Loretta will head straight down the Lakefront Trail, past the aquarium and Hyde Park and the science museum. She'll run all the way to Pittsburgh and then through the Pennsylvania townships and down the 355. She'll race across the Civil War battlefields of Monocacy and Germantown, running through Gaithersburg and Rockville and Bethesda, Maryland. And then she'll arrive in DC.

The last forty-six days of her trip.

The point is: the finish line. She can see the end of this impossible journey she started way back at Dick's in Seattle. It is thrilling, but it is terrifying. Seth Greggory waits for her at the end.

"Stop."

She does not shout this, but says it calmly, because she wants to take this in, this *now*. The Buckingham Fountain is in front of her, and this fountain in Grant Park is considered the city's front door.

She walks through.

She walks through, and on the big grass lawn around the fountain, among the dads with babies in backpacks and dogs and tourists taking photos, there's Gina and Grandpa and Dawn Celeste and Luke and Malcolm and Zach and Olivia, and they are all wearing leis, and they are holding this huge sign, and she recognizes Malcolm's big blocky writing on it. The sign says CONGRATULATIONS, GRADUATE.

Okay, it's all ridiculous and corny, because unfortunately and fortunately, some of life's biggest moments get wrapped up in corny, Annabelle is beginning to understand. Love is corny, when you get right down to it. It has two left feet. It trips over itself, because it is so large that it's awkward. It's sort of silly, done right. After all, how do you convey something that huge? Big signs made with colored markers and printer paper taped together. Plastic leis bought from Party for Less.

"Oh my God!" she screams in fake surprise. A gift for a gift; love offered, love returned. "You guys!"

"Happy graduation, baby," Gina says, and hugs her.

"I am so sweaty!"

"Do you think we care?" Gina says. Her eyes are teary. "I am so thrilled to see you right now."

"Happy graduation, baby," Malcolm, the smart-ass, repeats, and hugs her, too.

"Happy graduation, baby," Zach Oh says.

"Happy graduation, baby," Luke says, and Olivia says, and Dawn Celeste says.

And wait . . . They're all here together and they seem fine. Stuff worked itself out without her being around to make sure it did. It seems like a miracle, but it's just what happens a lot of times when you let go.

"Oh, you all are hilarious. You all are a big bunch of jokers," Gina says.

"Happy graduation, baby," Grandpa Ed says to Gina, and hugs her.

Annabelle takes the fastest shower of her life in her and Malcolm's room in the Best Western. She forgoes all of the usual motel thrills, like unwrapping the soaps and hunting for the Bible. Everyone is waiting in the lobby and she can hardly wait to get there. When she rides the elevator down and heads across the floor, she can hear them laughing and talking loudly. Her past and her present have collided to make something new. How has this happened? Annabelle thinks of the mysterious universe, how atoms of light can undergo fusion if they're squeezed under enough pressure. There is a transformation, a balance of forces. A star is born.

They're a large group, so they pair up as they walk down Taylor Street, heading toward Festa d'Italia, the three-day street fair happening right now in Little Italy. They pair up and then change partners, like a variation on the tarantella, the Italian dance of celebration. Annabelle can hear the music just ahead, and there are red and green banners looped across the street. She is walking with Zach.

"Smell," she says. Garlic, olive oil. She is suddenly starving. "Give me whatever that is."

"A truckful."

"Dump truck, tilted into my mouth." Zach is so skinny that this makes Annabelle smile.

"I can't believe any of this, can you? Look where we are."

"It's always weird to fly on a plane. Seven hours ago, I was in my bed and my mom was hunting in my bag to make sure I had my toothbrush."

Annabelle looks over at Zach, at the profile she's seen sitting next to her at elementary school assemblies and high school basketball games and the floor of his living room, playing Minecraft. But he looks older. She suddenly sees him in his middle school PE uniform, and then in his orchestra suit at the funerals, and now, looking like a *man*. Her heart rises, falls, and rises again. "I'm so happy you guys are here."

Zach's heart must be rising and falling and rising, too. "I wish—" He swallows. His voice is a little squeaky. He clears his throat. She's afraid of what he's going to say. But someone should say it.

"I wish—" He tries again. "You know. That Kat was here."

Annabelle squinches her eyes up tight. She feels the gut-sock in the hollow spot where her ribs meet.

"I know." Her voice is barely audible over the music.

"She would have—"

Loved it. Been so proud. Celebrated harder than anyone. "I know."

Zach Oh puts his arm around Annabelle's shoulder and squeezes.

Grandpa Ed is devouring a meatball sandwich as he stands at the curb outside of Salvatore's. Across the street at Patio's, a man in a white apron grills sausages. On a nearby stage, a woman sings "Funiculi Funicula" to a background of mandolins and guitars. On another, a guy group called Grande Amore belts "O Sole Mio" as Zach and Luke and Olivia watch, Olivia licking the cream from the end of a cannoli. The street is packed. A baby cries; there is cheerful crooning.

"Pancia mia fatti capanna!" Grandpa shouts to his *famiglia* across the street.

"'My tummy, make yourself a hut,'" Gina translates. "Basically: Get ready to eat a lot."

"I love a man who enjoys his food. I love a man who takes life in," Dawn Celeste says to Gina.

Annabelle sees it—Dawn Celeste's adoring gaze on goofy Grandpa Ed, who wears his socks with his sandals and has a thumbprint of tomato sauce on his chin. Annabelle also sees Gina, witnessing the same thing. Hearing the same thing. The word *love.* Gina narrows her eyebrows, and then they soften. One corner of her mouth edges up into a smile. She catches Annabelle's eyes. Annabelle shrugs.

"You want a meatball sandwich like that, Malc?" Gina asks him.

"I want four of them."

"Come on. Let's get you as many as you can stuff inside of yourself," Gina says.

"Tummy, make yourself a hut," Malc says.

They wait in line at Salvatore's outdoor booth. Dawn Celeste wanders back to join Grandpa. It's the three of them now, Annabelle, Gina, and Malcolm. The three of them have been through a lot together. "So, he's in love," Gina says.

"I know nothing."

"More has been going on than just running across the country."

"What happens in some small town in Montana stays in some small town in Montana."

"Time marches on," Gina says wistfully.

They move from the street fair to an early-evening boat ride around the city. It's an architectural tour, but no one is listening to the guide. Zach and Olivia hold hands and gaze up at the buildings. Grandpa Ed holds Dawn Celeste's hand and kisses her cheek.

"Smoochey-smoochey," Malcolm says.

"Come here, dude. I'll hold your hand if you're feeling left out," Luke says. A giant green building slides past in the yellow light of the late hour.

"Road trips are cool," Malc says.

"Forget it," Gina says.

"The light looks pretty on your hair, Ma," Annabelle says. It does. The glow has turned everything golden.

"Every light looks pretty on your hair, my Bella," her mom says.

"I'm seeing why the Mim-Ed thing works." Luke pushes his chair back from the long table at Toscana's. "Food, glorious food. I can't believe I'm telling you this, but I wish I could unbutton my pants."

"There's a reason for this sundress." It's a beautiful sundress with sunflowers on it—a graduation present from Gina.

"Oh jeez. Don't look," he warns.

Three men appear with a sheet cake. It is her third cake on this trip, and each one feels different. Each marks a time, a place, and an occasion that is miles out from the one before.

"I am going to bust, but I have to try that," Luke says.

One of the men has an accordion, another a tambourine. After the cake is set in front of her, they begin to sing "Bella Ciao." It is a fast and festive song, with a repeated line that's almost shouted: *O, bella, ciao! Bella, ciao! Bella, ciao, ciao, ciao!* Each *ciao* is punctuated with a hearty tambourine hit.

The crowd, her crowd, knows what to do. They sing along. They clap at every *ciao.* Zach Oh is shouting the words, and so are Olivia and Luke and Dawn Celeste, and they've all caught on and are clapping, and Malcolm adds a little fist in the air at each punctuation. His fist is appropriate. The song is about Italy's freedom from invading Nazi fascists.

"Happy graduation, Bella," her mom says.

Annabelle is exhausted. The lights are off and Malcolm is already asleep in the bed next to her when she hears the voices in the Best Western hallway. The voices are intense but not heated, not yet. She knows who's out there, of course. Oh, God, she hopes this magical day doesn't end with a fight.

She creeps out of bed.

With her ear against the door, she can't hear all that well, but well enough.

Do you see, Carina? Something, something—Annabelle

can't make it out. But she hears her name. *Annabelle*.

No, it is more like: *Annabelle?* With a question. He is asking if Gina understands something now because of her.

"What's happening?" Malcolm says.

"Shh."

"I want to hear." He's beside her. She can smell his warm toothpaste breath.

I tried, Carina. God knows.

She's as willful as Mom was.

Oh boy. Let me tell you.

You can't stop a person. You can't force your will.

That's it, Carina. That's right. The will comes right down the line with those two.

Malcolm pokes her. She hits him.

Come here. Give me a hug.

Love you, Pops.

Love you, Carina.

Get some sleep.

There's the sound of key cards in slots, the *kashunk* of doors opening and shutting.

"We've just eavesdropped on a miracle," she says.

"They'll be fighting again by tomorrow."

"Have some faith, butthead."

He smiles. Raises one eyebrow. Stupid genius Malcolm. He realizes before she does: She just told him to have some faith.

Two miracles in one night.

• • •

Annabelle takes the next day off, and the group goes first to the Field Museum of Natural History and then to the Museum of Science and Industry. Dinosaurs to rocket ships: the oldest things, and the ones still in the future. Dinner is hot dogs on Navy Pier. She loves this city so much. She has maybe had the best time she's ever had in her life.

She tells everyone this the next morning as they all hug good-bye. She's suited up and ready to go. Her family and friends will head out to the airport at various intervals.

"I've had the best time," she says to Zach, and Olivia, and to her mom and Malcolm.

"I'm going to miss you," she says to Luke.

"I'm going to miss *you*. Mim has already been asking about meeting you guys in Pittsburgh for your talk at Carnegie Mellon."

"Oh my God, I am so scared for that. I still have no idea what I'm going to say. I would love to have you guys there."

"You're going to be great, no matter what you tell them."

"Is your grandma serious about coming? It's so crazy, going to these random places because of me."

"We like your random places. But I don't want to keep crashing your party unless you want that, too." He takes her hands.

"Is this going to bother Sammy? You guys spending so much time with us?"

"Sammy?"

It seems cruel of Luke, to forget his girlfriend like this.

"Sammy *Jackson*? Your, um, *girlfriend*?"

"Sammy? Sammy isn't my girlfriend. I know I've maybe mentioned her a few times, but she's my . . . my Zach equivalent."

"She is?"

"You thought I had a girlfriend all this time?" He starts laughing. "Oh man! You must have thought I was such an asshole."

"I didn't think you were an asshole, I thought you were—" Safe. She doesn't say it. "Friendly. Being friendly."

He stops laughing. "Oh, shit. Oh, wow. I like you, Annabelle. Maybe I haven't been clear about that. I just thought . . . I mean, after what you've been through, Jesus, I'd be a dick if I didn't understand we need to go slow as hell here, right? Does this change things?"

She's not sure. Does it? It should. But standing there, he's just the same Luke Messenger from yesterday, the one who sat beside her on the Ferris wheel at Navy Pier and wouldn't open his eyes the entire time.

"I don't think so," she says. "No, I don't think it does." This is a surprise. She checks in with herself, as Dr. Mann has suggested. It feels calm in there. It feels calm and even accepting. Her palms are a little sweaty, and her heart is beating a bit fast, but it's just her and Luke here, and everything's okay. *Slow as hell* means time to breathe and think and say what she needs to say. *Slow as hell* is a capsule of respect for her boundaries. Respect for her boundaries equals safety. She wipes her palms on her shorts.

"Well, that's a relief. Because I *really* like you. I like *this*." He ticks his finger in the space between her and him. "Apparently it's a generational Agnelli-Messenger thing."

"Apparently it is."

"Give me a hug," he says. She does. She hugs him hard. She lets the hug say all the things she can't. He kisses her cheek. It's a kiss that's as sweet and relaxed as the one Grandpa Ed gave Dawn Celeste on the boat ride. "See you in Pittsburgh?"

"See you in Pittsburgh."

"I'm just going for the nearby Buchanan State Forest, home of old-growth hemlocks."

She smiles.

And on her run that day, and for many days after, when thoughts of Luke kick up nerve-dust and angst-gravel, she tries to think of those hemlocks. The way they grow slow as hell. The way they last.

30

1. In 1651, a freak accident leaves the son of an English aristocrat with a gaping hole in his chest. This allows people actually to look inside his chest to observe the heart, and to even reach in and touch it.
2. In 1818, physicians attempt to operate on the heart. Napoleon's surgeon, the baron Dominique Jean Larrey, performed the first operation. The patient dies within a month.
3. In 1896, English surgeon Stephen Paget says that heart surgery is impossible. "No method, no new discovery, can overcome the natural difficulties that attend a wound of the heart."
4. In 1925, Dr. Henry Souttar performs a successful heart operation on a young girl and saves her life. However, the medical community ridicules him for the effort, and he's never able to repeat his success.

5. Today, hearts can be repaired and even transplanted. Still, there's not much that can be done if a bullet rips right through the center of one.

He is waiting for her, of course.

The Taker.

Did she really think he'd go away for good?

He's been waiting it out, and so has Seth Greggory. She's had her fun, her little party, all those distractions in the Windy City, but there are a lot of miles of farmland in between Illinois and Pittsburgh. In the 154 miles from Chicago to Fort Wayne, Indiana, there are only three large towns, and the 240 miles across Ohio are primarily pasture, hay, and row crops of corn. This is twenty-four days of heat, exhaustion, and monotony. Grandpa Ed must meet her every five miles with water. She tries to approach every day as if the run is her job. She puts her head down, concentrates. But The Taker stalks her, like a cheetah stalks a gazelle in the open savanna.

He will make her look. He will force her to see the misery she's caused. She hasn't looked, not really, not since that night. She's only allowed little pieces in. Brief images, flashes, no story lines. No *from here to there*.

But out here, there is only *from here to there*. She is way, way too alone. She is way, way too close to the end. When you're trying to go forward, you can't escape going back.

She tries to keep him away. She listens to Luke Messenger's tape, and to the other music Zach gave her as a graduation present. She counts—silos and hay barrels and barns. It doesn't matter if she loses track; the only thing that matters is that she keeps counting. She keeps him away by chattering with Grandpa about meaningless facts of various small towns, keeps him away by answering the encouraging texts from Luke, keeps him away with calls to Dr. Mann. Keeps him away by talking with Olivia about the growing, growing numbers of their GoFundMe, about the invitations that are piling up for her to visit schools and community centers. She can't make any plans past September, though.

Silly. He can't be kept away! He will never, ever be away.

There he is. He is sitting on the porch of a farmhouse on Liberty Union Road in Scott, Ohio.

She shuts her eyes. It's heat exhaustion. She drinks water. She tries to flush him out. It is August. He shimmers in the sunrays on the Crawford-Huron County Line Road in Ohio. He sways in the alfalfa of Seneca Township.

She sees him in the cornfield several miles past, in Sullivan Township. Township to township to township, she counts and taps her fingers together. The Taker is getting like this, stalking her, pacing, because she's getting nearer and nearer to the point where she will stand on a stage and tell his story.

The dead heat of summer in farmland almost kills her. Outrunning The Taker is the only way she stays sane and goes on. But The Taker just waits. He wins, remember? A gun always makes you the winner. Violence does. That's the point of it.

She is in Chippewa Township, Pennsylvania. The farmland

has briefly changed to a forested trail surrounded by low mountains, and this is likely what does it. The forest looks more like home. It looks like the trail that she and Will hike after the night he comes over. Will packs a lunch of his favorite peanut butter and honey sandwiches and chips and Gatorade. They go on that trail, and they are happy. They barely make it to the end, because there's so much kissing and so much happiness.

They're together again. Within days, they're in their usual routine of calling every night before bed and texting in the morning, except it's better. It's all new but not new, sweeter from the longing and the reunion. She doesn't know what Robert and Tracie think about this. She doesn't care. No, wait—what's better is that *Will* doesn't care. Will is going against their wishes, and this says something to her, something large.

"Are you sure?" Kat asks. "He put you through so much."

"Very sure."

Something old but new again, and it feels completely right. His hands do. And so does his laugh, and the passenger seat of his car, and his favorite hoodie, with the string lost in the laundry long ago.

"You seem happy," The Taker says at lunch. She hears the question in it.

"I do?"

"Very."

Clearly, some part of her knows it's dangerous to tell him about Will, because she doesn't tell him.

"What's there to be unhappy about?"

"Umm . . . ," he says, meaning, *I can give you plenty of reasons.*

And then, a few weeks after he appears at her house, Will comes to school to pick her up. It's Friday, and school is almost out, and she is taking the day off from both work and volunteering. It's sunny and warm and they're going to go swimming at Green Lake, and then out to dinner at Serafina, a real restaurant. A date.

Will's out front, waiting. He's talking to Geoff Graham. Lots of Annabelle's friends had become friends with Will, too, and they're happy to see him.

Happy to see him . . . Oh, God, running on that wooded trail in Chippewa Township, Pennsylvania, it fills her. The joy of seeing Will standing there in his shorts and T-shirt.

"See ya," Geoff says, because it's very clear that Will's attention is elsewhere as soon as Annabelle comes out those double doors. She runs to him, and he picks her up. Her feet are off the ground. It's silly and sappy and teen-movie-ish, but who cares? She kisses him.

They kiss and kiss and he sets her back down on her feet. And when she's on the ground again, when she opens her happy, happy eyes, she sees him: The Taker. He's standing by the gym doors. He's staring at them.

Annabelle feels a terrible rod of guilt jam through her heart, guilt and . . . what? Something else. Unease.

"Let's get out of here," Will says.

• • •

Annabelle is meeting Grandpa in the small town of Beaver Falls, Pennsylvania. The forested trail lets out onto a two-lane highway with a scary, narrow shoulder. Finally, she drops down into a valley where there are houses on large parcels of land. She spots a young woman, walking with her phone crooked between her shoulder and her ear. She is getting the mail in the box by the road.

The Taker isn't letting go, is he? He is not letting her go now, just as he did not let her go then. This is Annabelle getting the mail. Wearing her shorts and a tank top and flip-flops. She gets the mail, and there's an envelope. It's from The Taker. She opens it right there, because it is strangely thick. It is so thick that she doesn't know how he even fit whatever it is into that envelope.

When she pulls it out, she gets a horrible, sick feeling, because it's a letter. An actual letter, written in tiny handwriting. Who writes letters anymore? She counts the pages. Thirteen. She has never written thirteen pages about anything in her life.

She reads the first few lines: *I just needed to put down into words how it felt to see you with the guy I know is Will. The reason I even know it's him is because Geoff told me. I had to ask, since you decided to keep it from me. I guess you were going for the maximum pain, letting me find out by seeing you like that.*

She stops reading. Or, rather, she skims the pages and sees that the content is all about the same: *How could you? You hurt me. I* loved *you. You* knew *that.* There's something about his birthday, him turning eighteen. How he was all alone and forgotten. How she ignored him on that day, after he'd made hers so special. She didn't know it was his birthday. No one did.

She's shocked. It's one thing to suspect what's in a person's head, and another to see the truth in actual words poured out page after page. There is the word *love*, but it's been stolen and used wrongly. Other words are used wrongly, too—*beautiful*, *future*, *us*. They sit beside a windstorm of rage. It's unsettling. She doesn't know what to do with this letter. She brings it inside, with the coupons for Papa Murphy's and QFC and the Puget Sound Energy bill. She leaves the letter out there on the counter.

She forgets about it momentarily because something else happens: He calls. When she sees his number appear, she recoils, as if she's just seen a poisonous creature. After that letter, she doesn't want to even touch her phone. The ringing stops. And then starts again. Stops. Starts. The poisonous creature retreats and appears again. She has to deal with it. As much as she doesn't want to get near it, it's her job to get the creepy thing out of the house once and for all. When the phone rings again, Annabelle answers, cringing as if the despicable creature is wadded up in a paper towel in her own hand. Her phone is crooked between her shoulder and her ear, just like the young woman who is walking into her front door right now in Beaver Falls, Pennsylvania.

"Belle," he says.

No. He *cries*. He is crying.

He is losing it. He is freaking out. It's like everything that was contained and hidden has been let loose. Abandonment has opened the door to the dark and ugly basement where the monsters have been waiting.

"What is this, Annabelle? What is this letter?"

"Mom!"

She is so glad to see her mom home from work. Gina is holding that letter. "This scares me, Annabelle. This is some scary shit."

Malcolm sits on a counter stool. He is still. He has stopped midway in the peeling of an orange. He does not interrupt to say that Gina owes him money for the swearing jar. He knows that this is too serious for that.

"He called. It's been a weird day. He saw me and Will yesterday."

"I think we should call someone. I don't know who. A counselor someone. The school counselor, maybe. I don't know. But we can't just let this—"

"He's just upset."

"Clearly. Thirteen pages of upset."

"I talked to him. I think he calmed down."

"Jesus, Annabelle. Thirteen pages."

"I talked to him. I think everything is okay."

She didn't think that, though. She didn't want Gina to worry. She told Will about it. He invited her over. They sat on his couch in the bonus room, same as always, and he wrapped his arms around her, and—this is awful, this is an awful thing to remember—she felt like it was some large drama that he was protecting her from. It was ugly but nice, the way his arms were around her.

The self-hatred floods back.

Yes, The Taker says. *Yes, yes, that's right. That's as it should be.*

She runs along the road, house to house. Two boys toss a baseball to each other. They are thin-legged and are wearing uniforms—striped pants and tall baseball socks, blue and red jerseys. It is cruel, this road.

Now she sees this: Malcolm—reader, scientist—is attempting his first sport, baseball, at the long-distance urging of That Bastard Father Anthony, former athlete. Former athlete fathers cause a lot of misery. Malcolm is gamely hanging in there, though he clearly hates to stand at home plate as the ball whizzes toward him. The tragedy that's coming will finish the season for him, the only good thing to come out of what's about to happen.

Annabelle and Will sit on a blanket on a grassy hill at Challenger Elementary, watching the game. Malcolm's uniform is blue and white. He is in the out-outfield. Gina is in the stands, but Annabelle and Will sit closer to Malcolm's outfield location, because Will is helping him. "That's the way, buddy! Mitt to the ground. Eyes on the ball." When it's Malcolm's turn to hit, they move the blanket. Malcolm loves Will. Annabelle does, too, and this is just one of the reasons.

Her phone buzzes. It's sitting on the blanket between

them. She looks at it. The Taker. She ignores it, and it buzzes again. Again. Again. The poisonous creature returns, no matter how many times she thinks it's finally gone.

"Who *is* that?" Will asks.

"It's him."

"If he doesn't knock this off, I'm going to handle him myself."

Annabelle looks around. She doesn't want to say it, because it sounds too dramatic, and she's not sure anyway. But she thinks she sees The Taker's car pulling out of the parking lot by the school.

31

Stop! she tries.

No good.

Stop, stop, stop!

There is no stopping. No stopping The Taker, no stopping her thoughts, no stopping her pumping legs, because she goes and goes and the thoughts come and come, and he's here. She is calling him. She is in her bedroom, and she calls him because she can't stand a minute more of this. She needs to smack that creature dead, because *enough is enough!* He picks up on the first ring.

"Belle," he says. "You're killing me, here."

"You've got to stop this. You're a great guy, but we were just friends. I care about you so much, but you've got to let this go."

She's lying. She doesn't care about him so much, not right now, not anymore, because he's scaring her. She just wants him to go away.

"I know we're supposed to be together. I *know* it. If I don't have that anymore, the hope of it . . ."

"Do we need to call someone? Are you—"

"What, going to hurt myself? Like you'd care?"

"Of course I'd care. I love you, like a friend, but I do. We all do. We care about you."

"I can tell," he says.

He knows she's not telling the truth. She doesn't love him. He's acting too frightening to love, and her lies are another rejection, but she's in an impossible bind she can't fake her way out of. She is tired. He's wearing her out. Enough is enough? Enough is *never* enough.

It gets worse, because he keeps this up. For days. He texts late at night. She spots him parked outside Sunnyside Eldercare. She switches tactics. She manages him. She *tries* to manage him, by being nice but not too nice, present but not too present. She thinks that if she just helps him through to the other side, kind of like Kat, kind of like how Kat helped Annabelle to the other side of her hurt after Will, then The Taker will be fine. She's responsible. She caused these feelings. She encouraged him, she was unclear, and now she's finally being clear. She hurt him, and dealing with that hurt is her job now. It is a big, uncontrollable, scary job. An exhausting one. She can't even run. She hasn't laced up her shoes in days. They sit empty by her bed.

After a week of this, he calls at two a.m.

"You need to stop calling me," she says. She hangs up. She

shuts off her phone. There are no tactics left except this one: no contact. None.

And then, the next afternoon, right after school, she calls the QFC, where The Taker works. She asks to speak to Lucy. She asks to speak to Adrian. There is no Lucy. There is no Adrian.

She can't believe it, and yet she suspected this all along. She is utterly and completely done now. A big X goes up in her mind over every single piece of the unnerving, unsettling idea of him.

That's it. Over. Finished. Discard.

Annabelle runs and runs down this awful Pennsylvania road, because now there is a car in a driveway, and its stereo is on, and music is pumping. *Stop! Stop!*

She puts her hands to her ears and presses. She can't. She can't go there or do this.

She has gone thirteen miles. Three short of her destination. After all of those lost days in Hayward, Minnesota, she has to stay on track now or she won't get to DC before she has to appear in Seth Greggory's office.

She wants to call Grandpa Ed to pick her up. She has been running a half marathon every day for nearly a month since Chicago, and her body is suffering. Suffering? It's been doing *that* for weeks and weeks. No, it's breaking down. It is saying *no more.* Way back in Cherry Valley, she started feeling the pain of runner's knee, and she's been trying to shorten her stride and avoid hard downhill runs, icing and wrapping it afterward, wearing a compression sleeve during the run itself. And every morning lately, she's also been dealing with a dull ache along the arch of her foot and a constant jab in her heel, which surely means plantar fasciitis, tears and inflammation of the tendons from her heel to her toes. Right now, her head starts to throb in the way that she knows means dehydration. She is breaking down and depleted and her mind is too full and she just can't go on.

She just can't.

"I'm taking you to a clinic."

"No."

"Don't argue. You're dehydrated. You're . . ."

Brittle, breaking, destroyed, because The Taker is sitting right next to her. She feels his warm breath on her cheek, hears him whispering in her ear. It's happening because the Carnegie Mellon students are waiting. Seth Greggory is waiting. The Taker himself is waiting. He is waiting, because he'll always be waiting.

She feels his fingers, pressing into her arm as he grabs it outside of class. After she hung up on him at two a.m., after she's gone 100 percent No Contact, he was absent for three days, and she's almost surprised to see him. In those three days, Gina called Mr. Curley, guidance counselor, and Mr. Curley pulled Annabelle out of class to tell him what was going on as she sat in his office surrounded by posters of Whitworth. Geoff's dad called Principal Garvey, too, after The Taker posted a photo of a gun on social media and then told Geoff that he was *feeling fucking dangerous.* It shook Geoff up. He thought it meant *suicidal.* People were talking, whispering. Making guesses as to why he was out of school. Rumors swirled, but then they heard that The Taker was getting help. It was all under control. Annabelle felt terrible, but after that call to QFC, she was glad he was gone, too. *It's not your fault*, everyone kept saying. She felt like she was walking on glass, and the three days of his absence felt pretty great. He was getting help, and she could breathe.

But now, here he is. Standing outside her last class. He grabs her wrist.

"We need to talk," he says.

"I have nothing more to say to you. Nothing," Annabelle says.

Geoff spots them. "Hey, man. Let her go," he says.

Let her go? Never.

Grandpa Ed has all three fans going in the RV and all of the windows are open, but it's still so hot in there.

"*Porca miseria!* I am not a doctor!" *Porca miseria*: Damn it! Literal translation: pig misery.

"Please. I just need to lie down."

"It's been over eighty all week. What if this is heatstroke? I don't know nothing about heatstroke."

"I'm fine. I promise you. Let me just lie down. Please. Please, no doctor."

They park at a rest area next to the Ohio River. Olivia calls. Grandpa Ed answers Annabelle's phone.

Annabelle listens to the low conversation. Grandpa Ed tells Olivia that he's not sure how much farther Annabelle can go. The summer heat is more than they anticipated. It is brutal. She's killing herself, he says. He tells Olivia all of the things Annabelle hasn't—how her knee pain has grown so that even prolonged spans of sitting hurt. How the compression sleeve doesn't seem to be helping anymore. How she's been popping anti-inflammatories and rolling her foot on a bottle of water to ease the agony in her arch. How her eyes are vacant and her body is so thin, because her muscles are actually shrinking and breaking down now. Her shorts barely stay up.

He buys food in town. Grandpa Ed and Annabelle eat burgers outside by the river. She is too tired for food. Too tired for nature. Too tired for whatever is living and flowing around her.

She sits in a camp chair and stares out until it is cool enough in the RV to sleep. She climbs into her bunk. Grandpa Ed begins to snore. The Saint Christopher medal shines in the moonlight, but even a saint seems small and powerless against what's coming.

She closes her eyes, and when she does, Annabelle hears the *thump, thump, thump* of the bass from the car she saw in that driveway today. She puts her pillow over her head, but she still hears it. *Bump-tha-thump-bump*.

"I have nothing more to say to you. Nothing," she says again to The Taker.

"Hey, man. Let her go," Geoff says again and again.

Because she knows then, doesn't she? The way The Taker's fingers drop suddenly from her wrist—Annabelle knows it's bad. She knows, because she's suddenly scared. Really scared. Something is coming. She knows and she doesn't want to know, so she tells herself she doesn't.

She tells herself he'll go away. She tells herself that everything is fine. She tells herself that it's no big deal. She tells herself that people older than her have things under control.

She tells herself that violence is something that happens to other people.

Annabelle gets dressed for the party at Geoff Graham's house. She wants to get excited for it, but she isn't. She feels sick about The Taker grabbing her at school, sick about shaking him off like that. She saw his face as she walked away. He wasn't just tearful and hurt. He was *pissed*.

Well, she's pissed, too. She's sick of him. She is so entirely, completely finished with him.

Annabelle tilts her chin up toward the bathroom mirror at home, puts her mascara on. It's a barbecue, a backyard party. It will get chilly later, so she wears her jeans and an orange T-shirt. Geoff Graham's parents have a hot tub, so she wraps her bathing suit up in a towel. She calls Will. He's meeting her there. He's working late, and he's driving over from the Eastside.

"I'm bringing my suit," she says. "In case we get a chance to get in the hot tub."

"Oh, nice," he says. "I'll bring mine, too. See you soon."

"See you soon."

She hunts for the keys to Gina's car. She spots them in a heap by Gina's purse.

"Don't be too late," Gina calls. "You know I worry. You know I wait up."

Of course Annabelle knows.

Annabelle stops at Greenwood Market. She buys a package of chips. She buys some mints. She plans on kissing Will a lot, and dancing, and having fun. All of her friends will be there—Kat and Zach and Olivia and Zander, lots of Geoff's friends from band. But The Taker won't be there. Geoff told him it might be best if he didn't come, and The Taker said it didn't matter anyway—he was going away for the weekend with his parents. What a relief. It's going to be nice to shake off some of the weirdness of what's been going on. School is almost out, and this'll be pre-summer fun.

There are lots of cars already. Annabelle parks behind the last one in the line on the street. Music is bumping. She can hear it from where she parks. *Bump, tha-thump, bump.*

She feels good. She feels mostly good. She's relieved to be there. Relieved that The Taker is gone and that Will is coming. She sees Kat's car, meaning Kat has already arrived.

She rings the bell. Geoff Graham answers. "Hey, chips. Thanks." He squeezes the bag twice in appreciation. "No one else brought anything. Losers."

"Hey, thank *you*. I mean, I smell *barbecue*."

"My brother's in charge of the hot dogs, because I cremate them. Beer's over there."

She shouldn't, her mother will smell it, but she does. She gets a beer, pops the cap, and takes a swig. It's cold and great. She rarely drinks, so the alcohol hits her immediately. She starts to relax. She can't wait until Will gets here.

"Belle Bottom! Get your sweet little ass over here!" Kat is in high spirits. She's talking with Sierra and Destiny. Zach and Olivia are dancing, and more people are pouring in. Annabelle hears loud laughter out in the backyard. People are getting into the hot tub already.

"Sister," Annabelle says to Kat, and flings her arm around Kat's shoulder. They have to shout a little over the music. Kat kisses her cheek.

"Oh my God, you guys are too much," Sierra says. "Did you plan that? You look like twins."

She's right. Annabelle and Kat are dressed alike. They both have on their jeans and orange T-shirts.

"Best friend mind meld," Kat says. "We don't have to *plan*, we just *know*. Is Will working?"

"He should be here any minute."

"Aww. Young love. I miss being in love."

"Poor Kit-Kat." Annabelle makes an exaggerated frown.

"Actually, I don't think I've ever really been in love."

Kat's at the end of her beer, maybe a second one, who knows. She's a tiny bit goofy and sloppy. But when Annabelle looks over at her, she realizes that Kat's serious.

"What?" Annabelle says. "What about Noah? You were crazy about him."

"Nah. I don't think so. It hasn't happened yet."

"That makes me sad!"

"Don't be sad, be glad. It's still *coming*."

"Yeah. That *is* good." Annabelle smiles. "God, I can't drink beer. I've got to go pee."

"We'll save your place," Sierra says.

Annabelle goes upstairs. She passes Trevor Jackson coming down. Two girls from band, Desiree and Hannah Kelly, wait in line by the door. "A line, really?"

"Josie's been in the parents' bathroom forever," one of the girls answers.

Annabelle waits. Finally, it's her turn. She's fussing with her makeup. She's putting on lip gloss. She wants to look good for Will. Her beer is on the bathroom counter. She washes her hands. She's about to grab the bottle, when she hears it.

Downstairs, someone screams.

Someone screams, and at first Annabelle thinks it's a play scream, but it doesn't sound like a play scream. It sounds like a terrified scream. And now, someone else screams, a guy, and people are shouting. These are the sounds of something awful happening, and so Annabelle thinks, *I've got to leave.* She wrongly thinks she must get out of this bathroom and this house, and she is at the top of the stairs when she hears a *pop-pop-pop*. It is a horrible *pop-pop-pop* and then lots of people are screaming, and there is the sound of something large falling, a sickening thud, and Annabelle is terrified because she knows, she *knows* that whatever just happened is bad, bad, bad, but she goes down those stairs anyway. It is the wrong direction, but she goes down and the front door is open and she can see the back of him. She sees The Taker, it's him, and she doesn't understand because in her mind he is not going to be here tonight, but that is his coat.

That is his coat, and he is fleeing, running from the house and down the sidewalk, and he is carrying a rifle. He is carrying a *rifle*, and Geoff Graham is yelling and sobbing, and when Annabelle gets to the bottom of the stairs, she sees something unreal, so unreal. People are crying and in shock, crouched down and covering their heads, and nothing is making sense. Sierra has wedged herself into the far corner of the room, her face in her hands, her shoulders heaving, and one of Geoff's friends from band is half hanging out a window attempting escape, and she sees Zach and Olivia hunched behind a chair, holding each other. There is blood everywhere, *blood everywhere*, and pieces . . . and pieces of—

She sees Kat on the ground. Kat is on the ground! Her face is to the floor but that is her orange T-shirt, and blood is flowing down her back into her jeans, and beside her, lying beside her—Jesus, no, Jesus, God—it's Will. It's Will! He's here, and he is on the ground, and he's in his jeans and his favorite hoodie, but he is crumpled and folded strangely, and some of his face is like . . . It looks like . . . It's just raw flesh and blood, it's gone, and his eyes are flat, just *flat*, and his chest . . . There is blood and blood just flowing and flowing from him.

Annabelle is screaming now, too; it's coming from her unbidden, and she goes to Will and Kat, the people she loves. She goes to them, but they terrify her. Their bodies terrify her, and someone grabs her. She feels the tight squeeze on both her arms, but she screams and screams and wrenches away and runs outside, into the street. People are in the street, too, kids from the party, kids trembling in their swimsuits wet from the hot tub, neighbors coming from their houses. The music is still going. The *bamp, thump, ba-bamp* goes sickeningly on and on in the background of the sobs and the crying, and now, the sound of a siren.

Annabelle crouches on the pavement, just crouches, because she was in the bathroom and then she heard a *pop-pop-pop* and then she came down the stairs and then there was Will and Kat and blood was flowing down the back of Kat's orange shirt, and Will's face—Annabelle shuts her eyes and puts her hands over her ears and she rocks and rocks back and forth because nothing is real. There are cars coming already, more sirens, lights. They've arrived so fast, but who knows how much time has passed. She is out in the street rocking and she throws up right there, and hands are on her, lifting her from the ground. *Are you all right? Are you injured? Are you all right? Are you injured?* they keep asking and asking. She doesn't know. She doesn't know, she doesn't know. Nothing is real. None of it can possibly be *real*, but it is real. It is.

She is crying now. She is sobbing and crying in her bunk of the RV. Grandpa Ed is awake. He's there with her. His arms are around her.

"Sweetheart," he says.

"I saw, I saw, I saw, I saw, I saw," she says.

32

1. In the cold of winter, the wood frog's heart freezes and stops, waiting until spring until it thaws and beats again.
2. Sometimes, humans must also attempt to come back to life.

She can't do it. Annabelle is backstage. She is trembling. Grandpa Ed has his hand on her shoulder. A woman, Ilene Chen, head of the Carnegie Mellon Gender Studies program, stands at a microphone and speaks to the audience.

There are a lot of people out there. Way, way more than the small groups of students Annabelle's spoken to before now. Ilene is introducing her. It's strange to hear her own name reverberating in the auditorium. Annabelle feels sick with anxiety. She tries not to listen to what Ilene is saying about her run and the tragedy. Instead, she concentrates on the tap, tap, tap of her thumb to her fingers, and on the weight of the Saint Christopher medal in her pocket. She concentrates on what her mom has said, and on what Dr. Mann and Malc and Zach and Olivia and Dawn Celeste and Luke have said: *Just be honest.* Luke said this to her only ten minutes ago, right before he and Dawn Celeste took their seats in the audience. She can do that. She can be honest. But honesty seems so small and quiet and insubstantial with all those people out there.

The microphone scares her. She's never spoken into a microphone before.

"I can't," she says to Grandpa Ed.

"Yeah, you can." He is sweating, though. His forehead is shiny, and he's so pale, he looks like he might throw up.

Now, the audience applauds. Jesus, they're clapping *for her.*

It is so wrong. After all she's done, after all she didn't do, they shouldn't be clapping.

"I can't."

Like a mother bird, Grandpa Ed gives her a little push.

And, oh my God, she's out here. Wow, there are a lot of people sitting in those red velvet seats. She might be sick right here onstage. Carly Cox did that during the second-grade play and never lived it down. Annabelle is going to do that now at Carnegie Mellon.

The microphone is up too high. She has to stand on her toes. Ilene comes back out and lowers it. Luke and Dawn Celeste are out there somewhere, but she can't see where. This calms her and makes her crazy-nervous both. Her throat is tight.

She clears it. It is a bad scene in a movie, because the microphone makes the throat-clearing sound like a rocket lifting off.

"I . . ."

Oh my God. It's quiet out there, except for the little shuffling sounds of waiting. It is a room of mostly young women, she sees. They look friendly. They smile at her and look up at her with kind eyes. But there are so many of them.

"I—the first thing I want to say is . . ."

They wait. She's had a long time to think about what she wants to say, but it's still hard to articulate. How is it possible to have words for this?

"The first thing I want to say is that that he, *he* . . . I can't say his name. But, the shooter . . . He sat in his car before coming into the party, and he read the instructions on how to work the gun he bought the day before."

The audience murmurs. There are exhales of outrage. It reminds her that those people out there want to hear what she has to say. Plenty of others won't, but these people do. She tries to breathe. She will just be honest, like those who love her have advised.

"I don't know why I feel like I have to start with that. There are so many things to say about what happened. But this just seems particularly horrifying, you know. That you can have a thought to destroy people, and within hours, *hours*, you can be doing it. I just can't get that out of my head.

"The shooter . . . He was eighteen." She turns away from the microphone. She has to clear her throat again. "I knew him, of course. I knew him pretty well. Sometimes he was funny and sweet, but he was also depressed and moody and vindictive. Clearly, he was vindictive. But, I mean, he couldn't take criticism. He'd get furious if someone teased him about what he was eating for lunch. And this boy, who just had his eighteenth birthday, who could get furious if someone teased him about what he was eating for *lunch*—all he needed to buy a gun was enough money and a pen to fill out a background check. He was born here, and he never committed a crime before, so just like that, he walked out of the store with a rifle. Buying a car takes a lot longer. Buying dinner in a restaurant does.

"This boy, he took his new gun and he shot my best friend, Kat Klein, because he thought she was me. *He thought she was me.* Her back was turned. We look alike. He shot the boy I loved, Will MacEvans, through the heart. And then, to make sure the job was done, he shot off part of Will's face. Her, Kat, my friend's last words were . . ."

Annabelle doesn't know if she can do this. Her throat squeezes with tears. It is so tight, she can barely speak. "Her last words to me were about how she hadn't fallen in love yet." She can't do this. She can't, and now she's crying. "How that was still coming. His were . . ." She swallows. She tries to hold it together. "His were 'See you soon.' Their futures . . . held things. They were kind and funny and cherished people with futures that held things. I loved them both so much. I love them both so much right this minute."

It is hard to talk now. She is crying. She has to stop and get herself together. She wipes her eyes. "Kat was murdered. Will was murdered. I was. The girl he thought I was, but also, the girl who truly was and will never be again.

"Mostly, I have a lot to say about what I don't have. I don't have Kat or Will or my old life. I don't have answers. I don't have big bunches of wisdom or statistics or facts to share with you, either. I don't have a slide show or charts. I'm scared to look at all the numbers. I peeked one day, so that I would have those things to give to you, honestly, but I had to stop when I saw the photos again of the kindergartners and first graders who were gunned down in 2012. I can't believe I even just said *kindergartners and first graders who were gunned down*.

"I don't have a great plan about the laws or regulations needed to decrease gun violence. I'm only eighteen. I don't have the knowledge required to devise those laws. But I'm old enough to know that even those words *decrease gun violence* are crazy. *Decrease* sounds insane, when we're talking about kindergartners. When Will and Kat were just at a party because it was almost summer. And the most insane thing of all is that it doesn't even have to be this way. In Japan, maybe two people a year are killed with guns. But not us, and this makes no sense."

Annabelle shakes her head, and looks out to the dark sky of the auditorium. Her tears have turned to anger, the kind of rant she and Kat might have gone on after watching some documentary. It's not a documentary, though. For the first time, she thinks about how pissed Kat would be about this if she were here. She thinks about Kat standing at a podium instead of her.

"When he . . . When the shooter was . . . *unraveling* after I rejected him, when I was scared that he might harm himself or me or someone else, I thought 'people' would handle it. 'People'—adults, people bigger than me, older, smarter, with more ability to do something, I thought they'd keep us all safe. That didn't happen. That still isn't happening.

"Most of all, I don't have a clear idea what I, my own self, can do about any of this. *Any of this* is big, too. *Any of this* is way larger than guns. What the shooter really wanted to do was control me. I understand that. He wanted to shut me up. He told the police that I was, um, his *dream girl.* He didn't want me to be with someone else. He made sure he got his own way. When I think about it in the simplest way I can, I see that his violence was just a show of power by a bully. Maybe all violence is. But it works. It sure does. Violence shuts you up, all right. A gun always gets the last word.

"I live in this system, you know, *you* do, *we* do, where the control and the shutting up is such a regular thing that we sometimes don't even see it. Where there are rules and rights for him and rules and rights for her and they are different rules and rights. The system says who gets to control who, and who is entitled to power and protection and who isn't, and every day I run because I just don't know what to do about it or how to change it."

Annabelle pauses to catch her breath. Her words have poured out. Her truth has risen and keeps rising like lava from a once-dormant volcano. *I am still here*, she thinks. *And this is what I'm made of, too.*

"When I am on a mountain road, say, and the wind is pressing me . . . I am pressing back. I am shoving against my helplessness. I put on those shoes day after day to fight and fight and fight the powerlessness I feel after what the shooter did to Kat and Will and me. I just keep running on those hot roads because I don't know if my country will protect me and my rights, as a female, as a person who wants to be safe from violence. It has not shown me that it will protect me, from males more powerful than me, from people who hate and intend to do harm. It has shown me that I am less than, that I am not worth being protected. It has shown recklessness with my well-being. So I run in the heat and I sweat and I push myself to persevere.

"And I run and run because I am filled with grief and sorrow, too. My running is crying and praying and screaming. It is saying that I don't know what to do but that I must do something. That I must use my voice, because it's the only thing you have sometimes when someone or something is larger and more powerful than you. My voice is here now, but it is mostly there in my running body. With every step, it is saying *please* and it is saying *must*. Please see my grief and sorrow. Must end this grief and sorrow."

She stops. She is exhausted and spent, in the same way she is after her day's work is done, her sixteen miles on the road. She is empty.

The audience begins to applaud then. The applause surprises her. She almost forgot about them out there, those mostly female students of Carnegie Mellon. She just stands in front of them. And then they stand. They are still clapping, but she looks at them and they look at her. They all look at each other. Standing—*still* standing. She is guessing that many of them out there, too, have felt her grief and confusion and powerlessness.

She is empty.

She is full.

33

On the banks of Shawnee State Park in Pennsylvania, just a few miles north of Buchanan State Forest, and 111 miles southeast of Pittsburgh, an RV with a CAPTAIN ED license plate and a HOME OF THE REDWOODS bumper sticker is parked next to a rented camper that smells of just-baked cinnamon rolls.

One old man grills sausages with the help of one young man with wild hair. One old woman, in a gauzy sundress, sits in a camp chair next to one young one, in a sundress splashed with sunflowers. They are not terrified astronauts floating in an endless atmosphere—they are just four ordinary explorers here on earth. And there are no great and dangerous slabs of ice that they must cross in spite of blizzards and starvation. There is just drying grass with a few dandelions poking up on a summer evening.

The sun is setting. The sky is pink, and it has turned the sweet ripples of the lake pink, too. Crickets are starting their evening chirp. There is not much of the trip left, and so Dawn

Celeste and Luke Messenger are now trekking alongside Grandpa Ed and Annabelle to the end. It is hard for Annabelle to believe that there is such thing as *The End*. She feels like she will run and run forever.

This is what she says to the old hippie sitting beside her.

"I feel like I am going to run and run forever."

"It's scary, isn't it, to think about stopping?"

She gets right to the heart of things, that Dawn Celeste. Annabelle wonders if her grandmother was the same. Tough but tender grandpas need someone like that.

"It is. I'm scared. Of Seth Greggory."

"He's on your side. He's there to help you and prepare you. You'll rehearse what's going to happen, so it isn't so frightening. I know about this. Do you know how I know? When I was twenty-three, in college, I was assaulted."

"Oh my God. I'm so sorry."

"It seems like a long, long time ago, except on some nights, when I am alone in my house and I think I hear something. Then it all comes back. The man broke into my apartment. He stood over my bed. He puts his hands on me. He fled when I screamed."

"That is so terrifying."

"It was. Like I said, it sometimes still is. Those assholes give you a permanent life sentence. Almost more terrifying than that night was facing him in court, like you're going to do in September. Being in the same room again with someone when you know what they're capable of . . . I'm not comparing what happened to me to what happened to you. But you know what? When I was done, after I saw him in court, I felt a little better. I'd done it—the thing I so feared. The thing you fear. I faced him. I used my voice to stand up to him. And he was the one in shackles, and I was the one who was free."

"I had no idea."

"Oh, every person is a book with chapters. Some are glorious and some are dark and ugly. Every person survives something. We should get a patch for it." She smacks her arm where her patch should be. "Like Cub Scout Troop one sixty-three."

"I just keep thinking of Ernest Shackleton and his crew on that ice. . . . Did you read it?"

"Yeah."

"You know how at the end of the book, they finally come across that whaler? I keep thinking of him, the whaler, how he breaks down and cries when he realizes that the haggard man in front of him is the great Ernest Shackleton, who's made it after all."

"Can you believe what they went through, just to survive?" Dawn Celeste says. "How awful and terrifying, that trip. Yet I imagine there were nights in Antarctica that were as beautiful as this lake is right now."

"Probably."

They sit quietly. Annabelle loves the quiet with Dawn Celeste, how it is absent of anxiety or expectation. Grandpa Ed loves that, too, it seems. Annabelle hears him laugh his big laugh when Luke cracks some joke over there. Grandpa Ed, in his socks and sandals, turns the sausages. On this trip, he's crossed the land and become a romantic hero, who would have guessed.

This is hard to say, but she has to confess it to someone. It's a big weight, growing bigger. "I feel like I need to study the heart."

Dawn Celeste looks over at her. She leans forward a bit in her chair. "Study the heart?"

"Before this, I was thinking of studying something science-related anyway, maybe astronomy. But now I think I have to study the heart. How to repair it. To maybe be, I don't know, a surgeon, I guess. Because of . . ." These words are difficult to speak. It's fine to run across the country and make speeches and face The Taker in a courtroom, but when she closes her eyes at night, she still sees Will and Will's parents. She sees Tracie, crying and staring at her with hate in her eyes. She sees Kat, who never got to fall in love; and Becka, Kat's sister; and Patty, Kat's mom, the way Annabelle saw her last, in a QFC, looking like a ghost, looking ruined, buying a box of cereal and a frozen dinner.

"I can understand that. But do you *want* to study the heart and become a surgeon?"

"I don't know. No. Not really. I just want to take some time to see what I want."

"I think you have studied the heart already. I think you will go on studying the heart, Annabelle, no matter what you do."

• • •

"What do you think 'going for a walk by the lake' means?" Annabelle asks Luke, who sits beside her. He's trying to whittle something using a pocketknife. It's almost dark. But after the hot days of summer, it feels good. It's cool there, on the bank by that lake. Annabelle's toes are in the water.

"Having a quickie, for sure," Luke says.

She socks him.

"You set me up for that," he says.

"Can you believe I only have a hundred and thirty-eight miles left? Nine days."

"Only? Only a hundred and thirty-eight miles?"

"I'll be done. I'll be there." *There.* Washington, DC, where she'll spend three days meeting her senators and the members of the Gun Violence Prevention Task Force, thanks to Olivia. "The thought of going home seems so strange."

"I bet."

"What then?" She is thinking a lot about this tonight.

"What do you mean?"

"I mean, will I ever see you after that?"

He sets down his knife and the little piece of wood. He looks at her, and she looks at him, and she knows what is about to happen. *About to happen?* No. She is not a passive participant, being acted upon. She is choosing, setting in motion. Her palms start to sweat. She wants to tap her fingers with sudden nerves. Will a kiss ever be simple for her again? Is a kiss ever simple for anyone? Every kiss is a story. And stories have befores and afters and . . . well, damn it, stories keep unfolding more than anything, don't they, and so she leans in, and so does he. The kiss is great and gentle, and it promises more, but the best part of it is that it is a bridge safely and sweetly crossed that she'd like to cross again. "You most definitely will, as long as you want that."

"I want that."

They hold hands. Her toes make circles in the water.

"I'll be in my new apartment in Portland, going to school. You'll be in Seattle, doing whatever comes next. One hundred and seventy-three miles between us. After twenty-seven hundred miles, that seems like no distance at all."

"You looked it up."

"Mm-hmm."

"You're not expecting me to run that, are you? I may never want to put on a pair of running shoes again."

"I have a pickup truck. I have a tent and sleeping bags. I am thinking nights like this."

It smells so good out there. The sky is black with shimmers of glitter, and in the lake, there's the sky's rippling twin. "I like nights like this."

"Olympic National Forest. I want to show you this wolf tree out there I saw once."

"A wolf tree? Right." She thinks he's setting her up.

"No! It's a real thing! An awesome thing. A nature thing, just like you love. A wolf tree is formed when it stands all alone in an area. Everything around it has been destroyed, by fire, by a natural disaster. . . . It's the lone survivor. Out there by itself, it gets damaged bad, usually from being hit by lightning. It should be dead. Burned up. Gone. You can *see* that it's been damaged in the past. It tilts from wind, since it has no shelter. Its heavier branches have been snapped off after ice storms. Those trees, let me tell you, they're gnarled and broken, twisted into some fantastic shapes."

"They sound hideous."

"Hideous? No way. The most beautiful creatures you've ever seen. And way up at the top, way up there, nearest the sun, new branches grow."

"Wow."

"Yep. The truest kind of beautiful."

"I will take your word for it. Oh man. Mosquitoes." She slaps her arm. "We should go in."

"Wait. I have something for you first." He hands her the little block of wood.

She laughs. "Raccoon turd of love?"

"I don't know. It doesn't really have ears or a tail or even a head, so maybe it should be just a turd of love."

A sweet kiss; a turd of love. Annabelle's heart fills. She feels choked up. There is so much good here that she aches. "It's one of the best things anyone has ever given me," she says softly.

She means it. And Luke can tell she does, so he puts his arm around her and pulls her close.

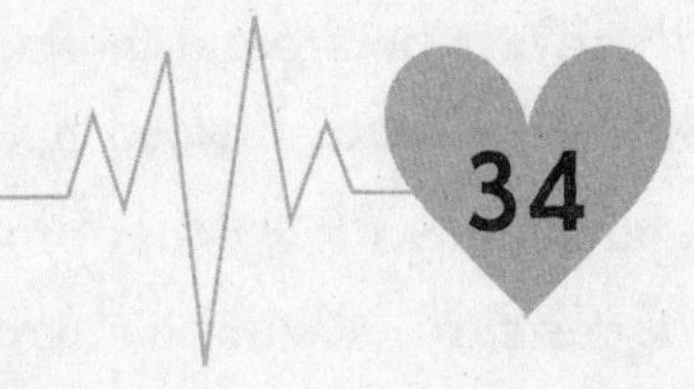

There are songs about the heart and poems about the heart and legends about the heart and facts about the heart. And, it's true—the heart sings and speaks and tells its story. There are exact miles of arteries; there is the exact force of its beat. But the heart is also quiet. It is also a mystery. No one really knows how it goes on after being broken.

How does it happen?

No idea.

How do we endure?

No clue.

What Annabelle does know now: The word *courage* comes from the Latin word *cor*, meaning *heart*. The ba-bump of the heart leads to the next ba-bump. One step leads to another step. We go forward. Sometimes against our will, sometimes against all odds, we go forward. We have crossed the glacier, the dark land of grief. We have gone to the outer edges of our atmosphere and returned. The glacier and the dark land of grief will always be there behind us. The atmosphere will always be around us and above us. We'll feel all of it there like a presence. *What has happened* will be a wind to fight against and a force that propels; it will be a guiding light in the blizzard, it will be a wrong turn. The trip across the glacier and through the dark land of grief is crooked and dangerous but sometimes beautiful. The voyage past the last edges of the universe is frightening and impossible but sometimes astonishing. Regardless—the steps, the ba-bump of the heart, push us to what's next.

Annabelle feels these things right now, right this minute—the thump of her heart in her chest, her feet driving her forward. As Loretta steers her around Dupont Circle and down Massachusetts Avenue, Annabelle feels the wind, the force, the guiding light, the history, the story, the exhaustion and the grief and the triumph of the crossing.

Just keep going. Just a little farther, Kat says, or maybe that's the Antarctic wind, or the whisper of space, or maybe that's a gust through her own wolf-tree branches.

At Scott Circle, Loretta tells her to hang a right. Down Sixteenth Street NW, Annabelle runs. Her heart is galloping. She knows what this street is: her last one. And she knows what's at the end of it.

My God, she cannot believe it. Everywhere she looks, there's a postcard of an image that's here-and-now real. Her heart goes a million miles an hour and her feet fly. She has forgotten the ever-present pain in her heel and her knee. She has no idea what she looks like, her small, thin self shuffling forward in her red tank top, her ponytail still bobbing, her lips cracked, and her skin so tan after these long weeks in the sun. She focuses only on what's ahead, because there it is: Lafayette Square, President's Park. There's a statue in the center of a rectangle of beautiful red flowers. It is Andrew Jackson on a horse. The horse is up on its two back legs. Andrew Jackson tips his hat in the air.

Beyond him, Annabelle can see the White House. It looks astonishingly like the White House in photographs, but larger and living, and beyond that, there's the familiar tip of the Washington Monument, looking astonishingly like the Washington Monument in the books. Goose bumps shiver up her arms.

She made it. Her heart and her legs have brought her to this new place.

Now, she hears the cheering. *Go, Annabelle, go! You did it! Come on, Annabelle!* They are chanting her name. *Annabelle! Annabelle! Annabelle!* She sees them—her people, her familiars. Her team. There's a small crowd with them, on both sides of the street. Everyone is wearing red, and waving their arms, and jumping up and down.

Galloping now, too—Malcolm. Her Malcolm. He can't help himself. He runs, full speed ahead, his knobby knees pumping like pistons, the back of his T-shirt flying out behind him. He smacks into her like a linebacker. She picks him up. He is almost her size now; he's grown so much these past months. But he's still her little brother, and so she lifts him and she sort of carries him, and it's the most awkward finish, his butt practically hanging down by her knees, but it's the best finish, because he's her number-one sidekick.

There is a banner, and oh, it's big, and oh wow, her mother is crying her eyes out, and so is Grandpa Ed. His glasses are off, and he's rubbing his eyes, and it's his victory, too. He's been through so much with her. So many days and nights and miles in the RV, just the two of them. So many tins of anchovies, so much chainsaw snoring, so many tender offerings of water bottles and clean socks. So much silent, old-man presence, and loud old-man encouragement. Amid the shouting and cheering, she falls into his arms.

"Bella Luna," he says.

"Grandpa. Thank you, Grandpa."

"Thank *you*, Bella Luna. Thank you for keeping on, *mia cara*."

"Thank God," Gina says. Yes, Him too. Thank everyone. Thank Saint Christopher, protector of travelers, guardian against storms, holy death, and toothaches. Thank Grandpa Ed, thank Mom, who grabs Annabelle and squeezes her hard, thank Malcolm and Dr. Mann, and even thank Carl Walter, who Annabelle spots in the background, snapping photos. Thank Dawn Celeste and Luke, who is hugging her and lifting her right up off her feet. "You did it, Annabelle. You did it!"

"Sweetheart," Dawn Celeste says, her cheeks flushed with happiness. "You are a champion! A big, damn champion!"

Thank Zach and Olivia, who are hugging her, too. Everyone is hugging her, holding her, lifting her. Her feet rise from the ground as Zach picks her up.

"You are a fucking *survivor*!" Zach says. Tears roll down his cheeks.

"*You* are." She clasps Zach to her. They have been through so much together. And she and Olivia have, as well, and so has everyone who was there that night. The humidity is intense. Everything she is feeling is intense. My God, she is glad to be here. She is glad her heart and her feet have moved her forward to feel all of this.

"See over there? Reporters," Olivia says. It's true. People are taking her picture. There is a news van with a satellite on top. "Danisha Prince," Olivia reads from her notebook, which she's already pulled from her backpack. "From the *Washington Post*. She'd like to speak to you after you catch your breath."

"You're awesome, Olivia," Annabelle says. "Look at what you've done."

"Look at what *you've* done!" Olivia's eyes shine with tears.

Gina shoves a bottle of water at her, and Annabelle drinks. It is the most delicious water she's ever tasted. People are congratulating her. Strangers. They shake her shoulders and clap her back and ask her how she feels. It's hard to take it all in. Her family and friends are wearing the red shirts, but so are these strangers. Run for a Cause shirts are everywhere. Thank her supporters, too. Aunt Angie and Uncle Pat, and her old bosses, Claire and Thomas, and the people from Sunnyside; her teachers from Roosevelt, her friends and their parents, her old neighbors, and so many people she *doesn't even know*. Gina lifts Malcolm in the air next, and swings him in a circle.

"I am so fucking happy," Gina says.

"Twenty-five cents, Mom!" Malcolm shouts.

What does she feel besides guilt?

Joy. She feels joy.

Her feet go forward and her heart *ba-bamps* that night at the celebration dinner at Morelli's, where there's a surprise. Her father has just flown in from Boston, and he's wearing a dress shirt and jeans, and he looks like her father, not That Bastard Father Anthony. He looks like her father maybe because he's been acting like one, with the notes and the calls and the support. He is shy. He hugs her hard. He smells like his old, same soap.

"Way to go. Way to *go*. I'm so proud of you, Peanut."

She's struck, because she hasn't heard that name in years, the name he used to call her when she was a little girl, the name he'd use when she'd bring him her report card to admire, when they practiced her spelling words, when he'd cheer her on as she raced around the yard as he timed her with his stopwatch. She hugs him back. When they separate, he holds her arms, and looks at her in the eyes, and she looks at him, and they see each other. She gets that sense, that they really do *see*, and she is Peanut and she is the young woman she is now, and he is the lawn-mowing young father and he is the man who's made mistakes and is trying to do better. He kisses her cheek. He sits down at the end of the table by Dawn Celeste and Malcolm. He compliments the waiter on the mostaccioli. It is maybe the beginning of something.

Her feet go forward and her heart *ba-bamps* the next day, too, as she walks down a red-carpeted corridor of the US Capitol. It *ba-bamps* hard. Senate is in session, and she meets her senators from Washington, who invite Annabelle to the State of the Union address in February. She gets her photo taken. She meets elected officials from Oregon and California, before being led to the south side of the Capitol, where she talks with the chair and vice-chair of the Gun Violence Prevention Task Force, who also invite her to speak as a panelist at their upcoming forum in December. There is a student group the next day at George Washington University. Annabelle doesn't think she can do it. Grandpa Ed pushes her out. She walks up to a microphone, which is tilted too high. The faces look at her, and she looks at them, and then she is honest. She remembers that everyone has a story. That the people in the audience have likely felt grief and confusion and powerlessness.

Her feet go forward and her heart *ba-bamps* three days

later, as she walks down the ramp to their airplane. Luke and Zach and Olivia have already left, and Grandpa Ed and Dawn Celeste are taking the long way home in the RV, via every national park they can hit until the trial starts, but Annabelle is flying home. Gina and Malcolm sit next to her. Gina reads the plastic sheet about the emergency exits. Annabelle closes her eyes and feels the liftoff.

Her feet go forward and her heart *ba-bamps* as she walks into her room at home that night. She is scared of her own house and her own room. She fears she'll be transformed back into the girl she was. But, no. Bit hops around at her legs in joyous reunion, and she kisses him, and she holds her pillow to her face and smells its beautiful familiarity, but she is still the Annabelle Agnelli who ran across the country.

And she is still that Annabelle the next week, too, when she walks into prosecutor Seth Greggory's office. Her feet go forward and her heart *ba-bamps* even as the Antarctic wind kicks up. She walks hard across the glacier and her extremities freeze. Crystals form on her eyelashes, or maybe they're just wet from tears. Seth Greggory is firm but gentle. He grills her, as The Taker's defense attorney will. He brings her coffee. He brings Gina coffee. They start again. And again. She must remind herself—as terrifying as he is and this is, Seth Greggory is on her side. He is part of Team Endurance.

Annabelle's feet go forward and her heart *ba-bamps, ba-bamps, BA-BAMPS* three weeks later, when she walks into a courtroom. She remembers the muscles in her calves and the strength in her thighs, and she remembers the heat of the farmland and the slope of the mountains and the miles and miles she's crossed. She remembers her strength. She tries to, because there are his parents, Nadine and Gavin, and there he is, The Taker—his hair is different, and he is wearing a suit and tie and, dear God, dear God, it is that tie he wore to the winter dance, and this is awful, awful, but Annabelle looks at him. She looks right at him, and she answers the questions about him, even though the microphone is tilted too far up and even though she'd been throwing up from stress all morning. She says the names of the people she loved. Kat Klein. Will MacEvans. And she looks right at The Taker, right at him, because he hasn't won. He needs to know he hasn't won. Her heart has. The way it keeps on beating, the way it survives in spite of how it's been destroyed—it has won.

"What shall we do tonight for dinner?" Gina asks as they get back into the car after Annabelle's awful two days of testimony are over. Grandpa is already heading home, to call Dawn Celeste with the details. It's just the three of them.

"Dick's," Annabelle says.

"Really?"

"Really."

They drive up. There is the orange Dick's sign, spinning around on top of its post. They order burgers and fries.

"You're not going to take off again, are you?" Gina asks.

"Hmm. My knee *is* feeling better. . . ."

"Awesome. I'll come, too," Malcolm says.

Gina socks him. "I hate it when you guys gang up."

They eat in the car. Annabelle loves eating in the car. Outside, there are customers in line ordering food. The air smells like fall coming, plus French fries. There are no intoxicated guys trying to grab her. There are just people with their stories, getting dinner.

The muscles in Annabelle's legs and arms are hard as baseballs again. Her voice is still rising from where it has been under her surface for so long. But her feet are planted. Her heart still thumps along in her chest.

"Too bad Bit isn't here. He loves French fries," Malcolm says.

"Even though they make him fart," Gina says.

"He could sit on your lap, Annabelle," Malcolm says.

"Non mi rompere i maroni," Annabelle says. She learned this from Grandpa, of course.

Translation: *Quit being annoying.* Literal translation: *Don't break my chestnuts.*

Her feet go forward and her heart *ba-bamps* when she must see The Taker once again, at his sentencing hearing. She does not look at him when she makes her statement. She looks at Judge Samuels, as she describes the ways her heart has been broken. She speaks about its shattered pieces, and the way it must go on beating, in spite of being wrecked. She summons the strength and the anger from the miles and the crossing and the people she's met. It is the hardest thing she's ever done, harder than running 2,700 miles. She is exhausted and spent when she sits down. Even her fingers are too tired to tap. When Gina wraps her arms around her, Annabelle closes her eyes and remembers Will's arms around her like that. They were lying on a blanket at Green Lake one spring day, and her head rested on his chest, and she could hear his heart thundering. She sobs when the judge sentences The Taker—Daniel Wainwright—to two consecutive life sentences.

Her feet go forward and her heart *ba-bamps* as she walks along a wooded trail. It is January, a new season, a new year. It's cold out there. It's not *Endurance* cold, not Antarctic cold, but a crisp, lovely, blue-chill cold. She breathes it in. Her lungs say *thank you*. Her muscles are happy to be outdoors again. She's been spending lots of time inside, inside classrooms and auditoriums, inside the little office in the new apartment she and Olivia share. They have a lot of work to do. There are a lot of people to talk to. Now, she tilts the microphone herself before she speaks. Now, she looks into the faces of the people in her audience as they look into hers.

But today, it is a forest-and-damp-earth afternoon. Out in nature, her anxiety rests, breathes a sigh of relief. Since her body has healed, she's been going on short daily runs again, and she's in good shape. Luke, well, he's another matter.

"Slow. Down. Please. Annabelle," he puffs.

"I can't wait to see it."

"It will still be there even if we slow down. My cramps have cramps."

There's a clearing. They stop.

"Voila," Luke breathes.

Oh, that wolf tree is ugly all right. It is no one's idea of beautiful. A stumpy, gnarled beast, alone in a wide area of open woods.

"Look right there. You can tell where the lightning has hit." Luke points.

She sees it. There's a distinct black gouge, the mark of a terrible moment in its life.

"Oh wow," Annabelle says.

"But look. Look up."

New growth spurts out from the top. It is winter and there are no leaves, but it is clearly still alive. "It looks like Malcolm after Mom cut his hair."

No. Actually, it's astonishing. God, she loves science and nature. That tree is ruined but not ruined. Rooted, in spite of the storms and the ice. There are no real words for it, so she's silent for a while, staring in respect and awe.

"I told you. Beautiful, right?"

"Yes." Yes, most definitely.

Annabelle Agnelli gazes up, up past the tree now, into winter-blue sky. She imagines that she can see 2,700 miles up into the atmosphere. She imagines that her love can rise farther than that, much farther, up into the universe, into unreachable places, and to unreachable people. *Kat. Will.* Her breath puffs clouds into the air.

It's getting cold. It's colder when you stand still. Luke cups his hands around his nose and exhales hard to warm it. "It's freezing out here. You ready to go?" he asks.

The chill wind presses, and her eyes are watering, but there is still so much more beautiful stuff to see.

"I'm ready," she says.

ACKNOWLEDGMENTS

My there-are-no-words thanks go to Michael Bourret, of Dystel, Goderich & Bourret. Your presence in my life and work has been downright transformative. I'm so happy and grateful you're on this ride with me. And to Liesa Abrams—your support, vision, and firm place in my corner has meant more than I can say. As well, I just plain respect the hell out of your intelligence, your passion, and your commitment, to both books and the subjects of deep importance to our readers. Thank you. We joke about having the dream team, but it's true—we do.

There is no other way to say it—publishing books is a labor of love. I thank every one of these people for the heart and dedication and talent you put into mine: Jon Anderson, Mara Anastas, Chriscynethia Floyd, Lauren Hoffman, Caitlin Sweeny, Anna Jarzab, Michelle Leo, Anthony Parisi, Sarah Woodruff, Katherine Devendorf, Elizabeth Mims, Rebecca Vitkus, Sara Berko, Christina Pecorale, Leah Hays, Victor Iannone, Christine Foye. Some of us have been doing this together for many books now. Thank you for being my publishing family. As well, my appreciation to Sarah Creech and

Daniel Stolle, for your work on this beautiful cover.

Much love and thanks, as always, to my family. And to the Seattle literary community, especially my friends and colleagues of Seattle7Writers. Thanks, guys, for being a clan of kindred spirits, and for always being there with your rare and particular understanding.

This time, too—a special thank-you to my readers. You've shared your stories, followed every book, expressed your love and excitement, and some of you have even named your babies after my characters. You always—every day—remind me in one way or another that you are here. Thanks for bringing the meaning.

TURN THE PAGE FOR A LOOK AT THIS SIMMERING THRILLER FROM DEB CALETTI. . . .

Exhibit 1: Recorded statement of Sydney E. Reilly, 1 of 5
Exhibit 2: Aerial photo of 716 Sea Cliff Drive
Exhibit 3: Photo of Lila Shore, Giacomo "Big Jake" Antonetti, and Sydney Reilly, Original Joe's, North Beach, undated

I had a bad feeling, even before I left home. A strong one. If I'm here to tell you what actually happened, well, it started there. With a sense of dread. Like some pissed-off old ghost was going to haunt me until I heard whatever she had to say. It was eerie and unsettling like that. Urgent.

The feeling was there late at night, when I was alone in the dorm showers and the hot-water pipes creaked and groaned like a dying man, and it was there when I lay awake in the dark, watching headlights flash across the ceiling in a way that made me pull my covers up. But it was there in bright daylight, too, when Hoodean and Cora and Lizzie and Meredith and I went to Cupcake Royale and we made fun of Hoodean for getting vanilla (he always got vanilla). It was there on those last weeks of school, when the sky was blue and the sun was out and the air smelled delicious.

I tried to tell myself there were logical reasons for it. I didn't want to go to San Francisco anyway. I know it sounds crazy, since Lila lived in that Sea Cliff mansion perched above the Pacific. But I was happy at school—just being in class, or walking around Green Lake with Meredith, picking out what dog we'd want. Or sitting on my bed with Cora under my Frida Kahlo poster, playing our favorite songs to each other. Volleyball in the fall, crew in the spring, dim sum in the International District with Meredith's parents.

Leaving my friends for the whole summer—*that's* why I felt dread, I thought. Especially since things were getting so good lately. I felt like *IT* was about to happen. I didn't know what *IT* was exactly, just something large, something that would change everything. Maybe *IT* was love, the passionate, all-encompassing kind, or actual sex, or maybe something else. Whatever it was, I wanted it bad, this something-big. I could feel it coming. I could feel it when my group of friends would be walking down the street, elbowing each other, laughing too loud, and people watched us with what I thought was envy. Or when we'd stroll into Victrola and the men would look up from their laptops to stare, even when Hoodean was with us. God, if I missed *IT* because I was stuck in a jillion-dollar house with my famous mother, I'd be heartbroken.

Which was another logical explanation for the dark feeling that followed me. Three months with Lila. She was a celebrity, and she was beautiful, but she was still my mother. The summer before, when I was fourteen, I wanted to tell her everything, to be best buds, to do stuff together. And then suddenly I didn't. Moms—they can be like a winter coat, helpful and warm and cozy, but then spring comes, and it weighs you down and maybe you just want to feel the cold anyway.

But I'm supposed to be telling you the truth, aren't I? And the truth is, Lila was never like that. She wasn't a warm and cozy mom like Meredith's, even if I felt the weight of her.

And the truth is, nothing made that sense of doom disappear, no explanations, no blue sky, nothing. It was persistent. It was spooky.

I didn't know what that feeling was. I didn't know which exact ghost from the past was trying to warn me. But she was real, and I didn't listen.

Exhibit 4: Yearbook photo of Sydney Elizabeth Riley,
Academy of Arts and Sciences, Seattle

A few weeks before I left, I tried to get out of going. I was at Edwina's for dinner. "Hey, I could live with you for the summer!" I said. I made it sound like an idea that had just come to me, when actually I'd thought about it every night since the ghost started talking.

My grandmother scowled.

"I don't *want* to go," I whined.

But she was having none of it. "Sydney. Stop that. Of course you do," she said.

Of course I *didn't.* The weekend before, Cora and I had gone to her cousin Simon's baseball game. A cute boy had talked to me by the concession stand and played with my hair, and who knew what else might happen if I stayed for the summer. *IT* was everywhere, though maybe *IT* was just *more.*

"Pleeeease?"

Eye roll.

Because of my mother's career, and also because Lila wasn't exactly what you'd call maternal, Edwina pretty much raised me. You probably already know this. She lived with us wherever we went, from our first apartment, to Papa Chesterton's estate, to the modern house in Topanga Canyon. When I left for Academy in the fifth grade, Edwina came too, sitting beside me on the plane with her purse on her lap so no one would steal it. They chose Academy because Edwina used to live in Seattle when Lila was born, and she liked it there.

I passed their old house often. You picture Lila in *Nefarious* or in *What the Neighbor Knew*, and you'd think, *No way*. Now it was a tiny, crappy rental for university students, with a beat-up couch on the porch and a Huskies blanket covering one window. It was right next to a Wing Zone, which was pretty hilarious. Seeing that house—you understood why she changed her name from Linda Short to Lila Shore. A shore—all that wide space. Solid land on one side, the open sea on the other.

That night at dinner, in the nice craftsman house that Lila bought her, Edwina carried a big platter of ham to the table using pot holders that had seen better days. Ham for the two of us kind of cracked me up. It was probably on sale at Fred Meyer, since Edwina loved a good sale. My friends always liked going to Edwina's because she cooked big, old-fashioned food, food you barely saw in Seattle, stuff like *gravy*, like *roast*, and also because they thought Edwina was *colorful*. That's the word people use when someone has a big personality but you're kind of glad you don't have to deal with them yourself.

"You'd rather stay here with an old lady than go to that big, fancy place?" Edwina stabbed a slice and slapped it on my plate. I had a brief desire to become a vegetarian, because ham always has a way of reminding you where it came from.

"There's a new boyfriend," I said.

Edwina met my eyes, and our gazes played a whole film of the past.

"Well. You never know," Edwina sighed.

"Jake Something-Italian."

"She likes those tough guys. The Jets and the Sharks."

"The Jets and the Sharks?" I laughed. "What are those, made-up gang names?"

"You're kidding me. *West Side Story*? You never seen it?" She snapped her fingers, danced toward me like a gang-member grandma getting ready to rumble on a dark street.

"Ooh, scary, haha. Especially in those slippers."

That's how it was, you know? Lots of things were funny. I folded a piece of ham into a buttered roll. It was so good. I ate one and then another. I wasn't in that part of womanhood yet where your body was something you were supposed to keep one nervous eye on all the time, like a bank balance. I still belonged mostly to myself, but not for long.

"She's all gaga in love," I said with my mouth full.

Edwina waved her hand as if the new guy were a pesky insect. "That beautiful house right on the ocean? You should've seen the Mission District, where I grew up. Six miles from there, but another universe. You're a lucky girl."

"All my friends are here." There was no way I could tell her how great things were getting lately, let alone about that uneasy feeling. The way it felt like the shutter of a camera, briefly opening, revealing a dark and gaping hole.

"Remember how much fun we had when we went to Mexico? It'll be fine."

"I was *eight*."

We did have fun in Mexico. We had an amazing time. I was a little kid, and I wanted nothing more than to be with Lila. She was the treasure you were only allowed to peek at, until one astonishing day you finally got to run your fingers through the pile of gold coins and try on all the gold jewelry and drink out of the golden goblets. Plus, she made whatever we did exciting. We sat under umbrellas and walked through markets and bought stuff and ate in nice restaurants and spent a lot of time staying out of the sun, even though sun is something Mexico happens to have a lot of. I could never really see her eyes in those sunglasses, but she held my hand and it made me happy.

I didn't know her as a person then. I knew her as a thing I didn't have in the way I wanted, though maybe that's true about most parents.

"Cora's taking a pastel workshop this summer. She wants me to go too." A last plea. I wasn't an amazing artist like Cora, but I loved my pastels—the colored dust on my hands, the way you could disappear into an image you created. "I'd be so busy, I wouldn't even bother you."

Edwina ignored me. "How about a haircut before you go? I'll make an appointment. Your hair is a big wall of brown." This was how Edwina showed her love. Feeding you, buying you a six-pack of underwear at Target, watching the way you looked even if you didn't. Being brisk and bossy and occasionally critical. Sometimes you had to remind yourself it was love.

"I like it how it is."

"No one likes a big wall of brown."

I put my hair over my face. "I prefer to call it a waterfall of brown." When I peeked through, Edwina was rolling her eyes again.

When you picture Lila Shore in *Nefarious* or in *What the Neighbor Knew* or in some article in a magazine, you can't imagine her growing up in a house like that, but you wouldn't have imagined *me* right then either.

I always felt too regular to be hers. I was just me, a girl. I was never beautiful. I was never desired.

And then I was.

Exhibit 5: Framed promotional film poster with partially shattered glass, 27" x 41" featuring Lila Shore in Nefarious

A week before I boarded the plane, Lila called. After that phone call, I felt an actual pulse of worry, a skitter of anxiety under my skin, something more definite than the ghost whisper. I almost didn't answer. The Mayor's Cup Regatta was in two days, and I was about to go to practice. Coach Dave gave extra crunches if you were late. The Mayor's Cup was supposed to be just a fun, end-of-the-season thing, but Academy was always competitive. We were good, and being on that team mattered to me, like it mattered to all of us.

"Baby!" Lila sang. "So, here's the deal. Don't be mad. I know I promised it would be just us, but Jake wants to come when I pick you up at the airport."

"Liiiii-laaa," I groaned, because, well, typical Lila. A man, a lie. "I haven't seen you in months. And I don't even know the guy. It'll be weird."

"We'll have *plenty* of time alone. Plus, you two need to meet! You're going to be seeing a lot of each other."

She'd just contradicted herself, but whatever. The more important thing was, my head began to throb with tension. History was flashing before my eyes. The bad kind of history, where people do horrible stuff for generations, not the good kind where they learn and do better. "Just don't marry him before I get there."

"Oh, baby, don't. Come on."

She was exasperated. I could hear her nails clicking against a hard surface. It wasn't an unreasonable thing to say. As you know, she'd done that before. Lila and men—ugh. *Of course* I felt uneasy.

There was a long, strained silence. I looked out my window toward the Montlake Cut, the slender neck of the Lake Washington Ship Canal, where the crew team was already gathering. I could see the satiny blue and yellow of their uniforms, the same satiny blue and yellow I was wearing. Meredith would be knocking at my door any second.

"I've got to go. Practice is about to start."

"Oh, not yet! Don't leave mad. Please. Talk to me some more."

Lila, well, she could be a conversational hostage-taker, letting you free only after you met her demands.

"I can't."

"Syd! Don't be like that. Stay. Let me just read you this letter I got today. You'll laugh your head off. An actual *letter.* Who writes letters anymore? A *seventeen-year-old boy*, that's who."

She laughed, because we always laughed at mail like this. It was one of our things. But I didn't feel like laughing. I was fifteen, almost sixteen. I went to school with seventeen-year-old boys. I mean, yeah, the whole world watched her, but seventeen-year-old boys were sort of *mine.*

Right then, Meredith popped her head into my room, and I was so glad to see her, it was like I'd been stranded at sea for years and she was the captain of the tanker who spotted me. I waved madly and gestured for her to come in. Meredith had her Academy crew bag over her shoulder. She tapped her wrist where a watch would be if people wore watches anymore. "We're late," she mouthed.

"Meredith's here. I need to go."

"She can wait! What have I told you a million times?"

"Don't be the first one anywhere."

Meredith pretended to gag.

"Precisely. Oh, you should see the handwriting on this thing! So tiny and restrained! 'Dear Ms. Shore: I've never written anyone a fan letter, but ever since I saw *Nefarious*, you've tormented my imagination. That scene where you're on the ladder and Brandon Searing lifts your skirt and we see your legs and the white lace of your—'"

"Lila, I'm hanging up."

"Tormented his *imagination*! Isn't that a riot? I think he's got his anatomy mixed up."

"*Stop.*" I was pleading by that point.

"Oh my God! I'm late for my manicure. Baby, I have to rush out of here. I love you, I love you, I love you."

She waited for me to say it back. But I was irritated, plus all kinds of other things jumbled together like the pile of dirty laundry in the corner of my room. I didn't *want* to say it. I could hear what I owed just sitting in the silence.

"I love you, Lila."

Ugh! Whatever. I hung up. Meredith and I took the steps out of Montgomery Hall. "We better hurry," I said.

"You okay?" she asked. Mer was my best friend. She knew me. She knew the me I was then.

"Yeah," I said, even though I wasn't, not by a long shot. And that irritation I felt? It was going to get worse. A lot worse. Outright *fury*. "Hey, cute hair."

Meredith made the ends of her braids dance. And then we heard Coach Dave's whistle and had to run.

In the boat, out on the water, I looked down at my own, regular legs. I remember this so clearly, how I examined this one body part like it was the malfunctioning O-ring that might make the whole ship blow up. Those legs were long and skinny and ended with my feet in a pair of Nikes. My knees were knobby as a couple of oranges. I had a scratch on my calf from when I missed the hurdle during the track unit in PE the week before.

There were little golden hairs that shimmered in the sun.

The thing was, my legs were just plain old things to walk on. They had regular jobs. Like running to catch up. Like riding a bike. Like screaming in pain when they hit the sun-hot seat of Meredith's mom's car. Those legs would never torment anyone, I was pretty sure.

Here was my experience with desire right then: picking out the cutest boy in my class on every first day of school since I was five and admiring him from afar. That thrilling note-passing in the sixth grade, when Emma English told me that Jeremy Wykowski liked me. Middle school slow dancing, a probably-not-accidental boob touch. That boy from another school who suddenly entwined his fingers with mine at a basketball game, who I fantasized about for months afterward, probably because his real self wasn't there to mess things up. The last six months with Samuel Crane, involving phone conversations about stuff that seemed deep, kissing behind the metal shop building and a few times in his parents' basement, hands up a shirt, hands down pants, more like hunting around in your backpack for your phone than anything else. And most recently: the men looking up from their laptops in Victrola. A boy twining my hair around his finger, the smell of hot dogs and mustard around us.

Torment—I had no real idea about any of that, honestly. I wasn't sure I even liked Samuel Crane the way I should. He liked me, and it seemed like reason enough to kiss back. Obviously, there was some hidden door to the bigger world that I hadn't walked through yet. I heard about that world in songs and saw it in movies, but it wasn't mine. It was an intriguing mystery, or maybe an outright lie.

I could feel it stirring around in there, though. Desire. Or desire for desire. I wanted to feel deep, aching *want*, but I wanted to make someone else feel it too. That was maybe even more appealing—the power to make a guy want me, badly. I would never have admitted this. It seemed wrong, especially since my own mother had made a career out of being a sex object. It was a truth I kept buried, like a secret from myself.

"Syd-Syd!" Meredith called from her seat behind me in the boat. I looked over my shoulder. Meredith made a face, and I made one back.

"Sit ready!" the coxswain called. My hands gripped the oar and I buried the blade in the water. This was the moment we steadied the boat before we rowed like crazy, deep in the intensity and the speed and the high of the race. And these were the moments before I found the hidden door. Right then, I didn't have a clue where it was.

I would find it, though, as you know. Along with everything that lay behind it. And sixth grade was like two seconds ago, and my hands still had pastel dust on them, and Samuel Crane couldn't even drive yet.

One last thing. I should also tell you this:

We won the Mayor's Cup Regatta. And afterward, we squirted juice packs at each other and ran around screaming.

We were excited to win, but even more, school was almost out, and that's the best feeling there is.

I was so tired that night that I conked right off. That dark sense of being haunted, the ghost—there was no way she was going to keep me awake. So of course I had a horrible dream instead. Warnings are persistent, until they just plain give up on you.

I realize this sounds like something out of one of Lila's films, one of the scenes where a woman walks into a couple's shadowy bedroom and you see the glint of silver in the moonlight. But this is the truth: I had a dream about a knife. I woke up and my heart was pounding. It was the kind of terrifying dream that feels so real your hands shake. When I tried to explain it in the morning, though, it seemed silly.

"A horrible person got stabbed in the chest. It was you but it wasn't you," Cora repeated in the dining hall, as she chased some Cheerios with her spoon.

"It was so real," I said, but I could see the little smile at the corner of Cora's mouth.